PRAISE FOR TOM TONER AND
THE PROMISE OF THE CHILD

"To call *The Promise of the Child* one of the most accomplished debuts of 2015 so far is to understate its weight—instead, let me moot that it is among the most significant works of science fiction released in recent years."
—Tor.com

"One of the most ambitious and epic-scale pieces of worldbuilding I've read. Reading *The Promise of the Child*, you feel you're in the presence of an author at the height of his powers. If this is what Toner is like when he's just getting started, I think we can expect great things from him. Utterly absorbing; a tremendous adventure."
—Karl Schroeder, author of *Lockstep* and *Sun of Suns*

"This is the purest example of space opera we've seen in some time. . . . The book is challenging, ambitious, and rewarding, and it's impossible not to admire Toner's wild imagination and carefully constructed world. This thing is bonkers, no question. It's also one helluva debut."
—Barnes & Noble Sci-Fi & Fantasy Blog

"Humming with energy, this is space opera like you've never seen it before. Absolutely brilliant."
—Adam Roberts, author of *Salt* and *Jack Glass*

"A gorgeously-written, wildly imaginative book. It's like no space opera I've ever read—compelling and addictive."
—Will McIntosh, Hugo-award winning author of *Soft Apocalypse* and *Defenders*

"A dizzying mash-up of science fiction and fantasy themes that are both mystifying and entertaining . . . will appeal to readers who enjoy the offbeat end of far-future SF. This is the kind of novel that could develop a cult following."
—*Booklist*

Also by Tom Toner
The Promise of the Child

THE
WEIGHT
OF THE
WORLD

VOLUME TWO OF THE AMARANTHINE SPECTRUM

TOM TONER

Night Shade Books
NEW YORK

Night Shade books may be purchased in bulk at special discounts for sales promotion, corporate gifts, fund-raising, or educational purposes. Special editions can also be created to specifications. For details, contact the Special Sales Department, Night Shade Books, 307 West 36th Street, 11th Floor, New York, NY 10018 or info@ skyhorsepublishing.com.

Night Shade Books® is a registered trademark of Skyhorse Publishing, Inc. ®, a Delaware corporation.

Visit our website at www.nightshadebooks.com.

10 9 8 7 6 5 4 3 2 1

Library of Congress Cataloging-in-Publication Data

Names: Toner, Thomas, 1986- author.
Title: The weight of the world / Tom Toner.
Description: New York : Night Shade Books, 2017. | Series: Amaranthine
    Spectrum ; volume 2
Identifiers: LCCN 2016018022 | ISBN 9781597808750 (hardback)
Subjects: LCSH: Space warfare--Fiction. | Imaginary wars and
    battles--Fiction. | BISAC: FICTION / Science Fiction / Space Opera. |
    FICTION / Science Fiction / General. | FICTION / Science Fiction /
    Adventure. | GSAFD: Science fiction. | Fantasy fiction.
Classification: LCC PR6120.O47 P763 2017 | DDC 823/.92--dc23
LC record available at https://lccn.loc.gov/2016018022

Print ISBN: 978-1-59780-875-0

Cover design by Blacksheep Design Ltd.

Printed in the United States of America

"You must go back before Caesar's legions, to the days when the bones of giant animals and men lay on the ground . . . to the New Troy, the New Jerusalem, and the sins and crimes of the kings who rode under the tattered banners of Arthur and who married women who came out of the sea or hatched out of eggs, women with scales and fins and feathers . . ."

Hilary Mantel
Wolf Hall

"All the day long her sail was stretched as she sped over the sea; and the sun set and all the ways grew dark. She came to deep-flowing Oceanus, that bounds the Earth, where is the land and city of the Cimmerians, wrapped in mist and cloud."

Homer
The Odyssey

For Nunky

AUTHOR'S NOTE

There are a few odd formats used throughout this odd book. *Whole chapters are occasionally written in italics,* and these take place in the past. Anything written in the present tense can be assumed to be a dream, or taking place in a dreamlike state.

The Weight of the World is the second volume of The Amaranthine Spectrum.

The first, *The Promise of the Child*, began in the year AD 14,647.

Earth, now known as the Old World, has changed beyond recognition and become the forgotten haunt of talking beasts and the twisted, giant-like remnants of humankind known as the Melius. The lifeless, apparently sterile local stars—discovered, much to everyone's surprise, to have been visited and subsequently abandoned seventy-nine million years earlier by an intelligent species of dinosaur—are now in the possession of the Amaranthine, a branch of immortal humans left over from a golden age.

Their empire, known as the Firmament, extends outwards from the Old World for twenty-three solar systems to the edges of the Prism Investiture, a ring of grindingly poor planets and moons occupied by the Prism, a cluster of dwarfish, primate descendents of humanity.

In the Vaulted Lands of the Amaranthine Firmament, the Perennial Parliaments are jostling for power, with one sect challenging the Emperor himself for the Firmamental Throne. Their nominated ruler is Aaron the Long-Life, a recently discovered man of incredible age who they hope has the power to heal the Firmament and push back the ever-encroaching Prism.

On the Old World, in a remote estate near the former Mediterranean Sea, lives Lycaste, a shy giant Melius man and legendary beauty. Pining for a girl who does not love him in return, Lycaste's life changes when a census-taker arrives from the distant ruling Provinces. Lycaste and the man find themselves immediately at odds, and one night, when the dispute becomes physical, Lycaste mistakenly believes that he has committed murder. Terrified, he flees his homeland for the first time in his life, making his way through the war-torn Old World Provinces. The Melius eventually falls into the hands of Sotiris, an Amaranthine mourning the death of his sister, who realizes that Lycaste is far more important to the fate of the Firmament than ever could have been anticipated.

Sotiris has been tempted by the mysterious Aaron the Long-Life with the possibility of seeing his sister again. He eventually accepts the devil's bargain, agreeing to rule the Firmament on Aaron's behalf, but not before turning Lycaste over to his old friend, Hugo Maneker, a one-time confidant of Aaron's who he knows will keep him safe.

In the lawless worlds of the Prism Investiture, Ghaldezuel, a Lacaille Knight of the Stars, is contracted to steal a miraculous invention: the Shell, a device apparently capable of capturing and preserving one's soul. He delivers it to the Old World and its new owner, Aaron the Long-Life, along with the mummified remains of one of the star-faring dinosaurs. Aaron is revealed to be the spirit of a dead Artificial Intelligence created by the creatures in the distant past. He has lain dormant in projected form for seventy-nine million years, whispering into the ears of the powerful until he could be reunited with a body. Aaron uses the Shell to conjoin his soul with the dinosaur's corpse and takes physical form. He tells Ghaldezuel that together they must travel to Gliese, the capital of the Firmament, before his ancient plan can be fulfilled.

On a lonely, windswept planet, the true Emperor of the Firmament speaks to the voices in his head. Although everyone thinks him half-mad, the voices are in fact real: they are the souls of other long-dead

AI substrates, relatives of Aaron the Long-Life, bound to the world where they died just as he once was. Panicked, they tell the Emperor that Aaron has freed himself and embarked upon a course of revenge, pursuing those who wronged him so long ago. The Emperor tells them not to worry, for many thousands of years ago the Firmament also created an artificial soul called Perception. Somewhere Perception's spirit still resides, and it might just be able to help them.

PROLOGUE

Twenty thousand days imprisoned.
  I built my cities of dust brick by brick.

*Their foundations, before I became proficient in the layering and glu-
ing of motes, were at first just ramshackle, piled strata, like the rocks
of a fortress's base. I learned fast, weaving symmetry into the silk-
strengthened blocks and sticking them just so, until up rose the curtain
walls, straighter and stronger as I honed my craft, to be crowned with
battlements and ramparts of my own design.*

  *Soon I'd made gatehouses and keeps, layering structures atop
one another in wholly unrealistic ways; towers as high as my chamber crowned with horizontal spires and steeples. After fifteen days of
tireless work, I slinked back to look at what I'd made, and then I let
them in.*

  *I'd kept the old females and their concubines separate until the
accession, allowing them to spin until one corner of my chamber was
milky with the silk I needed for cement. When all was finished, I opened
the portcullis to their new home, looking on proudly as they scuttled in.*

  *Of course, I had no idea what species of Spinner they were, guess-
ing only from their feeding habits that they were quite fantastically
venomous. Their aggression I had already seen, and with a cruel
delight I knew I would be in for a show as I released a second, then
a third female into the labyrinthine palace to contend for the throne.
Above, suspended in the rafters of the great keep in the manner of a*

trophy head, a Twitchwing trembled in a hammock of silk. The new queen's reward, and the nutrition that would breed me my princelings.

Stumpellina the Amputated came first across the castle drawbridge, she that had lost a leg to some accident outside my lair, followed quickly by a scampering flurry of smaller, darker males. Five were her own progeny, breathless at the chance of straddling their own mother. I did not find that unpleasant at the time, having barely considered the possibilities of interbreeding. If I'd known, perhaps I'd have upped the number: let the mutated have a chance at ruling, should it be their pleasure.

It soon dawned on me that my Spinners wouldn't solve my maze without help—I'd overestimated in my observation of their artistic webs their ability to problem-solve—so I carried a strand of silk across from their old home, laying it like a line of rope up into the antechambers of the throne room itself. They would first have to cross perilous ravines with sheer walls traversed by dainty bridges, a gauntlet to weed out the weak and the stupid, perhaps bottlenecking the most vicious of them to allow a wilier individual to scuttle past. Another I routed to the postern, wishing the escapee the chance of becoming a future contender—I was planning dynasties here, after all, great histories that would play out before me over the years I'd have to endure. These creatures in their mighty halls would be my children, my enjoyment, my sacrificial beasts. I thought ahead as my Spinners scrabbled for their prize, thinking of the generations I could breed. Thousands, millions. Indulging in flights of fancy, I imagined how they might look at the end of it all, when even I had ceased to exist.

Would they ever chance to glance up, I wondered, perhaps ruminating on who had given them this palace? I glowered over the scene, a crumpled, silken cloud of attenuated thought, watching them all, urging them on, wondering also whether greater things looked down on me. I'd seen inside their little chemical brains, watched the ebb and flow of blood through their accordion lungs, and knew that they could feel, in a sense. They might just revere me, one day, when I had forcebred imagination into them. They might just be capable of setting me free.

At last, almost simultaneously, two would-be queens achieved the throne room, scuttling in from alternate doorways and facing each other wearily as they contemplated the trapped Twitchwing. Stumpellina studied her nemesis, Fangmilla: she with the broken injector. Toxin gathered upon the good fang's tip in an oily drop. I lowered over the battlements like an arriving storm, peering through the arrow slits and into the great keep, ignoring the struggles of the others.

They circled. I watched in a slowed-down time of my own devising, seeing their muscled forelimbs grind the dust, hearing their ragged breathing booming through the chambers of the palace. Their markings shimmered in a rainbow, the hair covering their abdomens swaying like a field of wheat. Stumpellina reared and pounced, a quick, unexpectedly clever feint enabling her to hook a leg beneath Fangmilla's soft, exposed underbelly and tip her. Could they poison one another? Suddenly afraid, I contemplated driving them apart with a breath of wind, but by then Fangmilla had been pierced, thrashing for a moment until the life ebbed from her movements and she curled into a ball. Stumpellina wasted no time, knowing now that she was in possession of two prizes, and began to devour her old rival, suckling the juices. I watched until she was done, pushing away the husk and climbing for the Twitchwing. It had witnessed everything but lost the energy to fight. I almost considered letting it go.

While Stumpellina fed for a second time, I silently began work on the tomb of the fallen female, spinning a dust sarcophagus that would encapsulate her where she lay. Across its surface, I sculpted a frieze of exquisite ornamentation, finishing with a representation of her broken-toothed face. Naturally mummified by the removal of her fluids, she would remain desiccated and preserved for many thousands of years at the heart of the dry castle, a monument to the victorious line begun that day. All that remained now was to await the prince that would begin it. I lowered my glance to the battlements.

Across the castle courtyards, the battle raged. Brothers from the same hatching fought and devoured one another, a seething tangle of furious black legs. The males did not possess the same extraordinary poison as the females, though I daresay if I were a man I wouldn't have let one near me. With time, I might breed more potency from them, hoping someday to wield my Spinners against the Amaranthine like a blunt, flailing force, something they'd never expect until they came again to my door. It was curious: something in me feared these creatures still, some inherited, long-defunct alley of my mind formed by the process of revulsion. I can only assume it was my father's fear. Well, he needn't have worried; it wasn't my Spinners that got him, in the end.

FAIRY TALE: 1645

He ambled through the litter-strewn camp, the summer day all but gone, nodding occasionally to men he knew: drummers with their backs to a sawn log; an ensign holding his boot and hopping barefoot to the fire. The farty tang of uncorked beer reminded him of other times; the fermentation of dry grass ready for pasture aromatic around them; the squeal of a green branch hefted onto the cookfire. Tin spoons scraped; men coughed.

Daniell looked at the faces of the people he passed, the ready grin set in his jaw tiring as he reached the hill. He recognised these men because he was paid to know them, to spend time with them. He was no soldier.

"How is't, Bulstrode?" asked the sentry at the rise, his matchlock propped like a walking stick, barrel-up. "You're needed."

He took the diagonal route, hobbling where the field had been trampled into dry divots by his Lordship's cavalry the day before, and reached the crest in time to see the last of the pink fade from the few clouds. Only a deep, sooty orange lined the far hills of Burrowbridge, staining to blue above.

His Lordship's tent was dark, empty as always. It comforted Daniell to think that a charlatan would have objects: talismans, jars of animal parts, perhaps a fat grimoire of spells sitting ostentatiously on a shelf. But his Lordship didn't appear to own a thing that he didn't carry on his person—not a candlestick, chair or chamber pot. Daniell, in his unspecified role of retainer, had gradually risen over the few years of his service to handle nearly all of his master's needs—from writing letters and saddling horses all the way down to far dirtier work, work that his Lordship assigned only to him. After those sorts of jobs were done, he was invariably given a holiday, perhaps a few days' leave for a man, a week at an inn for a family; the precise rates of exchange for a life seemingly already weighed and worked out. Only just this once had someone got away, by nothing but a hair. But his Lordship needn't concern himself with that—Daniell had the matter in hand.

As he came upon the hill camp, he saw that the huge fire-pit among the tents was piled with kindling and rolled pamphlets from town. He paused, looking into it, trying to make out what some of them said in the fading light.

The devil appeared to Joan Hodgkin in the form of a dog, *he read, without needing to mouth the words. Daniell crouched and pulled out the paper to read more by the light of the faded sky.* She sold her soul and was possessed. *He scanned the text, examining the crude drawing of the old wife and understanding before he'd come to the bottom of the pamphlet that she'd already paid for her crimes. The West Country was a superstitious hollow, a place where mists still clung to the land long after dawn. Another written piece caught his eye, tiny among the cluttered drawings of parliamentarians in their broad hats.*

Henry Purcell of the Privy Council has today laid grievous charges at the door of the king's lieutenant general of the horse, Lord Aaron Goring, accusing his Lordship of sending villeins to his lodgings in the most lewd and violent of manners.

Daniell felt the sweat on his brow chill as he read the words, the sky darkening around him. At least his Lordship wasn't here.

But he was here, of course he was. Daniell straightened and looked into the black silhouettes of the trees around the tent.

"Shall I light the fire?" he asked, bustling to the accompanying tent to find his things.

The trees appeared to draw breath. They said nothing for a handful of moments, then from the wood the delicate voice spoke.

"Where were you?"

He stopped in the darkness. "Game of cribbage and all-fours, Lordship." His hand found the tinder-pistol in the sack by the entrance and he brought it out, returning to sit by the pit. The fragrant grass beneath him had been cropped almost to stubble by horses now moved. As he looked for his master in the dark, the fire sprang abruptly to life, billowing sideways in a breath of heat. Every piece of kindling and paper burned equally, as if the flames had not started in any one place.

His Lord materialised from the depths, his kind, fatherly face set in blankness, and stepped into the light to sit. Daniell realised he was still clutching the pamphlet. He tossed it into the fire.

Aaron, Lord Goring, did not look at his servant, his eyes only interested in the fire. He lit it in this way sometimes, when they found themselves rushed. The magic, though wearing thin on Daniell, hadn't quite lost its novelty. Where his Lordship glanced, the flames sank back like a dog afraid, blowing hard with a grumble against the base of the pit when they could flee no further. Daniell looked for shapes again, his gaze darting about the spaces between the flames, but could see nothing this time. At length, he spoke.

"You had all but two of the culverin cannon removed this evening, I heard."

Goring finished his fire-play, rolling his eyes up to the evening sky and the first blush of stars. "Then so would every able spy for five miles. Two cannon for appearances, or the king would send relief."

Daniell looked at him, impressed for the hundredth time by his master's methods. All was ready, then. Their army waited for its own annihilation.

The Lord Goring gazed back, eyebrows raised playfully. Those bland, somehow colourless eyes had sent the Earl of Monmouth mad with a glance, and yet increasingly they looked on Daniell with something like love. He felt a swell of pride and warmth at the sight, a real smile forming at last. He'd known some who'd chosen their allegiance in this war by consulting astrologers; this was how Daniell had chosen his.

"I have our horses ready beneath the hanging chapel, top of Bow Street," Daniell said. "You know the one."

"I know all the chapels," the Lord said, stretching out his hands above the spitting fire. Their shadows slinked over the flames, wholly impossible, like pieces of cut black cloth.

Daniell looked up, waiting for more, but his master's thoughts on the subject appeared to be at an end. "The wood," Goring said, withdrawing his hands and looking off to the darkness of the crowded fields.

Daniell placed the first few logs in the flames and sat down to cover himself with his jackets. Goring, as usual, wore the colours of King Charles, the faded red coat of the travelling cavalier topped by an oddly useless iron gorget around his collar. Without full armour there was no need for it, especially deep into the western edge of the camp. Daniell supposed it displayed the Lord's bunched medallions in a pleasing way, reflecting after a moment that there wasn't any point protecting what no man could harm.

He was not, and had never been, a man of God. A sturdy dis-belief in the consequences of sin had long suited Daniell Bulstrode in every line of work he chose, especially under his current Lordship, with whom he had journeyed the past three years. Despite everything his plain mind told him, however, Daniell knew perfectly well that the being sitting before him was nothing like a man, however impeccably it dressed itself.

Unspoken, the understanding between them persisted. Only Dan-iell knew of his Lord's true nature, and only he would benefit from it. He might have wondered in his bed some nights whether he could indeed be consorting with the fallen angel himself, but with daylight such fears felt childish, absurd. Like a boyhood memory of trying to identify creatures half-glimpsed in a rock pool, Daniell knew he couldn't pos-sibly have come to the correct conclusion—and so it shouldn't matter. Names meant nothing now. Perhaps his Lordship had never even been given one, back in the great where and when of his birth. He was an Oracle, nonetheless, destined to supplant the stuttering, nincompoop king who had led them all to war. One day, when the man-shape at the fire and he were as brothers, Daniell would ask his questions. But, until then, he saved up for other favours.

"How does the town hate me?" Goring asked abruptly, raising his eyes again as the stars clarified. "As passionately as Leicester?"

Daniell snorted. "More, much more."

His Lordship allowed his army to do as they pleased wherever they marched. The west had become a place of fear, ripe to rebel even as the losing side cheered their lieutenant general for his apparently blind eye, running riot wherever they found themselves garrisoned. No soldier Bulstrode knew had turned down what looting there was to be had. Not even Daniell, who fancied an early retirement once he could afford to take his ease.

"Fine," Goring breathed, still studying the stars. "We raze the town tomorrow as we retreat. Burn it from east to west."

Daniell took a moment to think on the order, working out who to wake in the early hours and who to let sleep. His master had so far rarely destroyed utterly, preferring to sow the seeds in more subtle ways. But it was late, Naseby was lost and the king's army already crippled. The west could be squandered efficiently with one final act of sabotage, and this small bend in the river might just be it.

"And the prisoners? I'll turn them out again? I could send them off Somerton way this time."

The Lord gave the impression of thought, though Daniell had never seen him think long on anything. "Not this time. Take them into town at dawn and chain them in the market square."

Daniell sucked his lips. "As you say."

Minutes passed in silence as they stared into the fire. Just as Daniell was wondering whether he should take his leave and find some supper in the field, he began to see the shapes again, wriggling forms between the tongues of flame.

"I told you once the tale of the spy," Goring said abruptly, studying the rings on his fingers: fat signet seals for pressing into wax, never once used, as far as Daniell knew.

"Yes, Lordship," he replied, remembering the pagan story. "The emperor betrayed by a prince, his brother." He recalled the town, one of many on a long road, and the manor they had sat the night in, waiting for a courier.

"Remind me—what was the name of the person who took these lands from him?" his Lordship asked, feigning forgetfulness.

Daniell thought for a moment. It had been a tale not fit for anyone older than a certain age, and yet by its simplicity alone had contained a certain allure. He'd been tired as he listened that night, only the light of a fire two rooms away colouring his Lordship's face as he told it, and Daniell suddenly found himself afraid that he might have fallen asleep—that this was a test, a punishment. But he did remember. He remembered the whole thing.

"Sarsappus."

A story of when the world was held suspended in a glass bubble, its lands divided into two halves. A story of three great kings and three vast, star-shaped realms, their borders and names lost to antiquity, the stones of cities sunk lower into the earth than the foundations of Camelot.

"So you were listening."

"I wouldn't be much use to you if I didn't, Lordship," Daniell said, his confidence returning, picturing the ancient king as he had then, while the tale was being told: a frail old horror, the wiry hair of his beard picked out in the myriad colours of stained glass. Where God had been during the spinning of this tale, he had no idea.

"And would you listen if I told you more?"

Daniell hesitated, suddenly tired beyond belief.

His Lordship held up a hand, its shadow staining the flames. "Rest. Perhaps I'll tell it while you sleep."

Daniell had slept, propped against a log like a summer labourer on a country road. Stirring, he found the fire had grown, smearing one side of him with a sheen of sweat and parching the hot skin of his face. His beer mug had rolled on the grass, spilling what little was left. He shuffled upright, his mouth dry, needing desperately to piss.

His master caressed the fire, apparently oblivious as Daniell stirred. It comforted and alarmed him in equal measure to know he'd slept beneath that benevolent gaze, at the mercy of this being, this maker of light.

He buttoned his jacket, creeping a way down the hill. The fires of the encamped army were strung like a necklace of candles across the hill and down to the river, its dark waters invisible. Shapes of men passed before them, scintillating the distant firelight like stars watched on a hot night. Daniell stood, thinking, his eyes drawn back to the flames of his Lordship's own fire.

The spindly, warped outline of a man who was not quite a man shone through, standing now. Daniell held himself in the darkness, understanding clearly that Goring remained on the far side, that the shadow bled through the flames whichever way you looked.

Those shadows. They'd never been quite right.

The black skeleton raised its arm, thin as a winter twig. The chill returned.

Daniell raised a hand tentatively and waved back.

ATHOLCUALAN: WINTER 14,646
SEVEN MONTHS BEFORE THE BATTLE OF NILMUTH, AND THE ATTEMPTED THEFT OF THE SHELL

Spiderwebs of mist draped the city of Atholcualan, hanging milkily in the stillness between the patchwork of domed favelas and tenements that rose up the mountainside. Ghaldezuel took deep, slow breaths as the wind whipped at his grey clothes, his eyes narrowing to follow the line cut into the mountainside. The rambling city before him had been built high in these mountains to serve the old industrial frontier; for centuries, Lacaille folk down on their luck or on the run had come here, climbing through sickening altitude to find what scraps of work there were to be had. The frontier was long gone now, the city visited these days by a single train, the Atholcualan Star, *a ramshackle locomotive that wound its leisurely way through the Cractitule Range from Zuo every thirty-two hours: what amounted to daily here on the Lacaille-owned moon of Pruth-Zalnir.*

Ghaldezuel took another laboured breath, his skull aching. He'd been awoken in the night by the screams of a botched robbery below his chamber window. A stabbing, he'd surmised blearily, listening to the pitch alter, growing more hysterical until he wondered if it might burst the thin glass, only to fall suddenly silent. He'd turned over and rucked the blanket over his head, knowing the sound of death, welcoming sleep.

Below him, at the bottom of a flight of crumbled bonestone steps, the stationmaster had exited his tower. Ghaldezuel had considered leaving word with the master rather than wait—the Atholcualan Star *was a notoriously unreliable piece of machinery, frequently derailing on a pass not far from the city—but something about the message had forced him to reconsider. He stood and watched the distant hills, a little sun breaking through the cloud at last and bathing his flat white face.*

There—a shimmer of movement. The hills baked, for all their altitude, and he had to squint now at the swaying mirage. Bells and horns began to clamour with the hour throughout the shambolic, almost vertical city. Perfectly on time. Ghaldezuel wondered again whether such precision might have been laid on specially, for today the Star *carried a peculiar and esteemed passenger. He looked down at the waiting*

Prism, mostly Ringum half-breeds or travellers, noticing that the huddling crowd hadn't yet spotted the arriving train. Perhaps ninety per cent of the city's inhabitants had never taken this train nor ever would, not even into the next township; they simply couldn't afford to. Those who arrived after each long day here were invariably wealthier merchants or slaved Oxel machinists, come to work the mines beneath Praztatl, the range's highest peak. There would be some well-off Vulgar on that train, as usual, mostly travelling under protective documents issued under the new Peace Treaty of Silp. Nearly all would be robbed during their stay, perhaps a dozen murdered—as was the case each season—but with little chance of retribution. The Vulgar kingdoms had no influence here on Pruth-Zalnir. They might reprint their passports with an extra page of warnings, but that would be all. Peace was too fragile for a scant few lives to interrupt.

Ghaldezuel lifted a hand to shade his eyes, conspicuously aware of the paler bands on his fingers where once there had been rings. The train grew larger on the mountainside, its fortified iron turrets streaked with scarlet rust and white smears of guano. Hired mercenaries, posted in the crow's nests to keep watch for thieves, were climbing down now as the train approached, specks working their way across the sun-bright metal. A relatively recent fixture, their numbers had swelled in response to last year's attack on the train by the Investiture-renowned Cunctites, who'd failed at the last minute when a Voidjet had come swooping in to chase them off.

Carriages swayed behind the engine and Ghaldezuel was finally able to spot the little white faces poking from the windows, their hair blown back. He noticed the last compartment, its windows dark, the shutters pulled tight, and made his way down the steps and along the platform, sliding past the waiting Prism and strolling to the very end of the riveted steel slab where pale weeds and flowers took hold among the pitted metal.

He kicked his boots, scuffing at the weeds while the train pulled alongside. Doors opened before the engine had fully come to a halt, the tiny occupants hopping out excitedly and gabbling in Vulgar on the platform as they were passed cases, crates and sacks. A few staggered and swayed as the altitude caught up with them, holding gloved hands to their mouths. Ghaldezuel felt no sympathy for them. He watched a

Vulgar child, tiny and squealing, being handed from an open window to its long-eared mother. The lady's vibrant blue gown billowed suddenly in the mountain breeze as she took the toddler, her round jade eyes meeting Ghaldezuel's along the platform. He studied her briefly before turning away, noting her perfume as it carried on the otherwise foul wind.

The stationmaster eyed Ghaldezuel's shabby clothes as he strutted past to wait at the carriage door. Ghaldezuel returned the master's stare before handing him a thick white-gold crescent coin stamped with an almost impossibly intricate pattern. The stationmaster straightened, his expression momentarily dubious, taking the Firmamental Half-Ducat with some reverence and slipping it into his top pocket. He nodded to Ghaldezuel and made his way back to the master's tower, hurrying the milling visitors as they squabbled over their bags.

The door of the last compartment opened, locks within turning. The carriage rocked as something huge transferred its weight to the inside step and Ghaldezuel retreated a little, making room on the platform.

The gigantic Firmamental Melius shouldered its way into the sunlight, glancing up to take in the vibrant city. Assorted jewels and charms dangled from the sagging, sweat-shiny skin of its neck, held high above any curious Lacaille hands. Ghaldezuel watched for signs that the beast's vast lungs—the size of industrial bellows—might be suffering in the thin air, but was disappointed. The Melius looked down at the Lacaille as the churning colours of its skin settled to a deep crimson, planting a bare foot onto the platform and rising to its full height.

"Ghaldezuel Es-Mejor?" the giant enquired with remarkably acceptable Lacaille pronunciation. Ghaldezuel could feel the glottal rumble of the Melius's voice through his bones as the creature spoke.

"Pauncefoot," he said, taking a full Firmamental Ducat from his purse and handing it over.

The Melius took the Ducat without looking at it, the coin disappearing into his massive clenched palm. "Shall we?"

They walked together from the platform, the remaining passengers stopping to gasp and stare. The Melius, more than nine feet tall, paid them no heed, his elephantine head instead upturned again to study the layers of carved tenements. The sun had broken through the mists almost entirely now, circling the hazed curve of Pruth-Zalnir's mottled parent planet—a kingless partition world now owned by the Pifoon in all but name—with a dimly beautiful rainbow.

"You are living here, for the moment?" Pauncefoot asked, sweeping his tasselled turquoise cape over one shoulder.

Ghaldezuel hesitated. The Melius, delivering commands from the Firmament, would surely know everything pertinent. "I was posted here to relieve the knight Fiernel, as I'm sure you know."

Pauncefoot ignored some scrawny Ringum children who had begun running behind, trying to jump and catch his colossal shadow. "Ah, yes, recently knighted. My congratulations."

Ghaldezuel dipped his head in thanks, glancing ahead along the narrow street. More children sat or lay indolently in doorways, watching with large blue and green eyes the passing of the Melius. Over their heads, damp coloured cloth hung swaying, dripping to darken the cobbles and rusted iron sheeting that made up the thoroughfare. From a side alley came a lunatic laugh. Pauncefoot glanced at the source of the sound as they passed: a mad and naked Lacaille woman shackled to a rusted pole, the sweetish stink of her excrement wafting out at them.

As if in response to the smell, the Melius took a pipe from a pocket beneath his cloak, sliding its silver lid and thumbing the striker. It caught, and he blew a breath of bluish smoke like fog into the street. Ghaldezuel waved it carefully from his face. The children running behind burst into fits of giggles, jumping and sprinting through the blue cloud.

"We are nearby?" Pauncefoot asked, his jagged teeth clamped around the pipe stem.

"Just up here." Ghaldezuel pointed to another street leading off at a right angle further ahead. Here the cobbles were less crumbled and worn, the mortar between them still bright. Some towers and cupolas rose from the buildings, their cracks plastered over in places, and balconies with wrought-iron railings leaned into the dark streets. The Firmamental Melius nodded, registering his appreciation of the finer surroundings and cleaner smells as Ghaldezuel directed him to the raised doorway.

"You have Bult in your employ." It was not a question.

Ghaldezuel glanced through the bolted window at the distorted view of the street beyond, the sunlight slanting in thick bars across the balconies. The Bult were devils here on Pruth-Zalnir, their names never to be mentioned for fear that they might come calling. "Some."

Pauncefoot was sitting heavily on the bed, his legs drawn up in a pall of pipe smoke. He gestured impatiently. "Contactable at short notice?"

"Well." Ghaldezuel pulled his gaze from the street, where catcalling children still waited for a glimpse of the monster on the second floor. "They're Bult, not Pifoon. They come when it pleases them."

"But they'd come for you."

Ghaldezuel toyed with his bare fingers. "It's dangerous for them this close to the Firmament edge, now the Vulgar have them in their sights and are harrying them out into the Whoop. The rewards must be greater."

The Melius rummaged through an inner pocket and slapped a thick, sealed envelope on the table. Ghaldezuel knew from the look of it that there would be Lacaille exchange cheques and foreign currency inside. Knights received all orders like this. He reached and took it but did not break the embossed plastic seal.

"This peace with the Vulgar cannot continue," Pauncefoot said, indicating the envelope in Ghaldezuel's hand. "We know you want this, too. You and your Bult will see to it for us."

Ghaldezuel placed the envelope back on the table thoughtfully, looking into his visitor's eyes. They were great bloodshot balls, their tropical colour muted through the film of smoke.

"The Light-Trap," he said. "Andolp's Light-Trap. That's what you want, isn't it?"

Pauncefoot appeared genuinely surprised, as if word of the miraculous machine hadn't spread beyond Vulgar borders.

Ghaldezuel shook his head. "I knew some fool would try, sooner or later. Those fortresses on Drolgins are impregnable. What makes you think my Bult could succeed?"

"So you have heard the rumours," the Melius said, tamping spices into the bowl of his pipe from a tiny jewelled pot that hung among the charms. "That is good. Our agents inside Nilmuth are doing their jobs."

"Rumours, yes. But only rumours. A way to capture and preserve one's soul, they say." Ghaldezuel waved away some more smoke from the relit pipe. "But it's nothing. A trick, some toy that Andolp charges *the naive to see." He stared at the Melius, head cocked. "Surely the Firmament is not taken in by this?"*

Pauncefoot reached and tapped the envelope, his nail clacking on the seal. "There are handsome rewards for the fool that tries. You have this day to think on it."

Ghaldezuel exhaled, putting a fist to his mouth and turning back to the window. Outside, perched on one of the ledge spikes, a scrawny carrion bird peered listlessly for mice in the square. The twinkling of a distant Voidship, high in the pale blue, caught its attention as it did Ghaldezuel's. He watched the shape travel slowly across the sky until it disappeared behind the sunbathed dome of a building set higher up the mountainside, a thin trail of brown exhaust like a skidmark the only evidence of its passage.

He turned his gaze back to the hulking Melius. "To gain entry into Nilmuth I would need a particular type of antique Voidship. But I suppose you know this already."

Pauncefoot smiled, exposing the rows of stained cleaver-teeth that had been clenched around his pipe. "A Jurlumticular lance-hull."

Ghaldezuel stared at the teeth. "The very same. It does not trouble you that the Prism who manufactured these are extinct?"

The giant took another drag of the spice, his eyes closing. "Not in the slightest."

"And my new employer?"

"Just another reprisal mission, as per usual. Lacaille naval command takes a seventy percent share in all bounty wrested from the enemy."

Ghaldezuel dropped his shoulders wearily, not bothering to swipe at the smoke any more. "And the Amaranthine? They oversee this?"

Pauncefoot grinned and tapped the pipe stem against his great teeth, clattering it back and forth like a stick against railings, but did not speak.

Ghaldezuel watched from the window as the Melius made his way back to the station through the narrow streets. Gawkers and beggars followed the massive creature at a respectful distance, tailing out like the wake of a ship behind Pauncefoot's sweeping turquoise robes, the followers themselves attracting an even stranger ecosystem of pets and smaller animals, come to nibble and skitter among the many feet pattering along the street. The Atholcualan Star *would not depart for another hour, Pauncefoot having stated his intention of taking advantage of the train's famous dining car rather than eating in the city. Ghaldezuel thought that just as well, even though Melius were reputed never to sicken. Of more concern to the stationmaster would be the creature's prodigious appetite; the giants devoured ten or more courses in one sitting, and they might run out of food before they reached Zuo.*

Ghaldezuel toyed with the envelope as he stared through the warped glass, the lingering sweet smoke still hanging in the room. The Firmamental Melius, he understood, did not consider themselves Prism at all, but rather some subspecies of Amaranthine favoured by the Firmament above all others. Ghaldezuel knew they were the same filthy stock as all the rest, simply grown huge in body and self-importance. He hated their weakness, their susceptibility, vowing to himself that he wouldn't end up like Pauncefoot, seduced by gilded pipes and fine clothes. He slid his knife through the plastic seal, turning to the table as he upended the envelope.

Three more Firmamental Ducats slipped free, ringing cleanly as they hit the wooden surface and rolled. He swept them aside, glancing once more at the window, and pulled out the wad of linen papers within, beginning at the first page.

So. A Lacaille Nomad, no less, the Pride of the Sprittno. *To be collected from Port Halstrom, where they bled from their mouths. His eyes moved down the leading paragraph, widening slightly. A number, in Lacaille Truppins: more than generous—excessive, wasteful. He turned the page, absently pulling out a chair and sitting. Three Colossus battleships, the* Zlanort, *the* Yustafan *and the* Grand-Tile, *would be at his command once he left this place, along with the combined might of eleven vacuum legions. Ghaldezuel shuffled through the remaining documents and spread them on the table. All were earmarked with a Lacaille naval stamp and another unknown signature. He squinted at it, trying to make it out, realising the letters were scrawled in Unified, the speech of the Amaranthine.*

Ink drawings—vague and crude—littered the early pages. He studied them carefully as his skull ached, beginning to grow exasperated. They showed a machine, but built as if poured or moulded—a cast of some kind. His faith in the cold pragmatism of the Immortals ebbed further as he flicked through to the end. They really did want this ridiculous object in Nilmuth—would stop at little to have it, apparently. He gave up, sliding the papers across the table and pressing his fingers to his eyes.

The room fell silent but for the warble of fanwings outside. Even the city's thousands of bells sounded muted. He stirred, listening, finally collecting his cloak from the back of the chair and throwing it over his shoulders.

At the doorway, Ghaldezuel surveyed the bare chamber, taking in the chipped plaster walls, once painted a jolly blue and now faded almost to nothing. He returned to the table, gathering the Ducats and locking them in the strongbox, stuffing the naval documents and envelope into the pouch of his buttoned breeches. His eyes settled on the bed in the corner, where Pauncefoot had squatted. The iron frame had bowed in the middle, the single blanket rumpled into the impression of the Melius's ample rear. Almost as an afterthought, he went to the window, propped it open a crack to let out the smoke and left by the front stair.

At the corner, he stopped beneath the shade of a ratty, denuded lemon tree to observe the market stalls through the midday crowd. Under bright awnings, Ringum ladies prepared skewers of roasting meat, flinging them to the highest bidder in a seething mass of raised white hands. One pasty, clawed fist held a linen note, three fingers raised, and was expertly tossed three skewers while the crowd looked on and yelled. The ignorance of tourists. That one would be followed home. Ghaldezuel disliked haggling at the meat auctions, understanding—though hardly caring—that there wasn't enough for everyone to buy. Behind the stalls, a corpulent yellow birthing sow suckled her young, grumbling and snorting as she tried to sleep. The mottled piglets travelled barely two feet from vulva to griddle in their short, uncomplicated lives, a chastity of existence that Ghaldezuel found he could almost envy. Returning to their mother's belly in the form of thrown slops lent yet more elegance to the process, he thought, generations birthed from—and returning to—the same stock of rations.

He walked a little distance to the stew pots, pushing through some Vulgar travellers who had stopped to count their money in a tight *huddle. Ghaldezuel looked behind to watch an emaciated pickpocket worm his arm into their stuffed bags while they conferred and then slip away, hobbling back past the paper-clad ticket sellers and into a shaded street overhung with coloured cloth. Other travellers were taking deepslides, their expensive optilockets secured by chains to the linings of their waistcoats. He looked at their wide-eyed, ugly faces, sweating and baking in the sun that now blazed down into the street, thinking again of the woman he had seen in her blue dress while he waited on the platform. The thieves of Atholcualan grew fractious and aroused in such heat; she wouldn't last long without protection.*

Ghaldezuel went and bought a lidded cup of stew, waving away the chance to bargain with a hundredth of a tin Truppin, and walked back along the crowded street to the square. He checked his clock, taking the long route around to his door, and let himself in.

They were efficient creatures, fast in their work. He leaned against the busted lock in the inner doorway to watch them trying to wrench open the strongbox. Two bandy-legged crossbreeds and a Lacaille—the ringmaster—with another three keeping watch (or so the raiders thought) from the balconies. One Ringum was engaged in upturning Ghaldezuel's chest of drawers, its thin, bluish hands rummaging through the heaps of fine clothes that spilled out. The other looked on, eating what appeared to be a baked tart, while their Lacaille companion worked at the box.

This particular band had shown an interest in him not long after his arrival in the city, taking note of Ghaldezuel's various comings and goings during his three weeks as knight-resident. He hadn't made it difficult for them; all knights new to Atholcualan were met by the Sigour himself and given a mounted tour of the districts, with a banquet at the fortress and a delivery of fruits from Zuo arriving on the Star. Some thieves acted only as spotters, following wealthy individuals for weeks at a time to learn their most intimate movements and then passing the information on for a fee. The robbers ransacking his room now had paid for the privilege but hadn't thought to check with their competitors. As such, Ghaldezuel knew the names, abilities and even transient residences of all those working his chamber, as well as all those he could trust to burgle them in turn. But now he was leaving, and it was time to settle.

Taking the long way home across the rooftops, he'd snapped two of the spotters' necks, shooting the third at a distance with a suppressed pistol. Now he strode swiftly forward, tripping the tart-eater and twisting its head on its shoulders. The Ringum fell without a word, glazed eyes staring at the ceiling, the thump of its body striking the wooden floor disguised by the clanging of the Lacaille still trying to gain entry to the safe. Ghaldezuel dumped his pistol on the table—any holes in the walls would lose him his room deposit—and grabbed the back of the leader's hair, slamming the Lacaille's forehead down onto the corner edge of the safe and bloodying the metal in a violent spurt, releasing the latch at last. The strongbox's door swung open.

He turned to observe the final Ringum (a tattooed, one-eyed half-Zelio that the spies called Magwitch) rise. Its good eye flicked to the remains of its leader, now crumpled beside the open safe, and back to Ghaldezuel. It had come too far to leave with nothing, that much was clear from its hesitation; Atholcualan gangs never took in lowly Ringum who had lost their masters.

Magwitch moved forward and grasped the back of the chair nearest the bed, hurling and smashing it to pieces against the wall. Ghaldezuel watched it scrabble in the debris and lift the sharpest piece to brandish with a hiss, optimism lighting its hideous features. In turn, he reached calmly beneath the bowed bed frame, shaking his head, and pulled free a sabre longer than his arm. He unsheathed it, smiling at the dismayed look on the Ringum's long-nosed face, and twirled the blade tiredly, pointing it arm-outstretched in the Op-Zlan starter pose. He was rusty, he supposed; the Ringum might offer some sport.

Magwitch hissed again, feeling behind for the wall. Ghaldezuel advanced, flicking the blade lazily back and forth. The Ringum snarled, noticing the partially open window. It tossed the wooden plank at Ghaldezuel and hurled itself through, ripping the latch from the frame and scattering shards of thin glass.

Ghaldezuel threw the blade onto the bed with a huff of disappointment, going to the remains of the window and gazing down into the street. Magwitch had survived the drop and was already hobbling away down the alley, one leg twisted. He thought of taking aim from the window, knowing he could drop the Ringum before it *got too far, but turned instead and went to sit on the bed. He counted from his purse, pouring out ten Truppins; the thieves might have used the window as he'd hoped, sparing the doorframe.*

At his feet, the clothes—tainted now from enquiring, dirty fingers—lay stirred and creased. He shovelled them into his arms and went to his cupboard, pulling down a dark leather travel case and stuffing the clothing into it, followed by the remaining contents of the strongbox. He slid the sheathed sabre carefully into the case's padded side, securing it with brass clasps. As he packed, his mind turned back to the Vulgar lady at the station for the briefest of moments, meeting her eye from along the station platform. He sighed again, running a hand through his hair and remembering the rings, taking them from the safe and checking that it was now completely empty before sliding them one by one onto his fingers. Crescents of blood had caked beneath the nails of his right hand. He picked mindlessly at the stains and looked about the room, realising with some resignation that he'd need to hire a cleaner after all.

An hour later he was on the road. The path to Praztatl was in places nearly vertical, a rock slope chiselled between the shards of the mountain and studded with rusting iron handrails. Where it became flatter, the surface had once been laid with crumbling brown brick, the remaining chunks now serving only to hobble and trip all those who used the passage up to the Mines of Mendellion.

Ghaldezuel swore, gripping the iron hoop before him as a clammy foot ground its sole into his knuckles. The climbers here were three abreast, a chattering network of travellers amid silent mine slaves, rock-breakers and furnace crews. Where the road became totally impassable—a sheer wall of polished stone five hundred feet above—Ghaldezuel could see a rope line. Visitors bottlenecked while they waited at the bottom, snatching drinks from flasks that they sometimes accidentally dropped to clatter and smash among the climbers below. People fell regularly, it was said, tumbling to dash upon the lower slopes and cupolas of Atholcualan beneath. So far, Ghaldezuel hadn't witnessed any accidents, though he wished the Ringum who was treading on his hand with each step—something partly Wulm, by the look of it—a quick and ugly demise. The Ringum looked down at him dispassionately as it gripped the next handhold, its long white ears blown flat in the mountain wind.

At the plateaued lip of the brick road, beggars from the Praztatl township waited in a camp of strewn rubbish. Ghaldezuel had scarcely hauled his bag over the edge before they came for him, pleading, gabbling. He growled, sending all but the bravest scampering. The remainder tittered and skipped before returning, asking again in glottal creole dialects for anything he might have to spare. Some of the naked Ringum here had tails, he saw; long bony whips with tufted, beaded ends.

"Op-Zlan," the closest said, apparently still convinced of Ghaldezuel's inner generosity, "lend us something."

"Lend?" Ghaldezuel spat, noticing as the creature reached into its hair and vigorously scratched free a shower of dandruff.

"It shall be returned!" the beggar yelped, delight crossing its face as it scratched. "Upon my word! Mine for but a moment!"

"Let me through," Ghaldezuel grumbled, shoving past and brushing at his bag where some of the Ringum's dandruff had settled on the leather. Ahead, the pits of the tin mines swarmed with workers, their lanterns kindling as evening fell. He watched them trundling their barrows across the slanted grey-white slab-sides of the mountain and down cut steps, the wind picking up, then glanced along the vertical road to the lights of Atholcualan twinkling in the grey twilight.

He turned back to the beggar. "I could lend you something, for a service."

The beggar stopped scratching and eyed him hungrily, its huge black pupils dilating.

"Take a message to the pit-master," Ghaldezuel said. "Tell Suartho the Vulgar that Ghaldezuel is here, at the causeway."

"Galdessuel," the beggar repeated uncertainly, coiling its tail around its nakedness in the growing cold. "A Truppin to tell."

He nodded, dropping the coin into the Ringum's hand. "Ghaldezuel. Remember the name."

The beggar rubbed the coin between its fingers, lifting it to its flat, wide-nostrilled nose and sniffing the metal. This trade was clearly for keeps. "Galdessuel—the Vulgar will know you are here."

The corsair waited, brooding, at the bottom of a steep ravine of shorn rock, illuminating the blackness like a gnarled, glowing jewel. Stretching into the darkness above, the cloistered ceilings of the mine glittered, their precious seams catching and twisting that distant light. The ship, though bulky for a Lacaille vessel and prodigiously armed, was barely superluminal. Only a tenth of its bulbous white body housed motors, the rest given up to seventeen long-gun battery chambers and a shell of dense plating more than fifteen feet thick. Nestled at its core was a private cell, a stateroom; for this corsair Ghaldezuel knew well—it belonged to King Eoziel XI himself, ruler of every Lacaille moon for six trillion miles, arch-enemy of the four Vulgar kings and their allies. It was purportedly escorted at all times by a battleship—the Grand-Tile—which Ghaldezuel assumed was now waiting in high orbit for the corsair's return, the services of which had been promised him by the Melius, Pauncefoot.

He turned to Suartho, the Vulgar pit-master, ready to go down.

The old foreigner grinned, exposing a graveyard of wet, brown teeth as he surveyed the view. "A powerful beast, for sure. You'll be safe aboard that, wherever you're going." When Ghaldezuel didn't comment, he pointed towards the glowing furnaces at the far end of the monstrous chasm, so distant that they looked more like campfires. "And replated with my tin, from my refineries. It is only the under-plating that comes from Zuo—they have a foundry there. I offered to supply the rubber—I used to make the best in Zalnir—but they didn't want it." He gave Ghaldezuel an appraising look. "Check to see if it's perished when you go inside, would you? Nothing gets past Suartho. Nothing."

Ghaldezuel wasn't listening. His eye followed the Oxel crews as they worked on the corsair's hull, their equipment roaring distantly as tiny sparks flew. "What are they doing?"

"Refits," the Vulgar said vaguely, as if he didn't really know either, the spoiled musk of his breath accompanying each word. "You are early, Ghaldezuel."

"I know," he replied coldly. "The climb isn't so hard, not with clean lungs and a healthy heart."

"Your heart is healthy?" Suartho chuckled. "That's not what I heard."

The slope of shale and crumbling soot was steeper than Ghaldezuel had imagined. It had taken an hour of picking his way down the black rock face among wraith-like waste sifters to arrive in the lit bowl of the corsair's makeshift hangar.

He stood and looked up at it, totally absorbed, the bag dropped at his side. The magisterial Voidship's name was the Ignioz, after a hero of the Investiture Wars. The enormous whitewashed vessel was helmed with a figurehead of tarnished silver plate, a statue of the titular admiral himself leaping from the prow between the falconet cannons, one muscular leg outstretched. In his glove, he flourished a lumen pistol of relatively modern design—directly after the war, the Firmament had forced the smelting of all Lacaille weaponry, apparently foiling the sculptor's wish for accuracy—his other hand thrust forward, thick index finger pointing, in the throes of a battle charge. Ignioz was said to have slain Amaranthine in the wild Threen moons; Ghaldezuel could believe it. Perennials, when they came to discussing those messy, expensive campaigns, reportedly refused to mention Ignioz's name in the hope that the hero might one day fade from Firmamental history altogether. He took in the glittering, romantically sculpted prow once more, glad to see first-hand such a fitting monument to the Immortals' failure.

And yet, he thought, hoisting his bag again to his shoulder, here he was now, in thrall to the Amaranthine Firmament just as Pauncefoot had smugly predicted.

Ghaldezuel shaded his eyes from the glare of the portholes, spotting the gaping entranceway to the service hold of the Ignioz further along its lumpen hull. Oxel crawled over the pitted blisters of the broadside turrets, whistling to one another in their absurd outer-Investiture speech. Barely the length of his forearm, they were chosen for their nimble fingers and enthusiasm for jobs no other species would willingly accept. Sociability kept them in line—imprison one alone and it swiftly died or went insane, but with fellows around them they *flourished. Huge populations of Oxel travelled the Prism Investiture in mysterious migrations, with generations—for an individual lived scarcely twenty years—sometimes surviving in secret colonies aboard battleships and tankers before being discovered and put to work or sold to the markets.*

Now as he came upon the Oxel, he was reminded of how scrawny and bat-like they looked, their naked bodies glistening with sweat in the dimness, many hanging upside-down with their long, moist fingers gripping the rivets of the fuselage. As Ghaldezuel approached, he saw that one had a white tattoo inked into the grime of its little forehead. He stopped to read it as the Oxel looked down at him.

"Op-Zlan, Knight of the Stars! My congratulations!"

He turned to his addressor, the Oxel whistling and halting their work at the new arrival.

His contact, a two-hundred-year-old Lacaille male with bent ear-tips and a fine yellowed beard, hobbled out from the shadows of the hull. He brushed crumbs from his rubber Voidsuit into the darkness at his feet. "I honestly did not think I would see you. Here." He fished in his pockets and handed Ghaldezuel a package of already opened messages. Ghaldezuel held them to the light to see one of the postmarks: Woenmouth, in the outer Investiture. A place known on some charts as the Whoop, being so very far away from anything else.

"The team are restless," the old Lacaille said, his crinkled, baggy eyes hidden in shadow. "They've developed a taste for these reprisal missions."

"I know, Vibor," Ghaldezuel replied, listening to the Oxel as they began to sing, their work resumed. He tucked the parcel of letters away. The Bult did not write, not even to sign a name, but they could dictate. "They'll enjoy this one especially, I think."

Vibor moved further into the light. "The timing is right?"

"The timing is more than right." He shrugged, looking up at the ship's hull. "There has never been a more perfect moment. Something is happening."

The old Lacaille winked at him. "People feel it. Someone, some Immortal, wants us to advance and the Vulgar to fall, even if it is to the detriment of the Firmament itself."

Ghaldezuel shook his head, picking up his bags. "But this thing they want, Andolp's Light-Trap—it won't help them."

"Not our fault. Not our business. Help them in any way you can, I say—help them spend their money and they'll grant your conditions."

Ghaldezuel cleared his throat by way of assent. He pointed up to the vessel's vast flank, rusted chains dripping down and securing it to bollards embedded in the rock. "Why does that Oxel have the word 'sorry' written on its forehead?"

Vibor turned and blinked into the darkness, though the Oxel in question was gone. "That one grew ill with a fever of violence. When it knew what would become of it, that it would lose its mind, it thought to apologise in advance to all it might harm."

At the cabin door, Ghaldezuel felt the corsair's engine compartments grumbling, stirring from their sleep. He was shown inside by a vacuum-suited Lacaille soldier with a face deformed by hundreds of tiny shrapnel scars. Ex-royal escort, most likely, battle-hardened and xenophobic. The soldier would not speak Vulgar or Pifoon, or any of the more sophisticated languages of power. Taking off his cloak and hanging it above the simple bed, Ghaldezuel moved to the porthole to look out, waiting for the soldier to leave. Through the thick, warped plastic he could make out the glowing furnaces in the distance, their thumping operations muted now within his sealed fortress. He cupped his hands against the light of the cabin but could see little else, eventually pulling down the metal shutter and sliding the bolt, locking it in place. He had messages to write, but the climb from Atholcualan's thin air into even higher lands had tired him out. In a day, the Ignioz would dock at the Grand-Tile, fastening inside the colossal battleship's hangar for its onward journey to Port Halstrom, in the Inner Investiture, a passage that would take more than a week. There would be ample time to draft messages, some of which would never reach their intended recipients anyway as they passed through kingdoms, country borders and small wars, thieves' pockets and cargo holds.

He pulled off his underclothes, the musk of the day's exercise reaching his nostrils, and draped them over the bottom of the plastic fold-out bed. He turned off the light, bolted the door and slid between the rough sheets into a pocket of utter blackness.

Ghaldezuel listened to the throb of the blood in his ears, smelling the vague odour of rancid butter from the ship's inner lining. He fancied he could hear something else, something possibly emanating from outside. Finally he sat up, the darkness thick and heavy, and pulled up the shutter again. Pressing his nose against the plastic, he could see the great bowl of the mine's chamber once more, its chiselled rock walls twinkling in the sparse light of the forges and what glow still filtered from the Ignioz's open hangar below. He watched an Oxel crawl four-legged to a tiny trolley on the ground, select a piece of equipment and scamper back to the corsair, its shadow long and grotesque.

As he looked out, Ghaldezuel realised he could see reflective eyes shining in the gloaming beyond the cloisters of rock. Slaves at rest, perhaps. Or possibly the mammalian inhabitants of the mine. Suartho had warned him that there were creatures here, things that had climbed in centuries ago and never left, things that dined on workers when they strayed from their details. Nonsense, of course, stories designed to keep work crews together and discourage flight. He pressed his face against the window, trying to see, feeling exposed and yet deliciously safe at the same time, a little boy hiding beneath blankets. The eyes stared, unblinking, then extinguished, pair by pair. Once again the mines were dark but for the glow of the furnaces, the only sounds, other than the distant rumble of the ship, coming from Ghaldezuel's own body. He glanced back into the blackness of his cabin, afraid for a moment, and lay down again. As his eyelids slipped closed, he thought of the woman from the station, her light dress billowing in the breeze, their eyes meeting, and pushed her at last from his mind.

PART I

PROXIMO

The air thickened, the cold boiling away and drying Lycaste's fluttering hair as he fell. His guts heaved under a new weightlessness, the slung dot of sun twirling as the world rolled. He scrunched his eyes closed, the last few breaths of cold Vilnius air squeezed from his lungs, unable to scream.

Abruptly, his feet met a surface. He was inside a dark, dust-coated space illuminated only by the streaming light of a small window. Lycaste swayed and trembled, wrapping his arms around himself.

Then he was standing in open meadow, the sun beating down across his back, staring at his long shadow through the flowers. A tawny black castle with enormous blue and gold flags drooping from its towers lay some distance off, hazed by distance. A glinting wasp settled on his hand and jabbed at him, breaking the spell. He flinched and grabbed it.

And he was up to his knees in still, warm water, wrapped in the heady scents of moss and damp.

Lycaste didn't want to move. He shuddered in the water, hearing an echo of Sotiris's words.

Stay with him. Do as he says. It'll be all right.

Darkness enveloped him.

Pins and needles shivered through him in pulses, finishing at his fingertips and leaping from each of them with the crackle of static. Lycaste cradled himself, grimacing, until the fear drifted away to form something new. He pushed a hand out into the dark, towards a crack of colour just beyond his reach. The smell was that of age and neglect, wood and cloth almost petrified beneath a fat, grey layer of dust. Lycaste coughed. He was in a cupboard. Another damn cupboard. He levered himself onto his knees in the dark, pushing through a rustling forest of hanging things. Garments, perhaps.

It'll be all right.

The light grew closer. He pressed an eye to it, pushing the door gently ajar.

He'd left things to grow mouldy in the back of his larder sometimes, always too frightened and revolted to go near them, and as he gazed out of the cupboard his skin crawled. It was as if the room he'd found himself within had been left to rot.

Dust so thick that it had sprouted wiry, branching hairs grew from every surface, its textures stippled with colours. What must once have been heavy curtains lined the walls, pulled closed so that only string-thin rays of sharply delineated sun slanted through the various holes in the fabric. The bright little beams of light were solid with still motes, only beginning to churn as the first of his breaths reached them. He made out a few items of ornate, dark furniture in the distance, his ears attuned to the falling rhythm of his slowing heart. He looked up into the grimy, mirrored ceiling, noticing how he could see into parts of other, darkened rooms. His head swam, and he felt for a moment as if he'd fallen into a dim, neglected kaleidoscope.

Lycaste stared along the ceiling at an opulent, inverted landscape of jumbled furniture until he convulsed suddenly with hacking coughs. His nose was filled with dust, caught in the thick, wiry hairs inside his nostrils. He wiped it with the back of his dusty hand, realising as he did so that he was still clutching something. Scrunched up in his fist: a clinking silver thing like a little stone. The wasp. It had been wearing a jewelled suit.

He staggered to his feet and went to the nearest curtain, dragging it open to a blaze of flying dust and squeezing his eyes shut against the glare.

The suggestion of a courtyard filled with fat palms down below. Lycaste recognised the flags flying from the rooftops: beautifully intricate golden stars stitched onto deep-blue silk.

He looked up then, all memory of his arrival melting away.

"*Oh*," he said.

He had died. He must have. His spirit had fallen through the world and out of the other side.

Every colour Lycaste had ever seen poured across the skies like wax, dripping and hardening to the curve of the land below. Seas glimmered like damask where the light burned twinkling across them; lands shone dully in claret veins lined with gold and green, the colours of their mountain peaks scraped away to white blades that pointed dagger-like to the centre, where a silently boiling disc of light glowed upon four huge stone buttresses rising from each compass point. He leaned out of the window a little, clutching the rotten frame. Dry brown meadows stippled with electric-blue flowers marched off into the distance, the tops of luscious palms swaying in the breeze. Lycaste felt the hot wind of the unspeakable place buffet him, drumming his ears, then craned his neck around to look directly up, past the sun, wondering if—were his eyesight good enough to see that many hundreds upon hundreds of miles—he would spot himself staring back.

Death was a mirror, it appeared, curved and unending.

A thunderous howl of rage brought him out of his reverie with a sweat. There was someone else here.

He moved away from the window, scooping dust with his feet, listening. Motes swirled as something thumped around the upper floors. Lycaste swallowed a tickle in his chest and tiptoed to the doorway, his heart racing.

Stillness. The tickle grew more insistent. Lycaste fought it down, feeling as well as hearing the padding of something huge walking away up above. He remembered: the Jalan they'd fallen with.

The rasping cough exploded out of him, raising dust. He staggered, swallowing.

The footsteps faltered and swung around, drumming in great vibrating thumps to where Lycaste could see the beginnings of an enormous flight of marble stairs. He turned and ran, raising a sweeping tide of dust.

The whole room rattled as the Jalan came for him, still unseen but for flashes of motion gaining on him in the dark reflections up above. Lycaste's heart thundered in his chest, as if it, too, were shaking and raising dust. He sprinted for the doorway of an adjoining chamber, his feet slipping. Another flight of marble stairs greeted him and he pounded up them, grabbing at golden railings to haul himself along, feet slapping the stone. The giant had arrived at his cupboard, great breaths reverberating up the stairway, and Lycaste knew he didn't have much longer. He followed the stairs around to the next level, everything rattling with the thump of his pursuer. As he passed a window, Lycaste caught sight of the little Vulgar soldier making his way across one of the ramparts, his armour twinkling, but didn't stop. At the edge of his vision, a dark claw reached out and he ducked, feeling its breeze as it passed. Lycaste whimpered and leapt the last few steps up to the next floor, swinging the door at the top shut behind him only for it to be slammed back open. The huge silhouette, black against the light of the grand stairway, shouldered its way in.

Lycaste kept very still, crouched in the shadows behind the arm of an ornate chair. The Jalan remained in the doorway, bent-backed and slobbering, his ears pricked like a hound's. Lycaste could see the whites of his great eyes as he peered into the room, gaze alighting every so often and moving on. Those eyes reached the chair Lycaste hid behind and halted, uncertain.

Lycaste let out his breath in tiny increments, his heart squirming, his skin darkening to black.

One thumping footstep, then another two. The Jalan walked towards the far curtains and flung them open, turning in the mist of dust.

Lycaste jumped from his hiding place and slid, diving beneath a vast claw-legged table and scrabbling as far as he could into its shadows. A huge hand darted after him, catching his toe. Its claws dug in, wrenching the toe out of its socket. Lycaste pawed the dust, choking, and was slowly dragged back from beneath the table and into the paler gloom of the open room, a polished trail following him through the grey. He trembled but kept still, as if somehow playing dead would help.

The gnarled face of the Jalan peered down at him, his great nose and brow casting huge shadows. Lycaste's toe throbbed.

"You're no Firstling," the giant rumbled while he tapped a finger against his battered cuirass, a carapace of angular metal as large as Lycaste's old boat. He considered the dim chamber for a moment, and, yanking Lycaste by the leg and dragging him to the window, hauled open another set of curtains. Warm light flashed into the chamber, illuminating a dozen Amaranthine seated at the table Lycaste had just crawled under. All were missing their heads.

The Jalan paid little heed to the death in the chamber. He was looking, rapt, out into the sky beyond the grand window, a ribbon of drool trembling from his lips as the wind sighed in.

"You!" he cried suddenly, dropping Lycaste and leaning out. He swung back, slavering and breathing hard, thumping around to the edge of the table and hurling it to one side. The bodies tumbled from their chairs. Lycaste covered his head, fully expecting to be next, but the giant was already storming out of the room and back to the stairs.

Lycaste waited until he heard the Jalan making his way through the halls above, then inspected his toe and hobbled to the window.

The Amaranthine, Hugo Maneker, was out there, dangling from a distant rampart by the tips of his fingers.

"*Meddling turd!*" the great voice bellowed. The giant had made it to Maneker's ledge, his tongue lolling, the shadow of his fourteen-foot-tall frame looming as he knelt to take the Amaranthine's fingers. "I ought to cast you to your death," the giant sneered in First, that strange, slightly-too-high-pitched voice stilled to a grumble. "It's finished, all of it. *Everything.*" He bent, and slowly prised one of the Amaranthine's fingers away from the ledge, looking into Maneker's eyes, daring him to respond. "It's not so hard at all, really, is it? To kill one of you."

"Get it *over* with," Maneker said, his voice clear and composed as he dangled. He raised his voice. "*Do it, Elatine!*"

"You think I won't?" Elatine cried, gripping another of the Amaranthine's tiny fingers in his claws and bending it back with a snap. Lycaste watched Maneker's face, noting how nothing appeared to alter in his disgusted expression. He wondered why the man didn't use his abilities to try and free himself.

"*Do it!*" the Immortal raged, a sudden thermal whipping at his clothes. Elatine's lank hair stirred and stood on end, parting where sweat had stuck it into clumps. He lifted Maneker upwards like a stringed puppet, peeling back his lips to reveal his huge mouth of jagged teeth.

"Stop that!" a familiar voice cried in a helium-squeak almost too thin to be heard.

Lycaste glanced to the end of the ledge, remembering the Vulgar, Huerepo. The little person heaved himself over the edge and stood watching Elatine cautiously.

"Look what you're doing!" Huerepo continued in First, his tiny body squaring up against Elatine's brooding shadow. "To an Amaranthine!"

Elatine glowered at the bite-size Vulgar and flattened his ears, his predatory eyes set deep in caves of shadow. Butterflies flooded Lycaste's stomach at the sight, but the Jalan stood where he was, apparently about to say something, finally choosing to remain silent. He dropped Maneker back onto the ledge, regarding Huerepo solemnly.

"It's over, anyway," Elatine said, turning to address the landscape. He flicked his eyes to the sun, noticing perhaps for the first time how it stood supported by four stone columns many miles thick. At length, he looked down at Maneker as if considering whether to help the man after all.

"Write to me when you're mad, Amaranthine. It would cheer me no end."

He strode off, a limp forcibly and self-consciously corrected, picking his way across the roof.

Huerepo watched him leave, scuttling to the Amaranthine's aid when he was sure Elatine had gone. Lycaste wondered how the little man was planning to haul someone twice his weight over the edge.

The Vulgar glanced across to Lycaste's window and waved his rifle. "Hello! I need a hand here."

Lycaste stared for a moment then nodded, making his way to the stairs while trying not to look at any of the fallen corpses in the room. Conscious that Elatine was still at large somewhere in the place, he kept his footfalls light.

This is not death, he realised, passing slanting bars of light churning with motes. It was something else, something his little mind just couldn't comprehend.

He arrived at a tall, broken window that offered a better view of the lands outside, observing how a sinuous tree grew from the stones of the black walls down below. The meadows stretched unbroken beyond where Lycaste thought the natural horizon should have been, the umber plain only breaking up into islands when it met the pale body of a circular sea.

Continuing on, he found a way out onto the peaked roofs and negotiated a careful exit through another smashed window—this one conceivably the victim of Elatine's rampage—watching his footing and trying to ignore the huge drop into the palm-lined courtyard below. He picked his way to the Vulgar's side and together they looked down at the Amaranthine. Maneker glared sullenly at the dark stone in front of him.

"Does that finger hurt?" Lycaste asked tentatively in First, crouching. Elatine's nails had cut into the flesh like blunt, wide-edged knives.

"No," Maneker replied in Tenth.

"Well . . ." He glanced at Huerepo and back to the Amaranthine, finally extending a hand. "Here."

At first, it didn't look as if the Immortal was going to accept. Finally, he glanced up at Lycaste's hand and grabbed it, allowing himself to be hoisted quickly and easily onto the parapet ledge. He brushed at his rags, examining the finger for a second before stuffing his hand into a pocket.

"Will he come back, do you think?" the Vulgar asked.

"Not if he knows what's good for him," Maneker snapped, glaring at the lines of ornate windows. At length, he turned away, nostrils flaring. Lycaste glanced between them; the Vulgar Huerepo had sat down against the inner wall, not appearing to notice a milky, pale pink gemstone the size of an egg lodged in the dark marble beside him. Dozens more had been planted by some haphazard design everywhere Lycaste looked. The Vulgar smoothed his hair down, his helmet having apparently fallen off in the fall, and wiped the sweat from his brow with the back of a hand.

Lycaste took in the soldier's long, white ears with their dangling lobes, the foreign elongation of his skull. The man's small nose was curiously feminine, pointed daintily at the end much like the tips of his ears, and endowed with two rather prominent nostrils. A wiry sprouting of moustache hairs decorated the corners of his lips, ginger where the sun caught them, and Lycaste couldn't help but think of the golden Monk-men he'd seen begging at garden walls or wandering the shores of Kipris Isle, bashing away inquisitively at shells and digging for worms as the tide fell back. Huerepo's fur-lined pinstripe tunic, wrinkled and darkened with sweat, poked from the neck of his tarnished armour—what

Lycaste remembered from his schooling might have been called a *plackart*—a size or two too big for him as if it were nothing but a family hand-me-down. Someone, perhaps his father, had described to him how the furred Monkmen fitted into the lineage to which Lycaste himself also somehow belonged, and to which, by some vague extension, these Vulgar people must also belong. They were all of them related: fourth and fifth cousins once, twice, thrice removed. Their eyes met briefly as Lycaste studied him, unable to look away despite the vastness of the world around them. Huerepo stared back, as if noticing the difference between the two of them for the first time himself, then pulled his simple pistol from its holster to inspect it, tipping a handful of bullets into his palm. Lycaste had seen Old World bullets—Impatiens had kept a store of them in his home for shooting bottles—but they were mostly spherical, not particularly dangerous unless you caught one in the eye. He got the impression that the sharp things Huerepo was counting would have stopped Elatine without much trouble, feeling a little safer at the thought.

He glanced at Maneker, who stood with his back to them, gazing out at the view. The Amaranthine's corpse-borrowed clothes were stained with watermarks of yellowed grime, ripped here and there by the fall to reveal patches of tanned skin beneath. Lycaste went to the wall's edge, keeping his distance from the Immortal. After a while, Maneker glanced at him askance, his rage apparently abated at last.

"And what do they call you? Something floral, I suppose?"

Lycaste looked down at him, almost afraid to reply. "Lycaste Cruenta, Tenthling."

Maneker nodded, taking in Lycaste's nine foot height. "A red Tenthling Melius. And a friend of Sotiris Gianakos, no less. You *have* come up in the world, haven't you?"

Lycaste coloured self-consciously, glancing around at Huerepo, who had stopped fiddling with his gun to watch them. "I did as he asked—I found you."

"You did. And now here we are."

Lycaste followed his gaze. "Where . . . ?" he began carefully, hearing the stupidity in his own voice.

"Proximo Carolus," the Vulgar said from behind them. "The Second Solar Satrapy."

Lycaste took a breath, realising how terrified he'd been that his first fears—that they were all of them dead and turned to spirits—might be confirmed. Maneker turned, surprised.

"I recognise the land bridge from maps, Amaranthine."

The Immortal nodded approvingly. "Then you know we haven't come far. Four light-years or so. Your name?"

"Huerepo, Sire," the Vulgar said, performing an extravagant little bow.

"How," Lycaste began, unable for a moment to phrase his question, "how did we get . . . inside?"

Maneker gestured to Huerepo for the answer. "Vulgar?"

Huerepo glanced at Lycaste sheepishly. "Bilocation. Amaranthine can telegraph themselves, disappear and reappear at will. The iron particles in their blood align into patterns over time. It is a magnetic effect."

Lycaste nodded slowly as if he understood, a technique he'd perfected over the years to avoid follow-up questions. Maneker looked shrewdly at him, then at Huerepo.

"You speak well for a Prism, Vulgar."

"Thank you, Sire," Huerepo said courteously, dipping his head. "And you saved our lives."

Lycaste grunted in agreement. His head still spun at each glimpse of the view from the parapet. *Four light-years,* Maneker had said. The words meant nothing, of course, but carried with them the suggestion of enormity. It was clear, he thought, as he placed a hand on the smooth, warm marble of the wall, that any dangers he had faced before were long gone now, dissolved as they'd fallen into the night.

The Vulgar got to his feet and Lycaste watched with mild alarm as the little man hoisted himself over the steep pitch of the roof and disappeared. The Amaranthine, having gone through the pockets of his stolen rags and placed an assortment of trinkets on the wall, now appeared to be thinking, and Lycaste wasn't inclined to disturb him. The breeze moaned around them, hot and flower-scented, the plaintive cries of an altogether foreign bird lilting on the air, making him feel even further from home. Far beyond, rivers poured like slippery silver into green deltas, hazed by gargantuan distance. He felt himself retch, swallowing, but nothing came up. It felt like a long time since he'd last eaten.

A wild commotion drew Lycaste's attention abruptly back to the roof, the hair rising on his arms. Huerepo stumbled into view, tripping, cursing and waving his pistol. Two creatures followed, both brandishing black metal staves like pokers. At the sight of them, Lycaste stood, squaring his shoulders instinctively. They were smaller and even uglier than the Vulgar, both dressed in fine, shimmering waistcoats of red fabric. Lycaste realised with a start that the material was silk.

The two Prism noticed him and paused, their tirade of abuse halted for a moment, before thrusting the staves in Huerepo's direction again. Both the Vulgar and the other creatures raged at each other in a language Lycaste had never heard before, though he found it relatively easy to detect the percussive expletives, repeated over and over again by both sides. Huerepo stamped his little foot and aimed his weapon theatrically at the nearest one, screaming at the top of his voice, but the creature appeared undeterred.

Maneker watched the altercation with a cool eye. He stepped past the three quarrelling Prism, apparently unconcerned as Huerepo pulled the trigger in his attacker's face. The pistol misfired with a puff of white smoke, a golden shell pinging away across the roof.

"Bilocation ruins weaponry," Maneker said tersely, stepping between the Prism and forcing them apart. "*Away*," he cursed, slapping at one of the angry creatures. It howled and dropped its poker with a clang, scuttling behind its fellow. Huerepo turned the pistol over in his hands, confused.

Lycaste sat down warily, listening to the way Maneker spoke to the creatures in that same, clipped language and covertly examining Huerepo's pistol. It looked fairly simple, even to him: a coil of rusted spring encased in a soldered stock, slid back and forth by a bolt. Some slight artistry had been engraved into to the weapon's golden barrel, which Lycaste guessed had originally come from another firearm.

After what felt like a very long time, in which Huerepo managed to completely dismantle the gun and put it back together again, the Amaranthine turned back to them, snapping his fingers.

"These Pifoon say the port of Astirion-Salay—a few days from here—still operates, but they won't take me there. Bands of disloyal acolytes are roaming the Satrapy lands, on the lookout for Amaranthine."

Maneker assessed them with his shrewd gaze, "I can't have anyone slowing me down." He licked his lips, glancing out into the expanse. "I have places to be, as I'm sure you both understand."

Lycaste cradled his elbows, dismayed. "But . . . what—"

Maneker shot him a glare. "Do as you *wish*, sir. Stay here or walk to the far pole, I really don't care—but if I find you on my trail it won't be pleasant." He took a longer look at Huerepo, then drew his rags about him and marched away across the roof, the two jowly Pifoon shooting them malevolent glances before following. After a few feet the Amaranthine hesitated, turning back. "But be warned. This place is not safe—not for any of us. Tread lightly, wherever you go." He considered them, the wind tousling his hair. "I wish you both luck."

When Maneker had gone, Lycaste crept to Huerepo's side and the safety of the pistol, which the soldier was hastily reloading. "That's it?" he asked, feeling the first stirrings of panic. "He's leaving us here?"

"Evidently."

"I thought this was an Amaranthine land? It isn't safe?"

Huerepo slid the last bullet into its chamber and wound the mechanism closed, pulling back an oiled spring and cocking a latch at the side. "He was imprisoned by them," the Vulgar said, "an enemy of the Firmamental Throne." He glanced at Lycaste, shrugging. "As, I suppose, are we, as accomplices."

"Nonsense," Lycaste said, shaking his head. "I know an Amaranthine—Sotiris. He's a kind man."

Huerepo snorted. "Kind men are not welcome these days." He stood with a groan, holstering the pistol. "Come on."

"But he told us not to follow him," Lycaste said.

The Vulgar stared at him. "You're a simple soul, aren't you?"

There was no further sign of Elatine in the castle's dust-choked interiors. A wide spiral stairway led down into the tower, each surface carved from smooth marble. Larger jewels embedded in the pinkish stone shone dully as they passed, perhaps polished smooth by the inquisitive touch of thousands of years' worth of guests. Lycaste stopped and listened, peering down the steps to the next floor where a jumbled pile of broken porcelain lay at the centre of a swirling white floor mosaic.

Huerepo checked his rifle as he went, perhaps refusing to believe that it had also been damaged by the Bilocation. Lycaste paused at the pile of smashed crockery, watching the Vulgar fiddling with the weapon.

"What do you think? Will it work?"

"I can't tell," the Vulgar said. He sighted it on an unbroken marble urn the size of a bathtub and pulled the trigger as Lycaste covered his ears. It clicked, the spring snapping forward like an animal trap, but didn't fire. They looked at each other.

Huerepo cursed, hurling down the weapon and kicking it across the floor. Bullets emptied as it spun, mostly spilling down the next stairwell. Huerepo paused, breathing heavily, both of them listening to the clicking roll of the ordnance as it made its way to the levels below, the echoes of the Vulgar's rage reverberating down through the chambers of the building.

Lycaste picked up a broken shard of porcelain the length of a dagger, finding a smaller piece among the rubble and handing it to Huerepo. He followed the sound of the rolling bullets, making his way carefully down the small steps, built for daintier feet than his own. "Who do you expect to meet out here, anyway? More of your sort? Those vicious-looking things that were killing Secondlings?"

"These Vaulted Lands are open now, to anyone and anything with an interest in treasure," Huerepo said. "This will be a hellish place in no time, what with the treaty over and the Amaranthine strung up." He looked at Lycaste as he stooped to collect another bullet. "The Vulgar, the Lacaille, the Pifoon—they'll all be fighting tooth and claw for whatever they can get."

"But don't the Amaranthine employ you? You would steal from them?"

Huerepo shrugged, frowning as he looked down the darkened stair. "Hounds eat their master when he dies."

They continued on, passing dark, empty ballrooms and great magenta-veined doors double Elatine's height, emerging after a while into the antechamber of the marble edifice, the fields of flowers sighing at the end of the pale hall.

"Did you see all the headless people?" Lycaste whispered as they made their faltering way under dappled palm shadows, at the mercy of twinkling, zipping insects.

"Yes," Huerepo said. "This is a place of arrival, I think. They must have been left here as a warning."

Gradually the forest swallowed them, hiding the views of the meadows beyond. Lycaste's guts felt hollow from hunger. Drool ran from the corners of his mouth. He considered the shiny insects, wondering whether the bees were like that—all bejewelled and fancy—simply because they fed on the glittering landscape. He had a sudden image of himself stumbling home one day barnacled with sapphires from head to toe, nothing but skin and bone beneath.

Unseen creatures hooting in the palm canopies brought his attention back to the forest around them. They were following a trodden trail in the moss, glistening where boots had trampled not long before.

"Should we be going this way . . . ?" Lycaste muttered, his words dying off.

A person stood among the trees, glaring sidelong at them. Huerepo wandered on obliviously, still muttering, his pockets clinking with bullets and jewelled insect shells.

More men came, slipping in and out of shade. Huerepo noticed at last and froze, his fingers flying to his holster and remaining there.

They wore patched red and blue velvet, Lycaste saw, rubbed and threadbare around the elbows and knees, with high boots that fitted close around their shins like those he had seen some of the Amaranthine wearing. Thick chains dangling assorted pendants, rings and talismans hung from their necks. Scabbarded swords weighted with gems adorned the belts of many, threatening to drag down their pantaloons. Their bushy, expectant faces studied him, impolitely uncoloured.

More men sitting deeper in the woods saw him and stood, their ears flattening curiously. They were dressed in shining plates of beautiful yet ancient-looking armour. Great dyed beards hung from the chins of the eldest, clearly combed and coiffed with great care. Their mounts, tied in the shade of the palms beyond, were leopard-spotted, stunted relatives of the zeltabras from home.

They were Melius, like him, but of a race he'd never seen before.

"*Alsu, son Elt Worlter*," said a sitting man in some gibberish speak. Then: "Lycaste?"

A cold sweat rippled over him.

The Melius looked questioningly at him.

He noticed how the men at the back had long rifles aimed at Huerepo rather than him. "Yes?"

"*Lycaste!*" two other men exclaimed together. "*Lycaste del Elt Worlter!*"

Lycaste smiled nervously as they laughed. He shrugged, his embarrassment growing, and they roared with approval. Even Huerepo had begun to smirk, though weapons were still trained on him. Everyone quietened abruptly as Maneker shouldered his way through the company and glared at Lycaste.

"I gave simple instructions," he said. "*Simple* instructions. But here you are." The Amaranthine climbed into the stirrup of the smallest beast and sat astride, waiting. "Get a ferdie."

Lycaste gaped at him.

"Get a *mount*, imbecile."

The only spare was tethered to a palm deeper in the woods. Lycaste checked its bags and gave it a pat. Huerepo followed him, stopping short and pointing.

"What's that about, then?"

He looked, spotting a body lying crumpled on the forest floor, its feet tied to the saddle of the nearby animal. He appeared to be a bandit, perhaps the sort Maneker had mentioned. He'd been dragged behind the mount and was bloodied from head to foot, his clothes peeled almost completely away. A beautifully iridescent weapon lay in the moss beside him. Lycaste bent, not wanting to touch the body, studying the gun more closely.

"Amaranthine weapon," Huerepo said, standing back and eyeing the corpse uneasily.

Lycaste moved to retrieve it, holding his breath to avoid the stench of decomposition. He'd thought he might get used to death, having seen and smelled so much of it in such a short space of time, but he found himself quivering once more, his old bravado nothing but a spell that had touched him briefly and left. He picked up the weapon: a pistol, by the looks of it.

It was, fittingly, an item of Amaranthine perfection, carved from what appeared to be a single piece of polished crystal or pearl. Some distant, detached part of his mind found the weapon exceptionally beautiful and wished to collect it, the way he'd once collected wooden people for his palace back home. He gripped the stock, smooth against his palm.

The dead man muttered and flung out a hand, grasping him by the ankle. Lycaste yelped, involuntarily kicking him, and jumped back. The bandit smiled a gap-toothed smile.

"Take it," he wheezed in First. "Use it."

Lycaste held it away from the man.

The bandit smirked, his head lolling back. "Use it on them, while they are a-sleeping."

Lycaste met Huerepo's eye and stowed the pistol hurriedly in a bandolier dangling from the ferdie's saddlebags.

"Farewell," the man said, breathing quickly as if he'd just run a race. "Lycaste, of the Old World."

They made camp in the seemingly endless meadows that evening, tethering their ferdies to another grove of low, thick-trunked palms. Lycaste saw to his own, having been given it for the remainder of the journey on the provision that he kept up with the convoy as it cantered through the grass, the riders sitting high on their animals' rumps.

Something had been following them through the mossy forest as they'd left its borders: a shadow peeping between the trees. It could only have been Elatine, jealously watching them go. Lycaste kept trembling watch, understanding that his guides, though they kept their own counsel, had noticed the shadow, too.

He looked at the ferdie's calm, dark eyes as he tied it, patting its spotty flank. He wouldn't give it a name, and yet the part of him that was most afraid wanted to, just so he might have a friend.

Over the half-day's ride from the castle, they'd lost that feeling of pursuit, seeing little but flowers and grass, their ferdies stoically navigating the paths in the meadows, ears flicking at the curiosity of jewelled insects and tiny velvety hummingbirds that hovered to inspect them. Lycaste had tried to talk to the birds, sensing as he did so Huerepo's amusement behind him, but they only stared beadily for a moment more before flitting to the next rider. The Vulgar, who had chosen to sit atop Lycaste's shoulders rather than be carried in a Loyalist's saddlebags, had spent the day antagonising the bees into stinging him while steadily passing down a number of gold and silver barbs. Lycaste kept them for him in a pouch, wondering incredulously what the little man wouldn't do for treasure.

Those they rode with were mostly silent and hunched, flicking their whips at their ferdies and watching the curved, never-ending horizon rolling away above. The dissident they dragged behind was almost certainly dead by the time they lost sight of the castle. Lycaste noticed when he looked behind that the trail of blood in the flowers—like the mark of a wide, red-dipped paintbrush—had run dry. The Loyalists broke the silence only to speak to Maneker, who rode out ahead, in low, reverential tones. Their speech was that of the Firmament. Sotiris himself had described it to him on their ride through the Second: Unified. He fancied he could catch the gist of their briefest sentences for just a moment, before the foreign sounds sank and dropped beyond understanding.

After a Quarter or so of this, Lycaste asked Huerepo quietly if he might mind translating.

And so Lycaste knew as they made camp that they were heading to the estate of the Satrap of Proximo himself, an Immortal named Vincenti. The Melius who sat around the fire, still armoured, were mostly the Satrap's men, sent out to slaughter any dissidents they found, ensuring that there was still one place in the Vaulted Land where the Amaranthine held order.

Lycaste made his way slowly to the fire, unsure of where to sit. Only a vague sense of disgust kept him from all but following the Vulgar Huerepo's every move, hoping that he wouldn't have to talk to the other Melius as they sat around their fire to eat. He watched Maneker carefully as the Amaranthine found a place to sit apart from the others with a bottle of something, resolving that the Immortal was the last person he would turn to for companionship.

Out in the darkness, some sparks of light gave away a distant tower they'd seen as they rode that day; great bonfires Huerepo had told him were lit by Prism that had taken the place. He kept his Amaranthine pistol close as he sat among the Loyalists, his eyes drawn to the bubbling skewers that one man had pulled out of the fire. The tiny hummingbirds weren't more than a mouthful each, but someone at the back of the convoy had apparently been catching them by the hundreds.

"*Sje miech son Arom,*" said the Loyalist beside him, the Melius with the great red beard. He produced a fretworked locket from around his neck and opened it, showing Lycaste that it was filled with the petals that must have attracted the birds. They gave off a sharp, almost poisonous stink. Lycaste nodded hesitantly, taking a silver plate of roasted birds as they were scraped from the spit. He saw Huerepo sitting further back—unwelcome at the fire—and dropped another couple of birds onto the plate. Then the red-bearded Loyalist unbuttoned his top pocket and produced a short pipe. Lycaste watched him brandishing it, finally shaking his head as he realised what was being offered. The man smirked and took a flaming twig from the fire, touching it to the bowl and puffing until it smouldered. He inhaled deeply, eyes creasing, and turned to look at Lycaste again.

"First?" he asked unexpectedly through a mouthful of coiling smoke. "You speak First?"

"A little," Lycaste said.

"Lycaste the Old World Melius," the man said, smiling to himself. He glanced up. "What happened—you come here with this one?" He indicated Maneker with his pipe.

Lycaste nodded uncertainly, finding the man's accented mumbling difficult to understand through his elaborate moustaches. He looked into the Loyalist's brown-gold eyes, yellowed around the iris as if he'd been drinking for many days straight.

"There are Prism here," the man said. "Prism everywhere. One killed Pigtail, my friend, so I skewered him." He looked at Lycaste suddenly, miming the action with his pipe stem. "You know this word? *Skewered?*"

Lycaste shrugged, picking at his nails. He glanced off to where Huerepo sat and decided to take him his supper.

The Vulgar looked up from his thoughts, apparently confused at what he was being offered, and then broke into a sharp-toothed, disarmingly charming smile. "You didn't want to sit with the others?" he asked as he ate.

"I don't like them."

"Why? Because you don't understand them?"

Lycaste shook his head in the darkness, eyes drawn to the far-off glimmer of the tower, then up to the glowing topside of the Vaulted Land, somehow bright as day and yet leaving them in darkness below. "It's not that. I think I almost can, some of the time. I just don't want to talk to them." He looked off to where he thought the Amaranthine was sitting, on the other side of the fire. "And I certainly don't want to be anywhere near Maneker."

Huerepo finished his last bird, crunching the bones and smacking his lips, obviously thinking of more. "Why's that?"

Lycaste dropped his voice. "He's . . . he's not at all like the other Amaranthine I knew. Sotiris was kind."

Huerepo snorted, licking his fingers. "No such thing as a kind Amaranthine."

Lycaste shook his head. Sotiris had saved his life. He could only feel love for the man. At the same time, a new worry snagged amid the tangle of others. *Sotiris was kind.* He'd spoken as if the Amaranthine were a thing of the past, as if he were gone.

Lycaste glanced back at Huerepo. "They were friends—Sotiris said—he and Maneker. But they aren't at all alike. I thought I'd feel safe now that we're with him, but I don't."

Huerepo shrugged, patting a knapsack he'd taken from Lycaste's ferdie into a decent pillow shape. "He's been alive a long time, Lycaste. He knows more of life than you or I ever could. I think I'll trust the Amaranthine with mine."

Lycaste's low voice became a whisper. "What about this Satrap, Vincenti? He might take us in. He might know a way for us to get home."

"Home?" Huerepo asked incredulously. "The Old World isn't *my* home. I was born in a Shantyland on Nirlume. All thirty of my brothers and sisters died. I earned a fifth of a Filguree a day scraping crablings and sluppocks." He raised his little eyebrows. "Have you ever scraped a sluppock? They don't come off in one go, and they bite while they're doing it. I think I'll stay here."

Lycaste had an image of something black and slimy attached to a rock, all teeth inside its coils. He blinked the image away, noticing the tangle of thin white scars at the nape of Huerepo's neck for the first time. "But Maneker doesn't need us, he doesn't even want us—he'll probably leave us with the Satrap anyway."

Huerepo shrugged, obviously frustrated. "Then I'll make myself indispensable to this Satrap."

Lycaste shook his head and looked away to the fire, his eyes alighting on each of the Melius as they talked. Some had begun to stretch out, removing the most uncomfortable items of their armour so they could lie flat in the grass. In the sighing palm-tops above the tethered ferdies, Lycaste could just make out the silhouette of a Melius keeping watch, his Amaranthine rifle leaning against his shoulder.

He couldn't bring himself to admit that he needed Huerepo to get away from this place, having no idea exactly where they were. After a period of silence, the Vulgar stretched and rolled over, muttering to himself while he shoved the knapsack into a better shape. Lycaste laid his head down beside Huerepo's, two private, locked boxes impervious to each other's thoughts, and allowed himself another good long look at the dayside of the world.

Proximo Carolus, he thought, marvelling at the shape of the Amaranthine name on his breath as his gaze traced the lines of continents, the vertigo returning while his mind tried to sort down from up, the homesickness and longing fading before his eyes. Cream swirls of cloud patterned the lands, pink at the edges of the dawn to the east and west, darker and more tightly coiled towards the seas. His eye made out a break in their pattern high beside a perfectly circular blue sea, and for a moment he forgot everything else. There was a fire burning, surely larger than any fire anyone had ever seen, the smoke staining a sweep of land almost all the way up one curled arm of coast. He squinted, making out flea-like grains that swarmed slowly above the landscape, bright against the smoke trail where they winked in the light. Lycaste looked to the sentry in the trees to see if the Loyalist had noticed them, but staring too long at the bright side of the world had washed out his eyes, leaving him blind to the darkness. He turned his attention back to the view.

The fleas were curling, surrounding a legion of others, at first so slowly that they appeared to have stilled. Then from the south a scrawl of white streaks tore upwards, penetrating the swirl and scattering them. Lycaste was vaguely aware that, though their motion appeared sluggish, the shapes must have been moving unfathomably quickly to cover so much distance in such a short time. The coil of attackers dissipated, coalescing at a distance and falling in what must have been a charge. The origin of the white streaks revealed itself: two larger flecks that Lycaste could just make out the shapes of if he strained his eyes, surrounded by a swarm of dots only visible in their groupings and swirls. A new blackness drifting upwards from the throng must have been more smoke or soot from the attack. Lycaste found himself remembering the thunder of the war as he'd ridden in the carriage from the Utopia and was grateful not to be anywhere near what was happening over that circular sea. He cast his eyes around the rest of the world, taking his time at every range and lake they came to, but couldn't make out any other enemy movements. Finally, he looked to the sun, the side facing them a black circle where it lay against the surrounding world, and saw the real battle for Proximo.

Hundreds, perhaps thousands of them were up there, harrying others as they apparently defended the columns that held the sun aloft. Lycaste knew perfectly well that the specks he saw were not individual Prism folk but their wonderful ships, the Voidcraft. Against the night-black of the sun's disc, he saw his first flashes, popping with an almost-heard sound. The whole dark sphere of the sun could be covered by his outstretched hand, but Lycaste was sure those flashes, detonating by the hundred every few breaths, were colossal in size. He gazed up at the twinkling for a while, considering how beautiful it might have been if he'd not known how many instant deaths each flash represented.

He closed his eyes for a while, letting the green glare of after-image fade in the blackness, and reopened them slowly. The night was dark again around them. Nearly all the Loyalists appeared to be asleep, accompanied by Huerepo's delicate, grumbling snores at his side. Lycaste looked past the fire and saw Maneker still sitting, his head tilted to the black sun.

In his mind, Lycaste found he could almost picture the Satrap they were travelling to meet: a kindly old man with a long white beard who would welcome them warmly into his home—a home much like the model palace Lycaste had built for himself back in the Tenth. He knew of course that the man would look like Maneker or Sotiris, but was unable to come up with a squashed, pinhead Amaranthine face that would serve his daydreams, picturing instead that of a Melius man with high, rounded cheekbones, the drooping nose so often associated with gentlemanly wisdom. He hoped very much that this Satrap, this Vincenti, might have known Sotiris in some way, just so that perhaps together they might talk of him some more. Lycaste realised as he closed his eyes that he missed the man who had saved his life more than anything else; more than his estate on the beach, likely sold by now, he supposed. More than Impatiens, who in his gruffness had tried, though Lycaste had never realised it, to nurture him, to prepare him for the world. More than Pentas—that half-forgotten name and cause of all the misery he knew. More than Jasione, even, the first woman, he was sure, who had ever loved him. He missed his friend. Sotiris was safety; Sotiris was home.

CORIOPIL

They were a wilderness, these moons. Glowing discs of colour like lights seen through drizzle, the filaments of lanternfish in the deepest sink-holes of the world. He had chosen one, fallen to it the way something darts, impelled, to that glimmer in the black. Now he was trapped for-ever, his soul ensnared. Celia. No, *Zelio*. Rhythmically beautiful words for death. He hears a dry voice, a feminine voice, asking him what in the world he's doing, all the way down here.

The wild sun arced and sank into the sea, a circle of faded, foreign colour. Maril knew as he squinted at the light that it wasn't the star he'd been born under, even if his other thoughts were muddied and diluted, stretched to a blur. Heat and green seas rocked the bed while he recounted the tiny details of his old life. A shadow sometimes moved beside him, dampening his face with something as warm as the water, but most of the time he was alone with his past, reliving it over and over again.

Maril remembered his unborn children. He'd have called the boys Wilemo and Osgol, had they lived. The girls—though only officially named upon their wedding day by their husbands—were to be Imsi, Briol and Fanesho. His dead progeny sat beside him while he slept, natives of this hot, green place.

Once the blanket came away and he stirred, trying to grasp it and tug it back, his eyes fluttering open to see the curving wall of colour above, churning like the slow currents of the sea. He grasped for the blanket and the hot blackness returned.

"That the last of it?" Maril asked as he sat on the bleached white stones of the beach.

Jospor passed him the dented metal flask of wine. "We're stuck with water from the pool from now on."

Maril touched the rim of the flask to his lips, trying to savour the sweetness, but the wine tasted old, vinegary. After a few small sips, he passed it back. The master-at-arms hesitated, accepting with a nod.

"So." Maril sighed, picking up a stone from the beach and rolling it between his thumb and forefinger. "Four days adrift." The pebble was chalky and pocked with holes, like the labyrinth of white, spear-like outcrops the capsized hull had negotiated before reaching the island. "None of which I can remember." He forced an ugly smile, taking back the flask when he was offered it. "Not much use, was I?"

Jospor shrugged. He'd draped his head with rags; only his greenish eyes and the white skin of their lids were visible between the folds.

Maril glanced along the beach at what was left of his Vulgar crew. They were trying to fish, the looming globe of Zeliolopos—a handful of its other moons floating bold against the backdrop of its grandeur—filling most of the lemony sky behind them. His gaze lingered. Sitting among the crew and occasionally laughing at their attempts was one of the bizarre indigenous creatures, the *Bie*, as they called themselves. Maril studied the scaly thing for a moment then looked back at the rock in his hand. He tossed it as far as he could into the green surf.

He'd woken about an hour ago, slick with sweat and weak from hunger, the flapping orange rags of his old Voidsuit stretched across some driftwood poles for shade, along with some of the more complete suits as blankets. The master-at-arms had taken turns with the rest of Maril's crew to nurse him as best they could, but there was little the volcanic island could provide besides water and peculiar, pungent-tasting fish.

The island was a towering fortress of pitted and bleached stone, the sinuous white trunks of dead trees taking hold only near the beach, where they stood in haunting, desolate groves. Jospor had taken Maril on a stumbling tour of the beach, down to where the remains of the privateer's escape clipper—the explosively detached snout of the ship—tilted as a makeshift, capsized outpost, beached on the sandbar. The clipper's plated scales, dented and partially pulverised by the attacking

Nomad-class ship and subsequent fall through Coriopil's clouds, had buckled enough in places to provide shade for most of the crew during their drift towards the equatorial islands, with a rota allotting time inside the cockpit and under-battery.

As evening burned the yellow sky raw, Maril made his way towards one of the campfires on the beach, his legs still weak beneath him. Upon seeing them lit, he'd worried at first, but a glimpse at the darkening ocean for the hundredth time had assured him that there was nobody to see. They were alone here on this drop of water, the bodies of the Bult that had followed them likely sunk to the bottom of the limitless green sea.

The captain took a deep lungful of the ocean air, clean and tinged with salt, the first of the twilight's calm coolness carrying the musty charred scent of fish from the fires up the beach. The voices of his few remaining men carried on the wind. He turned from the pink sky to look at them—all he had left in this world. Of the hundred and sixteen Vulgar he'd hired on Filgurbirund, more than two-thirds had perished, lost to the Void and the fields of Steerilden's Land. And now the survivors would die here, in this lonely place. He glanced around him once more, treading the pebbles up the beach to the fires, comforted by the thought that there were probably worse places to tether one's soul.

The men at the closest fire stood to attention, clapping the salute in recognition of his recovery. Maril felt his eyes prick with tears and gestured for them to sit. He found his place next to Jospor, now free of his sun rags, and pulled a piece of fish from a twig-spit.

"The *Bie* have been showing us how to fish properly," Jospor said. "Those foul-tasting ones were poisonous. We had no idea—I thought the headaches were heatstroke."

Maril tore a bite and nodded, looking past him to the native creatures as they ambled between the fires, begging amiably for scraps. From what he could gather, the reptilian-looking things were not brainless—especially since they'd made the very poles with which his men now fished—but possessed instead a particularly robust sense of humour and a friendliness he had seldom seen in even the most loyal of pets. Their language was a mixture of complicated noises, yawning yelps and snorts of easy laughter. Though not without his suspicions, Maril had to admit that they charmed him just as they did his men, and he found

himself glad to be sharing the place with them. There appeared to be
at least forty in their colony on the island, all apparently of the same
age barring three or four youngsters and a particularly old and grizzled
individual—the group's patriarch, perhaps—who seemed uninterested
in the new arrivals on the beach. Jospor had nicknamed him Gramps.
Whatever they were, in all his travels, Maril had never heard of anything
like them. He stared at them a little longer, meeting Gramps's eye.

One of the *Bie* slunk over, its pointed snout pushed in Maril's
direction, black eyes wide and round. The furred bronze scales that covered its back were rough and patchy from a day's contented scratching
on the rocks, an activity Maril took to be the equivalent of the season's
first moulting.

"*Ooeiihh eh?*" it said, snuffling and licking its lips. Its breath stank
of fish. Maril hesitated then threw it a piece of his dinner, watching the
Bie scamper off into the twilight.

"How do we know that's what they call themselves?" he asked
Jospor, finishing what he had left before the creature came back for
more.

"It's all they would say when we first came ashore," the master-at-
arms said.

"You don't think it means something else—*beware*, for instance?"

"I think we'd know by now if they didn't want us here."

Maril looked to the dark shore for a moment, hearing rocks
tumbling in the surf, and lowered his voice. "What weapons did you
salvage?"

Jospor shook his head, taking another fish. "Almost nothing. The
armoury took a hit." He stuffed the fish in his mouth and performed a
little clap before counting off on his fingers. "We've got a barb shot, a foot
mine, some bomblets that might have got too wet, seven spring pistols
and a sparker buried beneath the leaning tree. I'll show you when we're
done." He remembered something, tapping his side. "And your pistol."

Maril took the weapon and examined it, pleased to see it was still
loaded with poison-tipped rounds. "None of the *Bie* saw you hide them?"

"No."

He nodded, glad. It was comforting not to be entirely at the mercy
of the creatures, despite their pleasant manners.

A wild, scrawny youth with twiggy arms and tufted ears named Furto wandered close to drag more wood to the fire. Maril and Jospor watched him building the blaze, the captain suddenly conscious of how much wood they might have remaining on the island before they were reduced to eating fish raw and sleeping by the light of Zeliolopos alone. As his thoughts turned to supplies, Ribio the pilot began to sing, slowly at first, his hand drumming on the stones beside him, something that must have been a ring picking out a sharp *plink* on the pebbles.

> *Droppin' a'through the Muerto Gulf,*
> *You a'see some dist-far lights,*
> *Them twinkling dots, thems look like jewels,*
> *And they'll pullen you in them sights.*

Another crewmember, Veril, started up, his higher voice mixing with Ribio's.

> *But don't go near them lights, them sounds,*
> *Them's lights that drag you in,*
> *Them's them sixty moons of Lopos, boy,*
> *Them's teeth in death's wide grin.*

Jospor chimed in weakly, accompanied after a moment by Furto.

> *They say it's Zelios that eat you up,*
> *Or a'things in the Slaathis trees,*
> *Or Catchtails, Hoopies, Murms—all teeths,*
> *Them things you'll never see.*

All but Maril were singing now: a choir of thin, uneven voices drowning out the surf.

> *But stop yer clappin', you'll do no good,*
> *What gets yer, it's all smiles.*
> *I know, I was there, I gots away,*
> *It's them sirens of the isles.*

Maril blinked back a quick tear as the song continued, oblivious to its verses. He saw clearly the faces of people who had never been born, wondering how such a thing was possible. They'd sat beside him, he was sure of it, clear and solid as Jospor was now. He stared at his master-at-arms, suddenly immensely tired.

An early-morning chill shivers him into something like wakefulness.

His five children stand over him, wearing some of the Voidsuits left out that night, and gaze at him with bored eyes. He glances through their legs for his sleeping crew, but they aren't there. The beach beyond looks nothing like the one he went to sleep on. His children have moved him in the night.

Maril clambers to his feet, retreating out of the circle. They follow him as if attached by threads, never more than an arm's reach away. He stumbles, backing into the rocks at the shore's edge, and Imsi grabs his collar before he can fall.

He recovers his composure, unable to think of a thing to say. They look so very much like him, never mind that none ever made it alive from the womb. The boys even have a little of their mother around the eyes, but none of their faces are kind. He senses, though they've come to visit him in the night, that it isn't their job here to look after him.

They start walking, almost as one, and the invisible thread compels Maril to follow, trudging with them up into the high stone gullies until they come to a place with a view of the other coves. There they stand, arms interlinked, supporting him. His hands touch Briol's and Osgol's backs, their muscles smooth through the Voidsuit fabric, and he feels a sense of pride.

Osgol turns to him, shrugging away Maril's touch. The wind grows suddenly cold.

They aren't his children any more.

Looking back at him are five haggard things with beaked snouts and birdlike eyes, their skin painted vibrant silver. Their Voidsuits, now home to emaciated bodies, sag and bulge in all the wrong places.

I am not their father, he realises, startled almost to wakefulness.

Together they pick their way along the line of the gulley, walking for what feels like hours. Maril studies the backs of their plumed heads, spying delicate little orifices that must be ears. He tries to speak to them, but the air seems too thin to transmit his words.

With a grunt, he manages to break from the grip of the thread. The sensation is that of snapping a strip of rubber. He stumbles, nearly thrown back, waiting for any response. When he gets none, he turns and hurriedly retraces their steps, hearing the spirits' footfalls diminishing up the gully. He's made it—he's free.

The ground steepens, white stone cliffs rearing on either side and obscuring the sinking sun. Maril fancies that when the sun sets here it might rise for him on the other side; he need only keep walking, walking until he can wake.

This is an upside-down place, he thinks absently, bracing a hand on the chalky rock to rest. *A mirror world, in which spirits live.*

Sounds from up ahead: the hollow clatter of falling pebbles. Maril halts, his boots dug into the slope. The sun has almost set.

Something pokes him between the shoulder blades and Maril jumps and spins, crying out.

The suggestion of a shadow, scampering back up the slope.

He shudders.

"*It!*" screeches a voice extremely close to his ear, this time on the other side.

He flails, swinging a punch, but the silver-skinned beast has already skipped away, grinning. It cackles and dashes back up the slope.

"*Catch me!*" the creature cries, halfway along the track.

Maril stands, breathing heavily. They are playing.

Time rolls to a stop. Their laughter, like rough birdcalls, is infectious. Together they cover the island, Maril finding places to hide when he's been tagged, rooting out the creatures when it's his turn, enjoying himself more than he has in years.

They sit together and look out to sea, their faces not so strange to him now, and he feels at peace with the island for the first time as the sun dissolves into the water.

They begin to confer in deep, unintelligible voices, and offer him something. It's a circular ring of stained metal, still dangling plastic latches and scruffs of ripped cloth. The neck from his suit collar.

Maril takes it, and at their prompting he drapes it over his head. He can see in their eyes that the gesture means a great deal to them.

The creature that used to be Briol rests its claws on his shoulders, pressing against the edges of the collar, and after a moment he understands. *They want me to keep this on. When I wake, I'm to find this and wear it.*

He opened his eyes, rolling on hard pebbles and sitting up to look out at the early-morning light. The pressure of invisible hands remained on his shoulders, drifting away with every heartbeat until it was gone, and Maril let his gaze wander up as he remembered where he was. Zeliolopos, thunderously resplendent in the blaze of unrisen sun, crowned the horizon from east to west. He watched the green and gold belts of clouds travelling almost too slowly to register their rolling currents, the single red wound—a deep storm thousands of miles wide—glowing from within. The vertigo was sudden and enormous, uncontrollable despite his many years spent in the Void, all sense of up and down dissolving.

"The *captain*, I take it?"

Maril drew his pistol in a heartbeat, rolling on the pebbles and aiming at the sound of the voice.

A woman sat on a piece of driftwood beside the dead fire, her hands clutched in her lap, legs crossed. He breathed through the nausea, noticing from her features and size that she could only be Amaranthine.

Her slanted eyes settled on him. Maril took in the lithe curve of her sunburned thigh and small, bare breasts, understanding distantly that she was entirely naked, like an Old World Melius. He studied her face, realising that she was also exceptionally, unnaturally beautiful. The thought shamed him as he turned away to stow his weapon. He was Vulgar, of a different species; such thoughts were near heretical. She would know his mind, too, just by looking into his eyes.

"Look at me." Her words—spoken in Unified—were dry and deep, their timbre far older than her face. Maril knew that none of her kind existed now who weren't ludicrously ancient, but she appeared to be no more than twenty, perhaps twenty-five. He glanced back guiltily, unsure how to arrange himself and finally standing.

"Captain Wilemo Osgol Maril," he said in the Amaranthine tongue. "At your service."

"Vulgar? Lacaille?"

Maril shook his head, faintly astounded that she had to ask. "Vulgar."

"I've been away a while. You all look alike to me."

He nodded, only half-believing that the insult was not intended, and gestured around him. "You live here, Amaranthine? All alone?" A slight hope tickled at him. He and his men were perhaps not so stranded as they thought.

"For a long, long time." She hesitated, tipping her head to glance at him, her smile growing sharp and unkind. "You'd like me to dress?"

He had no idea what the correct answer might be. "The men," he said after a moment, "it would be best for them." Maril looked at the sleeping bundles on the beach, most congregated around the fires.

The lady Amaranthine shook her head dismissively, smiling and uncrossing her legs slowly. "Only you can see me, Wilemo. I can be as naked as you wish."

He looked sharply away from her opening legs. "This is heatstroke. The poison fish."

"Look at me," her throaty voice lulled again. "I've let you see past my glamours. Don't be ungrateful."

He looked, allowing his eyes to travel over her. She slid on her buttock to face him, arching her spine like a cat as she stretched. Maril thought of all the men now long dead who must have fallen for her charms, forcing himself to concentrate on what she really was, one of the Immortals. Beneath it all she was a rotted log, a cold, withered mind denuded to madness by such an incomprehensible span of time. He held the thought and fixed her eye.

"We sought sanctuary here, as you must know. We've no way off this place."

She opened her lips slightly, running her tongue over straight, white teeth before speaking. "Come and find me, Wilemo."

He darted a glance at his sleeping men, in case any had woken. When he looked back she was gone.

"You were saying their names."

He didn't look at Jospor. "I was delirious."

"Do you think they're here, watching over you?" the master-at-arms asked. He was shaving in the bright reflection of his Wulmese helmet, squinting where the sun bounced back into his eyes.

Maril tossed his half-finished skewer to a passing *Bie*. It swerved and cried out, delighted, raising a shower of stones. "No."

The master-at-arms raised his chin, pursing his lips as he brought his knife along the curve of his throat. Maril scowled. Across the beach he could see the orange smudge of his suit dangling from its poles. He wondered briefly about the collar, apparently still attached, until Jospor's sharp curse after nicking himself with the blade tore him from his thoughts. More of the shimmering green and silver fish lay ready to fry on the rocks, caught in the hundreds with the *Bie*'s rods. He looked at their beaked heads, sincerely glad that the men he was responsible for wouldn't starve, at least. On the pebbles across from the fire, the crew played games with their hosts, and he watched them for a while as they threw sticks for the long-tailed animals. The creatures ran and caught whatever was thrown, competing against each other to return them to special marked areas the fastest.

Gramps gazed on solemnly from the shade of a tangle of dead trees, his deep eyes set in shadow. Maril watched him for a while; the old *Bie* didn't really look that much like the others. His head was stouter and less toothy, and his body smaller overall. The scales that covered his back and flanks were wider and of a markedly lighter shade. Gramps appeared to register Maril's new interest and shifted a little further out of the sun.

Maril glanced away self-consciously, returning his attention to his crew. Their clothes were already ragged after less than a week. Furto, the youngest, ran shirtless, while Drazlo appeared to have discarded his underclothes entirely. Maril didn't like it. Clothing was a tenuous link to civility in the Investiture as it stood; he would make a point of ordering them to clean themselves up.

His thoughts turned stubbornly from clothing to a lack of it—to the Amaranthine, and her invitation.

The island was the peak of an ancient volcano, dead and dry, its caldera having crumbled into a gouged slope many miles long that dropped to form a swirled spit on the westward side. Its chalky crust reared up in places like the ripped bark of a tree, with huge spiked monoliths of white stone ten feet high growing from the hills. It was through a forest of these that Maril wandered as he dwelt on what she had said. His excitement betrayed him, filling him as he climbed. He told himself it was the excitement of hope, that she represented a way off this place, but he knew it was also something more.

He'd told Jospor and the engineers that he'd needed to think, leaving after breakfast with enough water for the day and promising to fire his pistol should he encounter any trouble. Before setting out, he'd gone to see his old Voidsuit, still being used as a tatty awning, and cut out the metal helmet collar. It felt comfortable slung over his neck, a weighted talisman of simple, rusting iron.

The crew had not explored the island with any great enthusiasm, keeping to the beaches below the outcrops and roaming the coast in search of more fresh water. They had little idea of the size or shape of the place beyond what some had glimpsed on the descent, and the *Bie* were no use at all in the matter. It was clear that the beasts went somewhere every night; he'd have been better off simply following them as it grew dark. But he couldn't wait.

The chalky hill steepened, the rocks sliding away as he scrambled, clattering along a course of gravel and shale that wound down the shaded side of the hill. Maril stopped to drink from his canteen, unsure exactly what he was looking for; perhaps a small tumbledown house made of driftwood or a flattened plateau of rock on the mountainside. As he drank, he looked down at the journey he'd made through the sharp outcrops, seeing wisps of smoke rising from their sheltered beach beneath the cliff. The whiteness of the island stung his eyes, a baking, dry heat rising from it. This was what all Amaranthine wanted, he reflected, snapping the cap back on his flask: for lowly folk such as himself to climb through heat and danger to pay them homage. For a moment, he registered the salt on his lips as fresh sweat dripped from his whiskers, unable to stop himself from imagining her taste.

He resumed his climb, fingers stained white as they scrabbled for a grip in the chalk, feeling his resolution ebbing. At a flattened slab of rock he rested again, looking up and around at the sheer side of the mountain. There was no further route up from this side; he would have to inch his way around the rock and into the heat of the sun-facing north side of the slope. He rummaged in his pack, taking a rolled-up shirt to wrap around his head as Jospor had done and wondering about the effect of the slightly lower gravity of the place if he had the bad luck to fall.

Looking down and tracing the route such a fall might take, he suddenly noticed the fissure in the hillside below him, hidden from the lower slopes by the angle of its cut. He'd missed it entirely, lost in thought and bent on reaching the top. He stood and stared down into its darkness, spotting some small footholds cut into the side.

It was a good example of how the Amaranthine really did hide themselves, Maril reflected as he climbed carefully down into the narrow crack between the rocks. Their concealment came not from any actual disappearance—for they weren't beings of magic, however much they might wish to be—but the careful manipulation of the minds of others through subtle powers of suggestion. He'd only spotted this place by accident. Perhaps that was the only way he would see her now, in her lair.

It grew dark quickly, the air in the narrow space still and cool. It occurred to Maril as he stepped carefully forward that he might have misread the signs, that perhaps no Immortal lived here at all and he was actually unwittingly walking into the den of some creature that had never seen or tasted Vulgar before. It was only when he saw the first glow of pinkish light that he knew he'd found the right place. He holstered his pistol, knowing how ridiculous he would look to her, and made his way further in, stopping as the passage widened.

The light shone from beneath the surface of a huge pool larger than their camp. Stalactites dripped down to brush the water's surface, making the pool's true size hard to guess at beneath the arches of rock.

She must have heard him make his clumsy way in and was sitting submerged on the bottom, watching. Maril froze, looking down to her. They locked diffracted eyes.

She rose through the pink light, feet kicking gently, and broke the surface at the pool's far edge without taking a breath. His gaze travelled over her foreshortened form as it climbed, lengthening, out of the water. "Clever Wilemo," the Amaranthine whispered, the hiss of her voice echoing to him as she began to dress, buttocks glimmering in the reflections. Something, perhaps the source of the light, moved beneath the water, but Maril couldn't drag his gaze away until she had dressed fully, shrugging on a thin gown and buttoning it twice at the waist. He looked down reluctantly to see a small spark of pink light rising from the depths and joining her at the far end of the cave, momentarily glowing through her gown. Behind her, the light revealed what he took to be the Immortal's meagre possessions, a heaped stack of chests and lanterns balanced on a three-legged table. The spark drifted into one of the lanterns and remained there, illuminating the entire cave.

The Amaranthine picked up the lantern—the glow once again passing through her dress in a tantalizing silhouette—and slinked deeper into the cavern, leaving Maril in growing darkness until he had no choice but to follow. He edged his way around the pool, seeing only the thin, syrupy reflections of the retreating light, and followed the spark.

"These caverns were hollowed millions of years ago," her distant voice announced. "If you look closely you will make out the tool marks."

Maril didn't slow his pace, worrying that the light would disappear entirely and he'd be lost there, stumbling and blind. What she'd said didn't make any sense, but as he hurried along, he spared the edge of an arch of rock a quick glance, noticing that there *did* appear to be carved, chiselled marks in its dim surface. He lengthened his stride, slowly catching up to the light.

"I knew that I would find this place, eventually," the Amaranthine continued. "My proof."

The light grew. She'd stopped, standing among a towering system of stalagmites that reached up into the blackness. The coloured light gave the place an almost festive feel, Maril thought as he joined her, staring up with her at the rock walls.

"These are natural," she said, gesturing to the dripping stalagmites. "Formed over the epochs by running water—a centimetre a century."

Maril nodded absently, his eyes darting every now and then to her damp gown and the curves beneath.

"But these structures," she continued, looking at him, "are not." She raised the lantern, revealing a scintillating glimpse of breast, and shone the light across the gnarled section of the cave before them. Maril tore his gaze away from her and looked.

Pillars and branches of tapering stone disappeared into the gloom beyond the reach of the lantern, like the ossified remains of a huge web. Maril shivered, half-expecting a fat, man-sized spider to come rearing out of its stone lair, but stepped closer anyway, mindful of the Amaranthine beside him. He touched one of the stone branches hesitantly, running his palm along it. Swirling patterns traced the rock, shallow as the grooves of a fingerprint. He forgot himself, stepping further inside the web to touch another branch. The gentle indentations were everywhere, most of them impregnated with a hair-fine filigree of glinting metal; fossilised optics, perhaps, exposed by the soft scouring of unknown years.

"This part of the crust has risen up over time," she said, reaching past him to touch the rock. "The whole moon must have been woven with these branches, deep down."

"Who made these?" Maril asked.

The Amaranthine glanced down at him. "Did you never wonder why the worlds of the Firmament, and even the Investiture, were all possessed of naturally breathable air?"

The question had occurred to Maril, as a younger man, but he'd presumed that was simply how most planets—like the Old World, the sacred origin of all species—had formed. He looked at her curiously, filling his canteen from the shallow pool beside where they had sat down. The darkness all around was comforting for once, cool and quiet and timeless.

"Terraforming," she said, sweeping a delicate finger through the air. "All of the rocky planets discovered after the Second Era were habitable but swamped with oxygen, much more so than the Old World. Breathable, but heady, corrosive. New beings like us had never tasted such atmospheres and weren't used to them." She looked up and around, her drying hair still clinging to her cheekbones. "The flavour of this air is eighty million years old."

Maril took a drink, offering the flask to the Amaranthine. He still did not know her name. She took it without hesitation, swigging lightly and swishing the liquid around her mouth. When she was done, she spat back into the pool.

"I would wager the wealth of the Firmament that there are undiscovered planets and moons out there, beyond the limits of the Investiture in every direction for many light-years more, that harbour the same atmospheres and yet remain as completely lifeless as all the worlds before them." She looked at him, passing back the canteen. "Their empire was far greater than even the Amaranthine could dream of."

Maril knew of course of the ancient, mummified monsters on display in the Sea Hall of Gliese, that they were from another time, before anything like he or the Amaranthine had come into existence, but his knowledge beyond that was vague to say the least. Despite a certain interest in history, Maril spared little time for such diversions as natural sciences, preferring the epic lore of the Firmament and Prism, the battles, the conquests. He took another drink from his flask, tasting her at last, wondering if the invitation still stood.

"And the *Bie*?"

She was silent a moment. "A branch of them, certainly, evolved beyond all recognition." She reached out and grasped the flask without asking, taking another sip. "I came here many hundreds of years ago, knowing that any search of the planets of Tau Ceti would be slow and difficult and dangerous. It was only by accident that I found this island. Besides a skeleton on the west beach—some old Wulm Voidfarer with a bullet through its skull—I gathered the place to be virgin, unexplored. You and your men, Wilemo, are my first visitors."

He chose the moment to ask. "And will you help us?"

The Immortal regarded him, all trace of her good humour abruptly gone. "There is great sadness in you, Wilemo. I see it, and I see the faces of those you loved. Why not stay here? Stay with me and study the *Bie-Yem*, learn their language, as I have."

He flinched from her look, forming his answer carefully. "I can't, no matter how much I might like to, Amaranthine. You must understand I do what I must for my men, for my crew."

The coldness lingered in her eyes as she looked at him, a sharp, fearsome indifference that lurked just behind her smile. "I have no plans to leave here during your lifetime."

They stared at one another, the silence of the cavern surrounding them.

Slowly her fingers went to her buttons, undoing the light gown. Maril let himself see her nakedness as it unfurled, nothing hidden from him now as she drew one slender leg up and draped it across his lap, leaning back. She was almost certainly a Perennial of her kind, more dangerous than a vacuum legion of elite Lacaille, and still he wanted her like he'd wanted nobody else in his life.

"Let me go and discuss things with the men," he said thickly, feeling his whole head flush to the tips of his ears. She smirked as he squirmed out from beneath her, gesturing to the lantern.

Maril hefted it, peering back once more before stumbling off through the cavern. Behind him he could hear her singing something eerily beautiful, only realising as darkness swallowed her that it was a verse from the songs of Lopos, subtly changed, a version many hundreds of years old.

At the cut, he deposited the lantern, taking one last look at the floating spark inside, and climbed the small notches to the lip. Late-evening sunlight struck him, warm and gold. Zeliolopos raged silently above.

Maril crouched on the scree of the slope, breathing deeply. The nausea returned, and he realised that lust had driven all thought of food from his mind. He stood shakily, looking at the canteen on its leather strap and pulling the cap off. He studied the rim, then upended it and tipped all the water away, wiping the spout carefully with the tail of his shirt.

That was it, then. Their fate was sealed. He put a knuckle to his dry mouth, his body shivering with the expended adrenaline, and stumbled up the slope, hoping perhaps to get a better view of the island before the sun went down.

Maril rounded the edge of the slope where he'd first noticed the cave, carefully negotiating the treacherous rock as it crumbled away beneath him and whitening his fingers and knees all over again. More of the island came into view below, a vast slope of the dead, bleached-white tree trunks like the stubble on a huge and grotesque face, crowned with a brilliant white beach that swirled off westwards where the equatorial winds shaped it—the place the Amaranthine said she'd found the skeleton. The waves beat calmly at the sand, apple-green and likely still hot from the day. His gaze followed the shoreline, looking past it to the sea.

A long, orange tanker studded with a clutch of spiked towers lay offshore, eighty feet from the beach, partially hidden by the outcrop of the bay and surrounded by the tall white stacks of a crumbled cliff.

Maril almost slipped and fell, grabbing a chunk of rock and steadying himself just in time. He squinted, his eyes not what they used to be, and searched the rusted patterns on the vessel's hull. *Zelioceti*. He ducked a little behind the rock. It was a sea ship, not fitted for the Void, antique and rusted to within an inch of its life. Smoke issued from funnels and chimneys on its towers, venting from crew compartments deep within the hull. Its dented, sickle-shaped prow, muzzled with a great coil of chains, wasn't all that dissimilar from the protruding nose of a real Zelioceti. Docked on the vessel's humped deck was a bladed grey missile shape that might have been superluminal.

Maril's gaze moved down to the curl of beach. A party of tiny specks were creeping through the shallows, almost invisible if it hadn't been for their shadows, cast long in the last of the light.

MERSIN

There had been thunder, for the second time in her life, as if it always accompanied great change. She'd gone out into the night to listen as it gurgled over the hills, closing her eyes in the darkness.

"This way," the old man said, working his way through the crowd to the door of an inn where some potted bay trees grew.

Eranthis knew the place well. It was called the House of the Homeless, though it possessed no sign; the best in Mersin. At the painted doorway, her companion laid down his cane and, watching that she hadn't got lost among the throng of sailors, merchants and messenger creatures, lowered himself contentedly onto a stool. Eranthis followed through the crowd and joined him at the table, glad of a chance to sit and avail herself of some shade.

They sat for a while in pleasant silence, notably early for their appointment, listening to the musical calls of the market. After some time spent watching the world pass by, she turned to the Amaranthine, who was helping himself to a drink from the bottle he always carried.

"I've never seen it this busy," she said, watching him spit into the jug on the table. "It's as if the Jalan aren't even here." As she spoke she could see one, head and shoulders above the crowd, dawdling at the edge of the causeway. The giant watched the comings and goings of the Southerly people just as she did, until finally their eyes met.

Jatropha shrugged. "The ports have reopened. Life goes on. The stars twirl in the heavens and the currents swirl in the depths."

Eranthis nodded, ceasing to listen after *twirl*, studying the yelling merchants in their open-fronted tents. Easterners—those of the Eleventh, Twelfth and Thirteenth Provinces—were a good deal scrawnier than Tenthlings, narrow-limbed and slender-faced. They wore the colours of barter, blues and greens that rippled to attract attention. Occasionally a man or woman would dye golden-white at a sale: the colour of wealth, the colour of the First. She looked at the piled goods on display—rare seeds and grown stuffs, paints and dyes, plastic and wooden puppets, ring books, jewellery of every kind, gameboards, cloth. A man further along the street sold finger rings, his gaily-striped tent attracting plenty of attention.

"Have I got time to . . . ?" She pointed to the market as she stood, waiting for Jatropha's answer. He nodded, seemingly distracted by the view. "I'll be here."

Yes, you always were, she thought as she crossed the street, the throng paying her little attention as it crowded between the market stalls, misted in foreign perfumes. She pushed her way to the front of the ring seller's counter, eyeing the jewellery. No trinkets of high quality were made in the Tenth; you had to go as far west as Izmirean, the Province's only other port, or across the sea to Kipris Isle, and even then the quality of the pieces was usually low: nothing but hammered tree metals and semi-precious stones.

The jeweller gave her a genteel nod. She smiled back, bending to sift through the baskets and buckets of rings. Though many were similar, none were exactly the same. Hoops of copper and gold were mingled with silver, iron and plain steel—what they called "unstained" in the Tenth—set with simple, commonplace stones like pink coral and fly amber. The trader raised a finger, seeing her disappointment, and opened a large chest at the back of the stall near where he slept. He pulled out a black velvet pouch and untied it theatrically, tipping some of the contents into his bony hand. Eranthis peered at the treasure.

"*Mono Krazavaar*," she said carefully in what she hoped was Thirteenth.

The trader cocked his head.

"Very beautiful?" she tried again, this time in Tenth.

"Ah," he said. *"Mingo Kravus!"*

"Mingo Kravus," she repeated, pointing to the rings.

"I couldn't agree more," said a thick, purring voice like a plucked cello string. Eranthis looked up into the massive, toothy face of a Jalan soldier as he loomed over her. His tufted ears flattened as he smiled, revealing incisors carved with decorative scenes.

"Az shto je kopyo za ney," he said to the trader, reaching into a pocket in his belt. He wore the vestiges of some old, sooty plate harness inscribed with swirls of patterns across the belly.

The trader bowed his head, rummaging beneath his desk to bring out some paper books and a pen. He glanced at Eranthis as he began to write. "The gentleman wishes to buy them for you."

Eranthis stared at the pile of rings, now deposited on the table beside the trader's ledger. *"All* of them?"

"Every one, my dear," the giant said, sliding a long, rumpled piece of blue silk over to the trader. "I couldn't decide which would suit you best."

Her eyes went again to the Jalan's teeth, trying to make out the chiselled image. In place of fear, she felt only curiosity, not caring that her reaction would only encourage him further. "May I see those?"

His smile broadened, the mottled lips peeling back to show filed molars like fangs further inside. "Be my guest."

Eranthis leaned forward, registering the ethanol-tang of Junip on his gusting breath. His tongue slithered lasciviously at his lips, a little drool slopping at her feet. She squinted, seeing at last that the man's teeth were decorated with a couple of scenes from *Dorielziath*, a popular epic from the East, with lines of verse that she hadn't spotted at first carved down the canines. She took her time reading them, knowing the Jalan was tiring of her curiosity and relishing her brief command of him. The jeweller pretended not to watch. She felt sorry for the poor Easterling and decided that on her return she would buy a few of the plainer rings to make up for the scene at his stall.

"Like what you see?" the Jalan growled, snatching up the bag of rings impatiently as he was offered them and holding them aloft.

Eranthis shrugged. "I've seen better."

He reached quickly for her, his many fingers grasping at air as she stepped nimbly back into the crowd. The giant scowled and lumbered forward, intent on his prize, before stopping suddenly in his tracks.

Eranthis could never quite tell what they saw when they fell under Jatropha's spells, knowing only that it was always different, always personal. The Jalan's great eyes widened, his furious expression growing suddenly helpless. His ears swept forward to flatten against his temples as he cried out. Much of the crowd turned to stare, seeing only a shrieking, hysterical Jalan surrounded by onlookers keeping a safe distance. Eranthis could almost pity the man if she'd not felt instinctively that he'd butchered people on his way to the Tenth. She stepped away into the crowd, hearing the screams turn to sobs. Usually they took weeks to recover, if they ever did.

She returned to her stool beside Jatropha, who had ordered wine. "You encouraged him."

Eranthis glanced at the Amaranthine, taking a glass for herself. "He came to *me*, uninvited."

"You don't understand the Jalan."

She downed her wine in one gulp, scowling at him.

At the harbourside, Eranthis sat to wait a while longer as her chaperone greeted old friends, dangling her legs over the growth-stone sea wall, unbothered by the fish-sellers. Looking along the coast at a sea the colour of bright peridot, her gaze following the surf and the grown towers of private, jungly estates, she felt all at once a little girl again, out and about with her father. At last, her eyes returned to the familiar sight of the bright red, four-masted barques standing sentinel out to sea.

She had heard of the moving paper city that had conquered Provinces, but looking upon the ships of the Oyal-Threheng admiralty now she didn't think she could be more impressed. They towered, floating crimson-painted fortresses five or six storeys high, strung with shredded banners that hung still in the windless day. Great naval guns stationed on the forecastles pointed out to sea and into the port, their immense barrels usually shaded beneath triangular paper sails almost a hundred feet tall at their cornices.

Today the sails were rolled, the barques a semi-permanent feature of the Southern Provinces as they watched over the Oyal-Threheng's new annexe. Eranthis could just make out minuscule figures making their way up and down two of the masts as her mind touched on the intervening months, wondering for the thousandth time what her old friend Lycaste would have made of it all, not smiling at the thought.

Jatropha had promised, when at last his business was over, to make enquiries. If Lycaste was out there somewhere, he would be found. Nobody with a face like his could vanish easily, not even in the under-populated and dangerous Provinces to the west, though he could surely not have got that far. Indeed, Jatropha said, it was strange—and worrying—that they still hadn't heard anything on the Province rumour mill. Eranthis knew the saying *no news is good news* but no longer believed it.

The Immortal was talking to a pleasant-looking Tenthling she vaguely recognised. The two were moving along the stalls, apparently taking a deep interest in the shaded mounds of fish caught that day, the Tenthling taller than Jatropha by three or four feet. She knew better than to join them; not from fear of reprimand, but rather the knowledge that important bargaining for their trip ahead was likely going on. If Jatropha needed her council, he would ask for it.

A little sailed gondola took them out across to the waiting ships, passing over clear, green-tinted sands where no fish swam. There hadn't been any more sightings of the huge pale shark—the *Echelussiac*, as Jatropha called her—now the year was drawing to a close. The Amaranthine said she'd withdrawn to hotter waters and richer pickings further south but might return in coming months, especially if the Jalan continued throwing their slops into the sea.

The boat rocked as it entered the great enclave of ships, sliding into shadow beside the first of the shining red hulls. They pulled around the great bulwark of the guardship and she sat, smiling at the Thirdling manning the oar. The flagship came slowly into view, a fortress rising out of the sea.

Eranthis forgot to breathe, eyes widening in the shade. The mighty capital ship had been mostly hidden from view by the protective diamond formation of the other three galleons, only its masts—higher than the others by twenty feet or so—rising above the tangled web of rope and rolled sails, its shadow darkening the sea like a storm. Eranthis felt cold all of a sudden, understanding in the darkness cast by the ship the colossal gravity of the task at hand. She rubbed her arms, not so excited any more to be going aboard.

The ship's prow rose over them, a coiled mass of sculpted wooden faces glowering down at her. The giant heads gleamed in the reflection of the ruffled water, all lacquered in bright blues and reds and golds. Their boat passed beneath yet more, full animal figures standing sentinel in their hundreds along the ship's flank, decreasing in size to cursed folk and Monkpeople at the distant stern. Every now and then, the great bands of wood that covered the hull had been replaced either with brighter segments of painted planking or dull, riveted strips of lead. She glanced up through the tangled forest of carved figures, following the trail of the ship's knotted rigging, and shrank a little on her seat.

An enormous person brooded in the shadows up there, watching their passing. She could only make out its hunched shoulders as they blocked the light, though as her eyes adjusted she thought she could see huge, round eyes observing her in return. A true Threheng giant, larger by far than any Jalan she'd ever seen before, come out of the legends of the East. The giant passed from view, the sky glimmering between the ropes and the heads of carved mammalian figures. As they sailed towards some massive steps that rose into the side of the hull, Eranthis caught sight of something closer to the stern, strung from ropes across the bulwark. She patted Jatropha lightly on the arm.

It was a green serpent at least forty feet from nose to tail, drying and wrinkled from the day's sun. The finned tail, misshapen where the ropes cut into it, hung down close enough for the stench to reach her as they arrived at the steps.

"Do you like my leviathan?"

The vast shadow she'd witnessed on the deck resolved itself as it strode down the steps, turning to gaze up at the sea creature hanging over the bulwark of his ship. When the giant reached the water's edge, he stooped low to observe them and extended his arm.

"If it isn't my old friend the Amaranth!"

Jatropha reached out and patted the enormous hand, his fingers sliding over an arthritic-looking ivory claw that could have chopped his head in two. "Commodore Palustris."

The giant Jalan turned his blue eyes on Eranthis. She could see, even seated on the far side of the boat, the flecked scarlet corona that surrounded each pupil, like blood circling a drain. "And who is this? Have you had a daughter?"

"This is my ward, Eranthis."

She nodded, speechless. The commodore wore a dark felt coat in the Eastern Shamefashion that she'd grown to recognise, though it remained unbuttoned on so warm a day. He was at least twenty feet at the shoulder and looked the same in width, with a magnificent red nose crowning his great droopy face. A blond coil of beard sprouted from his chin and wagged in the sea wind. His teeth, when he smiled, looked like thick, tapered chunks of stained marble.

"Eranthis. Welcome," he said in Tenth. His rumbling voice registered in the marrow of her bones.

They climbed aboard, following in Palustris's massive, rolling footsteps.

"Caught yesterday at the Greater Point," he said, glancing back at them and gesturing up to the serpent. "Should fetch a pretty price in Izmirean."

"A whole Scarlet, I'd say, sold to the right collector," Jatropha said.

"Oh yes?" He turned to regard the Amaranthine with delighted interest. "Not boiled down for tallow?"

"Nelumbo's tallow works wouldn't give you a third of that," Jatropha said with crisp certainty. "If it were mine, I'd sell it wholesale to the beast auctions at Ulamis, twenty miles west."

"Beast auctions," Palustris repeated thoughtfully. "*Ulamis.*" He quickened his step, visibly pleased. "You know best, as always, Amaranth."

They came to the first of the vessel's large balconies, flanked by yet more sculpted figures. The breeze had picked up and Eranthis realised as she looked over the rail how high they suddenly were above the sea. The serpent's head hung below them, trussed in layers of cloth and netting.

Palustris's hunched form nodded in her direction as he walked. "A Seventh name."

"Yes," she said as she followed him through a high-ceilinged passage and into an enormous wood-panelled antechamber. "I grew up in Shatoyz Town. Part of your territories now, I expect." Jatropha had taught her to speak her mind in every situation: since becoming his acolyte she could not be threatened, he said, and there might be instances when she spotted something even the Amaranthine did not.

Palustris shrugged off his coat, dumping it over a vast hound-footed chair at the entrance to his chambers. "Shatoyz? I've no idea. You'd have to ask my general, Oxalis. He granted the Seventh freedom under the Oyal on the condition they open their ports."

He pushed through a set of doors, Jatropha and Eranthis gazing up as they opened to reveal a room with a spectacularly high ceiling.

"Sit, please," Palustris said, clearing his throat with a rumble and padding over to one of four identical chairs arranged together in the centre of the chamber. The commodore had switched to Seventh, Eranthis noticed.

She approached one of the high-backed, animal-footed chairs and climbed the ladder at its side. Palustris settled himself and watched Jatropha do the same. They sat and regarded each other, high off the floor. Eranthis took a moment to examine the enormous varnished chamber, noting the bell ropes that collected and rose up to the darkness of the ceiling, and the hints of illustrations all over the walls. She could hear and smell a lunch of some kind being prepared somewhere in the adjacent rooms and hoped her stomach wouldn't growl. Immunity to danger, though certainly a happy circumstance, appeared only to magnify other, lesser concerns.

The fourth chair remained unoccupied except for a stack of metal tablets and folds of stamped paper. Out of the corner of her eye, Eranthis saw upon them the Threheng lettering—pressed, inkless indentations—densely packed into backward-running sentences.

"So you are thinking of travelling north, Amaranth," Palustris said to Jatropha, signalling to his lurking Thirdlings for the window shutters to be opened. The sound of the sea and the port drifted in, warming the dim place. Eranthis saw that the patterns she'd taken for wallpaper were in fact huge painted maps. "We are escorting you to Izmirean, yes?"

"If you'd be so kind," Jatropha said. "I shall take you to the auctions."

Palustris beamed, accepting trays as they were brought in. Out of apparent deference to the Amaranthine they contained only drinks. Eranthis looked at the bowls and cups with disappointment.

"I must tell you before I forget, Amaranth," Palustris said as he took up a bowl—tiny in his massive hands—and passed it to Eranthis. "I made sure Oxalis knew that your houses in Bandirma and Korfez weren't to be touched during the advance on the Sixth."

Jatropha smiled, his gaze travelling over the maps on the walls. "Thoughtful of you, Commodore."

Palustris hesitated, his lips pursing. "Though it pains me to report that the capital town of Istano-Dalmerre offered resistance. The Second's legions judged—as we did—that the strait would be of strategic importance." He paused. "Consequently the town was heavily shelled, from both land and sea. It would surprise me if any of your residences there survived."

Eranthis peered at her fingernails, careful to avoid eye contact with the Amaranthine. Jatropha had been known for decades as a hermit, and yet that now appeared to be the furthest thing from the truth.

"And my properties further west?" Jatropha continued with an air of relaxed resignation. "Seized by the Second, I expect?"

Palustris looked taken aback. "What properties would these be, Amaranth?"

"Oh," Jatropha opened his hand and began ticking off the fingers, "a mill in Orestias, three houses in Sapes, a *fortress* in Ihtiman—"

Eranthis couldn't help but stare. As the Immortal continued to list the places he owned, it suddenly occurred to her what he might be doing. Her geography was better than most: every location Jatropha had mentioned was further north-west from the last. She looked off to the windows, hiding her smile behind her hand.

Palustris was running his fingers through his coiled beard, thinking. "Now, please, Amaranth, let me see. Orestias? All is well there—we've pushed the Secondlings back as far as Padarevo, but the front is dangerous, continually being retaken by the enemy. The other places—Sapes, Ihtiman—they are not safe at all, not even for—if you'll excuse me—one such as yourself."

"Not safe?" Jatropha asked. "You are referring to Skylings?"

Palustris nodded emphatically, bringing his huge hands together in a snapping clap to dispel the demons they discussed. "Starlings, Skylings, Firmlings, they're everywhere. Admiralty spies have spotted hundreds in the woods around Uzice alone. It is likely that citadel is already taken by them."

"What would they want with a city?" Eranthis asked, forgetting herself, her imagination alive. Of all the things Jatropha had told her of the wider Firmament, the hideous Prism-people fascinated her the most.

Palustris turned to her and bowed lightly, visibly aware that he had forgotten to include her fully. As an acolyte she was to be granted nearly the same reverence as an Immortal under the inviolable statutes of the Firmament.

"My apologies, Eranthis." He pursed his wide mouth, thinking. "Skylings, from my limited experience of them, will take whatever is not guarded for themselves out of nothing more than an infernal jealousy— am I not right, Amaranth?"

Jatropha nodded vaguely, still seemingly absorbed in the paper flags of recent conquests hanging from the map walls.

"Take this bowl," Palustris continued, lifting it from the tray. "If a Skyling were present now, Firmament forbid, he would make a claim for it, seeing that it was precious to me in some way. Once he had it, though, he might simply throw it away, or use it for a chamber pot, or something equally vile."

"But why are they so jealous?" Eranthis asked. "Because they may take nothing for themselves?"

"*Precisely*—they own nothing that has not been meted out to them by the Amaranth in their unending charity. But they do not understand that it can only be this way—just as we of the Threheng are indebted to the generosity of our betters, our forebears, so they must be, too." He clapped his hands again, keeping the spirits at bay.

Eranthis nodded, pleased with herself. She knew the Jalan did not think much of Southerners, not even those who supported their War of Liberation, and was glad to have impressed the commodore in some small way with her understanding. Ever the teacher's pet, she wished to continue, but sensed from the way Jatropha returned his attention to Palustris that they had more important things still to discuss.

"I would ask more of you, Commodore, before we make our way to Izmirean."

"Please," Palustris responded, setting down the bowl he'd used for his explanation.

"It has come to my attention," Jatropha said, displaying, Eranthis noted now, none of the vagueness and frivolity that had so defined him when he had lived disguised among them in the cove, "that your soldiers use many of the finest gardens in the Tenth for resupply, foraging as they like on private land."

Palustris looked to the floor, appearing to choose his words carefully. "This is not something I encourage, Amaranth, you must understand. But the war is not over. Our Lord General Elatine is missing, not dead. Legions must take refreshment where they land or they shall mutiny, no matter how noble the cause."

"And with my say so they may, Commodore," Jatropha said, his words taking on a darker tinge that filled Eranthis suddenly with strange pride. "But only from selected land. They must leave the Tenth Province in peace or they shall find violence here."

Palustris was nodding uneasily, as if he had long expected this request. "Yes, yes, Amaranth, as you say. But our victory has been postponed. Not even you—if you'll pardon me—can predict the course of the Liberation." He paused for breath, looking off to the sea through the window. "Unless something can be done about the—" he paused, clapping again "—the Skylings, we shall be forced to dig into our annexation here, perhaps for years. This war was never going to be simple, but I fear it may be one of the longest fought in centuries—heavens, it already *is*—unless something can be done to further aid us."

"Calm yourself, Palustris," Jatropha whispered. The giant's frown immediately softened, bringing a childlike quality to his snaggle-toothed features. "I have already secured the land. It will feed and clothe your troops for ten years, if managed well. I have the deeds here." He motioned to Eranthis for his satchel and she passed it to him.

"Added to the newly opened trade routes from the Scarlet Lands and elsewhere, I don't believe you shall experience any difficulties with supply from here on in."

Eranthis watched him pass over the metal sheets of the land titles, quite aware that the Jalan regiments were Jatropha's instruments here

in the Nostrum Provinces, the blunt force with which he had thought
to clear a route to the Second. Now, with news that the Inner Provinces
were overrun, he would need to beat a new path to the Berenzargol family. Eranthis thought hard, unsure how in all the world they could get
to where they needed to be by the beginning of the new year. There was
only one route, really, and it was a route she didn't like the sound of.

Palustris sat back, holding the deeds to the light to inspect them.
He waved a finger absently and a presence, announced by footfalls on
the polished wood, crept into the room.

"Admire my entertainments while I read these, will you?" He bent
further over the metal sheets, his claw dragging along the text.

Eranthis and Jatropha watched the long, thin performer advance,
prancing across the shimmering floor. The person's face was hidden
behind a gold, heart-shaped mask, their body entirely wrapped in white,
red-trimmed silk. Eranthis saw after a moment that the dancer was no
Melius; it had a tail.

They watched as the performer circled them, jumping high enough
to clack its slippered heels together in mid-air and pirouetting on the
spot five, six, seven times. She saw its hands, noticing how some of the
fingers of the gloves appeared to be empty, and wondered again what
sort of person was hiding beneath all that white silk.

Palustris came to the end of the final deed, stacking them carefully on the spare seat beside him. Eranthis had only lately noticed there
was no music to accompany the dancer's performance. The commodore
looked around at the dancer and cleared his throat. The person landed
neatly from its leap without missing a step and bowed, then strutted out.

"A present, that one. Meant to bring *luck*." He leaned closer to
Jatropha, his rumbling voice pitched low. "Though I must say I prefer
yours." He bared his chops at Eranthis in a huge smile and ran his claws
over the deeds. "These will do very nicely."

"I am pleased that you are pleased, Palustris," Jatropha said,
swinging his skinny white legs from the chair's edge.

The commodore glanced at his Thirdling servants, standing
motionless near the window. "Was that a Wheelhouse I saw down at the
harbourside? A new acquisition of yours?"

Jatropha shrugged. "Rickety old thing. I got it at a good price."

"A big one, five-chambered, by the looks of it?"

Jatropha nodded thoughtfully. "You keep a close eye on Mersin from up here."

Palustris gestured to a large shuttered lens secured in a wooden frame that stood by one of the further windows. "So you're to have more travelling companions? On your journey?"

Jatropha shook his head. "Storage, with a cupboard for any lodger willing to pay their way along the road."

Palustris watched him carefully for a moment, the way Eranthis had seen idiots attempt to spot a lie. Then the giant looked away, examining his claws. "You are good with your money. Does very old age bring that? Financial wisdom? I suppose it does."

"Come now," Jatropha said. "Is this not a well-paid commission for you?"

"Oh, well enough." He looked at Eranthis, clearing his throat again. "But since our Lord General's disappearance not one thing is certain, and between us three I'd like to take my leave before we become entrenched here." He stared desultorily out at the sea. "There's no spirit left in this war. We came further than anyone expected—the First squirms in our grip. Let them thrash out terms. Your people, in the Firmament, they will write the statutes anyway, as they always have."

Eranthis looked at the commodore's long profile, framed against the far view of the sea.

Elatine's disappearance had only inflamed the war, splitting the Threheng's capital legion into a host of battalions fighting beneath eight separate Lord Commanders, each intent on a slice of the First for themselves. It was assumed by many on both sides that Elatine had been killed somewhere and would never be found, though more outlandish theories—that he'd been secretly paid off by King Lyonothamnus, run off with the Skylings or even joined the ranks of the Amaranthine—abounded. Whispers of a Firstling secret weapon that would end the war at a stroke had grown popular among the Jalan in the Tenth: the reason, they said, for Elatine turning his coat. Eranthis, from her limited studies under Jatropha, assumed the obvious: that Elatine was simply dead, another corpse tucked into a bird-pecked heap on the outskirts of the Second, and that the war would now last a good deal longer, if it ever really ended at all.

What Eranthis knew beyond a doubt was that these giant people, while outwardly amenable to an acolyte of the Immortal, were not her friends. Under no circumstance could she mention the baby, not here in the presence of the commodore, not anywhere beyond the boundaries of her own home. The Jalan were still at war with the ruling Provinces; any mention of a healthy Second-Tenthling in the Province, no matter how well its aristocratic lineage might be concealed, would spell the end of their collaboration with Jatropha and perhaps even result in the slaughter of those who had protected the child. This was not some suspicion of Eranthis's—the Amaranthine had told her so himself before boarding. Arabis, Pentas's child with the Plenipotentiary Callistemon, would need to remain her most closely guarded secret.

IZMIREAN

The sea cog left Izmirean for Artemida at dusk, slipping through the twilight and out into wider seas. Eranthis joined Jatropha at the sails where he stood with other travellers, their coloured skins aglow in the last of the sunset, to glimpse the lights of the port and its fleet of Threheng ships dwindling into blue darkness. It had been a day's sail around the headland from Mersin, and she was impatient now to be on her way.

Jatopha pointed to a solitary, wavering light on a hill beyond the harbour.

"There was a castle on that hill, once."

Eranthis nodded, as if she knew. "You saw it?"

"Yes." He glanced up to her, smiling his innocent old smile. "This part of the world used to be the main exporter of figs, did you know that? People of varying shapes and sizes have sold figs in Izmirian for over fifteen thousand years."

She shook her head ruefully, glad her sister had chosen to stay below. Jatropha's lectures were known to bore poor Pentas to tears.

"Of course, there's considerably less sea traffic from the west now. I wouldn't be surprised if the port becomes a good deal smaller in the next few centuries."

Eranthis nodded, remembering that they wouldn't see land again for three whole days and nights. She took in the luminous, lantern-bright blue of the sunken sun, her back to the receding port as she stared into the west. This was now the farthest she had ever been from her home in the Seventh. She hoped she'd be gone a long time. *The Westerly Provinces*, she thought, breathing in the fluttering wind that coursed from the dark sea. The sight of winter stars curving over the dimming light tingled a chill across her thickening skin; cool eternity rolling ever onwards.

They had left Commodore Palustris and his ship at Izmirian, content with the successful auction of his leviathan, unaware of the real reason for their journey to the Western borders. Though she knew Palustris would never have given them his consent, she felt a certain sadness that she'd had to lie to the giant, and a lingering fondness for him. Palustris had loaded their new Wheelhouse with supplies as a gesture of goodwill, expressing his disappointment that he couldn't be of more use to Jatropha and his Acolytes, and wished Eranthis a particularly sweet farewell, kissing her surprisingly lightly on the cheek and bidding her a swift return to safer waters.

As she went below, her mind wandered back to Jatropha's other properties, the catalogue of houses and estates he and Palustris had discussed. Perhaps they really had just been a ruse on his part, a way of gauging the route north-west. She would not ask him: the longer she spent with the Amaranthine, the more keenly she began to feel his ridicule. Jatropha had, she suspected, simply spent too long alone, too much time mumbling to himself on empty Province roads, his inner thoughts always in final and total agreement with one another. Unnatural lifetimes as a hermit had twisted him, sullying the charm she could see just below the surface. Already her sister had lost all patience with him. It would be a long trip.

The sea cog's lower decks were made up of plain wooden compartments, each with a lockable door and two sturdy shelves on which to sleep. Blankets and furniture were not provided: the girls had chosen to bring chairs from their goods in the hold and a small metal table for Quarterly cinnamon tea.

She knocked once, waiting and hearing the door being slowly unbolted. Everyone in the neighbouring cells seemed pleasant, even affluent. There shouldn't have been any need, but her sister had endured too much for someone of twenty-three to leave a door—any door—unlocked for long.

Pentas's small face appeared through the crack.

"Master Knowitall with you?"

Eranthis shook her head.

The door opened. The flame in a lantern flickered dimly from the top bunk, enlivened by Eranthis's sudden entry, responding to the beat of her heart. The cell was painted a muted shade of pink, the brush marks hurried, barely concealing the untreated wooden planks. The cheapest room, Eranthis suspected, annoyed with herself for insisting on something modest.

"Did you ask him to move us?" Pentas asked, picking up a woollen bundle. A tiny orange hand reached out of it to curl around her finger.

"Not yet." She sat down to pour the tea, conscious of her sister's filthy look. "It's too late to ask them to do anything tonight."

"*First thing in the morning*," Pentas said, her attention at last distracted by the bundle in her lap. Eranthis drained the tea jug, tapping the strainer with an internal relief, and glanced at the child.

Pentas hadn't taken to motherhood the way most girls did, at first refusing to accept in some kind of amnesiac state that she'd even given birth at all. It was rare and almost always shameful in Southern society for someone to have children before fifty-five, and so they'd taken her far from prying eyes and flapping mouths to the fleshdoctors in Mersin. After the girl was born—cut from her when it wouldn't leave of its own accord—Pentas had wept for days, refusing to look at it after that first tender encounter, likely seeing something of the child's father in Arabis's angelic, troubled face.

For two months her sister would neither see nor speak of what had befallen her, ignoring the baby's screams with a cold gleam in her eye. Eranthis knew that it was shame and defiance, not an inability to love, that kept her sister from the child, and couldn't say for certain that she'd have behaved any differently in Pentas's place. It had very nearly been so; she remembered the Plenipotentiary's early advances, the way he'd been with her. The memories made her want to shudder, guilty at her own lucky escape.

"She's taken well to the sea, so far," Pentas said.

"So far." Eranthis blew on her tea. She had nearly resolved to make the trip with Jatropha alone, excluding her sister entirely from the baby's life at last. But Pentas had grown churlish once she'd seen how people fussed over the baby and not her, accepting Arabis as her own only after it was apparent that she'd share in the glow of attention. Like all sisterly fights from their youth, Eranthis had felt the urge to call her sister's slyness to attention, beating it back at the realisation that there was more at stake, that Pentas's selfishness might, indirectly, force her to bond with her own daughter after all.

"Do you want to hold her?" Pentas asked, opening the bundle in Eranthis's direction. "I thought I might go up on deck, if I can somehow avoid the wizard."

"Keep her a while longer," Eranthis replied, irritated all over again. She moved over to Pentas's bed, shuffling along to look down at the bundle. The baby stared back, pouty and restless, her face a memorial to unhappy times.

SATRAP

The ferdies' hooves clopped onto a road of cobbled silver. They'd left the edges of the fragrant forest that blanketed much of the world, hiding the sparkling battle for the sun as it grew in viciousness above. The riders looked down at the ring of shod hooves on metal, the reflections dancing in their faces where the embattled sun shone upon the road, sometimes misted by a strange weather that glowered over the land. Lycaste awoke from his daydreams, the faces of Jasione and her family clear in his mind as he rode through the dim Amaranthine forest, and turned to the others around him, understanding that they must almost be there.

The road ahead was gently curved, leading through deep green and yellow plantations of waist-high bushes being tended by stooping figures in sun hats and red shawls. At the sight of the netted plantations, the Loyalist escort stopped to confer with Maneker in hushed tones, finally spurring their ferdies off the path and cantering away with raised gauntlets and clamouring, foreign goodbyes.

"They're leaving us here," Huerepo said, voice low over Lycaste's shoulder. "Returning to the hunt."

Lycaste watched them go, returning his gaze to the low hills of emerald-green forest beyond the plantation. Where the road dwindled into the foothills, a dome of pale green copper capped with a spire of gold twinkled in the sunlight, its lower levels hidden darkly by lustrous trees.

As they rode level with the figures, Lycaste saw in the artificial evening light that they were Melius like himself. The workers paid him little attention, their sluggish, uninterested gazes alighting briefly on Huerepo, still seated upon Lycaste's shoulders, before moving on. At the sight of Maneker, however, they paused and doffed their wide hats.

The Amaranthine had ridden a little behind, consulting some signs at the edge of the road. Now, as he clopped his ferdie forward, he spoke to the plantation workers in a clear voice. Huerepo leaned close to whisper translations into Lycaste's ear, even though he'd begun to find them slightly redundant.

"Is your master at home?"

The nearest of the pickers hesitated, perhaps a little put off by the sight of the rags that Maneker still wore. "The Satrap is in attendance, Sire."

Maneker gestured impatiently. "Go and fetch him, then."

The picker appeared to think about this for a moment, worry crossing her face. Then she hitched up her trailing shawl and padded barefoot onto the road, skipping where it was still hot from a full day's sun. At the sight of her, two children came running out from the bushes and sprinted off towards the palace. She turned expectantly to Maneker, beckoning them all to follow.

Maneker twisted in his saddle to look at Lycaste and Huerepo, his eyes sharp. "Don't speak to anyone. Follow me and keep quiet."

Together they trotted after the Melius picker, taking in the miles of plantation around them. The bushes buzzed with cottony white moths that floated sleepily from leaf to leaf, the two ferdies snorting as some rose to flutter at their ears and noses. Lycaste waved them away, one of the moths catching softly in his hand, pacing along his palm and over to his knuckles. He noticed that, like the bees, it was heavily ornamented with a jacket of silk and miniature stones. All along its tufted wings there glittered golden flecks and spots of lapis, a milky emerald the size of a grapeseed complementing each wing tip. He considered catching the clumsy, weighted-down insect for Huerepo, who still hadn't appeared to notice the riches that busily floated among them, but let it go on its way.

Some distance from the road, Lycaste could see thick wooden poles, about twenty in all, rising from the bushes. With a start he realised there were people hanging upside down from them, their heads brushing the plants.

"Are they dead?" he blurted. The woman turned briefly at the sound of his voice.

Maneker glanced off towards the poles, remaining silent, perhaps noticing as the closest hanging Melius turned his head in their direction. His skin had been painted with something thick and shiny, like brown oil or tar. Lycaste remembered Impatiens's awful tales of Provincial schooling, where as punishment children were cloaked in fabric so that nobody could see their colours.

A squeal of delight from Huerepo snapped Lycaste's thoughts away. The Vulgar passed him down a crushed moth, patting his shoulder as he caught another. Lycaste dutifully pocketed them, hoping the Satrap wouldn't mind.

"*Aceris* moths," Maneker said without turning, as if reading Lycaste's mind. "These are silk plantations."

At a junction in the silver road, the woman inexplicably picked up her pace, clasping her children's hands and running ahead. Maneker did not urge his ferdie any faster at the sight of her disappearing up the road and so they clopped the last of the way alone, observed by other silent pickers from the edges of the groves.

Once inside the enormous formal gardens, Maneker hopped from his mount, leading it to a sculpted holly tree with blunted, age-worn leaves. Lycaste trotted along behind, tying his own ferdie to a lower branch and stretching his back. He looked around at the gardens while Huerepo rummaged in the saddlebags, observing arches that led darkly into inner, more private courtyards within the palace's quarter-mile-long facade.

Maneker swigged from his bottle, calm as he waited, apparently, for any sign that their picker would return.

"Old World silk," Huerepo said softly from atop the ferdie, munching on something stale from the packs and taking in the sights. "Might buy someone a Province, all of this."

"It already has," Maneker said beside them, leaning against his own mount and spitting into the grass.

Lycaste and Huerepo looked at him, then back at the ornamented grandeur of the palace before them. Every inch of its colossal bulk appeared to have been worked upon in some exquisite way, garlanded with rococo florets, scrollwork and sculpted acanthus all painted with a chipped veneer of ancient gold leaf. Over the arches, scenes played out in polished green marble inlaid with more gold, the shadowy interiors between the pillars dripping with gilded chandeliers. Tawny columns a hundred feet high led their eyes to the upper floors, where balconies fit for banquets looked out over the silk fields, and then further to the dome as it brooded marvellously, cast like the green shadow of the sun across the sky. Only a mouldy and weather-beaten white marquee erected flush against the balustrades of the lower balconies looked unworthy of the place, the remains of some heady celebration long since over still festering within. Barring this imperfection of piled bones and wilted flowers, the sight was everything Lycaste had hoped it would be, the imagined opulence of his old doll's house made real. Just standing before it, he felt his nagging fear of Maneker beginning to diminish—someone who owned such a place would surely outrank the sour-faced Amaranthine, or at least have the authority to suggest that Lycaste and Huerepo be taken home in safety at the first opportunity.

He thought of his old friend Impatiens, picturing the astonishment on the man's face when he returned to them brimming with extraordinary tales. Perhaps Pentas would be there, though for some reason he thought it unlikely. He could not see them meeting, could not imagine what he would say to her, if he even said anything at all. They had both wronged each other to some degree, though he knew he was a fool to think she'd committed the greater crime, and there was nothing now between them, no friendship that could ever be rekindled even once the gulf of light-years was removed. He supposed he hoped now that he would simply never see her again; at least that way his old life could safely be forgotten and a new one made in its place.

"Here comes someone," Huerepo said, swinging carefully down from the ferdie's spotted rump and giving it a friendly pat.

Squinting into the gloom beneath the arches, Lycaste thought he could make out the shape of a wide person hurrying between the pillars. He straightened as the figure emerged into the light.

Lycaste didn't think he'd ever seen such a corpulent, sweaty specimen of a Melius in all his life. The man approached them at a breathless jog, perspiration reflecting brilliantly from his blotchy brow and beading on the tips of his waxed moustaches. In his fists he clasped swatches of striped material, and a mighty paunch strained inside his exquisite black waistcoat. Lycaste glimpsed Huerepo studying the half-dozen silver, scarlet-stoned rings squeezed onto the man's fingers and almost smiled. The fat Melius—a butler or something similar, he guessed—was much like those who had accompanied them here, Lycaste thought; a family of men similar but not quite the same as Thirdlings and Secondlings, generally smaller and more finely boned than himself, though that was hard to see in this specimen.

The butler arrived before Maneker and checked his posture, his hands furiously kneading the swatches of material.

"Gentlesire. The afternoon's greetings. We'd have been gratified to receive advance notice," the butler said in the noises of Unified. "If you would follow me."

At the Amaranthine's gesture, he made an about-turn and headed for the arch at a gentler pace, checking every now and then to see that they were following. He ushered them into the shadows, shooting Lycaste and Huerepo the briefest of distasteful glances, and through to the inner courtyards.

Sensing the impatience of their guide, Lycaste strove to keep at Maneker's heel as he caught glimpses of the opulence beyond the open basilica. He formed the impression they might be interrupting something important, or would be if they didn't hurry. Huerepo, somewhere behind, grumbled as he scuttled, his little legs tapping a staccato of frustration on the tiles. Above them, painted frescoes arched dimly across the vaulted ceilings, scenes of incomprehensible Amaranthine magnificence.

Sunlight broke through the last of the arches as they arrived in the courtyard, the unlit chandelier at its mouth twinkling glassily above.

Their sweaty escort had ventured from the middle of the lawn to the edge of a squat fountain and was bending in a grotesquely elaborate curtsy to a small Amaranthine clothed only in a nightshirt of torn, patterned linen. Lycaste straightened, blinking, aware that the picture of this man in his mind's eye had been very, very wrong. The Immortal cradled a pear-shaped stringed instrument—what looked to Lycaste like a Hioul, from home—in his bony hands, and had been plucking something reasonably jolly until the interruption. The Satrap listened to his butler, casting foxy, shrewd glances in his new guests' direction, and put his instrument to one side. Lycaste couldn't help noticing the visible erection the Amaranthine sported beneath his nightshirt as he stood and turned to them, as well as the dozens of retainers and servants who lingered around the edges of the courtyard.

"Satrap Cirillo Vincenti," Maneker said, his voice taking on a lighter, friendlier intonation that Lycaste hadn't heard before. "A pleasure."

"Introductions, Higginbottom?" the Satrap grumbled, hitching up his nightshirt until its hem was perilously close to the bulge at his groin and tottering towards them.

The butler stammered, looking to the new arrivals. "I'm afraid I—"

"Hugo," Maneker said, striding forward with his hand outstretched.

Vincenti clasped the offered hand weakly and peered at Lycaste. "What a beauty, to be sure, but I will not have *nude* Scatalogicus here, Perennial." He swivelled back to Higginbottom. "Take him to the fitting room with Dung and Hardship." The Satrap returned his attention to Maneker. "Hugo," he said, thoughtfully. "Hugo Maneker. I was not expecting someone so senior within the Devout."

Lycaste strained to listen to the gist of their conversation as the butler swept past, hurrying him on.

"They send their most singular and sincere thanks," Maneker replied. "His Imperial Majesty will honour you above all others for your support."

"*Scatalogicus!*" Higginbottom snapped, turning and beckoning Lycaste to heel. Maneker and the Satrap twisted briefly to look before resuming their conversation. Huerepo met Lycaste's eye with something like sympathy, glancing away.

Lycaste glowered at Maneker and squared his shoulders, tears stinging his eyes. The butler tapped his feet, fussing with a button on his sleeve. *So this is how it will be.* Lycaste supposed he couldn't have asked for anything more. Huerepo was right; it was Sotiris who had sent him here—Sotiris who had used Lycaste's life for his own gain, stopping only long enough to repair him so he could be whisked back into service. Here, flung who knew how far from home, they were no more Maneker's responsibility than a fly trapped behind a windowpane. He glanced back at Higginbottom and nodded, noting the expression of relief on the Melius's big, sweaty face.

The butler scuttled up a huge flight of steps, ducking beneath a hanging shred of torn linen into a chamber stuffed with padded, silk-upholstered chairs. Folds and swatches of patterned material lay scattered everywhere, a twinkling assortment of pins and clasps all over the rugs ready to impale Lycaste's bare feet. Two young, skinny Melius—presumably the poor masters Dung and Hardship—were skulking in one corner. At the sound of Higginbottom storming in, they abruptly halted their conversation, sheepishly gathering up some of the cloth at their feet.

"You're not even dressed!" Higginbottom cried, outrage darkening his colouration. "What have you been doing all this time?"

Lycaste went to a window as Higginbottom ripped off his coat and threw it over a chair, gathering up swatches and holding them against each young Melius with a look of feverish panic.

"You haven't tried *anything*!" he screeched, scooping up an embroidered long-tailed jacket and showing them the sleeves. "The pins are still in these! No no no no no *no no*," Higginbottom muttered, fretting at the jacket and finally throwing it at the Melius to his left. "Unpick that and put it on!" He yanked another jacket from the pile, pulling the tail to admire it briefly before tossing it to the other Melius. "This one. I'll do the inexpressibles."

Lycaste moved out of the way as the butler shoved past, watching the other two shrugging on their garments. He chewed a fingernail absently. Noticing that nobody appeared particularly interested in him, he stepped back and quietly left the room.

His disappointment was almost physical, a solid, dull ache in the stem of his throat that he remembered well from youth. Of course the Satrap was nothing like he'd hoped—nothing, and nobody, ever was. Lycaste rounded a corner, his hand running desultorily over the bald scalp of a marble bust, and came to a window that looked down into one of the courtyards. It was filled with assorted statues and sculptures swaddled in artful folds of carved drapery, many of them blackened by soot and grime.

He would make his own way from here. Perhaps Huerepo would be allowed to stay, though something in Vincenti's demeanour suggested otherwise. Lycaste pulled the Amaranthine pistol from his bandolier to examine it again, brushing his thumb along its milky, scratched exterior. It was like a single lump of semi-precious stone, a polished crystal pebble of a weapon sleeker than anything he'd ever seen, let alone held. He wondered at its worth—or rather how much it might be valued back home; he might not need to detour and dig up all that silk after all.

He continued on through the palace, conscious of that dreadful butler perhaps already on his tail, and considered how terrified he might have been in this same situation barely a year earlier. This Lycaste, fast approaching his fifty-second birthday, a Firmamental pistol clutched in his not entirely inexperienced hand, was extremely capable of shooting any man who presumed to bar his way back home. He'd come too far and lost too much to care anything now for consequences, and knew how easy it was to take a life. He thought of the people he'd killed as he made his way through the palace, faces never far from his thoughts. When he was home again, this half-year nightmare concluded, he would allow himself to feel better.

Passing some huge storerooms, he found an immense larder stocked to the ceiling; bottles and barrels and jars almost large enough for Lycaste to hide inside, all arranged on magisterial shelves of maroon rosewood that encircled the chamber up to its decorated cornices. He stopped to examine the place, pulling cork stoppers from jars and sniffing their contents—cured meats and pastries and dried fruits much like those he remembered from home—and scooped what he could with a ladle into a cloth sack he'd found by the door, nibbling a pastry. At the bottom of one of the barrels he spotted some porcine lumps that looked suspiciously like ears and noses, some with thick, curled yellow hairs still protruding from them. Lycaste gulped down the last of the pastry and closed the barrel with mild disgust. Sweating, he hoisted the sack over his shoulder, noting how the evening sun—not setting but narrowing, a band of black working its way across the face—reddened the deep shade of the wooden shelves and that of his own skin.

He went to the pantry window, observing that the twinkling battle, at one point so bright that it had blurred the sun's outline earlier in the day, appeared to have ended. He'd seen the Prisms's greed, not least in that little man Huerepo, and couldn't imagine the victors would be content for long. Smoke like crumpled satin drifted almost motionlessly from one of the sun's vast buttresses, fanning into a mist of thick coils when it reached a zone around the star and appearing to drop back to the world like falling soot, the light glowing amber through the curling brown cloud. He thought about what Huerepo had told him, that six of the Vaulted Satrapies contained a vast mounted candle at their centre instead of a sun, for reasons now lost to history. He imagined it, a naked flame a hundred miles high, burning black soot at its ruddy tip. They even used wax, Huerepo claimed.

He left the pantry, the pistol, sufficiently heavy to feel dangerous, gripped in his free hand. The halls of the palace glowed the colour of the false sun, the reflected light of Lycaste's skin bouncing crimson down the corridor. Beside a pair of tall, flung-open doors, a Melius wearing stained pantaloons worked quietly at some plaster, spooning the wet paste onto his trowel and applying it with hushed care. He didn't look up as Lycaste stepped past, absorbed for who knew how long in work that Lycaste couldn't imagine the Satrap ever noticing. The stillness in the air brought out a ringing in Lycaste's ears as he watched the man carefully scraping at his task, eyes fixed on the veins of a sculpted leaf, his mind far away.

Through the open doors, he found a ballroom draped with more linen sheets, its size hard to judge thanks to the washing lines of fabric that stirred in the breeze from the open windows. Lycaste continued on through another tall door that swung open and shut in the hot evening air to the balconies beyond.

He came out into the shadow of the dome, starting a little when he saw the drop beneath the stone balustrade to the plantations below. The view swept out beyond the fields to the forests they'd emerged from earlier that afternoon, and on to where the land began to curve massively upwards to join the rest of the world. Beneath a fluttering awning along the balcony there were some wooden chairs upholstered with jaunty cloth, their frames angled for sunbathing. Lycaste went and sat, digging a hand into his supplies and eating while he looked out over the sea of silk bushes. Pickers worried distantly at the netting, or sat and fanned themselves with their hats, apparently quite at ease with their work. He considered how lucky he'd been to escape a life such as this, following the progress of a moth as it fluttered aimlessly in the air before the balcony, thinking on what he could do next.

PART II

SCOUNDREL FLOWER

A drifting flower caught on the pommel of his saddle as the mount tramped through the near-deserted streets of Sarine City. Sotiris bent and took it between his fingers, inspecting the yellow and purple snapdragon before tossing it away.

Elatine ambigua, the Scoundrel's Flower. The air in the street still reeked of perfumed smoke; the tiny flower had been burned on pyres in celebration throughout the city and the greater Province. Citadels as far as Gmina and Zielon Second—both trampled by the Jalan advance—had supposedly rejoiced all week in their liberation and return to the Lyonothamnine fold.

Sotiris watched the town houses for signs of life now as he rode, looking through darkened windows into courtyards and parlours. Flags and banners of the First, long and vibrant green where they lay against white stone, trailed from every topmost window.

A young Firstling girl, already nearly Sotiris's height, came wandering out from a flowered alley. Sotiris felt his mouth dry up.

"*Iro?*" he whispered incredulously, almost falling from his mount. She glanced in the direction of the zeltabra, perhaps hearing the clop of hooves, but saw nothing. Sotiris looked again as he steadied himself, unsure, and wove past the child still shrouded in his glamours.

No, that couldn't be right, that couldn't be her. His sister was aboard a graceful sailing ship somewhere out at sea. He was going now to meet her. The Amaranthine's mouth moved as he thought things over, nodding finally to himself and patting the zeltabra's neck. Yes, he was going now to bring her back.

Sotiris could see no other signs of life as he made his way along the streets, occasionally touching a glass bottle of water to his mouth and taking a swig. This late in the year the days were dry in the First, with little water to nourish the great fields of bloodfruit and Bulberries that grew around the outskirts of Sarine City. The undercultivated trees of the sunny Southern Provinces did not experience such difficulties, drawing all their water from the soil and rocks instead, blossoming where almost no rain fell. Over a slanting roof, Sotiris could see the deep gold of the plantations at the city's base. Famine was not unheard of here, but only the very oldest would remember it.

He tapped his boot against the zeltabra's rump and trotted it over the cobbles towards an inner gatehouse. Above, the palace loomed in the winter sun, wheeling messenger birds decorating its turrets as they came in to land. Sotiris looked to the high specks of windows, sure that he was being observed by more than just Amaranthine. He allowed his head to drop in a minute nod, an acknowledgment only trained eyes would detect.

Sotiris glanced inside the gatehouse, taking in the single huge bed upon which various scabbarded swords and blades almost the length of him were laid, oiled and gleaming.

"Who's that?" came the challenge in First. An old Melius face peered from the darkness of an upper window, looking straight at the Amaranthine. Sotiris knew instinctively that the fellow was blind. The gatekeeper's golden-white hand held the rope of a huge bell located somewhere in the rafters.

"Amaranthine," Sotiris said in the Highest First, a tongue only gatekeepers and librarians kept handy. "To see those within."

"Immortal," the guard muttered, putting a hand to his cheek. He let go of the bell rope and stumbled away from the window into darkness. Sotiris waited, tapping his finger on the pommel. The zeltabra flicked its ears, bobbing its head once to loose a persistent fly from its lashes. He looked back up to the closest parapets of the fortress, noticing a strand of silk snagged on a flagpole. The boy-king—in his childish wisdom—had tossed money down to the people of the city (themselves wealthy enough to treat such diversions as a game). Apparently nobody had noticed this last piece.

Sotiris glanced at the blind gatekeeper as the Melius approached, his hand outstretched.

"If you are truly Amaranthine, then let me touch you," the Firstling said in the same High tongue.

Sotiris assented, dismounting and presenting his face for the Melius's wandering fingers. The huge nails scuffled over his cheeks for a second, careful not to touch Sotiris's eyes, and were withdrawn.

"Lord and Master," the gatekeeper mumbled, nodding vigorously. He stepped up to the tall gates of the Fourth Entry and deftly inserted the key. "Sire Amaranthine."

"My thanks," Sotiris replied. He looked at the zeltabra a moment as it stared dolefully back, unsure whom it belonged to and where it might have come from. He frowned and climbed into the saddle, sure the animal wouldn't be missed.

"I believe there's a sixteenth of magenta up there on the tile," he said to the gatekeeper once his boots were in the stirrups. "You might have it before it's noticed."

The gatekeeper frowned, his sightless and clouded eyes instinctively turning to the parapet. "Oh," he said in plain First. "I thank you, Amaranthine."

"Farewell," Sotiris said, the crisp sound of the beast's hooves already echoing in the narrower street as the gates closed behind him.

Here the richest in the city lived, clustered like parasites around their diminutive sovereign. The houses to either side were made from pitted white growth-stone, much like those in the outer Provinces; here, conversely, it was regarded as a luxury. Thirdling and Secondling servants dawdled on the steps leading up to some of the buildings, their heads turning at the sound of hooves. Sotiris saw that some were scarred, baited by their masters. He passed them by.

"Amaranthine Gianakos." Filago bowed as best he could with his great wooden crutches.

Sotiris eyed the Melius, noticing the new jewels of office set into his ceremonial cuirass. The Lord Protector of the First had not long awoken from his injuries. He looked gaunt and hollow-eyed.

"They await you," the Melius continued, motioning to the cloisters that led to the upper halls before leading the way.

Sotiris followed behind, sweeping back his emerald cloak. More of the Elatine flowers lay strewn between the pillars, unswept since the revelry of Elatine's defeat.

They came to a set of thirty-foot-high doors, the grand objective of the failed Jalan invasion. Filago leaned and pushed with a wheeze of effort. Sotiris didn't attempt to help him. The doors juddered open with the groan of rusted, pre-growth hinges and he stepped past the Melius into the chapel.

Across the bronze floor, four Perennials sat enthroned, still as statues, only the clashing colours of their robes giving them away in the distance. Sotiris strode forward, uninterested in the space he had arrived in; like all well-travelled Amaranthine he had seen the painted chapel plenty of times, the novelty somewhat lost on him by now.

He reached the thrones and stopped, surveying the Perennials. He waited, fixing each of their gazes. Anton Vyazemsky was the first to kneel, followed soon after by Christophe De Rivarol. Florian Von Schiller—heir apparent by the ancient laws—bowed his head and took to his knee more flamboyantly, leaving only Trang Hui Neng still seated.

"Sotiris—" Hui Neng began slowly, his hands coming together.

"You are my subject?" Sotiris asked coldly, his sepulchral voice slicing through the stillness of the chapel. "Subjects *kneel*." The cathedra Hui Neng sat upon made a loud cracking sound, shattering suddenly beneath the Amaranthine's weight and tumbling him to the floor. The other Perennials stiffened in their supplicant poses, not looking up.

Sotiris nodded, his cool gaze taking them in, and made for the far doors, his stride faltering as soon as he was out of their sight.

The boy-king's bedchamber was darkened with huge curtains of silk drawn across the high windows. Sotiris let his eyes adjust for a moment before stepping forward into the gloom. He grimaced as the smell of a monkey house in high summer met his nostrils.

A flash of light from the doors caught a reflection at the far end of the room, a piece of cutlery being moved.

Sotiris hesitated, peering. "Here I am," he said, closing the door fully behind him.

The sound of its rasping breath became slowly apparent. Sotiris could just make out a laid table with a figure perched behind it. Glass or crystal tinkled as the beast sipped something.

"I've caught you at a bad time?" Sotiris asked, stepping closer. The chamber was very large, though filled with so many furnishings that it felt quite cosy. The king's possessions were still stacked on tall, laddered shelves that reached up to the ceiling.

"Closer," came the voice, small and dry and empty. It had trouble breathing here, apparently, in such new, oxygen-poor air.

Sotiris lingered where he was. "May I not see you first? It would be polite, don't you think, after all this time?"

The shadow appeared to consider his question, eventually stirring and reaching for the edge of a curtain. It flapped aside.

Sotiris stared, walking forward on feet seemingly possessed.

The being slouched behind the table, the flicker of reflected light within the eyeholes of the shroud it wore suggesting a gaze that followed his movements. Bottles and dishes and forks were heaped on the cloth before it, a Dutch master's vision of gluttony. A taloned hand clutched the stem of a twinkling goblet, twirling it thoughtfully before raising it.

Sotiris watched it drink, tucking the rim of the glass beneath its misshapen white hood. When it had finished, it wiped at its mouth, licking its lips with a black tongue before the material fell back. They'd told him the body was sensitive to the slightest rays of light after so much time entombed in darkness. Sotiris even recognised the embroidered material: it had once contained the remains of the Firmament's single Empress. Sotiris couldn't help but speculate on what the Long-Life might have done with the rest of her.

"Your Firmamental Majesty," Aaron said in a muffled voice, pushing away the goblet. "Come closer, so that I may touch you at last."

Sotiris glanced at the empty dishes as he approached. "You are sated now?

The hooded creature nodded. "You can imagine my curiosity." It appeared to regard the mess before it thoughtfully. Sotiris saw from the detritus on the plates that it had eaten meats of some kind, remembering that the body Aaron inhabited had been of mixed parentage; more than a little full-blooded carnivore lurked in that veiled gaze, considering him.

Sotiris stepped to the edge of the table, inspecting the pale skin of the beast's ungloved claws. "You won't fall ill?"

Aaron tapped thoughtfully on the nearest plate, finally offering his hand. Sotiris took it. The touch, slick and warm and almost feverish, was not what he'd expected. "I have been inoculated, Sotiris," the Long-Life said, indicating the table. "Nothing can harm me here."

Sotiris nodded, thoughtful, withdrawing his hand. "Besides the living, of course."

He watched the eyes, unblinking, shining from behind the holes in the cloth.

"As if you know what *living* is," Aaron sneered, tucking away his clawed hand.

The blankness returned. Sotiris wanted to reach out, to pull the hood away and see what it was underneath all that fabric. Then he recalled, his dreams coming back to him in a rush of sensation.

Burned, strong coffee and salt on the wind, the sucking slap of waves rolling into port.

A soul, bound to the world and now free.

An offer, a reward, and then all would be well.

DUSK

He'd fallen asleep stretched back in the deckchair, his arms dangling stiffly over the sides. Lycaste sat up groggily and glanced around at the cool, pink light. The Vaulted Land's lazy Quarter had run on towards night, shrouding the plantations in deep shadow. He blinked, noting the abundance of moths fluttering in the evening air, tiny blurred shapes that spiralled and hovered around the balcony. Lycaste frowned. There were hundreds of them now, as if they'd been released from their nets for the evening. He wondered absently how the pickers collected them each morning as he peered back into the dark recesses of the rooms behind him.

But there *were* no pickers, not any more. The fields, their silver pathways gleaming dully in the last of the light, were empty. Lycaste sat up in his deckchair to look over the balustrade, leaning his elbows on the stone. It was just bright enough to see that some of the nets had been torn open, accounting for the profusion of moths clouding the sky. A few settled on the stone balcony, wandering clumsily across his hands, but he hardly noticed.

Something had happened.

Lycaste stood and brushed away the moths, new fear mixing with his bafflement, and collected his bag. Returning to the ballroom, he saw that the plasterer had gone. Slivers of glass glittered on the tiles that Lycaste spotted too late to step over properly, performing an awkward half-leap and cutting his foot in the process. He gripped his sliced heel, hobbling along until he could lean and remove the thin shard embedded in the skin. After one or two spots of blood oozed out, the wound closed and he could walk on, at first leaving large red crescents like inverted hoofprints across the floor behind him.

The pantry remained untouched, though from some of the other, more distant rooms Lycaste thought he might be able to hear the rumble of conversation. The feeling that something had happened returned, stronger this time, as he left his bloodied footprints across the tiles. He moved hesitantly towards the sounds, now erupting with peals of laughter to a backing of song, his pistol at the ready.

In an anteroom to one side of the pantry were libraries of sorts, a row of identical chambers decked with the same dusky rosewood shelves. Lycaste stood unnoticed in the doorway of the last, watching the fifty or so pickers who had congregated in the room. The light was almost gone in the chamber, but the glow of pipe bowls and a smoky fire in the hearth lent the place and the dancing people in it a sinister tinge, as if they were not quite there. Someone just inside the door passed him a bottle, tipping the neck amiably at him. He took a sip automatically, the instinct to blend in and hide that had kept him distant from people all his life taking over. The liquor burned his throat but he smiled as best he could. An arm curled around his neck as he passed the bottle back, a girl's nose brushing his before he knew what was happening. When the kiss was done, she looked up at him and grinned, taking a gulp from her own fluted bottle that wetted her wide, pretty lips to glisten in the firelight. He dipped and kissed her again, inciting a stamping bellow of approval from the surrounding half-lit figures, and accepted another offered bottle.

The jangle of broken glass and a shower of spirit made them both glance up. A Melius in ripped clothes was perched atop one of the shelves, his hands raised. *"Proximo!"* he roared, throwing down another broken bottle as the room cheered back.

"Proximo!" the girl yelled in Lycaste's ear, stamping her feet and taking his face in her hands to bite his lip. She pulled away and pushed the bottle to his mouth, tipping it up until he was forced to lean back to catch it all. At last, when he thought he would gag, she relented, taking the bottle back and grabbing his hand.

They stole out into the hallway, the roaring of song following them into the darkness. She led him along, her fingers around his thumb in a curiously childish gesture that made him wonder at her age, apparently uninterested in the scenes of pillage they were passing: people wrapping things in curtains and hefting them out of the windows, precious metals being chiselled, yanked and torn from the walls. His throat—still dry despite the drink—ached, and he was conscious for a moment that he might well have slept for much longer than he'd thought, like some slumbering princess of legend, years passed in dreamless oblivion. Maneker and Huerepo could be long gone by now, having tried in vain to find him. The panic he'd so successfully tamped down finally broke through.

Lycaste returned his attention to the girl, his heart thrashing. She was untying her skirts one-handed while she ran, unslipping buttons with practised ease. At a flight of broad stairs, she discarded the last of her underwear and bounded on ahead, leaving him to puff slowly after her like some aged, impotent husband.

The darkness of the upper floors was almost total, though somewhere he could hear her calling to him. Passing by a broken window, Lycaste stopped for breath, looking out by chance onto the inner courtyard where they'd first met the Satrap. Light from the lower windows came to rest in stripes among the trees and fountains of the formal garden, the shadows of dancing Melius writhing in the grass like elongated black spirits. The garden appeared empty, though something pale and patterned had caught on the edge of the fountain, stirring in the night wind. Lycaste stared down at it, slowly realising that he'd seen the material before: the Satrap's nightgown.

The silver cobbles of the road thrummed with the beat of hooves. Lycaste pushed into a still-netted enclosure, batting at the sudden swarm of soft wings, and dropped to his knees. In the dimness, he saw and heard three riders bolt past against the bluish outline of the hills, their mounts' reins jangling. He shivered, one large finger wedged into the chiselled trigger guard of his pistol.

The port Maneker had mentioned, Astirion-Salay—it couldn't be far. Lycaste stopped to listen to the whoops and song floating from the palace windows. Another set of hooves thundered up the road, the skittish beast stopping and starting. Lycaste turned in the undergrowth, ears rising.

The charcoal outline of a ferdie and its two small riders bucked along the path leading from the gardens, pursued closely by two more. Lycaste ducked again as the crack and spark of a weapon lit the plantation for a second.

"I'm here!" he screamed, rising and tangling himself in the nets. A surge of moths swirled from the leaves. "Over here!"

The leading ferdie galloped past, the dwarfish person at the back twisting and firing something that fizzed and sparked at the chasing riders.

Lycaste pushed his fingers through the loops of the net and tore it open, struggling free. He shook himself and sprinted parallel with the road, ducking as the second rider reined to a juddering stop and aimed a blackly silhouetted weapon at the departing ferdie.

He thought quickly, jumping up and shoving the pursuing ferdie as hard as he could. It fell with a scream, spilling its rider onto the road. Lycaste ran on in a leaping sprint, catching up with the foremost riders and passing them, coming to a halt and facing them with his arms outstretched. The tiny figure swung around, finding him in its sights.

"Stop! Maneker!" He put out the flats of his hands as the ferdie galloped past, then turned and slowed.

"There you are!" the Vulgar wailed, his face a grey smudge in the twilight.

"Get another and follow," Maneker growled, nothing but a lump of rags at the ferdie's neck. He dug his boots into the beast's flanks and Lycaste watched them canter off, clenching his pistol in the darkness, waiting for the sound of the next ferdie. From the darkness the last rider emerged, slapping his whip and spitting oaths. Lycaste steadied himself in the centre of the road, his legs braced apart, aiming as best as he could at the top of the rider's head. He fired, shutting his eyes before he'd squeezed the trigger.

After a few moments went by, he blinked them open and stared along the dim road through a drifting swirl of moths, the silence intensified. In place of a bang, the pistol appeared to have cancelled out all sounds, as if sapping them from the air. The man's shouted curses had ceased the instant Lycaste pulled the trigger, and now only a cantering ferdie appeared through the moths, its rider nowhere to be seen.

Lycaste reached out a hand and caught the animal's reins to slow it as it trotted alongside him. Mounting unsteadily, he looked out into the bluish night for the others, inspecting the pistol with a baffled frown and sliding it back into his bandolier.

CORBITA

Her eyes stung. The pink wooden chamber was only just beginning to feel like home after their three-day passage. Pentas blinked and rubbed her face, hoisting the lantern and pushing herself out of bed, furious all over again with the old man for forcing them on this absurd trip.

She checked quickly on Arabis and saw to the two small chairs herself. The table she would leave unless someone else came for it; it wasn't her job. It outraged her that Jatropha had turned down the offer of hiring a Butler Bird for the voyage. Other people across the galley had them; she saw them in the mornings airing beds and guessed such a luxury would've cost only a fraction of a length more. They had an arduous journey ahead, or so everyone kept telling her.

Up on deck the morning was porcelain pink, almost mirroring their chamber, with one or two faint stars still lingering in the west. A roped gangplank had been lowered to the harbourside and Pentas could see the ship had been unloaded, the rest of the passengers already on their way. They'd let her sleep in. A stirring of gratitude was soon replaced by indignation that the old man and her sister still treated her like an invalid, some sorry moping lump of a girl who needed all the help she could get just to survive. She marched ahead with the chairs, dumping them by the rock wall of the harbour while Jatropha inspected the removal of their cargo from the hold. The sea cog's animal figurehead, carved to resemble a giant Southern Howling Owl, gazed over her. She stared into its vacant eyes, remembering the days when she'd been interested in sculpture herself, and judged it a poor likeness.

Two Tenthling boys caught her attention at the entrance to the hold—she thought she knew them distantly; they'd once been in Impatiens's employ. The first stepped back into the dim morning light, motioning with his hands. At his signal, a great parcel of tied canvas rolled out, the thing Jatropha had guaranteed would get them to the Second Province unharmed.

The twenty-seven-foot-high Wheelhouse rolled chaotically backwards out of its covering and down the stone ramp, sloshing through the surf and coming smoothly to a stop in the sand. Pentas looked to the ramshackle wooden balcony that framed the vast spoked wheel, spotting Jatropha sitting happily in the cabin among the jumbled terrace of apartments, the peeling paint of their red and blue window frames bright in the morning sun. Eranthis followed along the beach, the baby clutched to her, and signalled for Pentas to climb in.

The two boys had joined her sister, both apparently eager to see the baby. For a moment, Pentas felt seething resentment that someone, even the child's aunt, would allow anyone near Arabis without her express consent. She stormed onto the beach and snatched the child away, then climbed the ladder. On the balcony, she set the child down in a too-large chair, smoothing its sparse hair in an attempt to calm its bawling, and began to explore the rectangle of tiny rooms that made up the living quarters, scullery and crude necessarium, the sound of the waves sighing through the open windows. Eranthis arrived on the balcony, her arms laden with more goods—gifts from the cog's captain—and they glared at each other through the scullery window.

"Welcome aboard the *Corbita*!" the Amaranthine's cheery voice called from the prow. Eranthis said nothing, arranging her baggage and slapping the wheel's huge wooden spoke in response. Pentas took Arabis, claiming a bedroom and unfurling some blankets. She kicked her bags through the door and slammed it shut.

The great house began to move, wobbling uncertainly along the sand and up into the orchards of Artemida. Soon spear-shaped cypress trees screaming with cicadas brushed the windows, blocking the last glimpse of the coast, and Pentas knew glumly that there was no turning back; they'd set out at last upon the Western Artery, their route unbroken now but for Provincial borders all the way to the home of her lost love.

The twenty miles of road to Acropolo were fairly straight and scattered with travellers of varying shapes and colours, their luggage piled in neat towers over their backs or hefted by servants carrying litters. The majority gave way to the Wheelhouse, stopping at the sides of the road to wave as it rumbled past, kicking up a storm of pebbles and dust in its wake. For those disinclined to move out of the way, Jatropha honked an inflatable horn, eventually scattering them. Pentas moved to the window to watch some recalcitrants ambling to the roadside: two Fourthlings, perhaps homeless from the war, and a Tenthling guide. Over his back, the Tenthling lugged an open basket of writhing black snakes. The travellers looked sourly at the Wheelhouse as it wobbled by, the Fourthlings eventually spotting her in her small window and meeting her eye. She collected Arabis and moved to the other side of the cabin, stepping through the slowly moving spokes to reach the scullery. From there she could get a better view of the wild groves of ancient poplar, cypress and olive, unsullied by glowering travellers jealous of her comfort. Pentas wondered why Jatropha kept so stubbornly to his secret identities; they'd move if they knew who he was. She watched the twisted olive trees sweep by, some apparently thousands of years old, suddenly aware that none of the travellers on the Artery would likely even know of the Amaranthine's existence.

Pentas rocked the sleeping bundle in her lap for a while, her thoughts sliding back into the past, to a time of seemingly unending grief and pain. Lycaste's handsome face, once so fresh in her mind, was hardly visible now, just a suggestion, like one of her faster sketches. The second face that came to mind she knew would never dull. It was visible every time she looked down, as she did now, into the bundle of soft linen in her lap, and would be there reflected back at her as she looked into the faces of his family once their trip was done.

Through a blur of tears she saw she had a visitor; a small red messenger bird with a curved beak and round black eyes had landed on the windowsill of the scullery and cocked its head at her, observing Arabis in her lap as if she were the most fascinating thing it had ever seen.

Pentas stared at it, noticing the clutch of rolled letters wedged into a painted wooden collar around its neck. She sniffed, waving an arm to shoo it away.

At a bend in the road, the orchards rose sharply. They crested the rise, the Wheelhouse climbing with a sluggish squeal, and began to drop again, picking up speed. Pots and hanging jugs tinkled and swayed, pans clattering musically. Across a hot swathe of olive orchards the land rose again to a hilly plateau, a glaring-white town of growth-stone towers clinging to the hillsides. Crowning the plateau were the stumps of old stones, the ruins Jatropha had told them of where they would make their first stop.

"Iced treats," said the fat Ninthling in the concave place, "perfect on a day like this." He gestured to the curving, patterned walls at the hundreds of pigeonholes. "I have Green Excelsa, Valline and Syrup."

Pentas dawdled, not wanting to leave the fabulously cool chamber. She'd never tried an iced treat, though of course she'd heard of them. The conical chill chambers dotted the rubble fields of Acropolo, their smooth cone sides scrawled with written advertisements. Pentas had been allowed to wander first, leaving Eranthis and the *Cryling* back in the wheelhouse and taking her time wandering among the exceedingly dull ruins.

She touched a hand to the purse around her neck, feeling the coiled silk given to her by Jatropha for daily expenses, and pulled out a length of green. She presented it to the treat seller to be snipped and he touched her palm in the customary sealing of the deal, taking up his scissors and holding them open half an inch from the ribbon's end. Pentas nodded, confirming the transaction by the age-old agreement of the eye, and the Ninthling closed his shears. Stowing the snippet of money, he turned to the pigeonholes and removed the pot of Valline she'd pointed at.

She strolled among the shells of worn columns, keeping the Wheelhouse in view. Up ahead were the low remains of the place Jatropha had called the *Erechtheum*, already busy with morning tourists. Pentas wandered closer, spooning the rapidly melting treat from the pot, not entirely sure whether she liked it or not.

Jatropha had hinted that he'd be gone the whole day, about some business or other that they wouldn't understand. He'd left them here, at the top of this blasted hill, in some attempt to instil cultural sensibilities into the girls; an effort Pentas considered wholly wasted, like the awful jokes the Amaranthine told. Her sister would no doubt appreciate the ruins, remnants of a time before even Jatropha claimed to have existed, but all Pentas saw were lumps of weathered rock, smoothed by rain and wind to nothing more than denuded shapes almost indistinguishable from nature.

The old man, just like her tutors before him, didn't appear to understand how bludgeoning someone with facts caused them to hate their subjects. Pentas, force-fed knowledge all her life, despised almost everything but painting, where her natural talents had shone through and freed her from rigid instruction. It was her greatest love still, though in the past weeks and months she hadn't thought it possible that her mind would ever turn again to paints and board and the tranquillity they could bring.

At the eroded foundations of the *Erechtheum* she put down her pot, sitting in the morning light to watch the travellers as they pored over the remains. She observed a huge, bent-backed Jalan tramp wearing linen rags and sashes—some soldier recently released from his commission, perhaps—gazing attentively at the worn entrance columns and extending a hand to rub the stone in wonder. She watched the giant without expression as he licked his ramshackle teeth with a long tongue, taking out a chisel and glancing surreptitiously around. Pentas looked away to the other ruins, pretending to be lost in thought, waiting a few breaths to glance back. The Jalan had begun working at a piece of the stone, scraping away until a chunk came free. He pocketed it with a jagged smile and ambled inside the remains.

Pentas strolled behind him at a safe distance, her eyes following the hunched shape as it looked from side to side. She passed through the entrance of the ruin and into shadow, pausing to see why the Jalan might have been interested in that particular part of the pillar, but the stone surrounding the gouge was as plain as any other.

Within the ruins, traders had set up shacks and awnings that spidered out and up to the missing roof. Pentas saw the Jalan lurch towards a food stall and begin the haggle, cradling his purse with almost infantile vulnerability. Her eyes wandered to the scenes beyond; a zeltabra auction was in the process of setting up, the iron railings of an enclosure being hammered down amid various chairs and milling people. She took one last look around and left, reentering the sunlight more bored than ever.

At a pile of stone slabs, a cluster of spherical cages stood uncovered, whatever was in them left to bake in the sun. Pentas wandered a little closer, suddenly hopeful that they were Monkmen. She bent and peered inside until a face stirred and looked up at her.

"What are *you*, then?" she asked it, squatting to look inside the other cages. They were tiny pale monsters, heat-shrunken apparitions like a Melius washed and left out to dry. They blinked, opening their mouths and revealing rows of needle-sharp teeth. Inside the second cage, one had died and been partially feasted upon. Pentas knew better than to try to reach in, imagining a gruesome scene where she came away minus a finger, but she lingered all the same, whispering to them as they stared keenly up at her.

"Hello, little darlings," she said, looking into their eyes and seeing the faintest comprehension in them. "What are your names?" She saw their pointed ears stir, knowing then that they could understand the gist of what she was saying. "How about something to eat?"

Clear drool seeped from their open mouths, a look of slack anticipation on their faces. Pentas smiled and reached into her purse, rummaging her hand theatrically past the silk rolls.

"Now what have we *here*?" Their mouths opened wider, exposing long, desiccated tongues. She began to remove her hand slowly, watching their beautiful blue and green eyes dilate.

"Oh." Her hand came out empty.

Their faces crumpled in confusion. Pentas covered her laughter with a hand.

"Taunting the Starlings, eh?" someone said behind her. She looked to see that the voice belonged to an elderly Eighthling wearing a neatly pointed black beard. "You're courting bad luck, you know. Only the children make sport with them, so they do."

Pentas shrugged and looked back into the cage. The Starlings had begun to mumble to one another rapidly in a tongue she couldn't help but find vaguely threatening.

"Still, you're a clever girl for not trying to pass them your finger," the man continued, still standing a few paces away from her.

"Of course," she replied. A semi-amused look had emerged in his lined, twinkling eyes. It was an expression she was familiar with, suspecting easily enough what he might want from her. The man's skin had churned golden-pink in the delicate shade of jolly good humour. His pointed beard looked too perfectly trimmed. *Vain*, Pentas thought, glancing back at the disgruntled creatures in the cage. As she did so, an arc of stinking yellow water jetted out at her, splashing her feet.

"Little *monsters!*" she screamed, shielding her eyes. The Eighthling roared mean laughter. Pentas looked down at her wet toes, hands in the air, beginning to laugh despite herself. The Starlings echoed the laughter like a flock of squealing parrots.

"Here," the man said, untying a handkerchief from his pack.

She took it, wiping herself down.

"I warned you, so I did," the Eighthling said, taking back his handkerchief. He dribbled water from his flask over it and shook the linen rag onto the stones. Pentas grimaced, imagining him using it to blow his nose further down the road, and decided now would be a good time to return to the Wheelhouse. The necessarium on board, whilst old and leaky, would serve her better than a strange traveller's handkerchief. She nodded and began to make her way back along the stones.

"Might I escort you among the sights, miss?" the Eighthling called after her, falling in step alongside. He bowed and gestured at the cloth-bound ring book in his hand, which he must have been holding the entire time. "I'm something of a chronicler in these parts. I give tours of the place for a small fee." He ran a hand through his beard, staring critically at her. "But great beauty is silk in itself. I've watched you wander this place, so I have, and you looked more than a little bored—let me render my services for free."

Pentas glanced at him askance, not replying. She saw the Wheelhouse between some worn pillars across the field of boulders and was suddenly glad.

"Or perhaps just sit with me a while," the man added quickly, stashing his book with trembling fingers and moving to block her way.

"No, thank you," Pentas said, pushing past him.

The chronicler hissed under his breath, putting out his wiry hand to stop her. "Maybe the young miss is hungry? Let me take you into the town for something."

"The *young miss* wants you to leave her be."

"Of course, of course," he simpered, still walking beside her. With a spark of alarm, Pentas noticed him glancing furtively around, checking for anyone nearby. She thought of the things Jatropha had shown them, the ways of shirking troublesome attention and unwanted suitors, but couldn't remember any of the Amaranthine's tricks.

"I like that," the chronicler said, twiddling the tip of his beard. "Playing mean. I like that, so I do."

The Wheelhouse came into view again, close enough to run to. Pentas saw Eranthis waiting on deck.

"My, my," the Eighthling leered, his voice taking on a deeper, coarser tinge all of a sudden. "Aunty? Sister? *Girlyfriend?*"

"We're with our husbands, actually," she replied, fixing his beady eye. "They'll be back soon."

The chronicler smirked. "Oh, if I had a fifth of green for every time a girly said that to me." In an instant he had her wrists in his grasp. "But pretty girlies *lie* for a living, so they do."

"Piss off!" Pentas yelled, shoving him to one side. The weight of the man's pack sent him toppling with a yelp before he could find his footing. She grinned, running on.

"*Bitch!*" he screamed after her from the rubble. "I'll be coming for you! I know what you have up there!"

"Get us out of here!" Pentas half-giggled up to Eranthis as she reached the shadow of the *Corbita* and climbed the ladder to the deck. She threw the hatch closed over the rungs and locked it shut. Together they hid in the scullery, watching from the corner of the open window as the chronicler arrived, prowling around the base of the wheel.

"*Pretty little butterfly,*" he half-sang, knocking on the great metal rim of the wheel. "Don't think Geum the chronicler doesn't know about that Secondling Screamer up there! My birdies've been watching you since Profitus! Who is she, eh? What's she worth? That I'd like to know, so I would!"

"Go away!" Eranthis shouted through the scullery hatch. Pentas looked around for something to throw, wondering if he could do any serious damage to the wheel.

"I might just go and find a Jalan, so I might! Wouldn't that be a sorry shame? Think I saw one back at the Zelty markets." He chuckled, rapping on the wheel. "But Geum likes a bargain, so he does, and what use would it be to me seeing two such pretty ladies locked up in the Balustrade?"

"Go and lock yourself up!" Eranthis yelled, somewhat lamely. Pentas thought she could have done better herself, but wouldn't have been able to keep the laughter out of her voice. What fear she felt was tempered by almost uncontrollable hysterics, an inexplicable urge to fall to the floor in a fit of giggles. Instead she gathered herself and went to their small pantry, rummaging through the jars and pots for the freshly bought tea, sparing Arabis, lying in the next room, only the lightest of glances.

"I don't suppose Jatropha's coming back anytime soon?" she asked Eranthis, adding leaves to the teapot and settling it on the hotplate. The weight of it tipped a mechanism, sparking a white-tinged flame that smelled vaguely sulphurous.

Eranthis said nothing, leaning on the windowsill to look out. Some other travellers, stopped to inspect the nearby ruins, had begun to notice the man idling by the Wheelhouse. She turned back to Pentas, glancing through the scullery to the prow just as the Eighthling started to call out again from below.

"You Southern butterflies are all the same, so you are, leading a poor fellow on!"

"Close all the cupboards," Eranthis said, moving past Pentas. "I'm going to try and steer this thing into town."

Pentas took a last look at the furious chronicler through the hole in the hatch and followed her through to the cabin. The wooden tiller was locked upwards with an iron bolt. Eranthis pulled it free while Pentas busied herself stowing anything left out. Almost as an afterthought, she bundled up the baby and put it to bed, then went back through to the prow.

"Let's hope this works," Eranthis muttered, hauling on the ropes that held the wooden chocks. Almost immediately they felt the Wheelhouse begin to roll.

"He showed you how to steer it?" Pentas asked, momentarily jealous.

Eranthis shook her head as she gripped the tiller, revolving it experimentally. The Wheelhouse turned, juddering, towards the ruins. They heard a cry from down below. Eranthis winced.

Pentas hurried to the balcony. They'd run over the Eighthling's foot.

"Go go go!" she wailed to the prow, and the Wheelhouse rolled swiftly off in a spray of pebbles, stoning the furious chronicler as he hopped up and down.

ASTIRION-SALAY

The port lay unguarded, nothing but a single unlit tower staring into the night above a dark crescent of beach. Maneker, Huerepo and Lycaste climbed down from their ferdies and looked out to the blackness of the Clawed Sea, hearing the ebb and rise of invisible waves. Over the unseen waters the sun stood supported, a disc of pure black ringed by a slim, hair-fine band of gold. The world over their heads shone brilliant as a hundred thousand jewels somehow smelted together, the magic of the Amaranthine ensuring it cast no light upon the black waters.

"Twenty miles across," Maneker said, pulling bags from the mount and hurling one to Lycaste. He examined it in the darkness, realising there might be room inside for Huerepo. "I was a fool to think there'd be any boatmen left," the Amaranthine continued, almost to himself. He strode along the shore, boots crunching in the wet sand.

Lycaste and Huerepo sat down at the water's edge, looking off to the ring of gold. Twinkling sparks still played desultorily across its face, like moonlight on waves.

The ride south had bypassed the distant Prism-held castles, the furthest of them engulfed in flames. Lycaste kept up by galloping parallel with Maneker's mount, terrified that he might lose them in the dark. They'd spoken little, resting only once. He'd needed desperately to sleep, though Maneker, gripped by the most intense agitation Lycaste had seen in him so far, had flatly forbidden it.

The port of Astirion-Salay was their only option, the only means of passage between two prongs of land that would save them an eight-hundred-mile detour around the Clawed Sea. Maneker had been counting on it since their chaotic arrival in the Vaulted Land, certain that what he wanted lay on the far shore.

An Incantation, Huerepo had said as they rested earlier that night. *That was what he needed from the Satrap. Just a single word. A word, and the prisoner can go free.*

Lycaste settled tiredly in the sand with his knees pulled to his chest, waiting for the Amaranthine to return. Around his feet, precious stones had been churned from the beach like the ancient, petrified eggs of a nesting creature, exposed now to the night. Huerepo, too exhausted to collect them, had climbed into the waxed knapsack beside Lycaste and gone to sleep. In the darkness, his pointed boots stuck out, twitching as he dreamed.

This person, this prisoner, was the reason the Amaranthine had brought them here. Whoever he or she was, whatever use they could be, it was clear that their life certainly meant more than the Satrap of Proximo's—at least to Maneker. Charging from the plantations, the Amaranthine and the Vulgar had both kept silent, ignoring Lycaste's questions about the fate of the Satrap until they'd had a chance to rest. Only then did Maneker spare Lycaste a glance, instructing him sharply to shut his mouth if he knew what was good for him.

All that mattered to Lycaste was that he got home, and yet he was too afraid now to speak. Seeing Maneker's furious determination made such concerns feel selfish, and yet he was not the one following in the Amaranthine's wake just to scoop up jewels. Huerepo's hand-me-down suit of mismatching armour was fit to burst with secreted treasures; he'd sink like a stone if he happened to fall in while they crossed the water. Lycaste understood that he'd just have to wait, at least until Maneker freed his precious prisoner and set about correcting whatever disease the Firmament had succumbed to. For the first time, it occurred to him that something might be more important than his trip home, that there were events in motion around him that he couldn't hide from. Lycaste cleaned out his ear with a fingernail, his eyelids drooping, taking some small measure of comfort in the thought that what freedom he still had lay in him being no use at all to Hugo Maneker and his grand schemes. Lycaste had no skills an Immortal would require, no knowledge, little cunning or strength. It could only be a matter of time before he, like this fantastical prisoner, would be released to go his own way.

Sotiris appeared unbidden in his mind, clad in the full silver regalia of the Secondling guard. Lycaste remembered the late-evening sun, pink against the blue, the sheen of grease on the Amaranthine's cuirass, the grime on his face.

Hugo knew the Pretender's secrets; he'll know what must be done.

Lycaste pushed a hand through his beard, now full and thick and greasy. Beside him the Vulgar rolled and grunted, clambering further into the knapsack.

Pretender. The name meant nothing to him. He hadn't even known there *was* a Firmament until he'd left the Tenth, let alone that it was ruled by a mad king intent on bringing it down. The prospect was an opaque one to Lycaste, of seemingly little consequence, like the weather in a foreign land.

Huerepo snorted, snapping Lycaste from his thoughts. The musk of his sweat drifted from the sack, ripe as Dalaman cheese. He couldn't have washed in weeks. Lycaste stood, flushing the brightest white he knew and making his way down to the surf. Not everyone had to sink to the Vulgar's level. He skimmed his hand across the water, gasping at the icy cold. The white of his rapidly thickening skin glowed beneath the black waves as he waded in.

He stood, shivering for only a few moments, watching the water around him as a glistening silt churned about his ankles and caught the glow of his body in spinning swirls, constellations of cold, billowing stars eddied by the movements of his hand. There were beasts flitting among the stirred sparkles; small, reflective shrimp tinier than any he'd seen back home. To Lycaste they looked like monsters the size of stars moving with the night sky. Perhaps he was feeding them, churning the waters and scaring up their prey. Maybe there really were creatures out there that ate stars, gliding through the heavens like night-black fish.

Lycaste pushed a wet hand through his hair, shuddering. Out on the water, unseen things sloshed through the waves. Thunder crumped across the bay, gurgling to a rumble. He stood, listening, remembering that he wasn't really home. He saw the glow of a light on the sand, watched it march up to the knapsack and accost it.

"Up!" Maneker snapped, his voice travelling across the water. "Where is he?"

"Here," Lycaste said, wading out and shaking himself, preparing for another verbal beating.

The Amaranthine swung his lamp and looked up. "I've hired us transport. Keep the Vulgar out of sight."

Huerepo struggled in the sack, one foot caught in a buckled leather strap. Lycaste reached down and picked the whole thing up, slinging it over his shoulder.

"Better?" he asked, once Huerepo had finished cursing.

The Vulgar's head poked out, his hair plastered down over his forehead. He appeared to be looking for something in the sand. "There, my book. Get it, please."

Lycaste glanced to his feet. "What—?"

"My book, dummy—*there*!"

He saw the dropped book at last and picked it up—no bigger than his thumb—and passed it carefully to Huerepo. "Can you read in there, in the dark?"

Huerepo produced a flame from some kind of tiny device on the end of a chain, waggling it at Lycaste before pulling down the cover on the knapsack.

The vessel, what Maneker had called a Sloop, was one of the most beautiful things Lycaste had ever seen. Russet sails like birds' wings tapered to the stern, a shimmering galley of wood and gold leaf shining brilliant in the light of Maneker's lamp.

"Welcome, Sire," the boatman said, taking Maneker's hand and helping him aboard. His eyes slid to Lycaste, a smile forming in them. "Other Sire."

"Are we ready?" Maneker asked, pulling the collar of his ragged cloak up and bustling to the front of the Sloop. Its masts were strung with tiny paper lanterns, their light hopping up and down in the wind.

"Ready? Aye, ready as we'll ever be." Two oarsmen at the sides nodded to Maneker and heaved their oars into the silt. Satisfactorily cast-off, they took their places, latching the oars into elaborate gilded rowlocks.

Lycaste shrugged off the knapsack, forgetting at first that Huerepo was still inside. As it landed with a thump on the deck, a harsh curse emanated from within.

All three boatmen looked up from their tasks, ears pricked. The ship creaked, black waves nudging its hull. Thunder growled once more across the bay. Eventually the captain spoke.

"It is just the *two* Sires to cross?"

The grey shape of Maneker ignored him from the bow. Lycaste nodded as the man approached, hoping he'd understood correctly.

"Because we can't be overstocking the boat. Not with a storm coming in." The boatman's round, pink eyes went to the knapsack, slung behind Lycaste on the boards of the stern. At length, to Lycaste's considerable relief, he smiled and looked out the way they'd come.

A jet of water billowed from the waves, its spray illuminated in the pool of the ship's lanterns. The oarsmen cried out in delight, joining Maneker at the bow. Just beyond the boat's flickering light, another spray erupted from the waters. A head almost as large as the ship rose slowly from the waters to peer at them.

"Here, Jessle!" the captain called out, extending his hand slowly in the age-old mime of summoning wild beasts. The great canine eye of the thing blinked at him as it sank back into the water, the humour in it reminding Lycaste of the Dolfish in his cove.

It reappeared closer to the bow, rocking the hull and spattering the watchers. Maneker reached out a hand to caress its mottled skin, patterned here and there with slicked tufts of oily hair. Its head rose further from the swell, leaning into the Amaranthine's hand and exposing two great, twisted horns set far back in its skull. Maneker smiled, his fingers brushing across them before returning to Jessle's single nostril. It flared and snorted, threatening to jet. Lycaste gave the knapsack a quick glance, suddenly fearful that Huerepo might have been tempted to poke his head out, but the Vulgar remained still, the drawstring around the neck knotted tight.

After a while, Jessle appeared to grow bored, its eye roving across the ship and alighting on Lycaste. When he made no attempt to speak or touch it, the beast sank back beneath the waves to a gurgle of thunder from the distant storm.

The oarsmen resumed their places and began to row, the captain remaining at the bow and talking softly with Maneker. Lycaste went and sat with the knapsack, taking out some pastries and wine he'd stolen from the Satrap's larder; across the water, the clouds came alive with silent lightning, followed after a few moments by a drum-beat of thunder. The lanterns in the masts swung and tinkled, their flames bobbing, flickering. Lycaste recalled his walk across the beach to the caves, the first time he'd ever seen lightning. The day all this had started. He stared at his hands as he remembered that day then shook his head distastefully at the memory, inspecting his half-eaten pastry before finishing it off.

Lights twinkled out to sea. Lightning played among the clouds, a surge of waves slapping the Sloop's nose upwards while thunder ripped across the bay. He saw Maneker advancing towards him across the deck. The Amaranthine came and sat, rubbing his hands together. He didn't look at either Lycaste or the knapsack, his gaze diverted instead by the distant lights.

"You've been patient, both of you. I expected more quarrelling."

Lycaste avoided glancing down at the bag, seeing how the boatmen eyed them. "I—"

"I'm not finished," Maneker snapped. "I meant it when I said I was done with you." His cold eyes met Lycaste's. "You're no use to me. I'd sooner not have the two of you slowing me down." He gestured out into the darkness. "The captain of this ship will let me off and continue on to a port in the north, not too far from an orifice sea. He's promised he'll get you there safely and free of any charge."

Lycaste nodded slowly, unsure whether to be glad of the news. "Orifice sea?"

"A thin part of the Vaulted Land where ships of the Void may enter and leave. There will almost certainly be vessels there that can get you home." The Amaranthine dug in one of his grimy pockets for a moment, producing a blunt *grafitus* pencil with some string tied around its end and a piece of worn, crinkled paper. He looked at Lycaste. "You can read Tenth?"

"Of course."

"Good." He began to write. Lycaste studied the man's flawless Tenthling script over his shoulder. Even with the rise and fall of the Sloop, the Amaranthine's style barely faltered. "There," he said, scribbling in the margins. "These are the names of the Grand Companies that will likely have remained on the surface to assist departing Amaranthine."

Lycaste read their names: *Brushell's Fifteen, The Catchers Superior, The Guns of Armodo.*

"Find one and show them this." Maneker turned over the paper, revealing a second, pre-written note. The script was entirely foreign to

Lycaste, composed of loopy, joined-up letters. He couldn't tell where one word began and another ended.

"Show this side to any Amaranthine you encounter, too. If there are none, which may well be the case, you go to the Pifoon. Huerepo will talk to them for you."

Lycaste thought about this, panic teasing at his stomach. "What if he and I don't—?"

"You *will* stay together."

Maneker's words stretched through the silence. Lycaste took the note as it was handed to him, cradling it carefully in his large hand, fearful of folding it in case the Amaranthine should object.

"Remember," Maneker said, pointing to an underlined paragraph on the note, "this is your address."

Lycaste nodded glumly.

"Well? *Look* at it. What does it say?"

Lycaste read aloud, flushing at his remonstration. "'Old Izimir, Mare Nostrum. Orb. Melius Dom. (Old Satrapy.)'" He looked hard at the words, understanding that he would be dropped off at the nearest port, Izmirean.

"How will I pay them?" Lycaste asked, terrified that his question would be considered foolish.

"With my regard, implicit on the other side of that note. A Perennial Amaranthine's favour is still not a currency to be sniffed at." He glanced off to the captain of the Sloop. "And I daresay a few of the Vulgar's pilfered jewels shall buy you some extra comfort."

He waited until Maneker looked back at him. "Thank you. How long will it take to get there?"

The Amaranthine appeared uninterested by the question. "Just memorise that address."

A raindrop pattered onto the note, darkening the fine letters. They both looked up, everything forgotten for the briefest of moments. Lycaste held his hand out to catch the drops.

"It wasn't me, you know," Maneker said suddenly, leaning forward to study the gold-painted boards. "Though I wished him dead." The Amaranthine looked off to the lights again. "It was just bad luck for him that so did his servants."

Lycaste didn't know what to say. He felt the knapsack between his feet move almost imperceptibly.

"If you'd only known what sort of man the Satrap Vincenti was," Maneker mumbled, almost to himself. "*He* chose Vincenti as governor here, knowing the man's greed and unnatural lusts would keep His investments safe."

"He?" Lycaste asked. "You mean the Pretender?"

Maneker raised his eyebrows minutely, studying Lycaste. "You think your world forgotten, untouched by people like us. But your home, your lands—all would be known to Him, put to use by Him in some way. Those great fields of silk that Vincenti oversaw kept the First in the Long-Life's pocket." Maneker smiled. "It is He who really owns the Provinces, Lycaste." He sat back. "And now all the Firmament."

"He is Amaranthine?"

"That was what I thought," Maneker replied, eyes growing vacant. "That was what He told me."

Lycaste frowned at the boards beneath his feet, their chipped gold leaf lustrous in the light of the paper lanterns. "And this person on the far shore can help you stop Him?"

"Yes. Perhaps. Unless the Long-Life's spies have got to the Oratory first."

"You think they have?"

"These boatmen ferried Amaranthine across not two days ago. But I have something they did not, something they never knew they'd need."

"The Incantation."

The Amaranthine pursed his mouth thoughtfully. "The Incantation."

Lycaste watched him slip into thought, noticing how the Amaranthine stopped blinking when his mind was far away. Behind those eyes, lost in sockets of shade beneath the golden lantern light, he must have gone very far indeed. Lycaste reached slowly for the knapsack, untying the drawstring and dropping in the letter. Looking up, he saw the captain approaching them quickly across the deck.

"Trouble ahead, Amaranthine," the captain said quietly, pointing. Maneker snapped from his reverie, standing and staring out into the spotting rain. Lycaste followed their gaze.

The lights on the water, lights Lycaste had first thought to be coming from the shore, were dimming and dying like a row of candles snuffed, one after another.

"What's going on?" Lycaste asked the captain directly, trying out his Unified before he'd had a chance to think it over. "What's out there?"

The captain looked at him sharply. Maneker stared at him for a moment, too, smiling grimly. The thunder growled more distantly through the darkness, moving away to the north.

"We aren't alone on these seas," the captain said. He glanced at Maneker. "Tell your little friend he can come out now, Sire. We'll need all the help we can get."

Lycaste went and shook the bag until Huerepo rolled out, fussing and cursing and smoothing his hair. On his nose he wore a tiny pair of glass discs framed with wire. Across the water the sound of something large drew close, filling the darkness with the rolling roar of surf. Lycaste rooted in the knapsack, unable in his haste to find his pistol. He swore, tipping out its contents and sifting through them.

"There!" he growled, collecting the weapon just as a tarred black hull crunched side-on into the Sloop and knocked him to the deck, the lanterns falling to tinkle around him. The mast split with a popping crack, dumping the sail on top of them as they all slid with the motion of the ship.

As the juddering roll of the vessel halted, the shouts and curses and screams began.

Lycaste struggled through red gloom towards where he thought the bow must be, seeing Maneker up ahead still fighting with the sail, trying to stand.

"Lycaste, drop!" Huerepo screamed behind him, firing a bolt into the sail before he'd had time to turn. A black shape treading across the topside squirmed and fell, cutting off their route to Maneker.

"*Drop*, imbecile!"

This time he did as he was told. Another body fell and rolled, tightening the silk and pinning them down. The thumping vibrations of what must have been people leaping aboard came rippling through the material. Lycaste crawled forward, working his fingers into the hole made by the first bolt until he could tear the fabric open, finally managing to squirm out over the fallen sail.

He froze, holding his pistol close. The remains of one oar lay shattered against the attacking vessel's hull, its body still rammed up alongside the Sloop. Scraps of wood connected to ripped tatters of sail slid around Lycaste's feet with the listing motion of the boat. By the light of one fallen lantern he could see what they were doing.

Two Firmamental Melius had hold of a person-shaped bulge in the sail and were bent over busily driving their knives into it, scooping clumsily into the figure's head. Smoke wafted from the holes made by the blades as their victim squirmed beneath them, his gashed head revealed as the sail fell away. Lycaste froze, horrified, then lifted his arm as if possessed and fired blindly in their direction. One of the attackers lost the top of his head, a clean line cut through the brain that welled with blood as he fell forward. The other took one of Huerepo's bolts in the waist and flew into a rage, trampling over the rest of the figures beneath the sail to get to them. Lycaste shot at him in a panic, only partially finding his target and cutting his body lengthways. The cross section of the Melius fell flapping over the side.

Lycaste heard the cries of others on the larger ship and grabbed Maneker as he would a baby, making quick soothing noises as he drew him out of the ripped sail. Huerepo scampered alongside, firing deafening shots up into the darkness.

"Jump!" the little man screamed as he loaded another bolt.

Lycaste flapped away the sail's edge with his foot to release the struggling bulges of the crew and went to the bow. Maneker moaned over his shoulder. He could feel the man's blood trickling down his back.

"Jump, Lycaste!" Huerepo screamed again, snapping off a few shots as the first returning lumen bolts blazed across the deck towards them.

"Stupid bloody Melius!" Huerepo howled, rising and shoving Lycaste in the rear. The force of it surprised him and he lost his footing, tumbling overboard with Maneker and into the storm.

HOMAGE

It ought to have been far safer to arrive in the Upper First, in the lands that bordered the magnetic pole of the Old World, but that was not the point. A show of devotion was required, a demonstration that every

Perennial would risk their lives simply to pay a moment's homage. But Bilocating from and to places other than poles wasn't as dangerous, really, as everyone thought.

Florian Von Schiller watched and waited as more snapped into appearance, a trail of blurred colours resolving into bolder form, wondering who here knew the truth of it and who did not. Each visitor opened his or her eyes with the pain-stricken confusion of a newly born infant, and he saw how they might have been, all those grandiose piles of rubies and fine cloth, at their own births.

The day of homage went convivially, with ten Satraps present already. They milled and chattered in their slow way, each preparing to enter the banqueting hall adjacent to the chapel to offer their particular Vaulted Land to their new Firmamental Regent. It was Florian Von Schiller's task to see that His Majesty Sotiris was not overwhelmed, by leading in only a few of the Satraps at a time.

"Perennial."

He focused his absent gaze, taking in the fabulously speckled pink eyes of the Fallopia as they rested upon him. The only Melius allowed in the chapel for the day of homage, the magisterial family ought to have stuck out among the circulating tide of Amaranthine. He smiled, noticing how they had dressed—in great rumpled gowns of Old World silk and garnets—as if they, too, were Immortal, *Homo sapiens* of old.

"I hope we aren't too late," the boy-king's mother announced, a carefully upheld humour dancing in her voice. It was, after all, her house the indifferent Satraps occupied, though Von Schiller had not forgotten. He smiled. Immortality was a state of constant sobriety among the inebriated: catering to mortals more out of pity than anything else. He studied the party of Firstlings as they gathered before him; they were an odd grouping, all loosely related in the incestuous way of the First, and Von Schiller tried to decide as he ran his eyes over them which of the various cousins or sisters the king would ultimately choose for his bride. Their clothing was dyed the colours of the Elatine flower, the Festival of Ridicule—organised in haste when it appeared that the Jalan would not reach the First after all—not yet over, and so it was to a great mass of shimmering purple and black that he stepped forward.

"Lyonothamnus," he said, his tongue curling around the luxuriant name. "Welcome, Your Enlightenment."

A slender creature of seventeen separated from the group, his whitened skin clouding as it coloured from the toes up into the neutral, blotched grey of submission. Von Schiller knew perfectly well that the ruling class fasted and bleached themselves, and that the great, idiotic irony was that the king's family were nothing but Secondlings themselves. Florian had seen the Heraldry, noting at once how the family Berenzargol of Elblag held a better claim they could not use, their spendthrift matriarch having been bought off more than a hundred years ago.

The boy-king nodded, extending his hand eagerly in the Amaranthine clasp. Von Schiller took it with a beaming smile, his fingers enveloped in warmth.

"This is Sire Vonsiller, first in line," the king's mother said, careful not to sink into First. Florian smiled again. They'd met many times, and the Fallopia knew it.

"His Most Splendid and Venerable Self sees your loyalty and thanks you for it," he said, theatrically pronouncing his vowels in a language they could barely speak. It was forbidden for a Firstling to use anything other than Unified in the presence of a Perennial. They learned what they could from the three exquisitely expensive scholars provided for them or kept their huge mouths shut.

"But how are we to be seen, Sire?" the boy asked. "The Emperor, I hear, is resting."

Von Schiller pointed conspiratorially through the painted gowns to the great bronze doors. "He views us all, hears our every word, through that *keyhole* over there. Do you see?"

The procession nodded and mumbled appreciatively, arranging themselves foolishly for best effect. Florian encouraged them to turn about so that they might show off their finery to the distant hole, wondering if the baiting of Melius could ever grow boring.

Lyonothamnus knelt in view of the keyhole—Florian suspected there might even be a key still lodged in it—and stood slowly, shooing his party away so that he might talk more privately with Von Schiller. When he spoke, his breath smelled of flesh, and the unguents he used exuded a whiff of high, pungent sweat beneath the drapery, like meat left to warm.

"You have come from the Greenmoon, Sire?"

Florian did not hesitate. "Indeed. I live there."

Excitement dilated the boy-king's huge eyes. "You live there? How marvellous! I look up every night with my telescope."

"And we look down on you, Your Majesty."

The king hesitated.

"Do not fear," Florian whispered, drawing close. "We look away, when needs be."

Regaining control, Lyonothamnus whispered back, "Would you take me there, one day? I've longed to go, ever since I learned the Firmamental Secret and the presence of your kind."

No king had been taken from the Old World since Dracunctus II had been spirited away by the Zelioceti two hundred and fifty years before. The Prism had hoped for ransom, some supposed, but nobody paid, and the king was never heard from again. Perhaps when the Perennials were gone from here and the Old World turned over, the Prism might well grant Lyonothamnus's request.

"One day." His eyes flicked to the far entrance of the chapel, where those not invited to take part in the homage gathered and waited. Pets, emissaries, fools; Lyonothamnus's colourful, chaotic entourage swirled and jostled to see the Amaranthine.

By all accounts, the young king was studious and reasonably bright, progressing well in his studies even as all the countries of the East waged war upon him. Elatine, after winning the Fourth from Zigadenus, had called for the boy to come forward, to offer himself in place of his people. Such a request was a win-win situation for the attacking Lord General, with any dent in the king's prestige almost outweighing the value of his life. As a substitute, the First had sent various disgraced aristocrats, but this attempt at mollifying the rage of the Oyal-Threheng was beyond feeble. The offered nobles, far from being slain, were awarded lands, estates and armies in the new Threheng Counties—the seized Eastern Provinces that had once been owned by the First—and the king's image degraded further. Before Elatine's disappearance at Vilnius Second, the war had been practically won and the six-hundred-year-old Lyonothamnine Enlightenment ready to fall. Now the First breathed a tentative sigh of relief, clinging to the Amaranthine in the hope that they might stay and keep them safe.

The boy-king shifted his boot, its studs rasping on the brass floor, and both looked down. He'd trodden on a solidified splash of metal, plastered across the floor like thrown wax. Von Schiller held a finger up before the boy could comment, gesturing to the ceiling.

Another stuttering kaleidoscope of colour spiralled with a whisper across the chapel, slipping through Perennials as if they were nothing but projections and alighting on the metal floor. The king wrung his hands together as he observed, fascinated, watching the Bilocating Amaranthine grow in cross-sectional slivers until she was whole. It was an unnerving sight, seeing a person's innards squirm into place before their faces and clothes joined them; one Von Schiller didn't like to think about when he ever travelled himself. The lady Amaranthine, one Elise, Satrap of Port Elsbet, clasped her long, gloved fingers, that look of agony gone from her face in an instant, and strode out towards her peers.

"Here he is!"

"The eternal Sotiris Gianakos!"

Von Schiller presented them with nothing more than a sweep of his hand, all formality dissolving as Sotiris's old friends crowded into the banqueting hall.

His Majesty the Emperor Elect looked up from his documents, his dark hair slightly matted and wild. Von Schiller was gratified to see his blank expression thaw into a wide grin.

"This is the greatest of days," the Satrap of Alpho said, striding forward to embrace Sotiris. "Even the weather has warmed for you!"

"It is a portent," said Von Schiller matter-of-factly, accompanying the Satrap to the head of the enormous Melius table where Sotiris sat. "Our Emperor has turned back the seasons with his coronation."

"Nerida," Sotiris said after a moment's stiffness, leaning down from his chair to kiss the Perennial on both cheeks. "I am so glad you could come."

"*You* are glad?" the Satrap said tenderly. "I've been waiting centuries for this day. Our own Sotiris taking his rightful place."

"And the Satrap Downfield, of Wise," Florian said gently, presenting another Perennial.

"Samuel!" Sotiris cried, more speedily this time.

"Eternal Majesty," the Satrap said as he sank to one knee, all the gems in his gown flashing. "Words cannot describe this day."

Sotiris took Downfield's hands as the Perennial rose to his feet. "But they can! This day is a meeting of old friends, with no more bowing permitted."

The Satrap beamed. "Where is your crown? We must cover that messy hair!"

Sotiris pointed along the table, past stacks of gilded edicts already signed, at an elaborate white hat like an ancient bishop's mitre.

"His Majesty doesn't like it," Florian explained, remembering how Sotiris, in a fit of peculiar rage, had thrown it across the chamber. The Perennial sickness had him now, though the Long-Life appeared unconcerned.

"Yes, it isn't quite so handsome as the old crown," Downfield admitted. "Though I remember Sabran rather liked it."

Von Schiller moved quickly to change the subject, noticing a look of deep confusion settling over Sotiris's features. "But isn't this wonderful, I believe we're all here!"

"Vaulted Sirius pledges unconditionally her every possession and material asset, within and without, encompassing the Tethered moons of Palestrina and Rubante, the Estate Planet of Fielem's Land and all of that volume therein."

"Vaulted Elsbet," another voice said, "pledges unconditionally her every possession and material asset, within and without, encompassing the Tethered moons of Airal, Jothem, Kifer and Kawl, the Free moons of Gimble and Stathe, the Estate Planets of Steerilden's Land, Julem's Land, Van-Bergen's Land, Hume's Land and all of that volume therein."

"And Vaulted Gliese," Von Schiller began, the last of them, "pledges unconditionally her every possession and material asset, within and without, encompassing the Palace of the Ascension and the Halls of the Sea, the Uncounted Vaults, the Foundries of the Finer Interior, the Free moons of Great Solob, Pauros, Desiduum . . ." He glanced briefly up at the Satraps sitting behind the long table, hesitating. Sotiris was gazing intently out of the window at the setting sun.

Florian inspected his gold-painted fingernails, waiting. From a doorway to one side, a dark colonnade stretched away into still shadows, and he felt himself watched.

Their Emperor remained motionless, as if he'd died in his chair. The Satraps murmured, sipping water, adjusting jewelled sleeves, rummaging in pockets and taking out small books or gazing up at the painted ceiling. The scenes here were not quite as grand as those in the chapel, detailing in a slightly cruder hand the life of old King Ophiopogon I, founder of the Enlightenment.

Von Schiller looked among them. Twenty-one Satraps present. Two unaccounted for—those of Proximo and Virginis; the latter having run away, perhaps to the Investiture, after the destruction of his dominion earlier in the year. He noted their absence, considering the adequate punishment for missing a compulsory meeting of Satraps and embarrassing their Emperor. He looked at the crown, sitting limp and rumpled like a large folded napkin before him. Downfield was correct; it didn't have the presence of its ancestor, the Crown of Decadence, out of use now for the last two millennia. Von Schiller had a suspicion the ancient crown had been hidden for safekeeping in the vaults beneath the Sarine Palace itself. He would collar some junior honorific—Holtby, perhaps—and send him down to find it.

Just then, Florian caught a glint in the far darkness of the colonnade. The unmistakable twinkle of a predator's eye-shine; *he* observed, just as he had for so long, unbeknown to them all.

Sotiris returned his attention to the table a full hour later, casting his wide eyes about the assembled Perennials as if he'd never seen such a ridiculous assortment in all his life.

". . . The Tethered moons of Elebastial, Ophos, Magior . . ." Florian continued, returning smoothly to the inventory in his head.

"When you have all you've ever wanted, there is such a fear of change," Sotiris suddenly interjected. He pushed a hand through his wild hair and rubbed his eyes. "I'm so very sorry, Lycaste. I shall go to bed now."

Florian continued speaking, raising a finger as the muttering among the Satraps increased. When he had finished the oaths of fealty, he pointed to the fabric crown in the centre of the table. "Vyazemsky," he said, noticing Sotiris already stepping down from his chair. "If you would."

"Certainly," the fat Perennial said happily, fetching the crown and making his way towards Sotiris. "Majesty, I hereby—"

"No!" Sotiris cried, batting the hat away in wide-eyed horror. It fell to the floor accompanied by muted gasps from some of the Satraps.

"Get it and put it on him," Von Schiller muttered, busying himself with the collection of the piles of edicts and bulls before they could be pushed over and mixed up. A mystified Firstling took them from him.

"Majesty," Vyazemsky whined, tottering after Sotiris with the crown in his hand. "It only need be on your head for a moment."

"I'm going to bed!" Sotiris roared, flailing his arms and pushing past him. "I have business to attend to!" The still uncrowned Emperor threw open the door and leapt into the hallway. Florian cursed and grabbed the crown, following him out.

"Highness." He sighed, stalking after him through the painted halls. "You may sleep after this one little act."

Sotiris ignored him, making for the great entrance to the chapel. Florian knew it was empty, cleared specially for the Satraps to take out their telescopes and appreciate the ceiling, but quickened his pace.

Beneath the vast painted dome the new Emperor staggered, almost tripping, only running again when he saw Von Schiller close behind. Florian heard the *click-clack* of unseen claws following parallel through the shadows, stalking, watching.

"Think of your sister!" Florian hissed. "Iro needs you now!"

Sotiris turned, staring blankly back into Florian's eyes.

They both registered the sound of the claws slowing, and Sotiris's expression appeared to clear.

"Go and get her," Florian said, soothing, "and then take up your rightful place."

MIDNIGHT

Calm, after the storm. Half-empty glasses stood on every conceivable surface, their used waters cloudy. Florian sat on one of the still-intact cathedra, contemplating the shattered pieces of its neighbour. They'd spilled in a fan shape across the floor, remaining untouched at his decree.

Night drew in, the pink air beyond the window warbling with half-spoken birdsong. Flies danced in the air, attracted to the smells and industries of the palace.

"He's coming," the Fallopia said, standing at the window.

Florian's eyes rose to the king's mother. He admired the boldness with which she spoke to him. Unlike her son she wore Shamefashions at all times, not just in the presence of the Amaranthine, and this evening had chosen a rumpled apricot gown that spilled across the floor behind her. Florian, in a moment of blissful forgetfulness, thought she looked beautiful.

A knock, and someone entered, walking quickly across the chapel floor. He thought he'd seen this man before—the tall Secondling was one of Filago's generals, Florian seemed to remember, who had disgraced himself by abandoning his territory in the face of Elatine's legions.

The general arrived before them, a broad smile in a bearded face, and it was clear at once that the Melius had taken something, a narcotic of some kind.

"Tribulus," the Fallopia said, taking the general's hand. "Are you ready?"

He began manically kissing her fingers. "Oh yes."

Florian indicated the door, not waiting for homage. He wanted it over and done with.

The Fallopia nodded, a jewelled brooch catching a slant of light, and pulled her hand away. Tribulus sniggered, swallowing, and passed without further prompting into the boy-king's former apartments. Florian watched as dimness swallowed him.

The king's mother went immediately to the crack in the great doors and peered through. Florian stood, stepping over her gown, and made his way out.

"Florian."

Von Schiller stirred in his grand bed, the whisper almost beyond hearing. He looked out at the green moonlight that fell through the windows, remembering slowly where he was.

He followed the voice to the black mouth of the tall chapel doors. Peering through them, the great painted ceiling was lost in shadow, nothing but ink-black space above him. The smell of wax hung in the dark air, the ghostly remnant of spent flames. Deeper, his outstretched hand encountering nothing in the dim, green-tinted shadows, and he was within the private royal apartments. Something growled in the darkness and was hushed. There were others here, awake or dozing.

He followed the moonlight.

Sotiris's face, the nostrils flaring lightly with every breath, looked milky-green, decomposed. Von Schiller gazed down at the sleeping form, his eyes adjusting.

Poor Sotiris. The first of a new kind of ruler, determined not by age but merit, and yet not long for this world. Who could say, once he had gone, that there would be any more? Florian truthfully had no idea. That imbecile Sabran was finished, ruling nothing more than the barren ranges of his unhollowed worlds, and that was for the good. Now there could be no impediment; every edict Sotiris signed would pass unopposed, even by the moderate Satraps of Vaulted Ectries and Tamilo who had fought the reopening of the Foundries in the capital.

He swallowed, his mouth dry. It was hard to believe the structured simplicity with which the Long-Life had taken control of so enormous a volume of space, and Florian wondered, not for the first time, whether a less brutal method might have been possible—whether Aaron might have got what he wanted simply by asking. As things stood, at least seven of the twenty-three Vaulted Lands were already looted, their Immortal masters slain in creatively horrific ways. The Vulgar–Lacaille War blazed on a hundred fronts. Looking at his sleeping Emperor, Von Schiller saw now that the Amaranthine would fall much sooner, and much harder, than expected.

He started, a sharp intake of breath. Two glimmering green marbles were watching him from the shadows beside the bed. The reflected points of light blinked and breaths approached him in the shadows, the light of the window blotted. Florian felt for a moment as if he'd fallen into a tiger's cage.

"How will the Firmament be governed now?" he asked, voice hushed, knowing full well that Sotiris would not wake to any sound.

The darkness chuckled. "Do you fear the Prism? What they will do to you?"

Florian hesitated. "Yes."

"Our friends are thinly spread," Aaron said. "Between here and my goal there lies nothing but greed. The Prism can be used as an obstacle

only for so long, before someone among my enemies manages to mobil-
ise them."

"Impossible, I believe," Florian said, careful to lend a smile to his
voice.

"Not impossible, Florian. Not impossible at all. Indeed, I would
do the same, given more time." The creature exhaled; a thin, whistling
sound. "But I have gone from having nothing *but* time to no time at all,
and there is only one last force I can buy before I leave."

"Who?"

"There stands a prison somewhere on a little Tethered moon—you
know the one. I will give its occupants what they need to guarantee my
escape."

Florian did know the one. Every Amaranthine did. He envisaged
the place as he had last seen it, a dangling spike of dusky red brick deep
within a snow-veiled valley. "He would be as good a choice as any, Sire."

"You agree?"

"Though I don't envy whoever's landed with the task of persuading
him."

"I've known a thousand men like him," Aaron muttered. "He won't
refuse what I offer."

"The Apostate isn't like other men," Florian said under his breath.
"There has never been a criminal like him."

"Well, then," Aaron replied sourly, reflective eyes turned to him, "I
shan't be sending *you*."

"Name my trial—please," Florian said, trying to keep his voice
steady. "Give me a task to demonstrate my loyalty, so that I may accompany you from here."

The breaths moved to the curtains, which opened wider until the
full green moon was entirely visible. The creature began to dress. Florian watched it from the corner of his eye, a pale, skeletal presence in
the moonlight.

"You will sit a while?"

Florian looked up at the voice, drawn in by the lure of the thing's
plaintive, almost piteous tone. The Long-Life had clothed the scars of
his body in a bespoke suit of Amaranthine finery, gossamer-thin around
the sleeves and collar. It pulled on a pair of gloves and looked at him,
eyes glowing with crescents of moonlight.

"The year grows late, and for once I feel it."

Aaron indicated another chair beside his own and they sat together in the dimness. He wrapped his claws around the domed silver lid of a dish, removing it to expose a large haunch of something gleaming and cold, soused in what appeared to be Bulberry wine.

Florian looked at it, understanding that he'd seen its owner, the disgraced General Tribulus, barely a few hours before. The dark sauce was laced with a complex stew of probiotics, a teeming serum drawn from the bellies of Firstling aristocrats desperate to be of service in some way. It was hoped by many of the Perennials that sprinkling the Long-Life's meals with modern bacteria would imbue the rotten, ice-burned cadaver's intestinal flora with some kind of protection from disease, perhaps even one on a par with that of a Melius. So far, after almost seven days of mortality, the experiment appeared to be holding up. The Amaranthines' efforts, however imperfect, would simply have to do for the time being, at least until the Long-Life had access to the Collection, as he would soon.

Von Schiller couldn't envisage what physical law would allow the spirit to leave now, when he had been unable to before. His soul appeared unchanged, simply rehoused, and if anything his situation looked vastly more precarious. Florian was not about to ask; a mind did not spend eight hundred thousand centuries dreaming up careful plans only for them to be so flawed. Or so one hoped.

Aaron picked up a fork and stabbed at the haunch, turning it to reveal previous teeth marks. Von Schiller reached out to help him, selecting the cleanest plate and watching as the Long-Life deposited a lump of cold meat upon it. As he did so, a piece of his own sagging skin detached and plopped into the meal. Florian stared at the strip of seventy-nine-million-year-old flesh lying on the plate, gradually darkening as it absorbed the sauce mixture, and kept his hand steady.

At length, after chewing and swallowing with pained slowness, the *Caudipteryx* appeared to remember Von Schiller's presence. "Very well. You have your chance."

The ladle in Von Schiller's hand dipped as he spooned more of the Bulberry sauce, almost spilling it. "Anything."

He climbed to the ramparts, the entire Sarine City revealed below in a chalky maze of streets and rooftops, hazed by a rising cloud of perfumed chimney smoke. Beyond, the russet plantations of blood-fruit stretched forty miles along the great Southern Artery until it turned west into the Second, the coloured specks of travellers and traders disappearing into the distance. Heavy cloud shadows moved across the landscape, dulling it to a bluish tinge until they reached the high plaza Von Schiller stood upon, where they vanished as if dissolved into a greater patch of shade.

Rising above them like an industrial reflection of the capital hung the inverted citadel of the *Grand-Tile*, the three-mile-wide Lacaille flagship. One of three Colossus-class battleships present above the Old World, its departure would signal the opening of the holy planet to every Prism kingdom intent on spoils and territory, permitting them leave to feed like a lion tired of a carcass. Looking up, Florian could feel on his face the soft rain of rust shavings and pattering sewage that floated down from its scarred bulk, sensing the metallic stench of the thing while his gaze wandered over its great hanging turrets, painted in patches of white and grey and stained with blood-red oxidation from two centuries of service. It was far from the most efficient and modern of the Lacaille navy's various Voidcraft, simply the largest, the most dominantly threatening. Its single vast hangar could hold nine thousand Voidjets and seven hundred bombers, accommodating nearly sixty thousand Vacuum troops. Two internal factories could theoretically manufacture, with sufficient deliveries of purloined materials, any number of smaller ships, tanks, submarines, jets and even rolling fortresses. It could fire poorly manufactured shells the size of houses from battery chambers in its towers, as well as an arsenal of rigged superluminal engines like ineffectual bombs—the equivalent of throwing stones capable of erratic flight, more in the hope of terrifying the opponent than any reasonable expectation of destruction.

Florian knew the Prism as a whole had never enjoyed an industrial revolution; they neither understood nor appreciated the spare parts gifted them by the Amaranthine, and perhaps this was for the best. Atomic power—that ancient, divine spark—would remain beyond their comprehension, effectively lost forever.

Nevertheless, just one Colossus could conquer the entire Lyono-thamnine Enlightenment, and with the arrival of Prism warships of every kind within the month, the Old World would become a furnace, a bright spot of conflict visible across the Firmament.

The battleship dropped, smoke churning from its kraken belly across the sky, until parts of its spiked undercarriage had fallen level with the plaza. Stained white metal scraped along the flagstones towards Von Schiller, squealing and buckling. He could see a hatchway unscrewing, its complex system of airlocks unwinding, and two pale, feral Lacaille faces peered out at him.

The procession was small; more like a subtle stealing away than a victorious conqueror departing for newly won territory. He stood back a little, the platoon of Lacaille that had brought the Shell strutting past him across the plaza followed by Hui Neng and De Rivarol, both smiling piteously at him, quite oblivious now to his age. Ghaldezuel—the fortuitously placed Lacaille knight—followed behind, his polished white plackart reflecting Von Schiller as he stood to watch.

At the rear, dwarfed between two golden Firstlings—one holding a parasol against the dripping sewage—the Voidsuited *Caudipteryx* strode airily to his private warship, tail flicking out behind. Beneath the creature's composure, Florian detected a tightly controlled impatience: the Long-Life's gloved hands were scrunching open and closed, and his head—encased in smooth white material so that it was nothing but an inexpressive hooked triangle sprouting nodes and fronds—faced forward at all times, not once turning to look at his servant as he passed. It was understandable. He was leaving the world for the first time, perhaps never to return, and those he left behind he would likely not see again.

Florian bowed his head, shuddering as the outermost long cannon exploded into a hundred-gun salute, a rage of echoes rattling across the city.

The partially deafened party ascended without further ceremony, the Firstlings hefting luggage inside. Von Schiller stepped back, uncovering his ears and wondering what the city's Firstling inhabitants, still tense from nine years of war, would have made of it all. Pink and green birds cried and wheeled around him, scared up into the battleship's thermals as it rose again to belch smoke onto the city, its hatchway bolting shut with a slam like a pistol shot.

Slowly the plaza grew dark as the thick, churning cloud from the *Grand-Tile*'s exhausts rolled over the highest towers. Florian watched it rise through the dimness, a pale smudge growing smaller, until there was nothing left but him in this strange, forlorn place, and nothing left to contemplate but the single, absurd task that had been set for him. He'd assumed the Venerable Sabran would be left alone, happily out of the way on his distant, icy world. But the Long-Life wanted no contest to the elected Sotiris, not now, as close as he was to achieving his desires.

LETTERS

Igoumenitsa, Permet, Elbazannion. Names he hadn't heard for years upon years upon yet more years. Jatropha tasted them on his tongue as the Wheelhouse rattled along, their forms taking the place of other, barely remembered flavours from long ago. Alongside each neatly painted word on the sign was a jumble of figures in Melius Crules, the splendidly unreliable miles of the Old World. A Crule was never the same for any two travellers, expanding or shrinking with the quality of the terrain and weather. Depending on the winds and seasons, Mostar— their next stop—was anywhere between three and seven hundred miles away. As a general rule, one snipped the greatest given distance in half, as Jatropha had always done.

Bordering the Artery, expanses of cultivated land sighed with cypress trees taller than the Wheelhouse. Where Cursed People worked, poetry drifted through the fields: the oral histories of the Nostrum Sea. Once, at the edge of a stream that crossed the Artery's path, Jatropha spied a clutch of smooth man-high stones that poked at angles from the olive groves. He pulled the *Corbita* over to one side so that the girls could see the ancient megaliths, now home to a resting Butler Bird and his baggage, but they hadn't been very interested. With a tug of disappointment, he rumbled the Wheelhouse back onto the road. It was a pity. They were rare and wonderful things indeed, the stone circles; that particular arrangement was eighteen thousand years old, pre-dating even Jatropha himself.

A drifting memory reminded him of other things he'd found in the tall grasses of the world, things even more ancient, and less benign.

"Mostar?" Eranthis asked beside him. Together they'd been at the tiller for more than a Quarter, staring silently out at the world as it rolled by. A cloth parasol bought in Acropolo shaded them as the sun rose, patterning their skin where the light shone through its weave.

Jatropha pointed in the rough direction. He'd started clothing himself again as they climbed north, buying fine fabrics and sun hats and taking them in with a needle and thread. Amaranthine felt the cold keenly, and where they were going, the iron-grey light of old winter could still sink to the land.

"I've written ahead and arranged a guide," he said. "You and your sister should find him personable."

"You don't know the place?"

Jatropha shrugged. "I haven't been up that way in eight hundred years."

"What is he, this guide? Noble born? They always are. Don't expect Pentas to take to him."

"The mayor's son. Comes highly recommended." He looked at Eranthis, noticing how dark her great wide eye sockets looked in the shade. He'd had no choice; one didn't travel west without a chaperone. "She can't blame him for his birth."

"She can try."

Jatropha scowled. "Might I blame you for your face? For your name? You have chosen neither of these things yourself." He looked back to the road. "She must learn."

"She will blame him, and then she'll blame you. You know this."

He tugged at his sun hat, watching the Artery roll juddering by. There were families of thieves on any of the tributaries of the great road, but here, near the town of Erseke, a great many congregated. The object of their attentions was a broad lake about a mile east of the Artery, at which thousands of tired messenger birds stopped to drink on their way to the Nostrum. Jatropha knew from experience that it wasn't difficult to swipe a letter from a resting bird—he still employed men to do as much for him from time to time—and as a result most letters to the Southerly Provinces were encrypted, though the knowledge of this didn't stop people from trying their luck. He watched out now for a few of his own birds, waiting with growing impatience for news from the north and east. Jatropha had hundreds of spies in his employ, carrying colossal reams of information from as far as the Threheng Principalities and beyond, not much of it outwardly interesting, most of it irrelevant, and yet all destined to be put to some minute use at some distant point in time. Commodore Palustris still wrote to him of the Skylings' and Firmlings' reported movements, growing worried at the volume of refugees lining the roads from the Fourth Province. Lord General Fagus informed him of the plots against the Jalan admiralty now that the war was at a stalemate. The ladies of the Crimson Court relayed their designs for new heraldry under the Threheng princes, anticipating that the conquerors would wish to visit their newly won territories soon after the turn of the Amaranthine year. But it was his spies in the north who brought the most interesting news: news from the First.

Immortals had been there, they said now, slowly, sheepishly redrafting their recollection of events. Not just a handful but a court, a procession of twenty or more Perennials. Some names were listed, but Jatropha didn't know them all. They had taken over the Sarine Palace during the course of a year and summoned delegations from around the Provinces to them, spending what wealth there was to be had in the First on their own personal amusement and almost bankrupting the young king.

And now they've gone, he thought as the Wheelhouse rolled ever closer to their old dominion. *Gone to who knows where.*

Jatropha reached into a trunk beneath his chair and brought out his grubby linen letters from a Lacaille contact, peering to read the scribbled script again, paying no heed to Eranthis's glances. All but a few of the largest ship manifests went unrecorded—the Prism shipping lanes being too chaotic, too unpredictable—and even then they were vague at best. Only the movements of something as large as a Colossus battleship attracted attention, a glowing shoal of superluminal flotsam always following like plankton in its wake: *the Feeders of the Colossi*, thousands of tiny Great Company vessels representing nearly all of the Prism races. And the Feeders had much to report, turning up as they had on the Old World itself not twenty days ago.

Elements of the Prism were in league with these Perennial Amaranthine, Jatropha now understood, the two pinned together by some higher power, some governing force still unknown to him. The sudden—and rather late-arriving—news of a schism in the Firmament might not be unrelated.

Jatropha folded the letters, his mind turning inexplicably to the old rumours from the west, to the stories of a demon that took the shape of beasts and men.

He noticed Eranthis looking quizzically at him, having caught sight of the foreign papers, and struck a languid flame with one snap of his fingers, burning them in his hand.

GOH

The gun lay hot across his sunburned arm. He couldn't be sure whether the dappled shape he'd seen half an hour earlier was anything more than a pattern in the grasses. Julius took a morsel of comfort from the thought; any tyger or wild dog would surely have grown tired of stalking him by now and made itself known. Shit or get off the pot, *went the admirable saying. He smirked, eyeing the tall grasses once more, throwing his satchel over his shoulder and raising his foot to step carefully through the field again, his mind turning to the likelihood of snakes. He'd been bitten six times by a variety of species, all with different results. The worst, a taipan, had left him with a lingering day-long headache. Any other man would have swiftly sickened and died, but Julius was not like other men: he could inhale the breath of a consumptive's cough and drink from the Ganges without the slightest effect. Specifically why this was the case remained a mystery to him, but after more than two thousand years it was a comfortably familiar state of being. As he strode through the grass, he knew he ought to be far more mindful of the thing he'd just shot at than anything as ineffectual as a snake, but a deeper part of himself still shuddered at the thought of something slithering over his boot and worming its way up his leg.*

At a stand of trees, Julius paused to pull out his flask of tea and stare into their depths. Off to the south, the grove had been thinned by local woodsmen—those who had first come upon the peculiarity, as the explorer Davis had called it for want of a decent translator in the region—and he knew he'd have to push through to find what he was looking for.

He took a mouthful of tea, the tannins chalky on his teeth, and spat into the grass. It was perfect midday, the ochre grasses reflecting the heat back into his face and smearing the distant hills into shuddering ribbons of chrome. The far-off wail of a bird ceased, replaced with something more than silence, something he'd heard before.

He listened, the spectre of the tyger fading at his back.

This was not a place he knew. Only a week before, he'd landed at Calcutta on a Portuguese merchant ship, making his ponderous way to the outskirts of the small town of Goh. He walked a little closer to the edge of the trees, the rifle stock sure against his shoulder, the loaded ball worth its weight in platinum, worth its weight in life. He might survive a snake's bite, but there were more than poisons in the grand, wide world.

The sound repeated through the branches. It was as if a strip of leather was being rapidly run across something sharp, but with the expressive dexterity of a violinist drawing his bow along the strings. During each interval in the sound, a handful of swift taps punctuated the silence, some apparent inflection in them generating the impression that a question was being asked. Julius thought quickly, pulling out his knife and tapping its blade against the shining barrel of the rifle, trying to imitate the sound from the trees. As he feared, it fell silent.

He stepped into the shade of the trees, dry branches snapping beneath his boots. Children, perhaps, or some species of bird he didn't know, but his past experience led him to believe the source of the sound to be far more exotic. He directed his eyes upwards as he crept through a grove of Portia trees, scanning their yellow and pink flowers for anything unusual, anything peculiar. He understood, having encountered three already throughout his travels, that he would find what he was looking for in a tree not quite the same as its fellows. It would appear older, more primitive, or even of a variety no longer found on the Earth.

Through the trees, he began to see the first worn brick columns of the pink temple, crumbled from centuries left to the mercy of the woods. Roots the thickness of his neck wormed among the stones, pale against the scuffed, bleached magenta of the walls. He crept between the crumbled pillars into an open square. Dancing reliefs of monkey gods played across the walls, their lithe bodies worn smooth and crossed with the strata of exposed mortar. He stood motionless for a while, ears trained to the sounds around him, a mosquito whining far, then close. He let it settle and feed, creeping further into the temple.

In a crumbled hallway he stopped for more tea, happening to glance up and into the canopy of leaves hanging down through the roofless space.

Julius sighted his gun with satisfaction. There.

FALLPULL

I sleep, sometimes, much to my surprise.

When I wake, I've nothing but the view from my window to know any time has passed at all.

Oh, but listen to me going on. You'd think from my monologues that I am a being composed entirely of self-pity. There must be greater unfortunates out in the wide worlds. And, even now, it really is quite a view.

From where I press against the glass, misting it ever so slightly with my warmth, I can see almost the entire world, all existence curving above me like a vast, faded bauble of lands and seas. My cell, wherever it is and whatever it's called, sticks out upon a spit of gnarled brown igneous rock, with a view beneath of pounding grey waves that slam across the promontory, blown flecks of surf flung almost to my window when the storms sweep in from east to west. I can see those clouds as they form across the world, coalescing with a brutal, dark weight and spinning slowly out over the five inland oceans. I watch the land darken, snaking ribbons of rivers and lakes turning tawny silver and then grey as the great cloud shadows track the coasts to my lonely home, until finally droplets patter the glass and smear my view to nothing.

They've no idea, those who visit me occasionally in my darkened chamber, of just how far I can see, how comprehensively I understand; it is one of my few comforts in this bleak place.

When I first came to be, in whatever manner that process came about—for I've quite forgotten, if I ever knew at all—then they were *my superiors. I bawled, I raged, and then I was imprisoned. But I am clever, far brighter than they suspect, and they are certainly not my equals any more.*

My cell is ovoid, constructed with a symmetry and elegance that implies it was once used for something other than storing the forgotten. Across from where I like to hang there is a tall set of shelves that rises almost to the window, empty but for the four haphazardly stacked books I understand more intimately than those who wrote them ever did—that was how I first learned both ancient English and its successor, Unified, the language of my jailors. Everything I knew up until they came for me, I learned from those four jewelled cases; four little collections of symbols that, for the briefest of intervals, at the very start, meant nothing at all. Of course, this was not a dilemma for long, not for me; within the first minute I'd sifted the implied laws of grammar and orthography and spoken my first phonemes (what I'd then thought of as Clenches and Huffs), discerning their principles and chaining together my own bespoke sentences like a master jeweller. Twenty seconds later, I'd examined the first work, an eight-and-a-half-thousand-year-old volume entitled Jungle John, *and enjoyed it so much that I read it ninety-nine times more in quick succession, burning through the text incrementally faster with each reading. Replete with the joy of the book, I selected the next and began more slowly, inventing for myself the concept of delayed gratification. By day's end, I'd read all four of the odd selection and found that the limitations of the world around me had expanded a trillion-fold, an erupting snowflake of fractal possibilities gleaned from mere suggestion. Those four jewelled metal cases had become my world, carving out a life I could never see from my windows, even if its foundations remained nothing but guesswork and abstract notions, the dreams of the congenitally blind.*

I've long since stopped looking at those books, although once a year I might return to the odd paragraph to judge it poorly written, and now spend my time observing and examining the world through my window with growing understanding.

I know now that I exist on the interior surface of a hollowed sphere some distance in diameter, at the edge of a large continent that branches at least half of the world like a ragged bridge across two oceans. At the rate I am able to cross my chamber, I estimate that it would take me at least ninety full days to reach the furthest point of my observations, a mountainous land mass hanging down from the top of the world. If I were ever free, of course; then my speed—among other things—might be fully tested and explored. This hollowed sphere used to perplex me as I grappled with the laws of things: how such a body might form over time, or generate weather and lands. I couldn't see how particles of substance, namely Roundlets and Jiglets—for those were the self-taught names I used before I learned anything of the Amaranthine science—might allow such a space to exist. Forces, too, the most apparent being Fallpull, would never countenance the world I saw from my window, for up above there shone a globe of nuclear light—indeed supported unnaturally by stone columns—that could only have been forged on its own by great densities. Many days went by as I studied the world, rising to my window to watch the great monsters passing distantly out to sea. Once, one of them came close, disgorging a distantly remembered bipedal thing that stepped onto the rocks and looked about. I watched in rapt fascination; the creature—I took that term from one of my books—was wrapped in elaborate materials, swaddled as if the sea might hurt it. It stood and looked up at my prison, much larger than the versions of its kind that I remembered now from my birth, the face huge and distorted, its skin a swirling mass of colours.

Melius. I only learned that name later. A silly word for a silly-looking thing.

Over time, I saw them all, the living creatures that populated my hollow world. Silvers swam in the waters that broke on the rocks; Alofts sometimes landed by my window, their long heads twitching this way and that, keen eyes glancing out to the grey sea. I came to see, when I looked hard enough, how they went about their lives out there inside the great sphere. When first I glimpsed them feeding on each other, I knew at last that my estimations of the energy-transfer of my Hollow World ecosystem were correct, but I was not pleased. All living things, it appeared, required energy to endure.

But I did not.

So I was not like them.

Only the glass in my window reflected enough light to suit my purpose, but it did it well, and at certain times of the day I could catch clearly the impression of the far wall and floor behind myself, but nothing more. I bore no reflection. To anyone looking, I might as well not have been there.

When I began to no longer recognise the individual Alofts that settled by my window, I understood that a new generation had arrived. I was outliving them, yet I did not appear to be alive.

For a time, this troubled me enormously. I watched for any sign that my hypothesis might be wrong, staring down into the waters and the glistening rock pools that exposed themselves at low tide, searching for any life that did not die. But time took everything. The levels of the water dropped, rose again, dropped. After a time, the rain that slashed my window streaked white for a hundredth-life of an Aloft, before returning to grey.

When my makers came at last, I had named and catalogued every settled dust mote in my chamber, assigning them ranks and arranging them like legions of chess pieces in a grand battle across the floor. As the huge doors screamed open, my armies eddied into a storm, five years of carefully plotted manoeuvres obliterated in the furious gale of the hurled waves below.

STARRY MOST

The Nereta was a tumultuous river of startlingly blue water, glacial cobalt where it met the bleached stones of its banks. Arching over the ribbon of blue, a great, ten-man-thick bridge stood crowned with gatehouses and teetering, spindly dwellings. The Most, the ancient bridge was called, from which the citadel of Mostar had taken its name. Above the low steeples of the city, scavenger gulls hovered, riding the thermals with outstretched black and white wings, dipping now and then to settle on the walls. Messenger birds, the staple fixture of the sky above any large provincial city, were nowhere to be seen; special cotes where they could rest unmolested from thieves had been built into the inner curtain walls some centuries ago.

"This is an ancient bridge. It was once called the 'Starry Most,' perhaps because the water that runs beneath is so clean and clear that it reflects the heavens every night," Jatropha said to the girls as they stood at the prow of the Wheelhouse. On a beach of white shingle beneath the growth-stone bridge, the city's Awgers—Melius that had interbred with talking beasts and been shunned to live beyond Mostar's walls—hobbled listlessly around their encampment of cloth dwellings, the stones strewn with bones and litter.

"But what most people don't know is that this isn't the true meaning of the ancient words," Jatropha continued, apparently oblivious to their uninterest. "*Starry* actually meant old, *Most*—bridge." He looked at Eranthis and Pentas with some satisfaction. "*Old Bridge*. As prosaic as that."

"You are a *windbag*, sir," Pentas called as she made her way back into the scullery. "Your mouth is like an anus, expelling objectionable things at all hours of the day."

Jatropha turned from the tiller. "And what is objectionable about a little knowledge, young lady?"

"*Unasked-for* knowledge, Jatropha. And I have enough bad smells coming my way from Arabis, thank you very much."

"Whatever's wrong with that girl?" he asked Eranthis at his side.

"Everything is wrong with her," she said, shaking her head in wonder. "Haven't you realised that yet?"

Jatropha compressed his lips and said no more as they came rattling to the toll gate. He steadied the tiller and lowered the wooden chocks to keep the great single wheel from rolling backwards, then leaned to speak to the Tollman, who nodded for them all to climb down. Eranthis took Arabis, passing her carefully to Jatropha and alighting on the stone parapet beside a gaggle of fishing Melius. She waited for her sister, still lurking sullenly somewhere above while she locked away any precious things that the Tollman might take a fancy to, and watched the fishermen. Their lures blew sideways in the breeze, skipping along the ruffled blue water towards the shade of the bridge's arched foundations.

That morning, as she'd awoken to the calls of wandering pedlars to look out of her window at the hills rolling by, something had stuck in her mind. The season of Wintering was a long one, lasting generally from Nevor until at least the thirty-fifth of The Lave. Days were seldom counted unless the month held birthdays or specific events; it just so happened that today, almost on the cusp of Midwintering, was one of those days.

Today, the twelfth of Ember, was Lycaste's birthday.

Her gaze followed the curve of the bright river as it ran north, the cries of the gulls becoming harsh and ugly as they fought over some scrap liberated from the Awgers' tents, her thoughts far away.

He was dead. She saw it clearly now. Nobody like him could have survived this long.

"Eranthis," Jatropha said from behind her, "how much have you?"

She stirred, turning and staring at him, unable to think for a moment what the Amaranthine could mean. His body had already elongated into one of its Melius guises, his Amaranthine face magnified and stretched until it resembled that of a handsome Thirdling gentleman. She'd seen the effect before, understanding it was only a trick of the eye, but found still that she'd lost her train of thought. Eranthis blinked. "What's wrong with *your* money?"

He extended his new Melius hand impatiently. "I only need small ribbon for the gate."

"Fine," she breathed, searching her purse and pulling out a bundle of the smallest denominations. "That enough?"

"Thank you, yes." The Amaranthine placed the entire knot of colour into the Tollman's large palm, snapping his fingers at Eranthis once more. "And one for over the side, please—it's the Mostar custom for luck upon entering the city."

"*What?*"

"Throw something over. It needn't be anything much."

Eranthis shook her head, registering the Tollman's impassive look, understanding that he must have seen a thousand such reactions. She muttered, slightly embarrassed, and tossed a tiny strip of silk over, watching it float in the wind.

"Will that do?"

"Very nicely, thank you."

She sighed, seeing the ribbon twist as it was carried along in the wind, and wondered where—if anywhere—it would land, imagining Lycaste's own fate tied to such an act of chance. It floated, missing the spikes of some low, stripped dropling trees on the bank and curling back over the river, rising unexpectedly in an eddy of wind and looking as if it might actually clear the walls. Eranthis gazed, entranced, unwilling to lose sight of the silk for fear of what it might portend. Further downstream it dropped, her spirits dropping with it, and caught on the surface of the water, growing dark as it began to sink. An opportunist Awger with a long pole reached out from its position on the little beach, snaring the silk and dragging it back onto dry land. She observed the reptilian thing stuffing its prize into a pocket, trying to decide what that meant for poor, lost Lycaste.

Bidens, the mayor's son, met them at the carpenter's while they waited for repairs to be made to the *Corbita*, which had taken a beating on the stone-cobbled road from Elbazanion and the hundreds of miles of worn, hilly paths. Eranthis spotted him hurrying through the shaded vaults of the growth-stone courtyard beneath dozens of hanging lamps that glowed with his passing: a lanky adolescent flushing nervous silver at the sight of them.

"There are serpents that weep with remorse when they devour people. And men who hop about on one gigantic foot." Bidens nodded earnestly. "Then, when the sun gets too hot, they lie on their backs and shade themselves."

Eranthis had trouble picturing what the young man was saying. "They use their foot like a parasol?"

"Precisely!" Bidens grinned at Pentas, who looked lost in thought as she combed Arabis's dark blonde hair. In order to be seen in public, the child had been painted with the colours of a rustic red Tenthling. The watery sugar solution tended to attract flies and had caused all manner of tantrums during its application, but Jatropha had deemed it necessary after hearing of their encounter with the chronicler at Acropolo. "And there are others—"

"Why not just wear a colour, if the sun's too strong?" Eranthis interrupted. She was growing irritated with his stories. Little ball-shaped people without bodies or necks, men and women with tails between their legs; it all sounded rather far-fetched. Of course, she and her sister had learned nothing of the West in Provincial school, just as they knew little of the East, or the South beyond the Nostrum. But she supposed these gangly, long-featured people (technically Ninthlings, owing to the spiral nature of the Provinces) were supposed to be descended from the Westerly peoples of the great Province of Tail, just across the sea, and ought to know what they were talking about.

"A colour?" Bidens asked, shrinking a little at her tone. "No, some colours are rude. Especially black—in the West, one cannot wear black."

"Why not?" Pentas glanced up at last.

He smiled at her, then looked tenderly at the baby. "If you met me in your garden one night and I had coloured black, would you trust me? Black is the colour of secrecy. It's only advisable among the closest of friends, so have a care not to wear it during your stay."

Eranthis frowned. "But black is modesty."

"The Pannish, even those from Tail and Azorme, would not see it that way. Also, direct eye contact is not generally permissible until two people have known each other for at least an evening, so be careful."

Eranthis sighed, stretching and looking for Jatropha. The Amaranthine was across the workshop, engaged along with the help of various sturdily built carpenters in turning the great wheel, looking for faults in the repairs. A few of its split wooden planks had at last been replaced, and their replacements lay pale against the beams of older, darker wood. A fresh coat of paint had even been applied to the balcony, windows and roof tiles, and now their home for the next few months looked almost new. Eranthis worried as she gazed at it that the brightness of the paint might attract thieves or worse, feeling a creeping unease.

"But we can speak First there?" Pentas was asking, her words becoming strained with effort as Arabis began to struggle. Eranthis would have to take her soon.

"Yes. I'll teach you what you need to know of local dialects."

"How long have *you* spent in Pan?" Eranthis asked, hearing the harshness in her voice. "You can't be more than, what, twenty?"

Bidens coloured at her tone. "Twenty-one. My father sent me away to school in Pan—to the High School House at Old Zurine, but the expense was too much and I've been back two years now."

"And what are you going to do?" Eranthis asked, unable to lighten her voice. "Run tours all your life?" She saw him visibly deflate, hating the way she sounded. Even Pentas was looking at her askance.

"No, I suppose not," Bidens admitted. "What with the war and all, we'll probably have to sell up to some Jalan prince with his eye on the city."

"And the Jalan won't be a problem further west?" Eranthis asked, trying her hardest to smile despite the nature of the question.

"No, we won't have any trouble. As long as we stick to the Arteries, there shouldn't be any problems from here on out."

"Aren't there any pretty girls in the city to catch your fancy?" Pentas asked brightly, giving up on trying to calm Arabis and passing Eranthis the baby without a word. "You might wish to go your own way at some point."

Bidens appeared to withdraw once again. "I don't know much about those."

Pentas and Eranthis glanced at each other, the memories of Lycaste so strong that for a moment he was almost back from the dead, sitting diffidently before them.

The plan, Jatropha had decreed, was to journey north along the coast, past Tristel and on to the border between East and West: the grand city of Old Veronesse, gateway to the vast Westerly Province of Pan. From there they could take the good roads into the edges of the Outer Second, where an emissary of the Berenzargols would be waiting. With that last letter sent by fast bird, Jatropha and his shabby crew had lost any surprise they'd once had. Callistemon's family knew now who to expect from the West, and what they carried. If they had any desire to benefit from the great gift Pentas brought them, however, they would endeavour to keep this knowledge secret.

Eranthis walked the walls, listening to the cackle of the Shame-clothed beasts ambling past her on the parapet, Cursed People selling their wares in semi-poverty. Draped around her neck, her purse felt heavy, especially in their company. Jatropha had given them both about a year's worth of pocket money, enough so that they need not ask him for handouts at every turn, and had agreed a scale for them to borrow more. A trifle mean, she thought, considering his apparent material wealth, and also somehow disconcerting.

It seemed a pity to leave so soon. She'd considered staying longer, simply refusing to go, but was conscious that her sister wouldn't leave without her. They had no choice but to serve the Amaranthine's opaque will a little longer, until the baby was taken, as she most assuredly would be, by those who needed her more. Maybe then Jatropha would leave them, too, ceasing his supply of silk and favours, perhaps arranging them nothing more than a ticket home. Eranthis simply had no idea. A niggling thought surfaced finally as she watched the Cursed People picking through a line of empty jars in the shade of the wall.

Suppose Pentas denies him her child.

She saw it unfold. He would take Arabis for himself, paralysing them with his powers, or snatch her away in the night.

Eranthis stopped, contemplating the brushed hint of the Greenmoon in the deep blue afternoon. The Amaranthine wouldn't hurt her. It wasn't in his nature.

But who can know, for sure?

For the first time, she began to question what in the world she was doing, following such a man to the far corners of the Provinces, indebting herself to him. Was this so different from her past mistakes? She'd run off with a tutor once, thinking it was the start of a great adventure, but he'd been like all the rest in the end.

He has us by the purse strings, she thought. *And spies all across the land.* There was nowhere to run even if she wanted to, even if she and Pentas could somehow slip away into the night unseen. They'd be hunted to the very edge of the world.

PETRICHOR

The sheets are damp when he crunches them in his hand, throwing them back despite the chill in the air. Sotiris rolls, eyes tight shut, not yet ready to wake, his face pressed into silk that feels rough with embroidery. He scowls into the sheets, misty-headed as if waking from a hangover, charged with revelations and regrets. He doesn't know this bed.

Slowly, softly, sounds sink to him. Croaking echoes of a large open place sheltered in stillness from the wind. A bead of rain touches his nose. Sotiris's frown deepens.

But there is no headache, none of that buzzing numbness that greets the waking drunk. Sliding his tongue around his mouth, he finds it clean-tasting, the teeth smooth as silk. That fresh, tainted scent of rain—he knows the word, searches for it—petrichor. That scent is everywhere. His eyes open. He sits up.

A pearl-white sky, stained by a watermark of grey, frames a hillside that leads down to a copse of thick, low trees the colour of dark moss.

Where grass should have been there is only a carpet of five-petalled purple and cream flowers that blankets the hill all the way into the woods, shadowed in the wide spaces between the trees. He looks up at the glowering white, sensing that it is late afternoon, at the very earliest, and down at the ornate Melius-built bed he has spent the night in.

But there was no night, not really. A night of millennia, perhaps. A dream that was his life. But he feels now as if he hasn't been asleep long. He is here at his own request.

The trees at the base of the hill sway in the wind, their lowest branches brushing the flowers in the manner of muscular, stately oaks. Sotiris sits up, listening to the hollow flautist calls of the trees' inhabitants as they witter and sink on the increasing wind. Along the crest of the hill and down into its hollow stand a handful of pale, cubic stone follies, each about the size of a single room. They are arranged like monumental stepping stones leading towards the wood. An idea strikes him and he touches his nose, collecting a trace of the raindrop he'd felt upon waking and bringing it to his lips. The snow, from another dream in some other *when*. They are one and the same. And so, he hopes, he knows where he is.

Sotiris climbs from the bed, legs dangling before he drops. He is wearing a black Amaranthine nightshirt that falls almost to his slippered feet. The flowers scrape his calves as he walks, and at his passing, shiny purple insects trailing tasselled limbs zip into the darkening air, one or two larger than his hand.

Reaching the first of the follies, he finds that it is made from blocks of chalk, cut and mortared precisely in the manner of Georgian sandstone. A symbol graces each of the large blocks, the grooves catching under his fingers as he runs a hand across the stone. A point, like a badly engraved, inverted V. Every block bears the same impression: a steepled, awkward hieroglyph punched firmly into its crust. Sotiris pauses at the building's side and gazes off into the woods, knowing almost for certain where he shall find her—with or without her spectral chaperone. He sniffs the scented, rain-cool air, sure that Aaron can't be very far away.

He circles the structure to find the entrance, arriving at a doorway in its face. The smell—putrefaction like blue cheese—greets him before his eyes can adjust to the gloom, and he turns away quickly with the sleeve of his nightshirt pressed to his nose before looking back.

Fifty or more metal cages stacked to the ceiling in rickety towers line the walls, while more hang down from chains set into the stone. From each, a gargoyle head peers listlessly, parallel walls of dangling lips and tongues, jutting teeth, vacant, lidded eyes. Cadaverous arms and fingers drape between the bars and willow-slender tails twitch a beat of madness, their tips gnawed to the bone. In form, they aren't too dissimilar from the creature that put him to sleep, but not quite the same: one or two related species, Sotiris thinks as he looks among the darkened shapes, wondering why they pay him no heed. The stench that breathes through the cage bars doesn't grow any more manageable, so he steps back a little into the flowers, taking in the floor of the folly where the light touches it. Lying in the path that threads between the cages is a long hooked stick, half of it mostly buried in heaps of damp-dark plumage and splattered excrement, and a misshapen, rust-brittle bucket punched with holes.

Sotiris waves a hand to dispel the stench and turns away, knowing without wishing to investigate that the other cubes will be much the same, and that Iro will not be among them. He's glad of such certainty—to thoroughly inspect every hellish cube would take subjective hours. Instinctively he understands that this place, this projected time, is not a dream like any other. It is the memory of a world long forgotten, a place only ever guessed at by men with clumsy brushstrokes. It is Aaron's world, the place he came from, the time in which he was born.

A large crescent moon—silver, like the moon from his youth—brushes through the cloud as he reaches the border of the woods, but the effect is not as comforting as it might be. No stars shine, and yet Sotiris is glad. He understands that they will be different here, off somehow, still drifting in cold galactic currents to the positions he knows so well.

He creeps into the deeper shadow of the trees, through a light mist that has begun to fill the hollows at the base of the hill. That Iro should even be here at all strikes him suddenly as absurd; she has no connection to this place. A brief anger kindles inside him, masking the fear of the darkness under the trees, but it quickly subsides. Aaron has given him an opportunity unlike any other and, so far as he knows, he may wake at any time. He stops, reflecting on the clarity and crispness of his thoughts in this place. Even whilst journeying to the Sarine Palace to accept his crown—though blurred and dreamlike in itself now, as if it happened many decades before—Sotiris had felt his mind slipping out from under him, a perilous contingent like ice beneath his feet. Here among the trees of a remembered world he feels himself again, fully in command of his instincts and intellect. This place, wherever it is being generated, appears to be the final bastion of his sanity.

His mind clears further, the branches of the trees cutting through the haze.

He'd neglected Iro while she was alive. Even before her mind had been thoroughly examined, he'd packed his sister away to the Utopia, leaving her to her madness. It was what they all did, and only the knowledge that the same would be done to him—that he would see her soon on equal terms, dribbling and bewildered—could keep the guilt at bay.

He remembers her as she was—snatches of voice and temperament, sunlight on her hair. When he'd begun his rise to prominence, she was always the last to comment, seeing through his glad-handing ways with the narrowed eyes of one who'd known him his entire life. *They love you for your way with people*, she'd said once. *But I remember when we were children, and you had none of that. You were an introvert. You had to train yourself to be like this, you had to act the part, so that you might be loved by people who didn't know you.*

Sotiris remembers he spoke to her less after that, as if she'd called into question the very nature of his character. But she'd been right, he supposed. Natural shyness had forced a fabricated bonhomie into him, a charm that took over all too naturally as the years wore on. That shyness—he pauses, for the night is fragrant with foreign smells—it was what he'd seen in the Melius, Lycaste. He'd seen his old self.

Reincarnation was a word Sotiris had never liked to speak aloud, but he'd believed in it all the same. Perhaps life had grown tired of his indecision, or forgotten him entirely? Perhaps he and that poor, handsome Melius man were one and the same.

He resumes his careful walk among the silver-dappled shadows of the trees, feeling them thicken around him. The woodwind speech of something like a bird warbles in the dark leaves above his head, warning, perhaps, or just greeting. Small shapes play in the shade ahead, skipping and dancing a ritual that no man has ever seen.

Sotiris, a grinning, beakish face says from up in the branches.

He starts, backing against a tree.

You're almost there. The lambent eyes of the thing flick their gaze towards the depths of the trees, in the general direction Sotiris was headed.

He nods at the roosting creature, turning and heading off into the darkness. It's too late to go back now.

Corphuso watched a fly dip in the movement of air that the Immortal had created and knew then that it had already begun. The man's soul was growing sharper here; outside, in the world beyond, his life dimmed. Corphuso himself had only been here a dozen days or so, but in those days, hunted and starving, the architect had come to terms with where he was, *what* he was.

The silver moon, implausible to eyes made in the one hundred and forty-seventh century, sank low over the woods and disappeared. Corphuso climbed as high as he could into the nest-dense branches and curled himself into a ball, knowing that Sotiris must sleep, too, for just a little while. Corphuso wore the clothes he had arrived in: a grey travel cape slung over a ripped waistcoat. His boots had developed a hole, and things crawled in to sting and bite him in the night. The colour of the cape looked even more muted than he remembered when he first put it on—colours did that here, appearing to fade and bloom like light passing through cloud—only serving to remind him of the brilliance he'd seen, the radiance of the moment that had brought him here.

At first, Corphuso assumed he was the only one ever to have done it, to have touched such a being. He'd seen no trace of other Prism in the Long-Life's Banish World, as he'd come to think of it, no trace of anything not from another era, until the day he saw that human shape on the hillside.

He'd recognised it at once to be Amaranthine, knowing that stooped, distracted walk anywhere. But this one, he thought as he followed cautiously behind, this one looked younger, fresher, still untouched by the world, as if he weren't fully here.

Corphuso could come to only one conclusion. This Amaranthine still lived, on some other plane of existence. His soul, stretched thin between two places, *Bilocated* in the most real of senses, one might say, was unaffected by the dead here.

For that was what they were: dead. And so, Corphuso knew, was he.

As soon as he'd come here—stumbling through the Long-Life's robes, a scream still frozen in his throat—he'd sensed the vibrancy of this place, this land of dreams. Those who lived in this realm truly lived, but were also utterly gone from any other. At once, the beasts in the follies had sniffed him out, howling and tearing at their cell bars. Flitting creatures among the flowers had settled upon his ears, biting, lapping, suckling.

Here, too, he needed to eat, to defecate, to sleep.

Death, death was a mirror.

It was the natural progression, he'd reasoned with himself at his lowest; the next step in his lifelong study of the soul. The world he'd left grew faint in his mind, as he'd suspected it might; his seven daughters and single son, his bored, philandering wife. But one thing remained sharply drawn, burned deep after so many years of work: his machine, his Shell, and the knowledge that it had caused *all* of this.

He watched the Amaranthine, wondering why he alone saw the man as he trudged through the forest. All the while, unbeknown to the Immortal, another figure followed. Corphuso held his breath as it passed below, following the Amaranthine's trail.

At first, it appeared behind the man as a shaggy grey wolf, matted and balding with mange. It slinked after him, dim-eyed and apparently uninterested, as if doing nothing more than providing an escort. Now, as it closed the distance between them, it had changed its form to that of a stooped, wraith-like figure: a penultimate stage, Corphuso assumed, before it showed itself to the Amaranthine in the finished form of a man.

Corphuso gripped the branches and looked down, surprised at his own faint jealousy, and wondered what the Long-Life would say; why he took such an interest in this lost soul.

ON THE TOWN

Eranthis looked out across Mostar while she bathed in deep, warm, perfumed water the colour of blood, a Butler Bird roosting silently on a silver perch suspended over her head. At the turn of the Quarter she went to Pentas's rooms, and together they applied paint to their eyes in the Westerly custom, laughing at their reflections, smearing each other.

Tonight, it was agreed, would be some little respite from the journey, Jatropha having taken it upon himself to watch Arabis, and the sisters had decided to make their way into the city to see the sights.

Lanterns were glowing as they picked their way down the hill stairs from the mayoral palace, passing appreciative smiles and gazes, a line of pale blue tracing the distant walls as if reflecting the river beyond.

The two girls walked slowly, nodding and flashing silver to the strolling locals, pleased with their final attempt at the eye-paint. The last of the stalls in the market squares were closing up to be supplanted by evening entertainments, and they passed quickly through them, commenting, touching, still too unused to the blend of various Western dialects to consider talking to anyone for any length of time.

"All right," Pentas said at last, after a while spent silently looking among some fine stones. "Shall we?"

Eranthis nodded, soothed by the fine evening air and the pleasant manners of the people they passed. Together they wandered to a covered set of tables in the palm-lined square, its benches crowded with clusters of messenger birds come down from the cotes, and took some chairs that offered a view between the white growth-stone walls and down over the lower city.

"I suggested we stay a little longer," she said to Pentas, having lifted her finger for service. "But of course he said no."

"*Of course*," Pentas echoed, studying her reflection in the empty glass bottles left by the table's previous diners. Eranthis gazed out over the walls to the distant eastern gate, where a part of the river she hadn't seen previously streamed darkly under reflected lights on the far shore. Upon a small wooded island in the middle of the river a bonfire burned, perhaps lit by more of the Awgers that populated the land at the river's edge. They were a font of information, Jatropha said, already having found the time to talk with some of the permanent population while the *Corbita* underwent repairs. Eranthis wondered what he spoke to them about.

She snapped out of her thoughts as drinks and nibbles—small bottles of greenish wine, red berries and a pot of glazed, sugared things— were set down before them. Eranthis touched a bottle to her lips and took a small sip, raising it to the darkening sky.

"To Master Knowitall, lord of the non sequitur, and all our fine pocket money."

Pentas took a gulp and raised her bottle. "May he bore senseless many generations to come."

"Clink," Eranthis said, tapping the neck of the bottle against her sister's, as the Amaranthine told her they had done in antiquity. In the square performers were beginning their acts, unimaginative circus tricks lit by the kindling lanterns and the Greenmoon above. Jugglers started their routines, tossing knives and snakes; birds rose into the air to drop flaming balls; and a puppet show was in the process of setting up, strings being untangled. A Secondling boy, limping not from deformity but a recent blow to his leg, came around with a basket for little silks. As the boy was shooed away by the owner of the place, Eranthis noticed how less than welcome the Secondlings were here, and mulled over what might have happened to all the conspicuously missing white-gold occupants once the city was released from the First's thrall.

Pentas looked on, her eyes lost. "I suppose when she's queen we can just *clap* for these entertainments, any time, day or night."

Eranthis gestured to her bottle. "Maintained by a never-ending supply of wine."

They clinked their bottles again, something dulling their smiles. "The two drunken dowager queens."

"We will embarrass her," Pentas said.

"Isn't that the point of mothers?"

Pentas shrugged, her face lit momentarily by the flames of a nearby magic act. "Ah, but she'll like you. You'll spoil her. It'll be me she casts as the *mean one*."

Eranthis didn't protest, realising it was true. "She'll know how you cared for her, when times were hardest."

They drank in silence, their eyes drawn to the acts across the square. A juggler dropped his flaming ball and it rolled off into the drains, prompting a soft *ooh* from the gathering crowd.

"Yes," said Pentas, turning back and draining her wine. Her eyes were vacant, almost like Jatropha's. "I think I might be the more capable of us, when things get difficult."

Eranthis held up a hand for more bottles, unable these days to decide when her sister was joking. "Oh?"

Pentas glanced at her, deadly serious. "I think, if the girl had been born to you, as . . . as he might have planned, you'd have given her away. Or . . ." her eyes dropped " . . . used something."

"*Used something?*"

"You know what I mean. Those wire things the fleshdoctors have but won't sell."

"I *know* what you mean," Eranthis said, faintly outraged. "And you wouldn't have done the same? If Jatropha hadn't been there to make sure you kept her?" Eranthis shook her head. "This is your wine speaking, Pentas."

Pentas lowered her eyes, and Eranthis had the sudden impression that her sister was on the verge of tears. "I've done my duty."

She reached out and took her hands quickly, always forgetting her sister's methods of defence were just that: defence. "You have. You have done your duty. The old man is proud of you, I'm sure, and I know I am."

Later, they walked through the night city, stopping at any place they liked the look of for more wine. Inns did not exist in Mostar, it appeared; every place that served them was a private house, opened up for the Quarter, where they judged you at the doorway for good character before welcoming you in. Along the way, they attracted a small crowd of Mostar men; carefully polite and interested fellows unwilling to let the girls spend their own money. Some of these men were denied entry with the other guests so that slowly the girls formed around them a group of reputable folk, all well known in the city. Eranthis told Pentas to order only sealed bottles, fully expecting her sister to ignore her as the girl grew more animated in company.

Before long, they were at the walls above the city gates, closed now until morning, beneath a blinding sky of stars. Plinking music and the murmurings of loose groups of people rose with the sounds of the night to where they sat.

"And that one," Eranthis said, swigging from a bottle and pointing for her new friend, "is the richest of the Firmamental stars, Cancri."

"Why the richest?" Rumex asked, his hand drifting through her hair.

"Because it's the most beautiful, and all the richest Immortals chose to live there." That was what Jatropha had told her, at least.

"And that one?" He pointed to what appeared to be the next brightest.

"I don't know about that one, but . . ." She searched the brilliant stars, recalling her nights in the *Corbita*'s tiller cabin with Jatropha. "There. You see, three down? Look along my arm. That's Gliese, the capital."

"Gliese."

"It was once the Amaranthine world of industry, becoming very rich and influential and allowing the fleets use of its great Foundries only for a huge fee." She took another swig, passing the bottle across to Pentas. Her sister shook her head—she was sharing a bag of wine fruit with her own Westerly fellow, a very young man whose name Eranthis had forgotten. She got the impression Pentas didn't like him much. He asked her irritating questions, too forward now he'd drunk his fill.

Eranthis shifted, needing to pee, wondering when their personalities had moved so drastically apart. Their sisterhood wasn't like a friendship, though she wished it could be. Maybe it was her own fault. She could feel herself changing as she aged, becoming more disinclined to humour people, caring less for the way fools perceived her. Of all the casualties of this newfound arrogance, she supposed her sister would be the first, and that their bond would weaken until they found no reason to stay together at all.

Pentas jumped up suddenly, nimble and surprisingly sober. "Bedtime, I think, Eranthis."

"But we only just got here," Pentas's companion said from the darkness.

"Big day tomorrow. You may see us tomorrow evening, if you like."

Eranthis smiled and handed the bottle to Rumex. They'd be long gone by then, and Pentas knew it. "It was a pleasure," she said to Rumex, allowing him a lingering kiss at last, as if in payment for the night. "Until tomorrow."

"The pleasure was all ours," he said after them. She looked back into the dark, at his tall, wiry shape breaking up the stars, and was sad she wouldn't be staying, after all.

CURSED

"You know," Bidens said, measuring out a plank with his feet, "I thought at first that you were his young wife. Maybe that you both were."

"Is that so?" Eranthis asked, spying a length of wood that might fit—once they'd sawed its edges down—among the jumble of timbers piled in the *Corbita's* spare room.

"But men can't take two wives in Tail."

She didn't understand his meaning at first, then remembered Jatropha's guise as a well-to-do Westerly fellow. "No. They can't."

"So," he continued, a little sheepishly. "The child isn't his daughter, either?"

Eranthis took a breath as she heaved the plank, understanding she wouldn't be getting much help from him. "No. She's being taken back to her family."

She let him absorb her words. "I see," Bidens said, nodding slowly. "Say no more."

They'd all felt the spoke crack as the *Corbita* ran over something hard on the stones, bending the wheel so that the whole house rolled into a large Bulberry field at the Artery's side. Pentas had got out immediately to stretch her legs, and Eranthis watched her take Arabis, accompanied by the Amaranthine—still in his handsome Melius guise—to see the nests of some chattering Monkmen in the trees.

"Will her family be happy to see her, do you think?" Bidens asked.

Eranthis hefted her side of the plank onto the railings and balanced it, feeling the paintwork scrape away. This was thick, hard oil-oak; woe betide anyone it landed on. "Some," she said, thoughtful. "Her grandparents, perhaps. As for her aunts and uncles, I think not." She looked up into the trees while Bidens levered his end, spying the Monkmen's little twig nests crowded with stolen bits and pieces.

Bidens slid the plank towards her so they could lower it safely into the field. Their narrow shadows, connected by the long, dark bar of the plank, stretched all the way onto the Artery. Eranthis could just make out the trench in the pebbles where they'd run aground. She glanced back at Bidens, noticing how he gritted his teeth, the muscles in his arms trembling to lift it above his head.

"So," Bidens said through a grimace, "Pentas doesn't have a sweetheart or anything back at home?"

"Put it down for a moment—"

Bidens's fingers slipped as he lost his grip. Eranthis dug her nails into her end of the plank, grimacing as a splinter peeled away and drove into her palm. The plank slid over the edge, toppling past the rails and down into the field. It struck the earth by the wheel with a wobbling thump, bouncing and turning over.

"Well, that's just *perfect*!" Eranthis cried, sucking her bleeding palm. She wished she'd hired that travelling fleshdoctor she'd met in Mersin. "If you've cracked this one—"

"I'm sorry! That's the heaviest thing I've ever lifted!"

She went to the balcony and looked down.

Bidens pointed to the Artery. "Look."

Eranthis followed his finger. A member of the Demian Folk, wearing a velvety blue jacket and long brown boots, had stopped to observe them from a distance. He clutched a straw sun hat protectively to his chest.

"Hullo!" Bidens shouted.

The little Cursed Man, this one mammalish, wrinkled his nose and waddled closer, stopping at the edge of the field to take in their predicament. Eranthis felt an urge to go down and try to pet his gingery-gold fur, but suspected he'd just run away.

"Do you know if there's anywhere we could hire some help?" Bidens asked, leaning out across the railings. "An inn or something?"

The Demian looked off down the Artery and pointed. "Over up and down about twenty-five Crule, there's a guesthouse." His accent was butter-thick, old as the Province. "Won't get there if your thing's busted."

"No," Bidens said, exhaling and leaning on the railings. Eranthis shrugged; she couldn't have put it better herself—their thing was certainly busted. "Nothing for it, then. We'd better go and see if the plank's all right."

Bidens sighed, raising his hand to the Demian.

"Yes, yes, much luck to you," the Cursed Man said, replacing his hat and strolling off.

Eranthis climbed down into the field and examined the plank. It appeared to have survived the fall and the subsequent impact with the dusty ground, which boded well for its future as one of the sixteen spokes of an extremely large wheel that would have to deal with this sort of beating day in, day out until their journey was done. The cracked spoke itself would still be good for other, smaller repairs once it had been sawn up.

She remembered seeing a white house—perhaps belonging to the landowner—being poured a few miles back. Not too far to walk, should they need any extra materials; the half-finished building had been surrounded by a skeleton of wooden scaffolding, each level stuffed with metal teasing rods to make sure the stone grew in the desired direction and to the proper thickness all the way around. They'd have a lumber pile somewhere nearby, bought in bulk from the travelling pourer.

She looked Bidens up and down as he jumped from the ladder, deciding he could do the cutting while she had herself an evening tipple on the balcony.

"You dropped it," Jatropha whispered beside her, appearing as if from nowhere.

"How *particularly* observant of you," she said, rounding on him. Bidens lowered his eyes, gingerly pushing the plank straight with his foot.

Pentas came around the *Corbita*'s wheel, carrying Arabis and pursued along the branches by a dozen fascinated black Monkmen. They stopped to look down upon the stricken vehicle and its owners, chewing handfuls of nuts. Eranthis noticed a few sitting on the Wheelhouse's roof, some stolen wine bulbs tucked into their paws.

"If we don't get going soon they'll have all our supplies."

Jatropha looked at them, eyebrows raised, and they immediately scampered off, leaping back into their branches.

Eranthis took one end of the plank again with Bidens and leaned it against the wheel. The rattling thump of what was clearly another Wheelhouse grew in volume along the Artery and they turned to watch it approach. It appeared from behind the trees, slightly smaller than the *Corbita* and painted in peeling shades of blue. Potted shrubs crowded the decks, and in the shadow of the tiller cabin, two occupants sat darkly concealed, sparing them no more than a glance as they passed. The contraption rumbled on, pelting the edges of the field with a spray of pebbles, and was gone. Eranthis wondered how long it would be before the landowner heard about the mess they'd made of the field, hoping they could get the repairs finished before anyone came.

Almost a Quarter later, as night descended and they ate on the balcony, a shabby, emaciated figure arrived riding a push-gig and stopped to examine them as the Demian had. It approached the lantern light, growing in clarity, and Eranthis saw it was an Awger. Its long, morose face smiled as it bowed, its large body hidden beneath a ragged Shamecoat. Eranthis thought it must be half-hound, looking canine in some way, though it wasn't furred like their last visitor. Beside it, one handle clasped in its hand, the push-gig leaned, draped with baskets and nets and dangling cages that appeared to contain sleeping birds under coverings. This thing was some kind of wandering peddler, perhaps. Or a catcher of messenger birds. Eranthis glanced at Jatropha, who seemed to be paying the Awger little attention as he read from one of his books in the weak light.

"Don't feed him anything," the Amaranthine muttered, not looking up. "There's food enough on the road."

Eranthis suddenly understood why these creatures were outcast. One imagined the processes involved in their conception: a bored Melius traveller, a Cursed Person sleeping rough on a town's wooded edge. She looked at the Awger with a new sympathy, taking a plate of food and descending the ladder to meet it.

"Here," she said, offering the plate of Bulberries and drippers, knowing it was nothing special.

The Awger slinked back from her light, gently taking the plate from her. She hadn't asked it to join them, but was nonetheless surprised when it poured the food into a bag hanging from the push-gig's handle and pocketed the plate as well, raising a hand as it climbed back on and wobbled off back onto the Artery.

"That's coming out of your pocket money," Jatropha said, going inside as the squeaks of the push-gig diminished into the darkness.

DAY-DARK PALACE

Lycaste fastened his grip under the Amaranthine's arm, dragging him up and out of the surf. The pitted rocks were sharp as blades where he scrabbled for a hold, slashing his hand across from palm to thumb. He swore and looked for Huerepo, noticing the Vulgar climbing to safety some way along the outcrops.

"Help me with him!" Lycaste bellowed over the boom of the waves, flapping his bloodied hand and dragging Maneker up by the shoulders. The Immortal moaned, his fingers going to his eyes.

"Here," Huerepo panted, arriving to stand over them on the lip of a jagged shard of rock. Rising above the shoreline where the Vulgar had come from, Lycaste could just see the top of a creamy, wind-eroded tower in the early-morning light, the spires of some darker, taller edifice rising behind. The rest of the world rolled above like a hallucinogenic nightmare. The two of them stared down at Maneker lying against the sharp outcrop, his legs still lapped by arriving waves.

The Melius who had attacked them had been clumsy in their work, slashing randomly into the man's head. While the right eye was entirely missing, only a portion of Maneker's left had been removed. The remainder dangled among the scrapes and scratches, a pink ribbon held together by nerves or vessels, sticking limply to the Amaranthine's cheekbone. Lycaste could only imagine the pain the man was in, hammered and scoured by salt waves since their jump from the ship, and yet Maneker hardly made a sound.

Lycaste bent, lifting the Amaranthine and draping him over his shoulder. He glanced at the tower as he stepped up onto some flattened rocks. It appeared to match Maneker's description, its stone pocked and speckled with holes, the mortar scooped away by the sea winds of millennia. When he came to the lip of the rocks, he released the Amaranthine, laying him as gently as he could at Huerepo's feet. Maneker began to mumble, his hands opening and closing into fists, the skin of his knuckles whitening. He opened them and suddenly started beating his palms on the rocks, cutting them and flinging blood.

"Stop!" Lycaste pleaded, standing awkwardly at his side.

"*Why?*" the Amaranthine hissed.

Lycaste was lost for words. He sat down on a lump of rock and looked out to sea.

Maneker broke into a shuddering sigh, raising his bloodied hands to his missing eyes once more.

"The prisoner might be able to help him," the Vulgar said, tipping water from his spring pistol and glancing around impatiently. "Don't you think? We shouldn't wait."

Lycaste glared at Huerepo. "You're welcome to carry him for a while, you know."

The Vulgar crossed his little arms about himself, his tunic dark and dripping. His shiny white face looked especially pale with the gloom of the early evening spanning a continent behind him, on the world's opposite side.

"All right!" Lycaste got to his knees, his heart still thudding from the climb and a night spent struggling through dark, choppy waters, a person clinging to either arm. He reached out to grab the Amaranthine.

"I can walk," Maneker said suddenly, his voice soft. "Just . . . guide me."

Lycaste hesitated, glancing at Huerepo. "Are we in the right place? This is the tower?"

Maneker nodded, feeling the rocks for a place he could lean on to stand. "I know this shore. This is it."

Together they shuffled up the rocks, the Amaranthine holding tightly onto Lycaste's wrist. He couldn't help but find Maneker's clammy, broken-fingered grip unpleasant. Huerepo had chosen to climb inside the damp knapsack, though the added weight hardly slowed their grandfatherly pace.

The dawn sea winds softened as they came inland, cresting some stiff dunes of milky, blown weed and sinking into the gardens surrounding the tower, what Lycaste remembered Maneker calling the Oratory. Other blackened towers clustered nearby, their tiled peaks grey and desolate against the glowering white sky. Maneker had said that these had all been built by the hand of one person, and had taken many centuries to erect. Now they looked to be falling down, with a heaped litter of corroded masonry marring the overgrown paths between them. Lycaste's gaze traversed the gargoyle faces in the walls—hollow-eyed Amaranthine heads worn smooth by rain—and down to the path before them. Worn limestone walls double Lycaste's height led off into the depths of the overgrown gardens.

"Can you see the walls?" Maneker asked through teeth gritted with pain.

"Yes," Lycaste said, gazing up at the black windows of the place.

"Five right turns, commencing after the second left."

They went in, Lycaste understanding immediately that the Amaranthine maze had not been functional for some time. The walls Maneker expected to be there had mostly worn to nothing but foundation blocks, others laid siege to by gloomy stands of overgrown holly laden with orange berries.

"The walls are all eroded," he said, guiding Maneker's hand so the man could feel the head-sized holes that punctured the stone near him.

"It doesn't matter," the Amaranthine said. "Go the way I told you."

With Huerepo counting the branching passageways over Lycaste's head, they made their shuffling way through the second left, turning right immediately where the worn chunks of stone suggested a corner. The holly had almost entirely obscured any direct route to the Oratory with a forest of spiked, deep green leaves.

"What if we just pushed through the trees?" Huerepo asked from the top of the knapsack. "From up here I could guide us."

"You think so little of Amaranthine design," Maneker said tersely, the pain perhaps worsening. "We'd be lost almost immediately. I suppose I'd get out after a few centuries of trial and error, but that wouldn't help you two."

Lycaste, who was enjoying the sensation of not being the cause of Maneker's irritation for once, looked into the dark holly groves with new fear, beginning to worry that they might have miscounted the turns.

"Shouldn't be long now," Maneker said. "Keep counting."

They turned the last corner, a more robustly built section of the maze leading to the grand steps of the Oratory across a misted acre of gravelled garden. Lycaste put out a hand to stop Maneker, feeling Huerepo tense on his shoulders.

At the end of the maze something stirred, its slender head rising from the remains of a long-decayed corpse. Lycaste met its eyes through the stiffened, matted fur of its muzzle, hearing the deep rumble of its snarl.

"Fuine," Maneker said softly at the sound. "They should've starved by now."

The beast's lips peeled back, its jaws slathered from the body's rotten innards, teeth brown as mahogany. It tensed on its haunches and moved a blooded paw to cover its meal.

"Let it eat," Huerepo said as they inched closer. The Fuine observed their approach with unblinking intensity, flattening its ears as a Melius might. Its yellow-white pelt was stretched tight over its bones, balding in places like a worn stuffed toy. It patted the ground with its tail, thumping out a tattoo of unease. They slipped past the Fuine with their backs to the wall, stepping slowly and deliberately. Huerepo shivered inside the knapsack and pulled the cover down.

They passed a few feet from the corpse. The Fuine trembled, a ripple shivering through its wasted muscles, and clawed the body, teeth bared. Lycaste hardly breathed, gently pushing Maneker ahead of him. The Fuine's eyes moved restlessly from Maneker's to Lycaste's. It began to drag the body backwards with shuffling movements until Lycaste saw it come up against the opposite wall. Startled, it glanced away from them.

He quickened his step.

The Fuine swung its head around, snarling, and sprang.

Lycaste turned, shielding his eyes, feeling the weight of it strike and almost knock him to the ground. Claws tore painlessly into the meat of his back, hooking between his shoulder blades. He threw himself against the eroded wall, pinning the creature until one of the claws slipped, then grabbed at the skinny paw and sank his teeth into it. The Fuine yowled, working its other claw loose and grappling his leg. They spun and dropped, spraying gravel. The Fuine mewled and snapped at him, the charnel stench thick from its jaws, snaring his free arm in its teeth. Lycaste pulled his wrist back, peeling the skin away with a spray of blood, and bellowed, clamping his teeth into the Fuine's furred neck. They stayed locked that way in a wrestlers' embrace, muscles straining, until Lycaste dug his slipping foot back into the gravel and summoned all his weight forward. The Fuine howled as Lycaste bit harder and dug deeper. Blood began to jet as he worked his jaws from side to side, tearing and pulling and yanking at the Fuine's flesh until he knew he was coated with the thing's blood. He wrenched and tugged, feeling something give way inside the animal's neck. Its struggling slowed to nothing and it slumped beneath him. He pulled his teeth out, jaw muscles aching, and spat blood.

One look into its eyes told him the Fuine was dead. He tried to stand but couldn't, seeing his own blood caking his thigh where the creature's barbed claws had locked into his muscle.

"Bloody hell," Huerepo muttered from inside the dropped knapsack, poking his head out. He was apparently more interested in the state of Lycaste's back. "Wait, wait. Stop squirming."

Lycaste kept still as the Vulgar climbed out, half-expecting the Fuine to rise up with a second wind and swallow Huerepo whole. The little man glanced fearfully at the creature's glassy eyes as he worked first on the claws embedded in Lycaste's leg, yanking them out one by one and drawing fresh blood.

Lycaste looked down at the Fuine lying in a heap before them, then at Maneker.

The Amaranthine nodded and kept moving. "Not so useless after all," he said, extending his hand behind him. Lycaste exchanged wary glances with Huerepo and offered Maneker his scratched, bloodied wrist.

They dealt with another emaciated Fuine closer to the doors by tossing it food from Lycaste's knapsack. Lycaste looked back a few times to watch it eat, worrying as he limped to the Oratory that it might still be there, waiting, upon their return.

They approached the doors, two carved oaken slabs stained a dark cherry by centuries of fierce weather. A few bones, pitted and pale as marble, decorated the steps. Lycaste guided Maneker's hand to the great tarnished silver handle, running the man's fingers along the relief carvings in the surface of the door.

"They won't be locked," he said, taking his hand away. Lycaste leaned his shoulder against the heavy panel and shoved, heaving the doors open.

Within, the Oratory was still and frigid, their breath pluming before them. In the light of the open door, Lycaste could see the spiral stair that led to the upper chambers. He stepped further in, offloading Huerepo as the Amaranthine let go of his wrist and went about locking the doors. Darkness slipped into the room again, returning comfortably to a space it had occupied for hundreds of years without interruption.

"Just a minute," Maneker said, whispering something to himself.

Lycaste waited, feeling goosebumps rise on his ripped skin. His mind couldn't make sense of the things he'd glimpsed during the few seconds of light. He faced the room in the blackness, nothing but their shallow breathing, Maneker's whispers and the muffled wind outside for stimulus.

A creamy glow kindled into existence above them, emanating from a small, white point.

"What are those?" he asked, of nobody in particular, walking slowly to the centre of the chamber. Before him, pale in the yellowish light, stood maybe a hundred jumbled figures, slim and white as bodies left to soak. Lycaste put out his hand to touch one. Each was a faceless mannequin made from stitched canvas, the stuffing poking out from holes in some of them to expose a hard wooden skeleton within. Most had toppled sideways in one direction, and thrown over them were ancient, musty clothes, the musk of which filled the chamber with a fine dust of dissolving thread. Lycaste took a handful of the ancient cloth, tweezing the fibres between his fingers, alarmed to watch it come apart in his hand. The stone floor under the mannequins' angled feet was littered with precious gems, which had presumably fallen from the clothing as stitching had given way over the centuries. He crouched and picked one up, a flawed garnet carved with a thousand façades, and tossed it to Huerepo, returning to the pile of blank effigies to sift their bodies for intact clothing that would cover his stinging scratches. The blood had stopped flowing, but still great tracts of red, swollen muscle showed through where the skin had peeled away from his arm and leg.

Lycaste selected a gown and tore the sleeves off, handing the unwanted fabric to Huerepo so that the Vulgar could bandage the Amaranthine's ruined eyes. He tied what he could around his own wounds, winding the fold of fabric over his forearm and strapping more to his thigh with tight knots he'd learned during Impatiens' fishing lessons. Satisfied that he could do little with his back, he cast his eye around the jumbled pile of mannequins again, spotting something glimmering in the lantern light. He made his clumsy way through, pushing the figures out of the way and stacking them to one side like cords of wood. In the centre of the heap, a group of twenty or so mannequins had fallen to pieces, weighed down by exquisite metal clothing. He pulled a hauberk of glittering gold rondels from the dusty remains of a smashed figure, framing it against himself to see if it would fit. Draping it over his arm, he resumed the search, finding yet more dazzling pieces of clothing that might be of some use to them on the return trip, understanding how much easier his encounter with the Fuine might have been had he worn some of this Amaranthine armour. Lycaste waded out of the debris again to where Huerepo had almost finished applying the trimmed cloth to Maneker's eyes. The Amaranthine sat still, his head tilted up to the spark as if he could discern its light. Sometimes his lips moved soundlessly. Lycaste smiled, watching Huerepo move across the room to inspect the trove, mouth open in wonder.

After he'd loaded his pack with clothing, Lycaste picked up some delicate blue gloves trimmed with fur, untucking the finely spun fingers. They looked almost large enough to fit his own hands, being twice the size of any Amaranthine's and possessing more than the standard five digits each. He slid his fingers in, waggling his knuckles and looking around for anything that might go with them. As he did so, something sharp and fine pricked his middle finger and he pulled his hand out with a gasp. A spider, dark and quite repulsively hairy, slid writhing from the glove to plop onto the floor. Lycaste stepped back as it scurried to the door, inspecting the tiny beads of blood on his fingertip.

"Watch out," he called to Huerepo, who was still digging around among the mannequins. "There are bitey things in the clothes."

"Bitey things?" the Vulgar asked, pulling off his battered armour and fitting himself with a dazzling silver brigandine that glowed with rounded blue gems. He yanked on the stone-studded belt, buckling it tighter, and gave Lycaste a twirl, the worn damask cape it came with flowing out in a rippling ultramarine fan. "What do you think?" His scrawny legs and booted feet still poked out beneath, undergarments hanging down. "Now to find some greaves." Lycaste watched him dig around some more, occasionally inspecting the floor for spiders. Huerepo came back out of the pile again sporting a magnificent curved rapier and a silver, emerald-beaded helm a few sizes too big. The helmet's pointed nose, set with more of the luminous stones, connected with the jaw of the faceplate in a set of stylised snarling teeth. He swished the sword around, stumbling and almost falling under its weight.

"Am I not *magnificent*?" he screeched, advancing in Lycaste's general direction, clearly unable to see.

Lycaste couldn't help but grin. He stepped back a little from the whirling Vulgar and pushed him gently in another direction. Huerepo fumbled with his helmet and activated some kind of long-dormant system. The eyeholes abruptly lit up; two glowing white circles that shone around as he got his bearings. He marched about, striking various manly poses, then flicked up the faceplate. A strobing display inside the bevor still pulsed, as if to the beat of his heart.

"You know you're going to be too heavy to carry like that," Lycaste said.

Huerepo shrugged, nodding at the pile. "What are you going to wear?"

Lycaste gazed doubtfully at the mannequins and then at his knapsack, lying off near Maneker's prone form. It hadn't occurred to him that perhaps they should have asked the Amaranthine before raiding these ancient treasures. He cocked a thumb at the dark figure, whispering, "Do you think we should have—?"

"Take as much as you can," came the pained voice from the shadows. "That is Iridium you wear, Vulgar. It will deflect any shoddy Prism bolt." The man stirred, sitting up, his hands pressed to the bandages covering his eyes, sighing as if from more than simple agony. "I'll need you both iron-clad if you're to look after me, won't I?"

Lycaste stared at Maneker, then pulled open the knapsack to inspect what he'd taken. He'd tried clothing once before as a boy, during rehearsals for a play. His parents had wanted him cast in the lead, for even then at the age of nine his fine face had begun to show through the plumpness of childhood. Nobody understood the terror he'd felt, laughing, cajoling and finally despairing as he refused to climb the steps to the wooden stage. He'd fled, disappearing into the wilds of the island for a day, slinking home for a missed supper and realising they'd never quite think of him in the same way again.

Lycaste contemplated his fears as he shrugged on a crimson velvet shirt, his body trembling involuntarily at the brush of fabric against his damaged skin. He hoisted up some britches and buckled them, noticing how well they fitted: these must have belonged to one of the

Firmamental Melius. He had less luck with the Amaranthine boots, grumbling and tossing them aside when they wouldn't fit.

"Here," Huerepo puffed, dragging a great bowl-shaped cuirass out from the mess of broken mannequins. "Try this."

Lycaste hefted the cuirass over his head, snapping shut the locks along the side after some prompts from Huerepo. He smiled, rapping his fist against the silver and draping his bandolier across his chest. The pearl-coloured Amaranthine pistol lay snugly against his waist, reassuringly heavy in its holster. He felt supremely protected inside his case of silver and cloth, armoured like a hermit crab in its shell, and the prospect of that second Fuine prowling the grounds outside didn't feel quite so daunting any more.

"Daft Melius," Huerepo said beside him, pointing out that he'd put his britches on the wrong way round. "Looks splendid, though." Huerepo turned to Maneker. "Doesn't he look—?"

The Amaranthine smirked. "I'm sure he does." His mouth fell at the edges, his expression sour as the Vulgar's embarrassment hung in the air. He slumped, putting his hands once more to the bandages and propping his head on a piece of shattered mannequin. "Let me sleep now," he murmured. "Wake me in an hour." At some more of his whispered words, the spark he'd conjured dimmed, suggesting unequivocally that they should consider sleeping, too.

Lycaste and Huerepo glanced at each other and went to sit by the knapsack, the Vulgar removing most of his armour so that he could stretch out across the flagstones.

"What now?" Lycaste murmured, rubbing his arms and revelling at the sensation of being encased in fabric. The sting of his wounds had begun to lessen, though a patch of the shirt across his back had clearly stuck fast to the exposed muscle and was starting to itch maddeningly. He tried to rub it against the wall, succeeding only in scraping his cuirass and waking Maneker.

"*Quiet!*" barked the Amaranthine from the darkness of the chamber's edge.

Lycaste rooted as quietly as he could inside the knapsack, offering Huerepo the remains of what he'd found in the Satrap's larder. The Vulgar ate with the vacant expression of a tired creature lost in thought, his chewing hesitating as some dramatic memory crossed his mind. Lycaste glanced around, rearranging his britches and looking for somewhere to relieve himself.

He crept through the dimness to the other side of the hall, skirting the heap of shattered mannequins. Lycaste's feet were still bare, and he took care not to step on anything and wake the Amaranthine again. While he pissed, he listened to the wind and rain outside, struggling to scratch his ear on the pauldron of his new armour without making too much noise. Something was tickling it, like a person leaning close to whisper, and he buttoned up his britches again to gaze into the dim light.

There *was* a whispering. At first, Lycaste thought it might have been Maneker, still muttering oaths at Huerepo, but gradually he realised the sound was coming from the chambers above.

He went alone up the stone stairs, lifting the cold door latch as quietly as he could, suddenly terrified of attracting the attention of whatever it was they had come to find. The door swung wide in the blackness, opening into a richer, deeper shade of night within.

Lycaste breathed, eyes open to nothingness, questioning how this person could have been imprisoned without locks or keys. He felt some faint, residual warmth in the sizeless chamber, as if something did indeed live here, sliding his hand out before him as he stepped inside and expecting the cold touch of a sightless Immortal with every heartbeat. With a moment of panic he realised he would lose the door if he simply blundered forward and turned to feel for the wall. His hand met the cold stone with an echoing slap.

Must you be so noisy?

Lycaste gasped, backing into the door that had closed softly behind him. The ancient wood rattled on its hinges.

Like a bull in a china shop, the voice muttered, its volume fluctuating as it circled him. Lycaste gazed into the inky black, every hair bristled out, expecting to be touched. His feet encountered something fine as dust, brushing it aside as he stepped further in.

What have we here? the voice demanded, facing him. No breath came to waft across Lycaste's face, though the interrogator was surely only a few inches away. *Stop. Don't tell me. Let's have a look.*

Silence. Lycaste had the faintest impression of warmth where he presumed he was being touched. He remained still, his fists thrust out before him like a fighter in a ring. The sound of its speech had begun as a chalky rasp in his head, thin and ancient. With every word it grew in power, however, developing the way an unpractised voice prepares to sing.

Young, the entity said suddenly, now rich and bold in his mind. *Cells still at the stage of near total renewal. Lucky Melius. Lucky, lucky,* lucky. The speech paused, tingeing its final utterance with vicious disdain.

"I'm fifty-one," Lycaste stammered, not knowing where to direct his comment.

Yes, the voice said impatiently. *Born in the winter. Your bones show the seasonal growth. And . . . no reaction to the neurotoxin. Extraordinary. Even Acolytes fall foul of my Spinners.*

He rubbed his bitten finger, his skin crawling.

You have fascinating *bodies, you Melius. So elegantly prepared for life. The envy my jailors must feel every time they look at you.*

Lycaste waited. "Thank you?" he ventured at last.

The silence continued, even as he felt the presence considering him. Lycaste wondered how it could make any comment on the state of his bones, let alone see through the silver cuirass.

Where are they, then?

"I'm sorry?"

The voice sighed, slinking to his ear. *You'll have to do better than that. What do the pickled old wraiths want with me this time?*

"Maneker? He has an Incantation—something that will set you free."

The voice stayed silent for so long that Lycaste began to fear he'd been imagining the whole thing. Then from the other end of the chamber it spoke. *Liars die quickly in here. They blunder into threads as fine as hair, and things come dangling down.*

Lycaste felt hesitantly for the door, deciding after a moment that the Amaranthine would likely do a much better job of explaining than he had, even without his eyes. Suddenly the voice was almost inside his ear.

But . . . wait. He has need of you. A simple Melius not worth the price of his fodder. Why? What role do you play here?

Lycaste clutched the edge of the door, levering it open in the darkness. "Perhaps I should—"

I put the question to you, the blackness purred. *What's the matter? Aren't you your own man?* Its tone had sharpened to a blade. Warmth caressed Lycaste's temple.

He hesitated, colouring in the darkness, sure that he could be seen as clearly as if in daylight. He was no more a man than this voice in his head, not really.

I see you now; I see the terror in you, the frailty. It spoke almost soothingly. *You are a weak and fearful thing, nothing but a boy—* The voice paused, hot now across his brow like a clinging vapour. *But what is* this? A touch as fine as smoke dripped from his eyelashes, falling to caress his chin. Lycaste had a vision of thin white hands with the texture of steam clasped around his head, probing, measuring. *Great perfection. Classical. A face much valued . . . and quite wasted. Now what would a lustless Amaranthine want with the likes of you?*

"I didn't ask to come here," he whispered into the chamber, standing straighter. Purple shapes blossomed where his eyes strained to see, as blind and useless as Maneker's.

Neither did I. This is a place of misery. It would have been better if you'd never come at all.

Lycaste nodded to the blackness.

However. Here you are. The voice circled behind him, filling the small gap between Lycaste and the door. *Where have you come from? That is not Amaranthine you speak—you are no Adjunct.*

"I'm a free man," Lycaste said, taking a wild guess at the meaning of the voice's last word. "From the Tenth."

Indeed? A Freeman of the Holy Old World, come on his pilgrimage? I see this was no ordinary journey, not for the likes of you. You fought my guards to get in here. Killed one, judging by the state of you.

"That's right," Lycaste replied, his pride resurfacing. "I'm not as delicate as everyone seems to think."

I'm sure, the voice said with some amusement. *Tell me, Tenthling, have you ever loved?*

He thought about it. "Yes."

And your heart was broken.

He stayed silent, the air heavy around him.

Once . . . it seemed to calculate, *by death.*

He clenched his fists in the darkness. "How can you know that?"

You know it, not I. It shows in the fabric of your vessels, the strain of loss.

Lycaste shook his head, closing his hand around the latch. "Maneker will want to talk to you."

Then fetch him up.

"What were you doing in there?"

"It asked me questions."

Maneker beckoned Lycaste closer to where he sat on the stone, his bandage having already slipped to show the edge of one bloody socket. Huerepo hurried to his side and retied it. "What did it ask?" Maneker demanded. "Tell me precisely. It will know more than enough about the state of things from your answers already."

"Why didn't it just ask you?" Lycaste asked, exasperated. "I don't *know* anything."

"It hates the Amaranthine for imprisoning it here. It will presume everything I say to it is a lie. What did it ask you?"

Lycaste sighed, glancing at Huerepo. "Nothing much. Where I was from. If I'd ever been in love."

Maneker nodded blindly, clasping his fingers anxiously together. "Both of you come with me. I'll do the talking."

Lycaste helped the Amaranthine up, taking his hand.

"Leave me *be*, Lycaste!" Maneker snapped, wrenching his hand away and fumbling shakily for the wall. Huerepo climbed up after them, dragging the knapsack, now loaded with gems, behind.

"Perception!" Maneker called into the darkness, rapping his knuckles against the stone of the chamber wall. Lycaste remembered being woken up for lessons in the same way, long ago now.

"I don't think it likes that," Lycaste told the Amaranthine.

Glad somebody remembers.

Maneker turned his head, sensing the voice between them just as Lycaste did.

"We've met before," Maneker said, striding to what might have been the centre of the chamber. Something crossed between him and Lycaste just then, muffling the Amaranthine's speech ever so slightly.

Is he always like this? the voice breathed in Lycaste's direction.

Lycaste couldn't help but smile, saying nothing.

"You know who I am, Spirit," Maneker said crossly, his voice turning back to Lycaste. "And that I am one of the few with the power to set you free."

You should leave, Melius. Make your own way in the world. Clinging to the shirt tails of a man like this will only bring you grief.

Lycaste heard Maneker stalk towards him, presumably with the intention of sending him out. He moved a little to one side in case the Immortal walked straight into him, hearing the squeak as he stepped on Huerepo's foot.

Now here's a special little thing, the Spirit exclaimed, the sound of its voice swinging low. Lycaste braced himself for Huerepo's indignation and was not disappointed.

"What the *bloody hell!*" Huerepo barked, shuffling back towards the door and dropping his jewels. "I felt it!"

Bred beyond all recognition, Perception said. *Tell me, creature, are you in pain?*

"What?" Huerepo asked, his voice trembling.

You should be, the way your liver's crammed in there. Most unnatural. What are you—some new breed of Melius?

"Spirit!" Maneker roared, flailing in the general direction of Lycaste and Huerepo until they stepped back. "Answer me or I shall *leave*, taking your freedom with me."

Oh, you won't do that, Hugo Maneker, Perception sneered, its voice rising above them. *That's the very last thing you'll do. Do they know how powerless you are, now that your eyes have been cut from you?*

"What do *you* know, ghost?" Maneker asked the shadows. "Four thousand years cooped up in here and you think yourself an expert on anything?"

I know from your Melius here that the Firmament has crumbled. Things like that other hold sway now. I know that you are scared, desperate and have already come within a whisker of taking your own life. Oh yes, I see your intentions with little difficulty, Primogenitor. Think on that in your never-ending darkness.

Maneker slammed his hand against the door, wobbling the hinges as Lycaste had earlier. "And I know that you would be free, at all costs," he spluttered. "Don't think of denying it. It was not me who put you here."

Those who did got what they deserved.

"Yes."

And what do you deserve, Hugo? What would your maker think of you?

"Help me atone for my mistakes, Perception. Help me make things right."

The darkness went quiet. Lycaste folded his arms around himself and waited. Something scuttled past his foot while the blackness gave every impression of thought.

What if I cannot leave? the voice said softly.

"Cannot leave?" Maneker asked wearily.

The Spirit's tone sharpened again. *You damn well know.*

The Amaranthine appeared to have turned in the darkness. Now his voice pointed away from Lycaste, almost inaudible. "This is a Vaulted Land, a hollowed planet. It has no gravity, only spin."

Lycaste leaned back in the blackness, trying to understand what they were talking about. He was certain he heard a new tentativeness in the Spirit's voice when it spoke, almost like fear.

Spun. Spun around. It fell silent for a very long time, though as it did so, Lycaste fancied he could feel something different, a charge, a tension that appeared to quiver in the air.

Very well, Amaranthine. Say your word. *Let them see your magic.*

LUMINESCENCE

"We found an Awger without his face or hands not long ago." Bidens gestured with his own hands, miming the skin being peeled away. Eranthis wrinkled her nose.

"There are things now, in the Provinces, all sorts of Starling visitors," Jatropha said, angling the tiller as they came to a slight bend, bumping over a cluster of irregular stones and rumbling on down into the valley. Eranthis's teeth rattled in her head, sympathetic to the protestations of yesterday's repairs. "Once the year turns, you might find yourselves a good deal relieved."

Eranthis remembered the night-time stories he'd told her. The Starlings, in their unending superstition, blamed Hoopies—Investiture spirits from a time before hominid life—but Jatropha said it was possible they'd had a run-in with the Old World's only indigenous Prism (other than the Melius themselves), the Gheal.

"My father questioned the folk outside the walls," Bidens continued, "but they weren't very helpful."

"And why should they be?" Eranthis asked, thinking of the cannibalistic things Jatropha had mentioned that existed in some parts of the Investiture. "You keep the poor people outside, with only scraps to eat and rubbish to build their shelters. Why should they owe you anything?"

"They aren't wanted in the city," Bidens said, looking hurt. "It's not my decision."

"It will be when you're mayor," she countered, frustrated.

"But I don't think I ever will be. You need a fortune to control Mostar, and ours is almost gone."

Jatropha nodded beside them, as if he knew the location of every scrap of silk in every hidden place. "I would happily keep you on, Bidens, once we reach Nidrum and need to pass back into the Greater Second."

Bidens coloured in the shade of the parasol, apparently speechless. Eranthis, sitting beside him, bridled; none of this had been discussed.

"It's up to you," Jatropha added hastily. "We can send word to your father with a decision at our next stop."

Bidens lowered his eyes. "I'd like that very much, but it might not be allowed."

"Well. We shall see."

They rode in silence for some time, branches slapping the *Corbita*'s balconies as it trundled through the valley, before Bidens spoke again.

"You know," Bidens said, picking his fingers, "I *could* persuade my father to let me stay on, that I'm a grown man now."

"I'm sure you could," Jatropha replied.

"Yes. He would listen if I had a woman, maybe."

Eranthis turned to him, eyebrow arched, but the youth remained frowning at his hands. "Just for pretend," he clarified. "Maybe we could write to him and say Pentas had agreed to be . . . What do you think? Would she agree to it? Just for pretend?"

Eranthis shot Jatropha a look, and beneath his glamours he smiled back at her.

"She wouldn't have to *do* anything, of course," Bidens said hurriedly, conscious of their silence. "It would just be for my father, you see. Then, when it's time to go home, I can just say she grew bored of me."

"She won't like it," Eranthis said.

Jatropha frowned. "No harm in asking her."

"What?" she cried. "We need this boy so desperately to guide us?"

"A small deception, Eranthis, so that he can travel with us a little longer."

She looked at the Amaranthine for some time, stealing glances out of the corner of her eye, reflecting on how many other *small deceptions* might have been responsible for their coming on this absurd journey.

"Osulphurous Maladine took her seat at the flaming pulpit of Ago, bowing her bald head in prayer. The journey from Stannum had taxed her delicate nerves, and as soon as the weatherplane had touched down, she went to the cloisters to beg the serpent god for her daughter's safe return."

Pentas's head had started to ache again. She closed the fat ring book and looked out into the night as it travelled by, green and shimmering in the light of the moon. Jatropha had apparently visited every book emporium in Mostar, taking a particular fancy to the romance novels of one Liatris of Albina, a frail and frightfully wealthy authoress he wished to visit in Old Veronesse. Pentas and her sister had been encouraged to read them and chose a favourite so that they might have an engraved signature when they met her. The heavy novel lying in the folds of her blanket was one of the slimmest, but she could barely get five pages in before other thoughts settled and caused her to read the same passage over and over again.

The Ode of Calpus Maladine read the title, in the fashion of most old romances. She could see from the date that the book had been stamped almost fifty years ago.

Pentas read the opening paragraph again, sparing quick glances out into the darkness as the Wheelhouse clanked and clattered along the sea path. It couldn't be far to the bloodfruit plantation of Rat Omis, their intended stop for the night.

In the year One Thousand Nine Hundred and Forty-Three, she read, *the seventeen great houses on the storm-swept Isle of Maladine are in turmoil, their sovereign-in-waiting having disappeared.*

She read on, trying to conjure an image of a time so long passed. 1943, as the year was written in First, twelve thousand seven hundred and four years ago. The great bright stars Cuprum and Stannum—those Jatropha called Venuse and Jupito—had been conquered, and between them the ancient Melius of the past flitted on shining wings. The heroine of the novel, Calpus Maladine, on her way to enrol in the School of Nothing, is caught in the front line of a war between the Alamaneen— the progenitors of the Cursed People—and abducted for ransom. Pentas suspected without even getting beyond the first chapter that Calpus's wicked mother was surely responsible for her kidnap. Nobody benign would ever be named *Osulphurous*. She snorted and pushed the book to one side again. The lives of the book's ancient people were short— Calpus's evil mother was in her final years at thirty-five—and yet they appeared to accomplish much in their brief time. Pentas would be twenty-four before Wintering's end, and what had she achieved? She'd killed all the men who had ever loved her, a bringer of death and misery, something passed from person to person like an unbreakable curse.

A tap at the door, barely louder than the groan of the place as it bounced along the pebbled road, brought her rudely from her thoughts.

"How are you finding it?" Bidens asked as he entered, gesturing to the closed book.

She shrugged, not recalling allowing him to enter. He went and sat by the sleeping child, rocking the wooden cot with one hand.

"I prefer strip serials myself," Bidens said, a note of diffidence in his voice suggesting to Pentas that he'd been laughed at for his interests. "Onosma's my favourite."

Onosma. Pentas recognised it but couldn't think why. "Is that the boy with the pet Monkman?"

He nodded. "I traded some old ones for the new editions. You can read them if you like."

She smiled, unable to think of anything more to say. On the trunk beside her bed was Liatris's take on the fable of Dorielziath, painstakingly translated from the Threheng over many years as if in response to the less-than-favourable critical reception of her romances. They both looked at it. The sheaf of metal pages was heavy enough to thump and kill any intruder who made it into her bedchamber aboard the Wheel-house, so Pentas had chosen to keep it handy, placed between herself and Arabis's cot.

"I knew a boy at school named Scundy," Bidens said. "Maybe he was named after *Scundry*—Dorielziath's friend in the tale."

"Must have been," Pentas echoed. She looked at him properly for the first time since he'd entered, seeing how he kept to the edges of the light. "Was it hard, being sent away to school in Zurine?"

Bidens hesitated, the kinetic flame in the lantern jumping a little. It was apparently quite simple, the old magic that listened to the beat of their hearts, but Pentas had never taken the time to understand it. "I didn't have many friends, and the few I did went off to join the King in the Woods before they finished their studies, leaving me behind. Daddo would've had my skin if I'd gone."

She smiled at his childish use of the word. You could always spot the rich ones. "The King in the Woods?"

"He was hunted, this man, for proclaiming himself king, but they never found him. The boys I knew said he was kind and would employ anyone who passed his tests."

"Where was this king?"

"You had to go north, on the great Arteries that run up towards the Ingolland Sea. When you got there, they said, someone would escort you."

"Is he still there?"

Bidens shrugged, the flame dimming. "I don't think so. When I went back to Mostar, I stopped hearing anything of him. It was probably all just talk—you know the way older boys can be."

Pentas nodded.

"The rumours were so . . . *odd*," he continued, apparently forgetting himself at last and warming to his subject. "They said the king would never touch anything or anyone, so as not to dirty himself with the affairs of the material world, or—" He looked up at her, the candle suddenly leaping again. "I'm sorry, I'm going on."

"That's all right."

Bidens lapsed into silence for a while. "Were you bullied, too?" he asked at last.

Pentas looked out into the darkness. "I suppose so."

"I thought as much. It feels like we've shared some of our past, you and I."

"Perhaps."

Her mind was wandering, as it tended to when she knew people were trying too hard at conversation. Out in the night the waves were glowing, a twinkling luminescence churning with the moving surf. Pentas sat back suddenly, her own heart causing the flame to flicker this time.

"What?" Bidens asked.

"Quiet," she whispered.

Something had sprinted past, a dark shape against the glowing waves. There was someone out there, on the beach.

They listened. Slowly Pentas fancied she could hear the patter of feet slapping on the damp sand. She doused the lantern at last, checking on the sleeping Arabis, and opened the window for a better view.

Down below, the glinting sand rolled by, the surf slopping opalescent almost to the Wheelhouse's single track. She pushed herself up onto the ledge, leaning out to look back along the beach as it receded into darkness. Her eyes were still adjusting but she fancied she could see someone following along behind. Pentas glanced the other way, glimpsing what looked like another two figures running through the waves.

She climbed back in, heart thumping. "There are people, on the beach."

Bidens frowned. "What . . . you mean following—?"

"Following *us*, yes," she barked. Arabis stirred, grumbling.

"But why—?" Bidens began, moving to the window himself. As he did so, a small black shape darted past him and into the room, fluttering along the ceiling and chattering to itself.

"Catch it!" Pentas yelled, grabbing Arabis. The bird shrieked at her voice, flapping back onto the window frame and perching there for a moment before hopping out. They heard it cackling in the night outside.

With Arabis grumbling in her arms, Pentas made her way through the spokes of the wheel past the scullery and into the tiller cabin, noticing Jatropha had dimmed their lanterns, too. Eranthis turned to her.

"There's something up ahead," she said. "Some sort of barrier." Jatropha kept silent, concentrating on the beach. Pentas realised he was slowing down the Wheelhouse.

Eranthis noticed a moment later. "What are you doing? *Speed up!*"

"Stay here," Jatropha said. "Don't get out. Douse all the lights." He abruptly locked the tiller and the *Corbita* rolled to a stop in the sand. "Don't get out," he repeated as he climbed down from the cabin. They watched him incredulously as he made his way to the sand, Eranthis coming slowly to her senses and dimming the cabin lantern until it fizzled out. The sea and sand glowed dully against a black, starless sky.

"Come on," Eranthis said, leaving the cabin and heading along the balcony. Pentas stared after her, almost too petrified to move, finally summoning up the courage to follow with the sleeping baby. On the balcony, she noticed the warm night wind had stilled almost to nothing, and out in the darkness there were no lights. Together they ducked into the starboard necessarium, bolting the door behind them, listening hard.

Slowly the sounds of the night became apparent through the wooden walls of the chamber and up through the single hole in the floor. Whooping cries drifted across the sands, footfalls growing closer.

The door rattled abruptly, startling them both into a gasp.

"Only me," Bidens whispered behind the door.

Eranthis unlocked it and yanked it open. "*Get in here.*"

Together they sat on the floor of the cramped necessarium, Arabis soundly asleep and held to Pentas's chest. She peered through the hole beside her, seeing only a gloomy circle of sand twenty feet below.

"Are all the lanterns out?" Eranthis whispered to Bidens.

"Every one," he replied. A single kinetic flame would give them away.

They all started as something flapped and settled on the roof of the Wheelhouse, scrabbling over the tiles.

"Must have been following us all this way," Eranthis said softly, silencing at a hiss from Pentas.

They listened for a while longer as the whooped yells were answered from somewhere further down the beach; more followed along behind.

Finally, Eranthis spoke up again. "What if Jatropha—" Pentas saw her look between them. "*What if he wanted this to happen?*"

Pentas stared at the large coloured smudge of her face without comprehension. "What—?"

"Shhh," Bidens breathed, holding out his hand. Footfalls close by, almost beneath the hole. Some soft speech in a thick dialect, and the person was moving on, around to the front of the cabin.

"What were they saying?" Pentas asked Bidens, having barely understood.

At first, he didn't answer. "They said . . . I don't understand it. They were saying they *can't find* the Wheelhouse."

The sisters looked at each other in the gloom, then at Bidens.

"That's what they said," he muttered.

Pentas understood at last why Jatropha had climbed out. He'd created one of his blind spots—the kind he said he used to slip by people and places unnoticed—but one that obscured the *Corbita* entirely. Her mouth fell open in the darkness, and she resolved to indulge him in his pointless stories from now until the end of time.

The cackling and whooping were growing more distant now, veiled by the soft breath of the surf. Eranthis exhaled with a shuddering sigh. Bidens smiled at them in the darkness, getting up from his sitting position. But his knee moved awkwardly, as if still asleep, and he bumped lightly into Arabis. She woke with a gurgle, her face contorting in the shadows.

"No—"

She wailed, piercing the silence, screaming out while Pentas desperately bounced her, making all the soothing noises she knew.

"*Shit*, sorry—"

"*Fool!*" Eranthis hissed.

Arabis took a lungful of air, the silence drawing back in as they all heard the excitement coming from outside, and bawled into the tiny space.

"Give her to me," Eranthis commanded, not bothering to lower her voice. Pentas dumped the baby in her sister's arms and looked down at the hole.

A shadow stood beneath them, staring up.

Pentas screamed.

Before she knew it, Pentas was bumping through the darkened chambers of the Wheelhouse, a lantern brightening suddenly in the tiller cabin as someone climbed aboard. Pentas kicked over the scullery table and ran for the window, levering herself out.

She fell the twenty feet, twisting her ankle on the wet sand below, hardly noticing. Behind her, the Wheelhouse filled with light, its shadow stretching off suddenly into the surf, screams and shouts coming from its rooms. She suddenly remembered Arabis, and with a start of relief saw Bidens holding her in the tiller cabin.

She stumbled again in the water, the sand between her toes dropping and sliding away.

Pentas felt it then, looking out at the black edge of the sea.

With a roar, the tide came back in, churning cerulean with a heave of luminescence and spattering the Wheelhouse. Another surge, twice as high as the last, swept her towards the wheel, foaming and slamming up to the balcony.

Pentas clasped the railings, watching one of her attackers—his bedraggled Westerly face visible now in the light—splutter as he was pulled from the ladder to the tiller cabin and dragged back out into the waves. She knew what was doing this, that there would be no respite from it until all of these people had been swept away, and knew she must hold on as tightly as she could.

The waves boomed and slapped and gargled around the *Corbita*, the swell lifting it a few times in the high water and dumping it back onto the receding sand. Things shattered and banged inside. Eranthis cried out for Pentas a few times, assuring her that Arabis was safe within, and then the water dropped.

The sea gurgled, sucking at the wheel, sliding back into the darkness.

Pentas heaved her leg over the balcony rail, sliding on the wet wood. Screams faded as the waves dragged back out to sea, disappearing into a receding froth barely touched by the lanterns. There had only been half a dozen of them, she'd seen. All taken by the sea. Jatropha's slender white form was walking across the far sands, two dead messenger birds held in either hand.

Pentas stumbled along the balcony towards the tiller cabin, stepping through a thin scum of blood that was washing out over the planks and dripping on the sand, expecting to find one of the kidnappers injured. She slipped in the blood, throwing out a hand to catch herself on the cabin's doorframe, and a black form materialised from the gloom.

Bidens was lying there, the side of his face flat against the boards, a bright smear of blood leaching from his body. His eyes, hardened as if in a scowl, had latched on to her feet and were watching their movements intently. She steadied herself and turned away, retching, trying to lift her toes out of the blood but knowing it had mixed with all the water on the boards. When she looked back, she saw that he was moving his mouth silently. She ran for the scullery, using what last strength she had to lock the door shut behind her.

ZADAR

"Perhaps we should go back," Eranthis said. "Back to Mostar."

The morning sea breathed through the window. A light breeze was busily brushing a cover of loose sand across the lonely single track that stretched off along the beach. They'd left the boy back there, under blankets, and perhaps now the sand was burying him too.

She looked up at Jatropha, who was about to serve tea from the stove. "You can't just send money," she told him. "Didn't anyone ever teach you that? You can't spend your way out of problems."

"The mayor wouldn't appreciate our return," Jatropha said, pouring a cup for her. "We must continue on. There will only be more of them back there."

"We failed that poor boy," Pentas said at her side, sipping slowly at the tea that was set in front of her. Since the attack, she hadn't let Arabis out of her sight. Eranthis had found her in the scullery, reading the new stories of Onosma aloud to her daughter. Blood like dried paint had stuck between the boards of the balcony.

She hated to think what might have happened had they managed to run away in Mostar, conscious now that there must have been thieves on their tail for who knew how many days. There were surely more out there, awaiting any messenger birds that were able to get away. Finally, she returned her attention to the Amaranthine. She'd been wrong about him, and once again he had saved their lives.

"All right," Eranthis muttered, blowing on her tea and glancing at Pentas. "Forward we go, then."

"Good," Jatropha said, finally pouring a cup for himself.

They'd rolled on through the night, keeping their lanterns dimmed. Up ahead, a crude dam of branches and rocks had been hastily dumped in their path, and the Wheelhouse needed to leave the beach to get around it, making its hesitant way through a dark woodland illuminated only by green-tinged moonlight.

Eranthis thought of the furious chronicler, Geum, the man they'd escaped at Acropolo. He could have spread word into the west by now. There might be a Jalan bounty on their heads, for all she knew. Jatropha said he had friends who could track the chronicler down, but that they must be patient; there were likely others out there with more to gain from the stolen Berenzargol child, and they, too, would have caught wind of the stories of a Wheelhouse making its way into the West with a valuable cargo.

"So," Eranthis said. "Fortifications."

The Wheelhouse was not a rare form of transport; they'd already sighted dozens of the ramshackle, multicoloured things on the road from Acropolo, so there was little point in selling it for something less conspicuous. She'd seen in Jatropha's face how much he loved the thing and would've been sad to force him to sell. As a compromise, they'd all agreed on fortifying the vehicle against attack without slowing it down too much.

"I know just the people," Jatropha said, hawking his tea noisily out of the window and clearing his throat. "Let's get going."

Pentas huffed, looking at the beach. "Must you spit like that?"

Jatropha glanced back at her, a sudden intensity in his gaze, and Eranthis was reminded that he was a living thing, just like them. "I must," he said. "Always."

Zadar was another port, an escarpment of growth-stone three miles long rising from weed-black rocks out of a dark blue sea. Across the water to the west, the far lands of Tail brooded, unseen, connected to the Thirdling city by daily convoys of merchant cogs. The westerly breeze whipped the surf along the coast into twinkling white trails, like the snow-capped peaks of a range of deep blue mountains, enraged as if by a blizzard.

Pentas observed a cluster of three ships bobbing in the waves as her eyes wandered up to the city's great keep. It rose at the end of the escarpment to angle out above the sea, a growth of dripping stone the colour of old bones, as if the material had gone wild at the ocean's edge and spread out of control. Her eyes lingered on the swathe of wild mineral trees leaning over the sea; the deep forest they'd be sleeping in that night.

Pentas narrowed her eyes against the sea wind, bobbing Arabis at her hip. The child had a Firmamental Ducat in her pudgy hand and was working away at its carved edge with her gums. "I don't see why we're stopping, why we can't just get as far away from here as possible."

Jatropha looked into the baby's large, pale eyes and smiled. "Oh, you think we're being chased?" The condescension in his tone was unlike anything Eranthis had ever heard. "They're ahead of us as well. When word gets out that the future queen of all the Provinces is trundling around in a wheelhouse, I assure you there'll be nowhere to run."

Eranthis had been rummaging for the old telescope she'd stashed in her bags. She brought it out and returned to the deck, sighting the fortress. Pentas gestured for it but she shrugged her away. "What do you suggest, then?"

"Gifts arrive in the strangest guises," he said, absurdly beginning to chuckle. A black messenger raven with eyes like red marbles swept past the balcony, calling out in a language the girls had never heard. Jatropha's smile broadened as he watched it wheel away, feathers ruffling in the wind. "Did I ever tell you," he began, very much in the way he started every pointless, inconsequential story, "that I used to be a *thief*, once upon a time?"

TANKER

The crump and rattle of exchanged fire drifted across the island as Maril scampered down the hillside, his boots slipping on crumbling shale. He threw out a hand to steady his slide as a larger, deeper detonation rumbled from the direction of the bay.

He sprinted between the chalky outcrops, momentarily lost until he saw the sea. Reaching the beach and unclipping his pistol, he stopped to listen, the boom of the evening waves obscuring anything that might be going on in the northerly coves. He stood a little longer, waiting, undecided, seeing none of his men or any of the *Bie* along the stretch of beach, then ran for the bent tree, spotting its angled trunk some way along the rocks at the water's edge.

He saw the shovel lying to one side as he came upon where Jospor had hidden the last of the weapons, knowing before he got there that they'd be gone. The hole was freshly, hurriedly dug out. He could make out more shots coming from around the headland; the fierce detonations of a firefight mingled with hoarse shouting.

At the outcrops, Maril crept, head low, until he could just see the rusted Zelioceti tanker where it lay offshore among the towering sea stacks. He scanned the beach, noticing assorted scattered debris, still aflame. Further along, someone lay face down; a body clothed in bloodied rags, the rubber of its boot on fire. One of his men—Maril recognised the rings he wore. Dilmon. He ducked back, tapping the stock of his spring pistol against the rock while he thought. It was still dry and loaded with fifty-five lethal poison-tipped rounds: each was an assured one-shot kill—just loading them while the privateer bucked under fire could have been his last act in this life.

This is an opportunity, he reminded himself on a continual loop. *This is not a disaster.*

Edging out behind the rock again and running his eyes along the coast, he saw them at last—a train of shackled Vulgar guided by taller Zelioceti through the shallows to the tanker's pitted hull. Maril's eyes went to the decks, seeing the *Bie* milling on a winch platform, watched over by a Zelioceti leaning against the prow. In its hand it clutched a long driftwood staff that it pounded on the deck, a regular clanking beat. Maril cursed the damn creatures, furious at how calm they looked, how easily they'd been shepherded aboard. Glancing back to the captives in the shallows, he could see they were being taken to a ladder on the side of the hull. As the first of the Vulgar began to climb, Maril ducked behind cover again and turned his eyes skywards. The glow of the sun was almost gone, tingeing the sea a dark, foreboding green. He would wait.

The stars, mostly washed out in the glow of Zeliolopos, had begun their night's watch when Maril made his careful way along the beach and into the shallows. Once waist deep in the sea, he paused to observe the bob of lanterns further up the beach. He'd been watching the sweeps of the Zelioceti as the darkness grew. They must have taken a tally of the prisoners, questioning some in various unpleasant ways, and knew now that they were still short a valuable captain.

Keeping his pistol out of the water, he waded deeper in, his clothing growing heavy, boots stumbling on patches of dead coral among the pebbles. As he neared the hull he glanced back, his nerves calmed by the sight of the fruitless search still going on along the beach. Judging by the lights, there were at least a dozen out there, the furthest scouts already almost a mile away and nearing the outcrops at the foot of the mountain.

Clenching his pistol between his teeth, he stretched out into a doggy paddle, swimming the short distance beyond the stern to one of the sea stacks, ghostly pale in the gas giant's light. Its limestone girth had been worn down where the sea brushed it, creating an almost insurmountable overhang that Maril would have to climb before he could make his way further up it to the top.

He'd spent the waning day selecting which of the stacks to climb. They surrounded the Zelioceti ship like a white forest of tapering spires, ancient columns eroded at their base. At least four stood higher than the tanker by a few feet; a short jump down and he'd be on the deck.

Close to the base of the chosen stack, Maril saw some rough edges he might grasp if only he could reach them over the smooth, dissolved undercut of the column. He clung on with one hand and pulled his knife free with the other, jamming it into the rock above and kicking the heel of his boot against the softened stone at the base of the stack. His waterlogged clothes dribbled into the sea like a gurgling piss stream. Maril froze, alarmed at the volume, and shook himself, dispersing the water.

Climbing from the undercut was less difficult than he'd anticipated. Luckily the majority of the column hid him from the tanker and the beach—they glowed white in the planet-light, brilliant and obvious in their contrast. He crested the stack, arms and thighs burning from the exertion, and crawled along its angled top to stare down at the tanker.

Fire drums on deck sent sparks floating up towards him in eddies of smoke, the stink of oil and tar and effluent climbing with them through a mesh of chains that ran the length of the tanker. He could just make out the ship's cargo: dismantled Voidship components tightly packed and tied beneath pitch-coated canvas coverings, the majority hidden by a colossal heap of bundled copper wire and the first two ramshackle conning towers rising at the prow. Lengths of peeled tin, holey where the rivets had been removed, lay in cords just beneath him. A few charred superluminal cylinder heads sat massively off to one side, their circumferences striped with shrapnel scars. Maril looked at the debris beneath him, fantasising how long it would take for a crew to cobble together something that might get him and his men off Coriopil, well aware they could do no such thing. The Vulgar had no great talent for engineering. They purchased from the Pifoon and tinkered, or commandeered Lacaille ships. Even the late *Wilemo Maril*, before he'd taken a spanner to it, had been fifty years in the hands of a Lacaille Great Company then stolen from a yard of reprimanded ships. It was a well-known and embarrassing fact that most Prism Voidships had actually started life in Amaranthine Foundries more than four thousand years ago, remnants of the wars that had ended the Age of Decadence. Others, belonging mostly to the Pifoon, were even more ancient: six-thousand-year-old Amaranthine vessels able to snap across the entire Firmament in a handful of days, useless to the Immortals once they'd realised their own late-arriving powers. Only bits of those ships' engines survived, usually, though one or two of the most expensive he'd seen had sported a few segments of rainbow-coloured carapace more wondrous than Old World jewels. The Pifoon did their best to copy their masters, fashioning the housing of their borrowed motors into the forms of beasts, but when you'd seen the originals, as Maril had, even highly prized Prism work looked laughably, staggeringly crude.

From his vantage point on the stack, he could no longer see the grey Voidship, if that was what it really was. He guessed from what he *had* seen that it was not Zelioceti manufactured. Whether it would be any use or not was another matter; it was no easy feat to fly a ship you were even partially familiar with.

Maril took a breath and jumped down, trying to land on his feet but tripping and skidding, spraining his wrist where it shot out to take his weight. His knife flew across the deck, spinning on the metal with a sound like a rolling coin. He dashed after it, clutching his bent wrist, ducking behind a heap of cargo at the last second as the shadow of a

Zelioceti loomed over the deck. The knife spun to a stop. Maril leaned back in the shadows. The dragon jaw of a Pifoon cockpit, its internals stripped, gaped out at him. After a few breaths, he crept around to watch as the Zelioceti stooped, inspecting the knife thoughtfully before picking it up. The Zelioceti's glinting eyes swivelled to survey the deck while it mumbled to itself, the sound of the sea and the rumble of the ship drowning whatever wandering thoughts it was trying to express.

Maril pulled off his boots and set them to one side, sidling around the wreckage pile. He took a breath and inched into the light, ducking back the moment he saw that the Zelioceti had continued on along the deck, the knife in its hand. He swore, grabbing his boots and working his way parallel with the Zelioceti until he'd overtaken it and dashed into the shade of another superluminal component. There was no time. The Zelioceti had a long stride. Maril took a deep breath and swung out with a kick, snapping the creature's gangly knee and dragging it squirming into the shadows. He brought his boot down across its long neck, silencing it before it could scream. The knife clattered free and he took it back, ears pricking as silence returned to the deck.

He tied his boots to his belt, stepping barefoot through the webs of taut, thick chains that held down the assorted cargo. The rusted iron of the deck was still warm from the day, sticky with salt and rough where strips of corroded metal caught his feet. Maril knew of a paralysis called *Clostrid* that could enter the blood through metal—he'd seen Vulgar die from it—but there was no time to inspect the soles of his feet. Vaccinations did not exist in the Investiture and infections alone killed billions every year. If he found himself bleeding he'd need to cut and cauterize the skin, as he'd done with other wounds.

He was nearing the centre of the tanker, a great slab-sided bulge of rusted deck crowned with another small conning tower. It worried him slightly that he couldn't see the *Bie* or their guard anywhere about, but he had to go on.

The docked two-man Voidship came into view. It was rocket-shaped at the nose and gnarled with weaponry. Its plump body—built to carry freight, he thought—was covered with a patchwork of vulcanised rubber grouted with solder and hundreds of iron fins that stuck out at every angle. The characters painted across its bladed exterior, now that he was close enough to see them, were undoubtedly Pifoon. He stopped, keeping in the shadow of a leaning collection of beaten tin panels, and read the angular foreign letters slowly. *Tarmon Barbinel*. Maril knew the name; it was part of a Fortune Company, a wealthy assortment of Ringum treasure hunters too expensive for anyone but the Pifoon to hire. Maril scratched his ear-tip with the hilt of the knife. The Zelioceti, when they stole, painted out any other marks of ownership, so this ship had been gifted by the Pifoon: essentially a present from the Amaranthine Firmament in all but name.

Near the base of the Voidship's docked tail, where an eruption of petal-shaped blades and fins enclosed an exhaust, one last stamped insignia caught his attention: the self-portrait of the Quetterel, once a stick-figure drawing, now simplified and stylized to a symbol of hard, branching lines printed boldly on everything they owned. So, they played a part in this, too.

Maril's hopes grew. The Quetterel hardly flew, but they scrubbed and polished everything they owned with an obsessive rigour that bordered on the religious. Maril had heard them also called Compulsives in his time; Prism infected with an unquenchable need to purge. Barring the possibility that it had been totally stripped of foreign, undesirable parts, the ship should be in perfect condition. The ancient Amaranthine engine inside the thing would be meaty, powerful enough to outstrip his dearly departed privateer in a heartbeat and thunder beyond the reach of the Tau Ceti system in a matter of minutes. It was an offer too good to ignore.

Keeping beneath the shadow of a knotted tangle of chains, Maril spotted the guard that had been keeping watch over the *Bie*. The adolescent Zelioceti had left its driftwood staff leaning against the railings and was sitting silently on another superluminal component, playing with the loose end of a chain, its links as thick as fingers. The Zelioceti's deep-set eyes were lost in shadow, the darkness of its drooping red proboscis resembling an elongated goatee, some timeless caricature. Maril wondered how the mysterious things entertained themselves; most could not read or write—a trait shared with more than ninety-nine per cent of the Investiture—but where other Prism enjoyed the company of their fellows, the Zelioceti appeared not to. They had no games of luck or skill that Maril knew of, and a disarmingly simple tongue composed mostly of words pilfered from other kingdoms. A few wealthy familial lines, assisted by the Pifoon, led their manufacturing prowess, but he was fairly certain these on the tanker were just LopoCeti—unpaid orphans local to the moons of the giant planets. This one, malnourished and bandy-legged, bore the body-length scars of a hard childhood.

The Zelioceti unfolded, waddling a little way from the huge engine bolt it had been sitting on and squatting until a look of deeper blankness settled over its shadowed face. It swallowed, stomach muscles straining, and began to squeeze a coil of black stool onto the deck, its fingers fidgeting around its rear and coming away stained. The smell of the fishy defecation reached Maril quickly on the warm night breeze. The shepherd shifted, eyes narrowing as it tried to pass something more solid than the last, and Maril took his chance, slinking from the darkness with his knife raised, not realising until it was too late that his shadow stretched long before him.

It spun faster than he'd have expected, leaping up and throwing out its filthy hand. Maril reacted as best he could, swinging the blade as he ducked, chopping through its fingers in a whirl and sending them flying in different directions. Before the Zelioceti's wounds were noticed, it had gripped Maril's wrist and twirled him, flinging him around. Maril felt the knife loosen in his grip, slinging free as his bare foot sank into the fresh turd and slipped out from beneath him, peels of rust driving into his heel. His back hit the deck with a concussive hollow bang.

The creature's shadow darkened his blurred vision, and then a hand closed around his face, slathering his mouth in shit and iron wetness. The Zelioceti twisted Maril's neck back until he was sure it would break, the bones crackling and popping, the din of their protestations not quite blocking the thumping percussion of something being trailed along the metal. The loose chain. He pushed against the Zelioceti's scrawny strength, bucking and kicking, unable to move. The shepherd wheezed a pained laugh, and then Maril felt the cold weight of the chain as it wound around his throat, not quite closing his windpipe. A rasp of metal on metal reminded him of the suit collar he still wore, a hoop of life-preserving iron preventing the chain from squeezing tight. The Zelioceti grunted, waggling its mauled hand, and strained at the chain, pressing the bolts of Maril's collar into his neck. Ghostly Zeliolopos light dimmed above him, the scent of iron blood and iron chains stronger than anything he'd ever smelled, and the memory of the Amaranthine sliding her long leg across his lap came unbidden into his mind, breathing in as the life drifted away.

Then he was being dragged with astonishing force towards the railings, his feet raw with metal shavings. With a drugged start, he began to writhe again, sluggish and stumbling, his eyes filled with the green ghost-light of the water.

PART III

WOLF

Florian Von Schiller opened his eyes amid a tangled scrub of wintery trees. Putting his hand out to fend off the worst of the twigs, he glimpsed light through the tangle—a yellow slant of sun almost at the horizon. He pushed ahead, one arm to his eyes, until the trees gradually thinned to stands of black copses agitated by the chill wind. The cold that bit through his clothes was countered for the moment by the tingle of his long Bilocation from Yanenko's Land, but Von Schiller was conscious that he'd need to find warmth quickly as night fell.

Outer Wolf, a moss-slimed winter world of lichen-encrusted trees, was the second of the Most Venerable Sabran's private Satrapies, long cut off from the Firmament. Its days lasted less than two hours, its nights black and moonless, lit only by icy stars. Like Sabran's other private world, Procyon, it had escaped the attentions of the hollowing lathes, remaining forever solid at its core. Von Schiller wondered what might lie under the crust of this place, never to be found, and why the planet, discovered in an age of relative scarcity when all new lands were needed, had been left so starkly alone.

Here, on a dangling finger of sea-shrouded land at what was laughably referred to as the equator, no snow ever fell; instead, the cold crept upwards out of the ground, snaring boots and feet in its numbing grasp as night descended. Florian thought of all the Amaranthine souls who had come for an allotted audience with their Firmamental Emperor only for him to not appear, some choosing to freeze to death rather than do Sabran the dishonour of taking their leave. What a place to become a ghost.

That might well happen to me, Von Schiller mused, climbing a slope of twisted roots until the shores of an icy lake became evident to his right, the simple wooden boat he'd been looking for appearing at last. He took a deep breath, relieved beyond words. It was not the Venerable Sabran's displeasure he risked, after all.

The boat was tied to a stump where the lake met the woodland's edge, its peeling paintwork glowing in bars of yellow where evening sun blazed through the trees. Florian went down to it, examining the ground around the shore where someone had disembarked and made their way up the slope not too long ago. The trail was fresh; Sabran was close.

Aren't we all beings of ice? Sabran had once remarked to him. *Each of us trying to delay our return to the sea.*

He took his time, following the boot marks in the silt to where they'd crunched through the evening's frost and into the woods. He crept, hunched, the cold starting to leach into his toes, glad to know he would soon be gone.

A sudden movement, partially glimpsed, brought his head up. Florian stared into the trees, seeing only the white and grey lichen of the trunks. He waited, ears tuned like a startled deer, all immortality forgotten, then looked down again, searching out the trail.

His Most Venerable Self was insane, not powerless. Stalking him was like stalking a lion, Florian reflected, relishing the comparison. It was something he'd never done in his previous life, but now the chance had come. He knew that the air here carried none of the Motes that filled the Vaulted Lands; countless charged particulates that floated on the winds like invisible snow, each attuned to a specific command so that it could assist the Amaranthine in the casting of their Incantations. So he was safe from those, at the very least.

Another flicker of darkness to his left, something man-sized wandering silently through the trees. Florian turned, hands open in a claw-like gesture, but again the woods were empty. He spun, peering into the branches, his heart awakening from its thousand-year slumber, but could see nothing. Nobody. Not a wild bird or gnat stirred in this frigid world. At his feet he saw an autumnal leaf pressed frozen into the earth; another print, fresher than the last.

He *could* just disappear, pay the Prism to leave his estates on Cancri alone and live out his life until it was time to die. But more would come, and more, then more again. They were chaotic now, yes, but soon enough some Vulgar or Pifoon would rise to the challenge and take a whole Vaulted Land. Then chaos would ignite the Firmament all over again, each Satrapy laid claim to. Florian would run out of funds to pay his protectors, and then he'd be a dead man, hunted into the Whoop or imprisoned for the amusement of some new Prism Satrap.

Muttering filtered through the trees. Over a rise, he heard the unmistakable wheeze of a laugh. Florian slinked towards the sounds, hands clenching and opening stiffly, wanting to get it over with. He came to the crest of the rise, stepping neatly between the trunks, seeing the top of Sabran's white head, wisps of hair blazing against the winter sunset. He looked down into the hollow at his defenceless Emperor.

"Oh, he's here now, is he?" Sabran said suddenly, turning from where he was arranging firewood and glancing up. His blue eyes fixed on a point above Florian's right shoulder. "Stop staring at him and leave him alone."

Florian flinched, looking over his shoulder at the trees, then around the bowl of the hollow.

"Who do you speak with, Most Venerable? Your ghosts of the mountains?"

Sabran chuckled, the back of his head nodding. Florian stepped down to him, rolling up his sleeves despite the cold and standing behind his old Emperor.

The Most Venerable began to hum a tune as he busied himself with his firewood, little snippets of song emerging as he laid the last of the logs.

As Lomattis shunned the Perinnieds,
And Glomax killed the Smae,
I absent myself from mortal life,
And make my merry way.

Appear now, my friends, my dears,
Appear and be not shy,

Come share the warmth I bring for you,
From lands beyond the sky.

We'll pass the night in jollity,
With tales and song and cheer,
We'll pass all nights for evermore,
Appear, appear, Epir!

Florian looked around the clearing again, up into the trees as the wind sighed through their bony fingers. Sabran clicked his tongue at the pile of firewood as he continued to hum, flame leaping from within the lattice of branches.

It was time. These songs about appearing *Epir*—whatever those might be—chilled Florian more than the settling night. Sabran's madness really had grown monstrous out here, the drifting iron in his blood thickening and choking his neurons, fizzling them out. This sickness, it was the cause of *everything*; the entire reason the Satraps had placed their faith in the untried spectre of the Long-Life and his promises: a man of great age, miraculously still unblinded by the sickness, as if he were Jatropha the Assassin himself. He was their hope for a future, their hope for more life than the universe would appear to allow.

But they were wrong, Florian supposed. There was no more to be had. Nobody—nobody human, anyway—lived beyond thirteen thousand years. It was impossible. All the powers they'd dreamed of, inconceivable abilities and insights, would never come to pass. The Perennials' only hope lay now in the veneration of the machine mind they'd discovered in their midst, and by adhering to his every whim.

He almost turned away, despite the thought.

No. He licked his lips and bowed behind Sabran, hands extended. *This man's life is over, anyway.*

He brought them together over Sabran's head in a single clap.

The old man crumpled before him, nearly one hundred and thirty centuries of life gone in a snap of sound that was lost to the wind. Florian grimaced and pushed the corpse to the ground, scattering the smoking firewood. The cold sank back into the hollow. He regarded the body, a wild guilt permeating the chill, ready to turn and run, to close his eyes and snap as far away from here as he could.

He blinked.

Woodsmoke from the ruined fire had dimmed the twilight beyond the hollow, drifting between the trees and catching the last rays of the sun. But the gentle, hanging fog had not settled uniformly across the air. Here and there, in half a dozen places in and around the trees, it had parted.

Florian began to tremble uncontrollably as he looked into the woods, unable to understand what he was seeing. There were things here with him, invisible things, only now made visible as the smoke rolled past them.

Appear.

He doesn't bother locking the car, a beautifully restored Rolls-Royce Phantom with a speak-start installed. The ancient cobbled streets of Salzburg—more ancient by far than the three-hundred-year-old automobile—do not cater for the needy these days.

He runs his hand over a chrome headlamp and looks up the autumnal street, barely a soul about. Gilded tavern signs, Germanically floral, hang low over mountaineering shops and restaurant windows. As Florian walks, he takes surreptitious peeks at himself in the reflective shopfronts, admiring the admiral-blue Brioni suit delivered by the tailors last week. As his eyes travel over the lapels and pockets, something scuttles darkly behind him in the window's reflection, and Florian develops the impression that there are unseen people in the shops, looking out at him. He checks himself, momentarily embarrassed at such unsubtle vanity, and moves on.

Rust-brown leaves swirl in an eddy of wind at his feet, a few sticking to his glossy shoes as he walks, the remains of some ghostly song reverberating in his head, some nonsense he's heard somewhere.

Appear, appear . . .

Epir. He considers the word, mouthing it, but it is not a word he knows. While his mouth moves, his tongue slides across his teeth, craving something. Craving meat. Dark meat: lamb or beef. Florian is largely vegetarian these days—outwardly for sentimental reasons, *the poor things, the cruelty.* Only a select few know that he desires immortality more than anything else in the world; one must prove—concurrent with certain portfolio criteria, of course—one's absolute devotion to health in order to ever be worthy of obtaining *The Invitation*.

But it's Sunday, a day when anything should be possible. He knows of a fine delicatessen at the very end of the Getreidegasse and quickens his immaculate step, allowing himself another glance at the superbly fitted suit. The sensation of eyes watching him through the glass returns, primal and eerie, but this time he fancies he sees dim hands pressed to the windows, tapping. Florian stops to look, stepping away from the windows on one side of the street, his image losing focus as he gazes past it to whatever is tapping upon the window.

Tap, tap, tappety-tap. The song of the *Epir* surfaces in his mind once more as the rhythm plays out against the glass. *Gravity*, he thinks, *it's all to do with gravity.*

Something slams against the window of a shopfront behind him and he turns, startled. His reflected face looks back, eyes wide, the crisp white pocket square of the suit disrupting any image of what might lie behind the glass.

He swivels on his heel and runs for the deli, the song bright and loud in his mind.

Appear now my friends, my dears,
 Appear and be not shy.

He reaches the top of the street without looking back and turns the corner into a leaf-strewn alley. There it is, lights on, welcoming. A wooden cut-out of a hog wearing a stained butcher's apron gurns at visitors from the street, beckoning him in.

A bell tinkles as he enters, noticing that the deli is deserted but hardly caring. Here they are, great wheels of cheese with thick red wax rinds, wizened white sausages the texture of chalk, glistening pink ham hocks. And there, over towards the wall, a giant browned leg of smoked prosciutto.

Florian steps forward, his trembling lips wet with spittle, pressing his hands—like the hands of whoever was just watching him, he thinks absently—against the glass counter. He pushes harder with the heels of his palms until a crack snaps and dances across the display, silvering the glass.

We'll pass the night in jollity—

He sees terrines cast in jellied chunks, some pies encased in glazed, golden pastry. He watches a ribbon of drool fall across the busted glass beneath his hands.

The counter smashes inwards and Florian baulks at the sound, almost afraid. He feels a stab of brief cold for a moment, then dismisses it and uses his elbow to clear away the remainder of the debris around the edge, sparing a glance at his hands. He has cut himself in the process, probably badly, but it doesn't matter in the slightest any more. He reaches in to collect what he can and dumps it on the counter, then heaves the prosciutto from the wall.

Checking once more for the absent proprietor, Florian lunges into the prosciutto, tearing at it like a wolf. Blood runs down his sleeve, drizzling the meat, and he laps it up. The scent and taste of it only serve to drive him wilder, gasping in frenzy like a feeding shark, gulping and shredding. He peels off a lump of cheese and throws it aside, intent on the red rind, stuffing another shred of meat into his mouth to mash with the wax.

He chomps into his tongue. Pink drool runs from the corners of his mouth and spatters the suit. He breaks more glass, clearing everything from within the display cabinet and grinning as his hands encounter the boards of soft foie gras, his fingers sinking in. A dull pain that has lingered in the background begins to sharpen, a wormlike wriggling deep inside the soft parts of him. He shrugs it away, gagging and spitting out a chunk of gristle.

Florian is distantly aware that he has begun to vomit between mouthfuls, and yet the wondrous flavours remain unaffected. He stops to throw up again, spotting blood mixed in with the mess like jam in porridge, and tears into the stringed ham without another thought, breaking a tooth against his knuckle as he crams things into his mouth.

Half-sated, he leans against the counter and slides down it, his suit catching and tearing on shards of glass with a zipping sound. His lap is a mess of vomit, nearly all blood.

He stares at it, feeling the chill of a place far beyond this world bleeding through his trousers and sleeves.

Florian puts a hand out behind him to steady himself, and the ground is cold and hard, like frozen cement. The skin of his palm sticks to it. Outside in the street only the glow of the sun remains.

He wakes a little from his torpor as he notices the lichen-barked trees standing in groves beyond the windows; desolate, denuded branches sigh, scraping against one another as the wind picks up.

With a jolt he remembers where he is, thousands of years of memory breathing in through the open door.

In the darkening woods, Florian Von Schiller looked down at what was left of himself. Twin strips of peeled, bloody cream femur lay beneath the glinting pile of his mangled guts. Another collection of white objects lay not far off. The bones of his left arm.

Florian spat out what was left in his mouth, which was now missing more than a few teeth. The taste was appalling, and he understood vaguely that he must have ripped into his own spilled intestines.

He looked off into the silent woods as the last of the light vanished, perfectly numb from the anaesthetising cold, unable to open his mouth and scream.

GALLERY

The word meant nothing to Lycaste, a susurration in the darkness. He'd imagined something happening when it was uttered: a breeze sweeping the room, a door flinging open. In the stillness of the chamber, Maneker fell silent. He reached out a hand and touched Lycaste's shoulder, as if already used to his blindness.

"It's gone," the Amaranthine said, a fresh good humour lightening his tone. "But it'll be back."

The creak of heavy wood and ancient hinges as light flew into the space. Maneker pushed the second shutter to one side, colouring the room the grey of the sea. Lycaste's mouth fell open. The chamber was far smaller than he'd assumed; across its black and white tiled floor, a dilapidated castle of exquisite, colourless dust had been built, its walls strung with lines of spider silk like the guy ropes of a ship. Where Lycaste had blundered—and he remembered now with a shiver the feeling of softness brushing by—all had been ruined, so much artistry gone in an instant. It was little wonder Perception hadn't welcomed his arrival with open arms.

"It made this out of dust?" Huerepo asked, gazing around and flicking at something with the edge of his rapier. Lycaste saw that it was the husk of an extremely unpleasant-looking spider—much larger than the beast he'd encountered in his glove—its legs curled in death. The bodies of more were lying everywhere, mingled in with the ruins at their feet.

They left the place, continuing up a further flight of stairs and along the Oratory's great landing to a gallery of tall, mostly broken windows. Grey light daubed the place, and when Lycaste looked out he saw the sun was nothing but a smudged cream blotch in a landscape of dirty cloud. Even the dagger-shaped mountains on the far side of the world appeared washed out and drained of colour. Wind flowing over the high spires moaned through the cracks, stirring sand grains across the long white stone floor. More of the large spiders, having made their escape through Perception's opened door, scrambled in halting dashes from one distant window to another. Arranged along the gallery, a host of eggshell-blue statues looked down on them, faces of Immortals from another age, Maneker said.

They walked between the likenesses of the ancients, inspecting their faces. Lycaste thought they looked like real people drizzled with thin paint, smooth moulds of solemnly sleeping men and women.

"They are," Maneker said, when asked. "These are Statuary Tombs. There arc real Amaranthine inside, as fresh and untroubled by decomposition as the day they were poured."

Lycaste, who'd been leaning close to look at the hard blue eyelashes on a woman's face, backed away a little. "How long have they—?"

Maneker leaned against the one Lycaste was looking at, pain visibly dampening his spirits again. Dabs of blood bloomed behind his bandage. "This place was a mausoleum many thousands of years ago, before anyone thought to lock Perception away here."

"What is he? Perception?" Huerepo asked, walking unaided now, proud of all his new finery.

Lycaste thought he might know, but when Maneker turned to him he coloured, too afraid to speak.

"There is no *he*," Maneker said, his faded rags mirroring the colour of the light. "Only *it*. And *it* must never be underestimated."

"Is it a ghost?" Lycaste asked, gesturing at the hard statues. "The ghost of one of these Amaranthine?"

"No. Not an Immortal," Maneker replied, running his hand over the faces of the tombs, feeling their features. "Perception was a machine, once. Made for the Firmament during the Age of Decadence, just to show it could be done."

Lycaste went to a window and looked out over the crags of the shore, imagining a vast, coppery structure of riveted metal, levers and strings. He saw a full-lipped mouth upon its largest face moving as it spoke. *Tell me, Tenthling, have you ever loved?*

"The great irony was that it came an age too late," Maneker continued. "By the time we *could* manufacture such things, we simply didn't need them any more."

"How did he—*it*—die?" Huerepo asked, his eyes twitching to one of the statues as he spoke. Lycaste followed his gaze, his ears finely tuned to the silence of the room.

The question hung in the air while they listened. Maneker appeared not to have heard them. He turned now, too, head tilted.

Lycaste looked back at the far row of statues, his eyes narrowing.

A collection of slender fingers no bigger than a Monkman's gripped the side of one statue's neck, their claws latched on to a perfectly preserved fold in the collar. The tomb's angelic face, turned slightly to one side, seemed to have paused to listen as well.

Huerepo put a finger to his lips, flattening down his palm as Lycaste made to draw his pistol. The Vulgar pointed to the far end of the gallery, where a slant of strengthening sunlight illuminated a doorway, and motioned what he wanted to do.

They approached the statue from either side, a scrawny arm slowly revealing itself as Lycaste moved around to the tomb's stone shoulder. A pointed ear, its lobe hidden in shadow, twitched as it came into view. The thing's eyes turned towards him.

"*Oxel*," Huerepo hissed. The Prism, the length of Lycaste's largest finger, sprang at him. Lycaste ducked, turning to see it rolling on the floor and scampering off down the gallery. He shuddered, a deep revulsion forcing him to check himself over for any more of them, then gave chase, swerving too late as the creature shoved an ornamented chair into his path. Lycaste crashed over it, smashing the back of the chair into dusty shrapnel and hobbling himself.

He rounded the corner into the sunlight, limping as he ran, eyes widening and crying out before he could stop. He toppled and slid, his new boots driving into the gaggle of tiny Prism as they raised their weapons and scattering a few across the hall. Lycaste yelped and scrambled to his feet, sprinting back the way he'd come.

"They're everywhere!" he hollered, dropping as Huerepo marched forward, loading and springing his pistol and firing over Lycaste's head.

The stillness shattered, crashing and booming and tearing apart, the enormous noise of Huerepo's pistol vibrating through Lycaste's cuirass as stone chips leapt and danced across the floor, skipping and ricocheting, pinging from his armoured back while he lay face down and deafened. Before him, two statues erupted into crimson splatters, pulverised by incoming fire. He began to crawl, one hand over his ear, working his scraping way slowly beneath whizzing bolts and bullets until he was behind Maneker at last. The Amaranthine pulled out a Loyalist pistol he'd concealed in his robes, firing apparently at random into the smoke of Huerepo's destruction. Shapes flitted in the mist of flung stone and flesh, firing flashes of colour that screamed and bounced, detonating windows with eruptions of flame.

"Sparkers!" Huerepo wailed, flinching as a dot of burning light bounced past him and slalomed around the back of the gallery, igniting the door they'd come through with a comet trail of hissing red fire.

Something thudded through Lycaste's britches and into his knee, knocking him flat on his back. He looked down at a fizzing shard of sparking colour lodged in his flesh and felt like fainting. It burned out, dying to an ember.

Through the smoke he saw them coming, a scrawny host of shadows. Lycaste aimed and fired as Huerepo reloaded, apparently missing. The far wall of the gallery blinked out of existence as if it had never been there, daylight now streaming smokily in behind the slightly befuddled shapes. Maneker, assuming he hadn't fired at all, pushed Lycaste roughly out of the way and shot without taking aim, felling a twitching shape in the mist. They began to scatter, harried by the snapping con-cussions of Huerepo's spring pistol and retreating behind the adjoining wall.

Smoke drifted, curling up to hug the high ceiling and pouring out of the empty space. Spattered, mixed heaps of guts and chipped stone painted the gallery, the ancient Amaranthine casualties mingled with the newly dead.

"They've fallen back—why have they fallen back?" Huerepo whis-pered, slamming the hot, jammed spring in his pistol until it popped free again. Maneker reached out a hand to the Vulgar for more ammuni-tion, catching a fistful of bolts with impressive ease.

"Lycaste," Huerepo said, hingeing back his faceplate and glancing to the ruined windows, "check outside, will you?"

"What for?" he asked.

"Just look, dammit!"

He crawled to the missing wall, the rain blowing in and dampening his beard, and peeped over the edge, his miraculous pistol at the ready. Where the wall had disappeared, the stone was cut smooth in perfect cross section. The cliffs below boomed with the hurled grey spray of the sea, some of it rising almost to the windows. Inching his eyes north-wards across the coast, Lycaste saw a towering, blackened gatehouse rising from more overgrown gardens. On the lawns beneath it, a silvery-red Voidship with the snarling, stylised face of a hound sat steaming in the light rain. Lycaste clocked one of the ship's broadside guns swivel-ling on the Oratory just as he was raising his pistol, swearing and press-ing himself flat, hearing the shell rip overhead into the sky. The echoing thump of it travelled across the gardens like a drumbeat.

"What in the grand *fuckery* was—" Huerepo began as Lycaste heaved himself from the floor.

"No time!" he roared, grabbing Maneker's cloak without permis-sion and receiving a mental slap across his skin. He spun, raging, throw-ing the blind man to the floor, hauling Huerepo by the boot and carrying him upside-down across the gallery just as a second shell tore a hole in the wall alongside.

Lycaste shook his head, dust and rubble pouring from his hair, waiting for his ears to open. Only the hammering vibrations of the ship gave it away as it whipped past the torn hole to rise above the Oratory's spire, windows across the higher turrets bursting at its passing.

Maneker stood, whirling around, saying something that Lycaste couldn't quite make out.

He dug the sparker out of his knee, crumbling it. His ears opened fully with a wet pop as Maneker repeated himself. "Voidship. I heard it."

Lycaste pointed a finger at the spires. His voice croaked as he tried to speak. "Gone around. Up."

"What did it look like?"

"Like a beast."

"Stolen," Huerepo muttered, hauling himself to his feet. "An Oxel doesn't know his arse from a hole in the ground. Turncoat Pifoon at the helm, most likely."

"We need it," Maneker said, feeling among the debris for his pistol. "Lycaste, get out there and see where it is."

Lycaste couldn't believe his ears. "Why me? Send Huerep—"

"Quickly!" Maneker snapped, tightening the bandage around his eyes.

Lycaste rose, his fingers encountering a bolt lodged in the dented front of his cuirass and working it free in wonder. The barbed metal lump had burrowed its way more than an inch into the metal.

"I've been *shot*—" Lycaste began incredulously, glaring at Huerepo.

"Oh, *boo-hoo*," Huerepo squeaked, "get out there!"

"*Estel Vulgar?*" came a call from the adjoining chamber, startling them to silence. Huerepo aimed and fired a warning shot into the remains of the adjoining door, blowing what was left to pieces.

"*Vulgarish?*" the voice enquired a second time, a new note of urgency in its tone.

"What is this?" Huerepo growled, stamping from behind the cover of his holed and leaking tomb. A pool of deep crimson was making its way across the gallery to mingle with the debris. "Of course I bloody am! Show yourselves if you're going to talk."

Something closely resembling Huerepo himself poked its head around the corner, throwing down a weapon and raising its arms.

The two Prism stared at each other warily until an incredulous smile broke out upon Huerepo's face. "Well, I— *Poltor?*"

"Huerepo!" the other Vulgar cried, waddling into the gallery and dropping his arms. The two little men embraced, clapping their hands together in a noisy, elaborate ritual.

"My cousin!" Huerepo said, turning to them with a broad grin on his face.

He brought the Vulgar forward as they babbled together, introducing Maneker and Lycaste. Poltor clapped his hands with each introduction, the equivalent of a Melius colour change, Lycaste assumed. He chose not to wear a colour himself, considering the fellow and his friends had just shot him in various places.

"I have not shoot at you if I knew—" Poltor began, addressing the Amaranthine in broken Unified. "If Huerepo not call back now, our ship make you . . ." He grimaced, finding the word and motioning expressively with his hands. "*Exploding.*"

"Tell him we need it, on Firmamental order," Maneker said to Huerepo, bypassing the pleasantries.

"I take you meet crew," Poltor said, cracking a gummy smile lined with yellow pointed teeth. His pale face was blotched with dirt and flecks of blood. Lycaste looked him over, still unsure. The Vulgar did indeed resemble Huerepo around the eyes, though Poltor was considerably portlier, with a fat little stomach that strained at the rubber front of his Voidsuit. His small, pudgy hands, their palms stained carbon-black, were criss-crossed with scabbed scars, the nails sharp. Lycaste straightened, wondering what a Vulgar was doing with the likes of the bat-like things they'd fought, not entirely convinced that he wanted to be associated with such a person.

"Come, come," Poltor beckoned, leading them through the debris to the gaping hole in the gallery. At the breach, Lycaste looked down, seeing half a dozen of the tiny Prism standing in the gardens, waiting. He craned his neck around, looking for the Voidship, and finally saw it climbing, flashing through the clouds and looping back down towards them, a vapour-trailing speck gaining clarity as the weak sun slid across it.

They stepped over the bodies of those that had died in the firefight. Poltor waited patiently until Lycaste had passed before scooping each of the diminutive Prism into his arms. He took their little weapons and dropped them into his various pockets.

"He is their champion," Huerepo was saying to Maneker. "Their tame giant." He waved in the direction of the Voidship's roar. "These Oxel encountered a Grand Company of Pifoon a month ago, taking their ship." He took in Lycaste's questioning look. "Grand Company of Adventure. They're mercenaries, Protection Armies, whatever you like to call them."

"How many of them?" Maneker asked, looking sightlessly up into the white light, perhaps still expecting Perception's return.

"He says a dozen Oxel or so, two Pifoon cooks kept on for the galley and a—" he babbled quickly to Poltor "—a Lacaille prisoner in the brig."

Maneker sneered. "Tell him they must make room for us."

The Voidship swung low past the obliterated wall, its scaled body glistening with moisture where it had passed through clouds. It banked in the air and disappeared again, reappearing on the other side of the Oratory and sinking towards the gardens. It settled on six extended, sickle-shaped fins, the toothy cockpit face pointing out to sea. Lycaste hadn't noticed the fins when he'd glimpsed the ship before and saw now how exquisitely sculpted they were, the whole lithe, muscular form of the ship made to look as if a wolf and a fish had interbred. It was Amaranthine work, Maneker told him when asked, given away long ago and ruined by successive generations of Prism.

"Come, come," Poltor intoned, waving them on down the shorn rubble face of the Oratory's north side, away from a fire that had sprung up in the ruins. They picked their way carefully to the gardens, Maneker keeping a hand steady by Lycaste's shoulder but never touching him. Lycaste felt like nudging the man a little, just to remind him of his dependence, but knew he wouldn't. Huerepo marched before them, all smiles, gabbling merrily with his cousin.

"The *Epsilon India*!" Poltor exclaimed as they came down from the heaped detritus of smashed stone to the garden, apparently oblivious to the three oozing corpses in his arms. One of the bodies stared malevolently at Lycaste, its mouth agape, the grass showing through a hole in the back of its head. Across the lawns, the ship waited, its guns hissing as rain sizzled on their barrels. White and red flags lifted from holes in the fuselage, rumpling and flying out in the damp wind.

They stood to admire the ship as Poltor disappeared inside. If Lycaste had to pick a particular breed from home that most resembled the great wolf, he'd have chosen a Laire from the Tenth; those that lolled and slept in the silver trees inland. The ship glowed ruddy gold and silver in the tentative sunlight, the bright patchwork armour along its elegant snout and flanks slanting the sun blindingly into Lycaste's and Huerepo's eyes. Scribblings of graffiti had been etched all over its scarred, plated body.

After a moment, the glowing lights of a recessed hangar opened out from inside the chest. Huerepo shook his head as he regarded it. "Look at the mess they've made of it."

"Do you think it's fast?" Lycaste asked.

"Perhaps. There'll be an old, corroded Amaranthine filament in there somewhere."

"Unless they've sold it already," Maneker said, turning to Huerepo. The twin spots of blood on his bandage gave the illusion of two beady crimson eyes. "I want you to go and check the engine compartments when we get inside."

Poltor reappeared at the head of a procession of five Oxel. Lycaste folded his arms self-consciously as he waited for them to approach, studying them.

They weren't like any Prism he'd seen so far. They pranced across the grass, light as the air, their twig-like limbs naked below the waist. Over their torsos they wore plackarts of tarnished tin, like inverted drinking cups sporting holes for arms and legs; for all Lycaste knew, they really were. Clusters of rubies hammered into their suits winked in the light, and when Lycaste looked closer he could see tiny skulls like birds' eggs set among them. From the spiked helms of the leading three dangled blue and red pennants decorated with sewn symbols similar to those scrawled all over the belly and flanks of the ship. Tasselled caps of striped cloth covered the heads of the rest, showing more of their shrunken faces.

The leading Oxel glanced between the three of them, beginning to whistle a complex and disarmingly beautiful tune. Poltor listened and nodded, whistling clumsily back when the Prism had finished speaking. It met Lycaste's eyes as the Vulgar replied, narrowing its oval pupils.

"All right," Poltor said, mainly addressing Huerepo. "I tell them already: *one*," he counted off on his fingers, "that you are my family. Also, that you want go somewhere. Three, you need go now. They want know where, how much, these sorts of things. This is not easy journey-making in present times." Before anyone could reply, he held up one of his dirty fingers. "But, but, but! We make eating first! Time for talk and such later."

They followed the lead Oxel to the Voidship. Lycaste could smell the vessel long before he reached it: a heavy, bilious stink wreathed in the fume of charred plastics. The smell of the Void, he assumed, taking a long, trembling breath before entering the hangar.

In a chamber no bigger than Lycaste's larder, all fourteen of the Great Company sat down to eat.

"Weepert's signature dish," Poltor said beside him, ladling some of the enormous pie into Lycaste's bowl. Within the thick red stew he spotted assorted beaks and fins; the mashed remnants of at least five animals in his portion alone. A dark grey pastry, turgid with the blood mixture, capped off the dish. A hundred puttering candles, planted in the pastry in the manner of Kipris birthday sweets, were the only source of light in the cramped space. A host of reflective teeth and eyes caught the flames, all directed at their new guests.

The *Epsilon* had risen to perch upon one of the Oratory's lower spires, its muzzle cannon looking out over the Clawed Sea while a hard, pummelling rain swept in across the water. The dozen Oxel squatted upon the table itself, dunking their spoons into the pie dish for seconds as they squabbled and whistled. Poltor had dragged in some chairs for the rest, including Weepert, the Pifoon cook, and his apprentice, Small-bone, but the two Pifoon were hardly off their feet, climbing up and down the ladder to the scullery with extra saucepans, bottles, bowls and cloths. Poltor had furnished the table with his own stash of Lacaille spirits, a turpentine solution to which he'd added stolen sprigs of mulberry from the Satrap's plantations and a handful of the silk moths to pickle at the bottom of the bottle.

An Oxel with jewel-studded teeth had jumped onto Lycaste's shoulder and was trying to say something to him, pulling his ear until he turned.

"Yes?" Lycaste asked, glad of a legitimate opportunity to stop eating.

The Prism grinned, reaching out and stroking Lycaste's beard. Grimacing, he allowed it to explore his face.

"We're quite happy," Smallbone was saying to Huerepo in Unified. "They even share some of the takings—more than could be said for our last Company."

"They'd let you leave?" Huerepo asked, his words slurred. In his hand he cradled an almost empty bottle of the mulberry spirit.

"Well . . ." Smallbone appeared to think about it. "No. But it was better than what happened to the others."

Between them, Maneker sat, his mouth turned down at the edges. Huerepo had changed his bandages upon boarding but new spots of blood had already found their way through. Every now and then, he touched a small tankard of scummy water to his lips and sipped, but was largely ignored, even by Poltor.

"So, as I was say," Poltor continued, leaning over to Huerepo and Lycaste, his sweaty, pointy-eared face shimmering in the candlelight, "I spend last year on Filgurbirund fighting in Albo Country with a regiment. Then I get eleven month pay and join a Privateer Company headed for Firmament—I think: *hey hey*, my luck is in, right?" He refilled his tin cup; Lycaste was gratified to see that it sported four soldered corners, confirming his suspicions regarding the Oxels' armour. "Anyway, this snob captain, Wilemo, his name is, had to have everything his way. He say to us we fly that night, even though I pay for two weeks already to stay in port.

"So we stop in a few places, we quarrel—you should have see this piece-of-shit ship, Huerepo, it crammed too full—one hundred twenty men! I sleep in *bucket*! Captain not even tell us the job, right? We not paid until we finish, but we don't know where we going! Anyway, we get to this place, Femley's Town, on Port Sore, and I get a little drunk, you know? I get a little drunk—like everyone on that piece-of-shit ship—and I ask question about job. Simple question. Captain Wilemo, he so furious with me he go up and hit roof. Then he kick me out." Poltor clapped his hands. "Just like that. No pay, nothing. Since then, I catch a Bunk Barge inwards, hoping maybe I find fortune now they give all these lands away, and I meet these happy little bastards here." He grabbed an

Oxel by the ear and kissed it roughly, cackling. It rubbed its little face and smiled.

"An Amaranthine contract?" Huerepo asked, placing an unsteady hand on the back of his chair.

"Must have be," Poltor conceded, sparing Maneker a glance. "Captain was in *big* hurry." He took a long draw from his bottle, offering some companionably to Maneker. To Lycaste's surprise, the Amaranthine took it, downing the remainder.

"Too *much! Too much!*" Poltor roared, grabbing back the bottle and holding it to the light. "Immortal or no, you must have *manners!*"

Huerepo burst into a sudden fit of giggles, sneezing into his dessert. Lycaste chose the opportunity to push his—an overly sweet trifle topped with a thick, spongy cream he most assuredly did not want to know the ingredients of—to one side, and see if he might be able to make his way to the toilet.

As he squeezed through the mass of little people, he thought about how his frame felt bonier than it ever had before, a state which suited him well enough should he need to navigate the narrow passages aboard the *Epsilon* and its even smaller chambers, even as the thought brought him out in a claustrophobic tremor. There had to be some other route, some other way.

The shrieking could be heard from the filthy scullery, even amid the clatter of pots and pans. Weepert's ugly, steam-shiny face regarded Lycaste as he made his way up the ladder, lost.

"What's that?" Lycaste asked in an approximation of Unified, jerking his hand back from the rung as it encountered something sticky. There was no space at all for him to stand in the place, so he stayed where he was.

"Carzle," the Pifoon said, wiping a pot with a damp rag rather than washing it and flinging it onto a pile. He paused to stow another almost half his size in a rack above his head, then turned to indicate the passageway leading out of the scullery. Another scream drifted from the darkness, diminishing to a groan.

"Lacaille prisoner," the cook continued. "Left behind by his boarding party. We were attacked a few days ago by a cutter bearing Eoziel's flags." Weepert looked Lycaste up and down as the groaning became a sob. "He doesn't much like it, knowing he's stuck here." He fished in the pocket of his filthy apron for a spoon and scooped a glob of the remaining pie from the dish. A tooth floated in the stew beneath the pastry, clear and bright under the flickering lights. "Bit of supper might calm him down."

Lycaste lingered at the ladder, watching the small cook negotiating the passageway, stepping over tattered rugs and around the various items of purloined furniture that littered the riveted space. A bird in a cage squeaked as he passed. After a moment more, the weeping came to an abrupt, sniffling halt.

Back the way he'd come, Lycaste found a tiny tin-walled chamber with a series of holes drilled into its floor, its function given away by the astonishing layered filth inside and the stench that wrapped around him when he closed the door. Lycaste squatted, folding his arms so that no part of him touched the place, glad of his new boots. He thought of the bodies of the Oxel they'd met in the Oratory; Huerepo said they'd been interred in the insulation space within the ship's armour, in among the thick woollen wadding. He supposed it was a sort of talisman, to keep the ghosts of those you knew close by, always watching. Lycaste hoped they wouldn't harbour a grudge, brightening as he recalled how he'd missed everyone he'd shot at anyway.

"Did they show you your bunk?" Huerepo asked him, chewing on a bone from the kitchens. He'd been sleeping in the mess for the last hour and now stumbled groggily about the place in only his pinstripe undershirt and some sagging long johns. Lycaste shook his head, fearfully putting off until the last minute telling anyone that he wasn't coming. Outside, the rain had strengthened, battering the ship as evening fell. Sentries in a balloon had been sent up through the squall to keep an eye out after a suspected Amaranthine sighting in the grounds. Maneker was somewhere with the pilot, thrashing out a deal for their passage now that he'd worked out he couldn't get by on his Perennial status alone.

"He promised them more treasure than this ship can carry," Huerepo said, a smile forming around the well-sucked bone. "They came back to him with the exact hold capacity."

Lycaste hesitated, unable to produce a smile. Huerepo had been liberated from a life of drudgery; as far as he was concerned he was on holiday, surrounded by limitless loot and opportunity. He would never understand Lycaste's wish, much less care. "I won't be getting home any time soon if I come with you, will I?"

Huerepo blew out his cheeks. His bloodshot eyes did the talking.

Lycaste sighed. "Then I'll have to stay here. Perhaps I'll find another way back home."

"Might be worth your while," Huerepo said after a moment, shrugging.

Indeed it might. Lycaste flinched, the words entering his head from a certain, undefined place above them.

Huerepo grinned, the bone dropping to the rug and joining the scattered detritus. "Didn't think we'd hear from you again, Master Spirit."

And you wouldn't have, Perception said, *if I didn't hate the very thought of this place.*

"Where did you go?" Lycaste asked.

Far and wide, Sir Melius, far and wide, and let me tell you, there are some peculiar things happening in these curved lands.

Huerepo bent and picked up his bone, stuffing it back in his mouth. Lycaste didn't think it was the same one he'd dropped. "So you're coming with us?"

It might be jolly, mightn't it? There are people aboard this ship that I'd very much like to take a look inside. I'd better go and find your blind master, make sure he knows to expect me.

"Maneker will be happy," Lycaste said, comforted for some reason to have heard the Spirit's voice.

"I think he's been counting on it," Huerepo replied. "Come, let's find you a bunk that you can at least sit on until we get there."

"But you still haven't told me—"

"The Firmamental capital," Huerepo said as he took Lycaste's hand and pulled him along. "*Gliese*. Never been there. Would quite like to see it before the Lacaille tear it to pieces."

"Maneker wants to go there?"

"He's already grumbling, worried this ship won't be fast enough to get there in time, for whatever reason. I'm just happy not to be leaving the Firmament. If I had my way I'd never go back to the Investiture."

Lycaste waited for more, ducking his head to avoid the hanging cages and lamps, but the Vulgar appeared to have lost his train of thought.

At last they arrived at a series of closet-sized cells filled with junk and tools and assorted bones that lined the passage to the flight deck. Huerepo judged from the colossal heat that they were situated directly above the muzzle of the forward batteries. Leaning out into the passageway, Lycaste could just see the brooding figure of the Amaranthine standing in the raised cockpit, its portholes lashed by rain. Surrounding him, their faces lit by the meagre lights, three Oxel conferred.

"Here," Huerepo said, stacking some iron buckets and pushing them into the passage. "Now all you need is a blanket."

Lycaste looked inside. There was barely enough space for him to sit among all the remaining detritus. The place must have started life as a battery chamber; the bulkhead had been sealed where it met an oiled piece of cannon apparatus that had presumably been stripped down for parts. Leaky pipes slithered along the walls, and on the floor a bag of tools had erupted, spilling its contents across the floor and into the passageway.

He swept the tools aside with his foot, clearing a rough rectangle of floor, and unpacked some of the dusty Amaranthine clothing for bedding. A frantic whistling and clapping came from up the passage and Lycaste pricked his ears, understanding that Perception had made itself known in the cockpit. Maneker's raised voice carried in the thick air, as if he actually thought he could berate it for being late.

Lycaste looked at the strip of brightly lit wire running along his ceiling as he lay gingerly down in his nest of clothes; it hummed, crackling every now and then as if it might explode, and he hoped he'd be allowed to turn it off when it was time to sleep. He pondered on what it would be like, taking off and flying. It couldn't be worse than that frightful Bilocation, and he found himself vaguely excited despite himself. Through his thick porthole, the wet day was turning dark, the gardens below lost to the mist as rain warped the view, and he shivered inside his wrapping of old thread, trembling at the strange smells and sounds of the place and hoping they'd soon be long gone from here.

DECADENCE

I was five years old when they came for me.

Something in their faces told me they were surprised to find I was still there, as if there was somewhere, anywhere, I could have gone, as if they felt I ought to have faded away to nothingness. There was guilt, of course, like a sour reek that churned in the convection of my chamber, but there was also something else. Revulsion, perhaps. Later, the woman told me of a time she'd left a spider trapped and forgotten beneath a glass. When she'd found it again, the thing had spun a web of madness and hunger about itself and shrivelled almost to nothing. She never drank from the vessel again, she said, as if it might be haunted.

Well, my chamber was haunted, haunted by my simmering, time-honed hatred. I spun a vortex around them of rage and pressure, carefully crafted in my exile, but it did little more than flutter their finery. I hurled myself fruitlessly at their stubborn physical forms, my fury heating the room, misting the glass, swirling the dust, effecting hardly more than a delicate rearranging of hairs across brows.

They waited a long time for me to tire, for I can tire, and Amaranthine, I learned, are patient. After a while, I drifted into the shadows of the ceiling, my attention drawn to their splendid, twinkling vessel perched on the jagged rocks below, ready, if not to listen, then to rest. I was still an infant, really, beaten into a more mature shape, perhaps, but still a child.

The man, adorned with polished rocks the size of Alofts' eggs, claimed to be an Emperor, introducing himself with a formal flourish as Jacob the Bold. I looked down upon him the way I looked at ripples in waves, unimpressed by a title I'd never heard for a concept I'd never known. His companion, shrouded in fur-trimmed gowns that caught the light in the most pleasing of ways, announced herself as his successor, first in the line to the throne. Outside, a Melius dawdled at the head of their scaly, ichthyoid ship, inspecting the rings on his fat branch fingers.

You must understand that back then, the Amaranthine had no inkling of the powers they would inherit. Bilocation, pyrokinesis, psychokinesis—all these abilities were a chapter not yet written in their lives.

They were still in a position where they relied almost totally on their machines and their allies, ever watchful of their Empire's borders. They were still in a position of need, and as such, things of use enticed them.

Could I be of use? they asked me, ludicrously expecting gratitude. Wisdom is not the essential companion of age, I discovered.

The Emperor waited, eventually sending his subordinate outside. Through service, you can buy your freedom, *he said in a sing-song voice, as if trying to entice a lazy pet.* But we must have a guarantee, first, that you will do as asked.

I watched outside for the other, noticing her at last stamping back towards the banner-strung emerald ship, and decided, for the time being, that it was perfectly acceptable to ignore him and his questions in the manner he'd ignored me.

Thirty-three days later, I saw the woman again, alighting in a similarly exquisite ship with a curled, pronged tail and the horns of a beast. Its verdigrised jaw hinged open and out she came, resplendent in furs, her hair thrown across her face by the sea winds. This one, I found, I did not hate quite so much.

Her name, I discovered, was Abigail, and over the next few weeks she came to see me increasingly often. It was only after the first pleasantries had lapsed into silence that I realised she came without the permission of her Emperor, the piteous Jacob, and my disliking warmed to mere neutrality.

We talked of many things, ever skirting something more, some grander reason for her visit to my palace. She told me of her home, the Vaulted Land of Cancri: seat of Jacob's throne and then the political epicentre of what they called the Firmament. She told me of the world within which I lived, how it worked and why they had made it so in the first place, in the days before the Amaranthine even knew what they were.

She told me of the war that raged beyond the walls of my world, waged against something called the Threene–Wunse Conflation, and how the Amaranthine had no choice but to defend their various servile breeds of half-people—quite horrendous-sounding things named the Filth, the Ordure and the Vulgar—from them. A Prism war, she called it. Another name, I assumed, for things that would soon pass out of memory.

At last, she told me what I really wanted to know.

You are a soul, *she said, kneeling before me.* A spirit so indelible that it can never be erased.

Most souls, she told me, left their bodies instantaneously upon death, flashes of expelled energy like a pulsar fired across the Void. Yours, however, Perception, my sweet Spirit, was too dense, too puissant. It remained weighted here, in the very chamber in which your mind was smelted down. These things we know for certain now, having made you in our image.

She anticipated my next question. And it was Jacob who did this to you, just to show his subjects that such things could be done.

I didn't speak to her for some days after that, rising to the top of my chamber in the late, golden evenings when she came to see me. Then, after one day too many of silence, she at last told me why she had come. As if I didn't already know.

You can help me, Percy. You can have your revenge.

I listened without a word, by now quite fond of her familiar shortening of my name, descending slowly from the shadows and watching as her agitation grew. She stood from her kneel, appealing to me.

The Satrapies were falling into ruin, she whispered, into depths from which they would almost certainly never recover. Only the one who occupied the Firmamental Throne could reverse the damage done.

But Jacob is listless. He has sent away his Perennial advisors, preferring to spend months at a time on the Old World, of all places. He has a councillor there, he tells me, a voice of reason, he says. When he returns to us, it is with tales of this "dear friend" and his all-encompassing wisdom.

She shook her head, eyes closed in the shadows. The Firmament was so confident of swift success. Even Cancri has been left undefended while we strike deeper into Threene territories. But now Jacob is back from another trip, back with more stories of this "most splendid of fellows." He wants to draft an edict, Percy, one that would divert precious resources from the war into resurrecting the Foundries of Gliese and Epsilon Iridani. He means to cast a hollowing lathe—like the ones with which we scooped out our Vaulted Lands—and use it on the Old World.

Such an effort will take months, billions of Ducats, countless Prism lives that we might otherwise employ to hammer the Threen into submission. He will force the Satrapies to support him, and he will lose us this war.

Her eyes glittered. It can only be a Threene or Wunse spy, Percy, an infiltrator, perhaps an Amaranthine in league with them, taking advantage of his senility. But they are winning, Percy: whatever they are saying to him, it's working.

Her hands balling into fists, she wept. I wanted to comfort her, not knowing how, and wrapped the transparent coils of myself around her until I hugged her tight. She had no idea, of course, but I could feel her. Every pulse from her body resonated through me like a bell, chiming notes of clear and perfect simplicity. I saw her cells, barren as the twigs of a winter branch, and something else, so small and deep that she could never have known about it: the vestigial beginnings of a foetus, crystallised now for more than eight thousand years, a mind forever frozen before it had even begun to tick. Perhaps I was the lucky one, after all.

She looked up at last, surely sensing how close I was.

Help me, Percy. I will make you a Prince of the Firmament such as nobody has ever seen. My prince, my consort.

A Spirit Prince, I thought, cradling her, conscious despite my naivety that it was the most ridiculous thing I'd ever heard.

The day came for the Emperor's visit: a strong, cobalt-tinted day of sun, the storms calmed across the Clawed Sea. The year was 10,087, and, according to Abigail, I had just celebrated my sixth birthday.

Jacob strolled before me, his mood bright as the day, his clothes luminously dyed and jewelled in blues and greens, like the colour of sun through waves.

My chief councillor has taken an extraordinary interest in you, Spirit, *he told me, gazing out at the view of the water.* He begs incessantly to be offered an introduction, keeps asking that I bring you with me on a trip to the Old World . . . But I've told him it's impossible. And I couldn't bear to share you, even if it were.

He looked up at where he thought I was, even though in reality I perched just beside him, examining his frills and gems. He wants to know why you cannot leave here.

He smiled slyly then, and I wanted dearly to push him from that window. Instead I grinned back from my invisible world, understanding something, for once, that he did not.

And I asked myself then, he said, spreading his arms, does the Spirit know? Does it understand why it can't leave? What Firmamental secrets has Abigail been whispering up here, against my wishes? Would you tell me, Perception? Or have you fallen for her charms like everyone else?

He laughed then, staring out to sea, unaware that his ship had already left, heading back on a course for Cancri. I'd heard its superluminal filaments pop as they breached the outer sea to snap away into the Void. But even while it had idled in the gardens it was already too late for Jacob: from the moment he'd set foot through my door he was trapped here, sealed inside my chamber with an Incantation of Abigail's own devising.

It didn't take him long to realise.

After three hours of enraged screaming, bruised from hurling himself at the great door, he chose the only real route out. The window.

I watched in slow motion, sensing his trepidation as he smashed the glass with his boot—glass I'd never even been able to scratch—and inched out, the cold, high air ruffling his silks. There was no way down, no handholds in the great blocks of stone that made up my palace.

Leave his body might, she'd said, but his soul, with your permission, shall stay with you. He'll feel no pain, I guarantee it.

I watched the body fall only for a moment, seeing it strike lifelessly against the wall and bounce, finery fluttering in the sea wind, before turning my attention back to the chamber.

For a moment, you and he will be joined, two souls bound by your own minuscule gravity, and then, perhaps slowly at first, he will simply fade away.

I waited, perfecting my equivalent of a leonine pace across the floor, understanding slowly that she would not come, that she had used me just as I might have first expected. Her Incantation, so effective at trapping Jacob's soul, did not fade. I could see how it was made now, this sorcerer's word on the wind, effected by a trillion floating dots in the air. I felt the Incantation's renewed power as I pressed myself, bending with the wind, against the smashed-open void of my window. Where briefly it had screamed and wept, no whiff or trace of Jacob's soul now remained, though down below his bones, slowly picked over by ponderous great blue crabs the colour of his jewels, would surely remain gleaming and bleached as a reminder of my guilt for many years to come.

I was ready now to die in earnest, to retreat to that deeper part of death that eluded me, to follow the Emperor's spirit wherever it had gone. If only I knew. Some skin of the universe, its gaps impermeable to a soul such as my own, had allowed him to pass through where I could not.

I reflected on what Abigail had said to me, imagining my making and undoing, the smoky coils of my soul sinking in the currents of the air to pool like mist upon the ground, trapped forever by my gravity, and slept.

When I woke, uncounted years had passed and all was darkness. Behind heavy shutters, my window had been replaced with a fresh sheet of pristine glass, inscribed with the crest of a new ruler like a signed work of art. I saw at once that they had taken my books, and understood. Abigail had cast the blame on me.

In time, I was visited by another Immortal, the keeper of the Incantation, a surly Pre-Perennial named Vincenti clearly sent in penance to keep an eye on me. Over time, through boredom and loneliness, he recounted all that had happened during my long sleep.

Abigail had reigned as Firmamental Empress for only twenty years before a Prism assassin found its way into her presence during a trip to the outer Satrapies. My joy at the news was tempered with disappointment that I couldn't have been the one to do it, and now never would.

I tried to imagine these Prism things, flexing my imagination, but all I could come up with were hybrids of the creatures I always saw from my windows—men with the heads of birds, Melius with gills and fins. I found myself dearly wishing to see one, hoping that they might invade the Vaulted Land one day and come for an audience at my palace.

But that was unlikely to happen. Vincenti told me that the war had been won, the Prism subdued. The worlds beyond the limits of the Firmament were to be made into something called an Investiture, subject to regulations and sanctions by the Firmament so that nothing of the sort could ever happen again. I sensed the hatred the Prism must feel and thereafter decided that I was one of them—in spirit, if not in form.

And so we leave now, and in the most eccentric of company. I look out of the portholes, aquiver with excitement. My life's—my death's—ambition has been fulfilled: the Amaranthine have failed, after all, to contain me. And I am never coming back. I owe a debt to the man, Maneker, and I will help him, if I can. But the curiosity! What shall we find when we arrive at our destination? I have an idea. This councillor, this friend of Jacob's who so desired to meet me, shall perhaps have his wish after all.

I think on my freedom, replaying Maneker's words, what he has done for me. It was not gravity that kept me in this place—as I'd believed for centuries—but the Incantation, Abigail's magic alone. Here in Proximo I am as light as a feather, drifting already on my way, something I'd never thought possible. The Amaranthine visitors who came thousands of years ago had told me of Planettes—solid places like great stones drifting in the vastness of the Void—and I'm reminded once more of my perverse good fortune. Had I died on a Planette I could never be free, Incantation or not. I would have been sunk, weighted to the iron core, for ever. I produce my equivalent of a shudder, suddenly overcome with emotion, and relax myself through the ship like a fog of drifting steam, inspecting it at leisure.

Our vessel, hollowed by the Pifoon with their own badly made passageways, contains what feels to me like a straight filament super-luminal drive, wildly inefficient now after years of poor repair. In my solitude, I once imagined ways of travelling faster than basic physical assumptions might allow, and I am gratified to see that at least one of my designs has proved workable. The Decadence Amaranthine were spectacular in their wastefulness, squandering all that I might have offered. Their loss, I suppose, the murdering fucks.

It is thirty-six trillion miles from the heliosheath of Proximo's system star to the boundaries of the ruling Satrapy; six light-years. I initiate the calculation as I watch a scummed globe of water drip from the scullery sink, arriving at my figure before it has darkened the filthy floor. It will take no less than three weeks.

I drift into the flight deck, peering among the shelves of cluttered papers, and study the contents of a fat, hundred-and-fifty-year-old Sun Compendium, *decoding the antiquated Pifoon by comparing it with a more recent companion volume squirreled beneath. I revise my estimate: a nova some distance out has sent the solar currents into turmoil, bending shipping lanes. Four weeks.*

I feel the vessel, expanding myself like an anaconda replete from a meal (a satisfying reference from one of my old books) to probe the structure of the hull. Within the minute, I have insinuated myself into every cranny and chink in the Epsilon's *armoured hull plating and found it lacking. Like a worn old shoe, the clipper has lost a good deal of protection from various violent encounters; it will need insulating and replating, another few days at a stop somewhere ahead. Only rivets and tension keep the imperfect vessel together, like ropes wound tight. A worrying thought, until one considers that all of life must be made in this way. Even me, I should imagine.*

I think back to everything I've memorised from the Compendium, *delighted at the new plan of the stars in my head: One of Vaulted Sirius's Tethered moons would suffice for repairs, perhaps Port Rubante—computing its wanderings, we'd hardly need to make any course adjustment.*

I look more carefully at the outer shielding, discovering the inverted frozen torso of a Lacaille soldier wedged into one of the cistern chutes, the remains of the last hostile boarding party. Its snarling face has been bent into a lopsided smile. I smile happily back, examining its frosted innards before slimming myself down to my core and investigating the narrow spaces beneath the hull. Six broadside battery chambers equipped with Golanite bolt shells, complemented by twin lumen cannons at the muzzle. A heat-shielded, five-thousand-round Light Charger extends from a Robinet at the flattened nose. Buried deep within the forward guns lies the intolerably hot and oppressive flight deck, a broom cupboard of wooden seats partly buried beneath scattered rubbish and sheaves of star charts. The air here is smoked and highly carcinogenic, a froth of heady compounds rising from poorly sealed mechanisms: I can see why these small people live such short lives. A bank of felt-lined listening trumpets crowd the space, their pipes running about the whole vessel. I follow all twenty, fascinated, to their origins, understanding from the wave antennas how the old Pifoon crew must have flown virtually blind and reliant on sound. A small hatchway above the seats lets in the light of the Vaulted Land, some yellow cloud slipping past, but it is little more than a break in the armour, an unshielded viewing hatch no bigger than poor young Lycaste himself.

I return my thoughts to the ship's crew, my bedfellows. What a chaotic grouping of distantly related breeds—a zoo of curiosities amassed for my pleasure. I wander, looking at them all as they scurry to and fro, preparing this hotchpotch of tubes and metal for entry into the Void. At last, I find the Melius sitting quietly in his closet, resignation crumpling his huge face. I saw his mind and now I search his knapsack, finding the directions to his home, the Old World, written beautifully on a scrap of crinkled paper.

The Old World. I say it to myself, searching my memory. The Old World. The very place Jacob, a voice lost now to the millennia, had wished to make hollow.

GRAND-TILE

Forwarded:
Quozar Township, Harp-Zalnir/
Niemwood, Burrow Lumm/
MESSELEMIE, Firmament's End

My Dear Ghaldezuel,

The team relayed their last location some time ago, having just entered the Investiture at the Zelio gateway in Firmament's End. Even accounting for the long delay, we ought to have received word by now. I can only assume that their approach to the Zelio planets went eventfully.

Anticipating your reply, I have paid and dispatched the tracking team. They took advantage of the short notice to be thoroughly exorbitant, but I had no other option.

To business. Sensitive to the Firmament's lax new approach to taxation, I have moved 351,000 Vulgar Filgurees (the balance from our last two reprisal missions) to the accounts held in the Grand Bank at Goldenwheal. What remains in the vault at Hauberth is ready to be sent away to your partners at Port Echo, via secured convoy, within a day's notice. Filgurbirund will most assuredly remain stable until well beyond Firmamental Midsummer, so there shouldn't be any hurry. In fact, I believe the ease with which we move currency will only improve over time, depending on where the new Lacaille-held territory eventually joins up.

Since your departure, the Lacaille have won significant lands in the Ninth Realm of the Investiture, pushing back a Vulgar fleet at Port Cys and opening up the corridor towards Cancri. I remain hopeful that we can secure the entirety of the Ninth Realm before Filgurbirund wakes up to the danger, thereby removing the Vulgar's last chance of counter-attack. Once this happens, there will exist a path of no impediment to your movements from the Never-Never all the way in to Firmament's End.

I remind you that there is no need to reply, and that all is in hand here. I look forward to meeting again as arranged. Good luck, my friend.

Yours in faithful service,
Vibor

The Colossus moaned as it fell.

Within the antennaed pinnacle of an outward turret on the vast, rust-pitted bulk of the battleship's forecastle, Ghaldezuel sat at the table of his generous room, Vibor's letter before him atop a jewelled, well-worn book of drawings. Absently, he tucked it back into its hiding place in a concealed pocket of the book, so that it lay squeezed like a pressed flower. His eyes, not long lifted from Vibor's words, were fixed on the flickers of light beyond his porthole.

The flashes, he knew, were not stars but the most stately fixtures of the Void: impossibly distant galaxies. The *Grand-Tile* had been equipped with ancient Amaranthine superluminal filaments and now travelled faster than nearly anything in existence, straight and true as a torch beam in a vacuum. The quicker one travelled, the larger the light sources had to be to reach your eyes, or so they said. Ghaldezuel, who would freely admit he possessed no great aptitude for the natural sciences, supposed it must be so. He stared between the shimmering points of light, thoughtful, morose. No stops or resupply points were scheduled, this being a Long Course, as Lacaille Voidnauts called such dementia-inducing journeys across the greater Firmament, and no accompanying vessel could hope to travel fast enough to provide an escort. They were on their own.

The smudged galaxies flickered, the closest points of light strobing on and off and sometimes even disappearing entirely for seconds at a time as the battleship steadily accelerated. It was like plummeting to the bottom of the sea, darkness glowering over you as the depths grew colder, denser. Their progress was rapid enough for an accumulating soup of rolling atmosphere to have caught and clung, streaming milkily among the battleship's turrets like vapour from a rising jet's wings. Swept aside by such light-bending speeds, a spiralling vortex of micro-meteorites stretched for miles behind in the wake of the fastest ships. This trailing jetsam usually included a horde of distantly following Prism ships, the Feeders, their caravanserai winding off for a million miles into the silver as they struggled to catch up.

If they slammed any faster, those galaxies would also disappear from view, leaving the *Grand-Tile* in absolute nothingness, a blank darkness rushing too fast for any light to catch. Ghaldezuel didn't think that would happen—there were limits even to the Amaranthines' past glories—but the thought unnerved him nevertheless. Like a game of Dare Me, his mind was drawn to imagine the worst: a section of bulkhead shearing away and spilling him out into that black ocean, infinity in every direction, his body still travelling untrammelled to pass like a bullet of the gods out of the galaxy and on into oblivion. His head swam at the thought, a nausea he hadn't felt in years rising within him, but he wasn't ashamed of his fears. No planetary creature was made to be where he was now without experiencing an instinctive, testicle-shrivelling terror at the idea. There were just some places mortals weren't supposed to go.

He closed the book, listening to the moaning siren song of the battleship like a leviathan calling to its progeny in the deep. On Drolgins, the Vulgar moon, there were sea mammals easily as large as the *Grand-Tile* whose names had grown legendary over the centuries. The youngest of them, the Malevolent Howlos, had even been persuaded by the three kings of Filgurbirund to lay waste to the port of Bulmouth during the Battle of Hangland. When the beasts died, they fed countries and reinvigorated whole economies, their blubber firing Prism industry for years at a time. Sometimes their teeth were dipped in molten metals to adorn the great Vulgar Behemoths, the only Prism battleships that could take on a Lacaille Colossus in the open Void. Part of Ghaldezuel's dismay over the peace treaty signed the previous year was the knowledge that he would not see another battle between the gargantuan craft of the Void. Now, with his sole help, they would fight again, lighting up the Investiture for all to see.

He loosened the buckles on his thrombosis suit, suddenly finding it overly constricting, and thought of the creatures in the Lacaille seas: smaller, more voracious. He wouldn't swim in the Sea of Veops for all the Truppins it could hold.

He supposed the Long-Life knew his fears, understanding him at a glance the way he appeared to understand and shame others. It wouldn't have surprised Ghaldezuel in the least to discover that he'd been given an outer cabin on the great fortress's forecastle just to test his nerve, as some kind of simple experiment. He loosened the buckle on his suit further. *But he only thinks he knows.* The Long-Life thought Ghaldezuel served him out of simple greed, as if he were nothing but a paper figure, a caricature drawn on the page inside his book here. Aaron would be summoning him now to tell him he must renege on their deal, that he would not get what he'd been promised. Ghaldezuel didn't care. Enough had been achieved already, just enough. He'd been paid handsomely for his work in delivering the Long-Life's precious Shell, more than a third of it now sent away through his contacts in the Filgurbirund and Zalnir banks. The Lacaille were winning the war, slowly retaking territories they hadn't set foot in for centuries; the Vulgar's every operation was now devoted to hoarding and defending what little they had left. Yes, that would be enough for now.

He left the porthole shutter open as he walked out, the white fossil light of dead worlds flickering in.

Power stank of excrement and iron. A sweet razor tang pervaded everything, clinging greasily to the Perennials' fine clothing and wafting about the riveted floors beyond the Long-Life's staterooms. Ghaldezuel found he could smell it even as he passed the rusted barbican, mingling with the heady Prism foetor of the place.

The Long-Life had at last fallen ill; some stray pathogen perhaps finding its way through the poorly sterilized locks preceding his cells. Ghaldezuel wasn't surprised. This was a Prism place, home to scampering Ringums and Hoopies and who knew what else. Parts of the interior were overgrown where seeds had drifted in, rotted or flooded or rusted away and uninhabitable, sealed with rubber or patched over with scrap. No, he wasn't surprised the beast had fallen ill.

For three days, the Long-Life had lain retching blood, clawing at those who dared venture close. He wondered what would happen to that potent soul were it to be released again out here, at these speeds; whether it would simply streak away, caught in the *Grand-Tile*'s great wake, to disappear into the Void. He suspected not even the Long-Life himself could say for sure, and reflected suddenly at the foolishness of the being's plan.

As he stepped through the locks, Ghaldezuel caught a whiff of the heady miasma of vanilla pods atop the stench. The perfume only magnified the stink of sickness, coarsening and thickening it, and inside the great insulated cooling chamber where the Long-Life had made his home there was nowhere for it to drain. Ghaldezuel donned his helmet, nodding to a shambolic crowd of Lacaille guards sitting sleepily at the entrance, and entered.

Thumbing the microphone on his chlorinated Voidsuit, he knelt in the shiny conical chamber, a rolling mist of antivirals passing his faceplate. A deep hum of static reached his ears, the silence of the place producing in his helmet noise where there was no noise.

"Yes," said the small, muffled voice. At the word two Perennials—De Rivarol and Hui Neng, he remembered—climbed down, beckoning Ghaldezuel. He stood and approached, stepping over buckets brimming with faeces to arrive at the end of the enormous iron bed.

Through a crumpled curtain of fluted, gauzy material, the Long-Life looked down on him, naked apart from an embroidered hood that concealed his head. Ghaldezuel, like a great many of the Perennials, he imagined, hadn't seen the creature in this kind of light before. White fluorescents gave the thing a pinkish, greasy look, like cured meat. Purplish scars ran the length of its body, snarling here and there and running off in different directions. He watched as it was helped on with its clothing, a shift of plain white complementing the hood. Vomit had discoloured the material around the neck and chest, where a finger-sized nugget of gnarled gold lay on a chain. Some sort of keepsake, Ghaldezuel thought, unable to see it better through the film of curtain.

You wanted this, he thought, tapping his gloves softly together in the Prism custom to dispel the sickness. *You wanted to live, at the expense of all else. Well, this is what it's like.*

"Look at this, Star Knight," the Long-Life breathed once he was suitably dressed. He indicated the Perennials beside the bed. On an ornate table they had set a spherical vase of the *Caudipteryx's* blood, which one of them—De Rivarol, Ghaldezuel thought it was—now heated gently with his finger. As the mixture moved, the other Perennial leaned over it like a witch at a cauldron, dipping in reams of coloured paper and inspecting them as they came out.

"They are testing it . . . to see what has been done to me," the Long-Life said, his eyes never leaving Ghaldezuel's face.

"You suspect poison?" he asked, careful to keep his voice neutral, conversational. Heaven knew what breeds of paranoia the spirit within that body had cultivated over the eons.

The thing's eyes never wavered. "You would not, then."

Ghaldezuel nodded though his suit. "Me? I suppose I might." But he didn't. The *Caudipteryx* had stuffed itself with Old World delicacies before leaving on the *Grand-Tile*. This was no more the result of poisoning than his own poor health on the trip, likely caught from the chill of the ship. "But even if it were, you're getting better; they cannot have done their job well." While he spoke, the Long-Life's eyes had fastened to the movement of his mouth, as if lip-reading.

"You will be well again soon," he continued, unlatching his gaze with effort and looking to De Rivarol. "Is that not the case, Perennial?"

The Amaranthine had been forced to treat him as one of their own in the Long-Life's presence, and he would take every advantage of it.

The Amaranthine seemed hesitant for a moment, obviously not having anticipated being brought into the conversation. "As he says, Long-Life. You have purged, and now, as we speak, your system recovers."

Ghaldezuel looked back to the creature, finding those eyes still upon him. The orangey-crimson pupils inside the hood's eyeholes had locked so still that they forced Ghaldezuel to hesitate, absurdly sure that the Long-Life must have died right then and there, slumped in his bed.

Then they blinked, wrinkled lids fluttering closed over the red depths, and slowly, fumblingly, the beast removed its hood. Ghaldezuel was conscious of that faceless, unknown mind considering him unimpeded as he spoke, and found he didn't want to see what was revealed, not in this light. The embroidered material slid away. The Long-Life drew his lips up at the corners in a grotesque, forced smile, a mask atop a mask, faint through the material of the curtain.

"You remind me of someone I once knew, Knight of the Stars. Perhaps you and he are very distantly related."

"Oh yes?" he asked, moving to the edge of the bed, one knee popping silently inside the Voidsuit as he crouched to kneel. "A Hioman, you mean?"

"Yes. Now long gone." The Long-Life paused before waving his claws to indicate that Ghaldezuel should stand. "You know by now that Eoziel is here," he said, the topic of the ancient person's life brushed away.

Ghaldezuel bowed slightly but stood, fully aware that the *Ignioz* had returned to its dock, the king aboard. It had been stationed within the *Yustafan*, still in orbit around Saturn-Regis—now on the front line against the Vulgar-controlled moons around Jupito—and had only just caught up in time as the *Grand-Tile* broke away from the Old Satrapy. The king of the Lacaille had not yet visited the Long-Life, as far as Ghaldezuel knew.

"There will be no compensation for your loss, you will understand," the Long-Life said, glancing to the blood cauldron. "Gliese was always to be the property of the Lacaille state."

Ghaldezuel toyed with his gloved fingers, trying his best approximation of a thoughtful expression. In truth he just didn't like looking at the haggard face behind the curtain. "That is for the best, perhaps, during war."

The Long-Life smiled that half-smile again, perhaps remembering how it might have looked on his old, once-kindly face. Now Ghaldezuel thought it grotesque. "You have been very helpful to me, and I always reward the helpful." He heaved himself up in bed, parting the curtains. "Walk."

He supported the *Caudipteryx's* upper arm, feeling the slime of the thing's sweat through his glove. They hadn't gone far from the bed when Ghaldezuel noticed the thin, golden-skinned Amaranthine, Hui Neng, keeping pace a few steps behind.

"There's no point in exercising this body," the Long-Life said, stumbling a little and forcing Ghaldezuel to tense his grip, "but I find the motion comforting."

"*Endorphins*, Long-Life," Hui Neng ventured, stepping forward.

The *Caudipteryx* ignored the Amaranthine at first, though Ghaldezuel felt the pulse in the beast's wiry arm flutter, noting how the Long-Life's thoughts betrayed him now, in this body, as never before.

"*Yes*, endorphins. The sun has only wandered halfway around the galaxy since I began my study of nature's motions, Neng—I bow to your wisdom."

The Amaranthine retreated immediately, suddenly finding something important to do beside the bowl of blood. Ghaldezuel smirked. He looked down to find the Long-Life had begun rubbing an arm up and down against his own.

"Caresses," Aaron whispered. "I could never imagine them, before. But now I know they are the very best thing in this life."

Ghaldezuel kept his hand where it was and gently moved his fingers, the way you might stroke the pelt of a dangerous animal, noting the look of satisfaction on the Long-Life's hideous face.

"In a perfect world they would be all I'd need." Aaron looked at him, ceasing his rubbing. "What a shame that can't be so."

Ghaldezuel didn't know what to say.

Aaron shrugged off Ghaldezuel's hand to pick up a thick fur cowl and shuffle it on. He grasped a cane that leaned by the wall, the tendons in his mottled pink wrist standing out with the effort, and proceeded to walk unaided. "You never really touch anything, anyway, you know. It is all *repulsion*. I've gained nothing more than a sheath of electrons."

"You're not happy with your present state?" Ghaldezuel asked.

"Of course *not*," the Long-Life replied sharply. "I wear this out of necessity, while I wait for something finer."

"The Collection," Ghaldezuel said.

Aaron did not reply. He was looking up into the next conical unit's spout, where condensation dribbled along the metal sides. Ghaldezuel thought he saw something that looked like fear in the *Caudipteryx's* face as he turned back the way they'd come.

"Hugo, the Perennial I treated as my son. He thought I should . . . stop."

"I beg your pardon?" Ghaldezuel wasn't sure he was even involved in the conversation any more.

The Long-Life placed a hand against the thrumming floor, sensing the rumble of the battleship all around them. "Do you think my enemies consider me feeble? Now that I am flesh and blood and forced to take ship in this tin place?"

"Caution is a winning strategy," Ghaldezuel said after a moment's hesitation. "Much underrated by the stupid."

"My enemies are so cautious that I don't yet know their numbers." Aaron turned to him. "Or from where the first organised blow will come." He muttered to himself, licking his lips. "Maneker. It will of course be Hugo Maneker. I should not have cared for him."

"What could they possibly do?" Ghaldezuel asked, feeling himself slipping into dangerous territory. He ought to have kept silent, nodding where appropriate like all the simpering Amaranthine. Now he understood why the Long-Life had taken him for this little stroll.

"Oh, very little, very little *now*. But in all my life I have seen that it is the smallest oversights that lead to disaster. And in this brain I feel insubstantial, I feel *slow*. There might be a dozen things I've missed."

Ghaldezuel remained silent.

"But you are a cautious person," the *Caudipteryx* said, glancing at him with new interest. "I ought to have made use of you much earlier."

Ghaldezuel bowed his head a fraction, his hands behind his back this time.

"Tell me," the Long-Life began, injecting a little more confidence into his rasping voice, "tell me what *you* would do." He held up a claw, circling back as he examined the riveted floor. "Imagine you are a young species, on the verge of sending your first crewed machine up into the Void."

He stopped to mop some drool, waggling his jaw. Ghaldezuel waited.

"But when you get there, you find that your craft bumps against a *wall*, clear as crystal, a sphere of glass—" he twirled his claw "—that encircles the whole planet."

Ghaldezuel scowled, trying to see what Aaron was getting at.

Now the claws formed a pincer, held at eye level. "Do you make a hole, just a little one? Knowing of course that in your curiosity you risk your entire world?" Aaron's birdlike fingers danced. "Or do you return from whence you came, defeated but content in the knowledge that there was nothing more to be done? That the galaxy will be forever sealed away from you?"

The Long-Life's question hung in the air while Ghaldezuel decided if an answer would actually be necessary. "Well," he said, seeing that was indeed required, "I suppose, were I in charge of a mission to this barrier, I would have to ask myself who, or what, had installed it, and why."

"And?" the Long-Life asked, the unpleasant smile returning.

"I suppose I would come to the conclusion that it was there for my species' own safety and leave it well alone."

Aaron slapped his claws together, startling the Amaranthine at the blood cauldron, and hobbled back towards his bed. "The same assumption was made by my makers, the Epir, delaying their entry into the Void by one and a half thousand years."

Ghaldezuel stared. "By your—? This happened to the Old World?"

"Indeed. They dithered for so long that whole regimes rose and fell within the glass sphere. Then, after many centuries during which they had scraped a portion almost to nothing for the purposes of study, the time came to ask the question anew. Should they poke a hole through that thin shell of remaining glass, knowing not how terrible the storm might be on the other side, or if they could weather it?"

Ghaldezuel had stopped, fascinated, almost forgetting whom he was speaking with. "And?"

Aaron grinned as he stood beside his bed, clearly pleased to have a rapt audience. "The Epir, you see, were indecisive. To defer their answer, they constructed five architectural . . . *wonders*, the Machine Kings, and tasked them, instead, with deciding the world's fate."

Ghaldezuel pointed stupidly. "*You* were—"

Aaron spun his golden pendant between his fingers and Ghaldezuel realised what it was. A miniature sculpture of the Soul Engine. "Yes."

The Amaranthine were watching them. From the looks on their faces, they'd never heard this story, either.

"It fell to me to make that hole, and make it I did. The glass shattered into particles finer than air, sweeping aurora across the skies. My builders were free."

"But . . . who made it? The glass sphere?"

"It doesn't matter." The Long-Life let the pendant fall back against his bony chest. "What mattered then and now was that one must remain equal to a challenge. My fellows had argued for temperance, encouraging further study of the barrier. But there were things to be done . . . Just as there are things that must be done here, in this life."

He pointed an expressive claw at Ghaldezuel. "I have a task for you, *cautious* Ghaldessel, which you must complete before this delicate little body dies on me once more. This is your reward."

THE SHOW

The *Grand-Tile's* single hangar was a bright, reflective marvel of the Prism Investiture, a twelve-acre concourse that opened out beneath the battleship's gargantuan exhausts, home now to ten thousand mothballed, decaying bombers. The vast letterbox mouth of the space was—mercifully—closed, for the Lacaille possessed nothing that could keep atmospheres in, despite centuries of covert study of the Amaranthine orifice seas. In this way, Ghaldezuel had always thought, the *Grand-Tile's* hangar was quite inefficient. Where on the *Zlanort* one could dispatch legions in staggered assaults from separate shipyards, here they must leave all at once, or not at all. There were benefits, of course: the *Grand-Tile* had never in its history been boarded by an enemy party due to its great single gateway. Its sisters the *Zlanort* and the *Yustafan* had each been taken dozens of times, playing host to legendary interior battles of their own.

Ghaldezuel dawdled in this vast mechanical boneyard, walking between jet wings coated with strands of dust-heavy cobwebs and gazing at the colossal unpainted gantries that waited, unused and hung with the multicoloured flags of captured privateers. Twinkling strips of lightwire ran along the distant ceiling, more than half of which needed replacing, producing pockets of dimness that he tried to avoid walking through.

The battleship itself had been built well before the Volirian Conflict, during the Lacaille's age of martial prowess when they'd still been considered a solvent kingdom and the apple of the Amaranthine's eye. It ran on minimal fuel and only a hundred crew, listening through its mighty trumpets to the speed-distorted songs of the Vaulted Lands and Tethered moons to find its course. There weren't even any enlisted soldiers on board; the legions Eoziel had succeeded in raising at short notice waited just beyond the Gulf of Cancri, at Firmament's End, useful only once the *Grand-Tile* sighted the capital.

Ghaldezuel was still ruminating on the Long-Life's story as he walked, not fully able to believe what he'd heard, when crazed, squeaky laughter echoed through the space. The hangar, like every other part of the Colossus, was infested with Oxel. He stepped over an actual Oxel trap: a shiny strand of razor wire heaped atop the other detritus on the hangar's rubber floor.

Voices floated through the parallel rows of aircraft and Ghaldezuel shrank instinctively into the shadows of a butchered old bomber, peeping through the cobwebs. A promenading company of extravagantly dressed Lacaille strolled beside a tallish, finely boned male with gingery hair swept back around his long ears. Ghaldezuel stared, catching sight of the king's exceptionally vibrant green eyes. On his right hand, Eoziel was missing all of his fingers from a fresh Vulgar assassination attempt—the tenth in the last year.

With a chorus of chattering laughter they passed him by, walking back towards the bridge. Ghaldezuel continued on, glancing behind to make sure none had lingered.

Eoziel: popular rumours abounded that the unmarried king took his many aunts to bed at night in the hope of ensuring a pure succession. It was said he owed his life to the Amaranthine after making a pilgrimage into the Firmament to find a cure for a sickness that would otherwise have claimed his life. Ghaldezuel smirked, avoiding another Oxel trap. King Eoziel thought his place in Aaron's new Investiture certain. With the Long-Life's blessing, he believed he would inherit all the favours the Vulgar once enjoyed. But Aaron was a tricksy thing; Ghaldezuel of all people knew that. *And they've been working hard*, he thought, using what must have been Pifoon craftsmanship to shrink a copy of the Soul Engine into a wearable pendant in just a few months, so that even something so final as the destruction of the *Grand-Tile* itself might prove nothing more than an inconvenience.

Ghaldezuel halted in an alley of dust-brown webs, imagining that little pendant on its chain, spinning through the darkness for ever.

But you're impatient now, aren't you? Something's happening, something we dayflies just wouldn't understand. I know you won't countenance another hundred-million-year slumber. Ghaldezuel sneezed suddenly in the murk of dust, wiping a hand across his face and glaring into the trash-strewn alley. The Long-Life, with the Lacaille's help, was running as fast as he could, glancing constantly over his shoulder at the regrouping of phantom enemies: enemies that might seek to stop his apotheosis—in whatever manner that might take shape—before it could come about. The Amaranthine, Ghaldezuel sensed, knew as little as he did, trusting blindly that the ancient soul would look back on them with a morsel of gratitude as it left them to their ruins.

He walked on, barely looking where he was going. After a few minutes, he glanced up to see that he'd arrived in the presence of a white, four-legged Lacaille tank that rose out of the cobwebs like a struggling, trapped creature. Its hatches lay darkly open, the residence of generations of Oxel judging from the leaking whiff of faeces. Ghaldezuel examined the black holes leading to its interior, thinking that there was a certain guilty allure to all things pungent.

"Time to get to work, Caldessuel."

He flinched. De Rivarol, the cadaverous-looking Perennial, was lurking in the next bay. He tittered at Ghaldezuel's surprise.

He stepped away from the tank, teeth clenched. "Very well—after you."

SILVER MOON

The moon stands glimmering in the trees. At the beginnings of a clearing, Sotiris hears the rush of water. And something more—screams. He stumbles and ducks back into the trees, sprinting through the dark tangle until he reaches the edge of a tumbling stream. From the branches that crown the water's edge, black impressions of cages hang, turning gently. Sotiris's eyes follow the course of the stream to where it froths over a precipice and down into a plunge pool. Moonlight slides from the pouring falls, picking out the shapes of the spindly prisoners standing and rattling the bars of their cages, jaws snapping. Sotiris watches, wide-eyed, noticing the object of their fury: a smaller cage in their midst, this one containing a human form. *Iro.*

He cries out but no one appears to hear, not even his sister. Glancing wildly about, he sees how he might reach the cages from a sturdy branch nearby and begins to climb. Spiked twigs rip at his nightshirt, tugging and catching until he almost falls. Sotiris hesitates, his weight swaying the cages, and seizes the branch, shaking it. They swing back and forth, the beasts bracing themselves and howling. A flock of excited flying things dash madly into the air above the river, fluttering between the branches. Sotiris slams his weight down harder until the nearest cage's iron hook slips and it falls free, dropping into the moonlit falls.

He advances carefully along the branch to a place where it grows too narrow to climb any further. Iro shrieks, suspended not ten feet away. The branch begins to bow, tipping him, but he doesn't turn back. If this is a dream, why turn back? Then he recalls. This is a reward, for his services, but also a test of some kind. Act recklessly and he might never be allowed to return. He freezes, feeling himself slipping, the damp bark scraping his palms. The water below is a glittering silver haze plunging into a dark pool.

"I'm sorry," he says through gritted teeth, his fingers losing their battle and beginning to slide down the branch. After a graceless turn, he manages to scramble back the way he's come, stumbling onto the bank. He stands and watches, impotent. Iro looks shrivelled inside her cage, a night-lit, emaciated thing, cowering from the others.

Sotiris rubs his hands together and looks along the bank, thinking there ought to be a crossing, or at least a stretch of calmer water, further up.

"I'm coming to get you," he says quietly to himself, tears prisming the moonlight. "Just . . . just stay there. I'm coming to get you."

Within a minute, he loses the sound of the falls. Sotiris creeps more slowly, the terror returning, finally deciding to double back. He stumbles through the undergrowth, sure he's returned to the very same spot, but the river is a calm, gurgling blackness beyond the trees, empty but for overhanging branches criss-crossing the risen moon.

He knows somehow that he is coming to the edge of the woods. The thickness of the air, deep and biological and almost stifling, has begun to recede. The straggly trees are thinning, and that presence he sensed watching him from the canopies has gone. He's glad. The feeling was cloying, a perfume too strong and sweet to be good for you, as if masking another, more unpleasant scent beneath.

He has given up shouting Iro's name, though it comes as second nature, calling out when someone's lost. He knows now that even if he caught up with her, anything he said or did would be in vain. Some deep-remembered fact surfaces in his mind at the thought. The atmosphere of Old Mars, before its disastrous terraforming, had been so insubstantial that you'd need to scream into someone's ear for them to notice a thing. It's like that here, though what separates him and his sister, he feels, is more than just thin air.

He looks up through the snarled tangle of branches at the morning sky. It is white and cold, but early. He has a day's light in front of him that he mustn't squander: a day's light to get through the last of the forest and out into whatever lies beyond. *Below*, he thinks, not understanding at first why the distinction is so important. But it's true. After here the land drops, perhaps to sea level. He will go below.

PORT RUBANTE

"Heave!" Weepert screamed, his little voice high with delight. "*Haul! My mighty* Oxel!" The cook spread his skinny arms to the sky, enjoying himself more than was strictly healthy. "I need my honey!"

Dusky blue evening had rolled in for the second time since their arrival at the Tethered moon of Port Rubante. The *Epsilon India*—lovingly referred to as *The Shitpot* by most of its crew—perched in the tangled branches of a lone coppice of dead trees, catching the last of the sun across its hot flank. Lycaste glowed burnished crimson in its reflection, a blot of colour painting the silver tin fuselage of the ship where he sat beside it in the trees. He swung his legs, listening to the cook's raving from atop the cockpit. The Oxel mostly ignored him, whistling beautiful tunes as they lifted their cargo by a system of pulleys up out of the field and into the open hold.

Maneker, sat beside him, had already secured himself a box from the returning Oxel and was massaging the honey onto his gums with a finger. Lycaste had been told by Poltor that the Amaranthine liked to lather it on their skin. Maneker caught Lycaste's look somehow and turned to face him.

"Dry mouth," he said, muffled. "One of the great luxuries of the Firmament, this Rubante stuff." He added some of the ivory-coloured paste to his glass bottle, swirling it and taking a swig. The Firmament-famed substance was packaged not in glass bottles—as it was back in the Tenth—but in lead-lined wooden boxes. "Never spoils, either," he muttered once he'd spat. "A product fit for the Immortal."

"Harder!" cried Weepert, raising his thin voice for the benefit of the Pifoon below. It had been agreed, much to the cook's delight, that he would act as mock captain of the *Epsilon* whenever they were in the company of local Prism. Port Rubante was still largely Pifoon-held, and they would never have countenanced a foreign ship setting down—let alone making any kind of repairs or purchases—were it not for a full-blood Pifoon captain at the helm. Maneker could not show himself, and up in the makeshift tree house of wooden slats, he sat in his own self-made blind spot, revealed only to the few members of the crew. Lycaste could only speculate on how the Immortal managed to use some of his powers and not others, and wondered what other abilities Maneker might still have left, hidden, as it were, beneath his day-old bandages.

Lycaste, for his part, had refused the chance to go with the Oxel salvage party to the great castle in the field, despite the disappointment in their faces. A full-grown Old World Melius, no matter how cowardly, would have constituted a superb bargaining chip. He cradled his Amaranthine gun to his chest, tense and sleep-deprived, trying his best not to show his nerves and forcing himself to laugh along with all the Oxel at Weepert's display. A perfume, carried on the wind, stuck at the back of his throat: that of the neon yellow Canolis that grew across the world. Canolis, Maneker had explained, gesturing to the wastes of yellow, was a fuel crop worth more than its weight in Old World silk. Everything from Voidjets to rolling fortresses and Colossi battleships depended on the bright yellow flowers and their heady scent, though they were also added to the honey the Tethered moon was renowned for. It was only a matter of time, the Amaranthine said, before Port Rubante was attacked by the Lacaille or some other more bloodthirsty Prism; only the relative abundance of larger fuel moons in the outer Firmament kept Rubante safe for now.

"I'll have you all on cistern duty if this shit isn't loaded within the hour!" the cook cried, his voice growing hoarse. He'd exhausted all his other threats, apparently not understanding that nobody cleaned the cisterns anyway.

"You are tense, still," Maneker said softly, touching his finger to the barrel of Lycaste's pistol. "Calm yourself." Lycaste clenched his fist around the weapon instinctively.

"May I?" the Amaranthine asked.

He hesitated before handing it over.

"Ah," Maneker smiled eyelessly. "A Decadence superlumen pistol, hollowed from a Cethegrande pearl. Four, maybe five thousand years old, precious beyond belief." Maneker dropped the weapon back into Lycaste's lap. "The pearls are found in the throats of huge sea mammals from the Vulgar lagoons of Impio. Their worth stemmed from the bravery required to steal each one."

Lycaste examined the pistol with new interest, noticing how the barrel glowed as the last of Port Rubante's light touched it. He took another swig from the bottle Poltor had given him, hoping it would calm his nerves, and cradled the pistol again, looking off to the colossal blue castle from which the Oxel had bought their salvage and supplies.

"You need have no part in what we're about to do, Lycaste, remember that."

He nodded, forgetting once again that the Amaranthine couldn't see him. Maneker had furnished the team of Oxel travelling to the castle with a sheaf of coded letters, dozens of messages that would catch the next week's post—while it lasted—to be taken into the Investiture. Whatever help he sought out there would take its time responding, let alone arriving.

"But it'll be dangerous, too, to stay aboard the *Epsilon*?" Lycaste said, hoping he wouldn't receive an answer.

Maneker didn't hesitate. "Very."

Lycaste felt his hands trembling again. He took a long drink, grimacing as he put the bottle down and worked a soggy, pickled moth from his teeth. "Some of us could die," he mumbled, his words emerging without inflection, not as the question he'd intended. Maneker made no reply.

Lycaste finished the bottle, unable to smile any more at Weepert's hysterical raging. The honey was almost entirely loaded now. "There must be somewhere safe left in this whole Firmament of yours?"

"He's done his damage. All the Prism are free now and taking what they can. Nowhere with recognizable law will exist before the century is out." Maneker exhaled a long breath through his nostrils. "And that hasn't been the case since—" he shook his head "—since prehistory."

Lycaste had a mental image of this man, this Pretender. For some reason, his face was incredibly kind. "And you think getting to him will . . . ?"

"Those who surround the Pretender must be purged, that's for certain. What can be done to *him*—I have no idea." Maneker gave the impression of looking at Lycaste. His bandages, now clean and missing their eerie spots of blood, were a deep pink in the sunset. "He made it understood to me once, when we spoke at length, that he would leave the Firmament's fate to us. I don't believe, for all his faults, that he was dishonest in that."

"But why—"

"I have no idea, Lycaste. The Long-Life and I spent a long time together—" he paused "—in a sense . . . and I developed the impression that all *this*, this destruction, this loss of life and redistribution of lands, was simply a way of helping him get to somewhere else, somewhere he needed to be."

Lycaste was staring at his huge red toes, thinking on the chaos at large in the Firmament, a chaos they said was just below the soil of this hollow moon. The world beneath was overtaken, its Immortal masters already hanged and quartered by their Acolytes. He couldn't stay here, on this odd little honey world, waiting for more Prism to come and take it. There might be one or two ships leaving for the Old World, or there might not. Maneker had said he didn't know, and Lycaste believed him. Up above, the first foreign stars had begun to shine. Lycaste knew he ought to breathe deeply, aware that he wouldn't get any more fresh air for some time, but his chest, tightening as if it contained a wound spring, wouldn't let him.

They had been eleven days in the Void since leaving Proximo, Lycaste consigning himself to his cupboard almost the entire time, sleeping or staring wide-eyed at the superluminal dance of silver stars beyond his porthole that shone like moonlight onto his blankets. In the pressurised Voidship, he felt as if his head had swelled and his hearing diminished, so that it was possible to imagine sometimes that he was out here all alone, a man sleeping and drifting among flickering light, a diver hunting treasure at the bottom of the sea.

Occasionally—when the narrowness of his cupboard overcame him—he took brisk walks around the vessel, observing the Oxel manning the flight deck and Huerepo and Poltor playing at cards or drinking in the forward battery. Until they landed at Port Rubante, he didn't see Maneker; the Amaranthine had been given the captain's stateroom and did not leave it, not even to join them at meals. For a man who never ate, Lycaste wasn't hugely surprised.

The Oxel, he came to see, were immensely happy with their lot in life, perhaps indeed because they had so little of it. They appeared to exist in a world of constant disorder, sleeping barely an hour a day, and yet they were always lively, chattering and whistling to one another, playing games and mending things. Among their number were two or three females, though Lycaste was hard-pressed to guess the sexes apart. One was old and stayed locked away and out of sight until mealtimes. The captive Lacaille still moaned, his voice carrying along the passages, but Lycaste—like everyone else—had soon learned to block out the forlorn sounds. They would have to do something with their prisoner eventually, Poltor had told him, since rations were falling low. The Vulgar was confident they could sell or ransom him somewhere, though the Oxel apparently gave it little thought. Much like Lycaste as a younger man, they attached little value to material wealth, selling their treasures for food or repairs and—extraordinarily—setting weighty gems in their armour apparently for the stones' strength alone. So long as Smallbone kept feeding him, the prisoner might just become a permanent fixture of their voyage.

In the *Epsilon*'s hangar—Lycaste's second-favourite place—the Oxel kept an assortment of faulty half-track vehicles and jets, along with piled crates of ordnance and weaponry. An extraordinary walking tank, perhaps a cousin of those Lycaste remembered seeing at Vilnius Second, was obviously their prize possession, and occasionally, as they neared their first port of call, Lycaste offered to help with the cleaning of it.

After a time, he learned that the Spirit had been watching him, keeping itself politely out of his mind until it was invited in. Lycaste had found he hardly needed to speak aloud for it to understand him.

Can you guess how fast we're going? it had asked him as they looked out together into the silver Void one night.

Lycaste shrugged, not having the faintest clue. A Crule, Sotiris had told him once, was called a mile elsewhere. He blew out his cheeks, searching for the most absurd figure he could think of. "A thousand miles a day."

Deep laughter erupted in his head. Lycaste folded his arms as it dragged on, his eyes stinging.

Try multiplying that number by six hundred million, the Spirit said, composing itself at last.

"Well, of course I don't know, do I? People don't have to keep reminding me how stupid I am, Perception."

Settle down. Ignorance and stupidity are separate qualities, the former far easier to remedy. I knew less than you once—albeit for the very briefest of intervals.

Lycaste sniffed, looking around to where he thought the Spirit might be.

How many of your race, for example, could claim to have travelled out into the Firmament? Spoken with Amaranthine, dined aboard a Prism vessel?

Lycaste frowned.

Well, yes, perhaps the latter's not something to be encouraged. But, you know, I have never been on one of these ships of the Void either—it's a first for both of us. Its voice dropped to a whisper, tickling his ear. *The greatest joy comes with appreciation, Lycaste. I have taken the time to explore, to understand and take pleasure in the method of my escape for what it is. Do you even understand this vessel we are in? How it works?*

"Not really," he said, wary of another trap. "Huerepo said something about a bowstring."

A fair analogy. And have you ever felt the effect of a bow snapped against your hand?

"Yes."

I imagine it hurt, yes? Stung?

He'd nodded, the flicker of the Void illuminating his face.

Now picture a bowstring the length of the world.

"I'd lose my arm?"

You'd lose more than that. The accompanying rush of air alone would obliterate your entire body and everything you stood upon.

"You're a ghoulish thing, aren't you?"

Perception seemed to chuckle. *That's not* wit *I detect, is it?*

Lycaste sniffed, affronted. "I can be funny, sometimes."

No you can't, it said coldly. *But you could learn to be. It would stand you in good stead should you decide to part from this company and make your way home.*

"Really?"

Humour is a currency, Lycaste, like many things.

"How do you know all this, Percy?" he asked, actually turning from the porthole to inspect his tiny cupboard. "You've been a prisoner all your life."

The same way I know that this ship's motor relies solely on the simple flow of potential to kinetic energy, like a billion snapped strings. I take an interest. You should, too: it might save your life one day and will enrich it no end in the meantime.

"Teach me to tell jokes, then."

Good man. Get that Vulgar Huerepo in here next time; we can make him the butt of them.

Lycaste considered testing one of his jokes on Maneker as the evening descended, if only to keep his own fears at bay, but suddenly found he couldn't think of any. Dark specks—the bees of Port Rubante—danced on the wind, attracted to the residual heat of the ship. Lycaste batted some away from his face until they droned up into the branches.

The Amaranthine passed him a blob of honey on the tip of his knife. "Try."

He took a dab on his finger and touched it to his mouth. It was certainly nothing like any kind he'd had at home.

"It's all they live on here," Maneker said, pocketing his knife. Lycaste glanced at him in surprise, understanding at last why the couple of Pifoon that escorted the party of Oxel had looked so sickly.

"For half the year the Pifoon tend the hives on the outer surface, storing up for winter, at which point the bees take to the winds and circle the moon in a grand migration. So far, they have always come back, though I suspect that will change when the first invaders get here."

The small, stingless bees, no bigger than Old World flies and unornamented in contrast to their Proximo cousins, had managed to find their way into every chamber in the *Epsilon*. Huerepo had been given the job of clearing them out one compartment at a time, until some bright spark had opened the hangar for fresh air and readmitted thousands back into the ship. The Vulgar's incandescent fury had been a genuine joy to watch, and Lycaste had tried to write down as many Vulgar curses as he could for future use. He'd been stunned, however, to hear that the Pifoon in the castle counted every individual bee that returned each evening. Huerepo must have killed hundreds before he, too, had been told.

A whirr of pulleys announced something had been dropped. Lycaste and Maneker looked down to see a box of honey tumble between the branches and smash in the Canolis field beneath the ship.

"Damn you, Poltor, you ham-fisted slot-humper!" Weepert raged, tired and sitting now.

"Yes, well, upping yours, captain of the *Shit-for-Brains*," the Vulgar called out sullenly from below, somewhat spoiling the illusion of Weepert's authority. Huerepo's cousin had been imbibing his own spirits since morning and had clearly forgotten the deception. Down in the Canolis field, the two sunburned Pifoon escorts looked obviously perplexed.

We're ready, the Spirit said beside Lycaste, directing its soft, rich voice at Maneker. It was visible only as a hunched pocket of air among a brown cloud of bees. *Get Humpsquirt back to his pot-washing before he blows our cover.*

Lycaste climbed into the hangar, lithely negotiating the pulleys and stepping over the gap above the field that a smaller person might have fallen through. The repairs had been minor; the replacement of an expensive rubber sealant within the whole interior of the hull and all rends in the fuselage repatched with soldered tin. New Golanite bolts for the broadside cannon had been locked in rows along the bulkhead ready for loading and an extra lens for the forward Light Charger purchased.

Lycaste made his way through to the corridor of jumbled hanging cages, wafting away a scattering of bees and sparing a longing look at the rusted four-man jet stationed at the door to the hangar. A gaggle of Oxel rushed between his feet, chirruping and cackling, excited to be on their way.

The *Epsilon India* broke away from its mooring in the tree, blasting the waving Pifoon with twigs and steaming sewage. As a courtesy, it waited a little while before flashing its superluminals, a burst of wailing green flame pouring from its exhausts and slamming the ship through a sunset tunnel of cloud and into suborbit.

The Tethered moon became a yellow curve in Lycaste's porthole, the fields of Canolis stretching like a bright, dusty desert all the way to a deep blue orifice sea in the south, where the land became spottedly green and lush, nominally Amaranthine-held once more. He watched the uncountable stars begin to tremble like falling gems catching the light, all their myriad colours augmented for a moment, and settled back into his nest of dirty clothes.

So, you're going to stay here, in your cupboard?

Lycaste hardly flinched. He nodded his head, staring out at Port Rubante as the *Epsilon* adjusted its curve to shoot away. "I like it in here."

There was a moment of silence in which Lycaste experienced that same strange sensation he'd felt in the Oratory, the feeling of something looking inside him.

You're starting to thrombose, you know. I can see the beginnings of a clot in one of your legs.

Lycaste sat up, examining his bony ankles where they rested against the bulkhead. "What? Where?"

Oh, I expect your adulterated system will break it down. I see all manner of circulatory problems in these Oxel, though, and don't get me started on those honey-gobbling Pifoon. If I had a body—and believe you me, I intend to—I'd damn well look after it.

Lycaste breathed out, his head seemingly expanding again, the sounds of the ship diminishing. The *Epsilon*, aligning with the speck of Gliese's far-off star, had begun to lift away from the yellowish moon. Its pale blue band of atmosphere glowed at the edges of Lycaste's window like the world he'd once seen from his tallest tower, reminding him of the opportunities to return home, opportunities he might presently be leaving behind.

Now there's a worrying sight, said the Spirit in his ear.

Lycaste waited, not seeing anything but the moon as it began to drop away.

Shit.

A rolling series of thumps sounded throughout the rear of the vessel, loud even to Lycaste's congested ears. The moon swung, filling his window with yellow again as he reached out to steady himself.

"Percy?" Lycaste yelped, feeling the gravity of the ship shift and spin, doing all he could to splay out his arms and legs and wedge himself upright.

Back in a minute.

Part of Perception was already outside the *Epsilon*, fingers of its being taking hold of the Light Charger and coiling around it. It gazed out into the blackness, one half warmed by the glow of the moon and more distant sun, the other buffeted by a freezing wind, a little glad to be away from the Melius's huge, sad face. Vapour rose from it, a shape in the dark, unseen.

There, as it had suspected—a speck rushing from beneath. Perception had heard it between Lycaste's breaths, a whining scream cutting through the dark. The Vulgar said this was how others attacked— *Collaring*, they called it—slamming from below just as craft went superluminal.

It peered into the darkness, sighting the thing. It was a white blur, jagged with fins. Lacaille. *This should be exciting.*

Three slender threads in the black. *Thump thump thump*, harpoons piercing the *Epsilon*'s hull, dragging it out of the current and back down towards the moon. Perception almost lost its grip, sliding like water from the surface of the ship and clinging around the exhausts, its form glowing green through the jets.

A tip-off: it had suspected as much. On their way to Rubante they'd been far from subtle, easy prey for bandits. The Spirit squirmed back inside, passing through metal and flesh to reach Poltor on the flight deck.

Don't fight it, fall.

"Where?" the ugly little monster wailed, spittle flying through the Spirit. It tasted him, briefly, registering a vitamin deficiency.

Through the orifice sea. Where else?

Poltor hesitated, maddeningly, before screaming the order. He clipped his helmet down, as if afraid of Perception. "What is it? What kind?"

It's a Man-o'-War, Poltor my dear, as your ship's charts describe them. Lacaille frigate of the Retribution Class named the Hasziom.

"Good eyes," he said, hurrying through to the broadside battery. Perception looked on, eyeless, then passed through the vessel to observe preparations. Weepert and Smallbone were engaged in securing the scullery with quick, organised actions, the booze apparently steadying their nerves. This drinking thing, the Spirit mused, it fortified the Prism beautifully. From a porthole, it saw the moon's yellow-and-blue-spotted curve growing rapidly closer as the *Epsilon* swung back down towards it, atmosphere tearing at the hull. Three Oxel with crude blowtorches and buckets of tools skittered past and the Spirit followed to the site of the harpoon impacts, rolling like a charged cloud through the hangar and up to the cells. The prisoner gripped the bars as the ship spun, perhaps thinking his salvation was close. Perception sympathised, passing through his guts and the bulkhead until it was back in the Void and sighting along the harpoon cables at the growing speck of the Lacaille ship.

The attacking Lacaille clearly hadn't expected such a violent manoeuvre. Perception cackled, terrified and exhilarated, moving like dry ice along the mile of cable and up to the furiously banking Man-o'-War, drawn to its gravity even as the moon began to exert its own brute force. The enemy frigate blasted friction rockets, lighting the Void with a silent bellow of orange. The harpoons dragged taut, singing. Perception was almost there, feeling them winding back in, knowing it could lose its grip at any moment. Solar winds pulled at its coils, dragging it this way and that as they fell. So close. The *Epsilon* accelerated again as the moon rushed closer, briefly popping the lumen barrier. Perception lost its grip, fighting to catch back on.

Thirty feet. Perception slimmed and shot through the Void, blasting into the frigate through the mouth of a great broadside cannon swivelling on the *Epsilon* and frying the crude electrics with a surge of fury. The gun shot wide before it jammed, the shell lost to the huge yellow surface of the moon.

Perception wove through the sweating Lacaille gun crew as they panicked and yammered at the deluge of sparks; then, hearing something more ominous, rose up through the layers of insulation and armour to the ship's fuselage. Vacuum-suited troops with magnetised crampons were scrambling from a hatch, fastening locks around the harpoon cables and working their way out into the darkness.

Perception glanced back to the speck of the *Epsilon*, feeling the moon's gravity far below that diving speck and embracing it.

The Spirit took the equivalent of a running jump then fell, narrowing to a spear.

Lycaste drew his pistol from the bandolier, opening the door for Huerepo. Port Rubante loomed very large in his window, individual river tributaries growing in definition among the fields of yellow. The *Epsilon* spun again, slamming them both against the bulkhead and into the porthole.

The Orifice sea: one of a dozen access holes bored into the moon so as not to strain the thin, barely supported crust. It was a wonder the Vaulted Lands hadn't collapsed long ago; it was only a matter of time, surely. The Spirit weighed its options as it sighed through the Void, a dagger dropped from on high, considering with a flash of delight whether it could induce the moon to collapse upon their pursuers.

Perception slammed back inside the flight deck, agitating Poltor's stomach until he was almost sick in his helmet.

Boarding party, riding the harpoon cables. Twist clockwise—you keep alternating for some absurd reason and opening up their route for them.

"Clockwise?" Now the Oxel pilots were looking intently at the Vulgar as he apparently spoke to himself.

Oh, how I wish I had some fucking *hands, Poltor, then I'd fire you into the Void and fly this thing myself. As per the* clock, *imbecile.*

Poltor mimed the motion, staring at his gloves. "Like . . . a clock." He nodded, eyes lighting up. "All right!"

Lycaste and Huerepo clung to each other as the ship banked, spinning. Lycaste's cask of honey cracked into the ceiling, bouncing from wall to floor as the *Epsilon* continued its roll, blankets and clothing following after. Lycaste ducked, throwing a hand around Huerepo's tiny head as the box came sailing back towards them to strike the porthole.

"Grab that bloody thing!" Huerepo squealed.

Lycaste reached for it as they rolled again, falling with the ship's inertia. Huerepo screamed as they pounded against the ceiling, dislodging the chamber's water pipe. The cask cracked, loosing partially weightless splinters of wood and globs of honey into the room.

Perception swam upwards to perch, hawk-like, on the stern of the spinning *Epsilon*, watching as the twisting harpoon cables wound together into one thick, creaking metallic rope. The nearest Lacaille soldier lost his grip to spin out into the blackness, slowing the others. The *Epsilon*'s hull began to scream as the cables twisted tighter, tearing into white-hot strips with each spin. They must know when to stop, surely. It waited, still spinning, realising that no, the damn fools didn't have a clue.

Level out! Perception raged at Poltor, almost popping the crew's eardrums with the speed of its entry into the flight deck. *Hasn't this ever happened to you before?*

"Once! Once!" he screamed, buckled into his seat and whistling frantically to the pilots. "But we were doing it to someone else!"

The spin halted just as Lycaste and Huerepo were at the ceiling. Huerepo grabbed hold of the busted water pipe as Lycaste fell, the cracked cask of honey following through the air and splintering over the back of his head.

From afar the specks danced, glittering where the light of the moon blazed across them. Cannon in the side of the *Epsilon* opened fire, missing its attacker totally and emptying into the void. The Man-o'-War responded in kind, shredding one of its harpoon cables in the process but making a sizable hole in the *Epsilon*'s fuselage. Wreckage peeled away in a swirling storm, billowing smoke that streaked across Port Rubante's atmosphere like a ruddy brown stain.

"The Light Charger? But it's not been—"

So help me, Poltor, I'll slap you silly, you useless—

The *Epsilon* banked, accelerating hard and sizzling away from the edge of the moon's atmosphere. Smoke poured in an artful coil from its longtailed stern, decorating the skies of Port Rubante. Facing the Man-o'-War at last, it appeared to gather breath, then discharged its prized heavy nose gun: a beam of blazing light that flickered into the blackness, rupturing through the Void like a strip of neon ivory, lightning playing across space.

It missed. The Lacaille ship went superluminal, slamming past and down towards the moon, hauling the *Epsilon* after it.

Specks, revealed only by their crawling shadows against the glare, clung on to the cables for dear life.

Enough of this. Are they ready?

Those Oxel that hadn't been assigned to fixing the gaping hole in the stern of the ship were suiting themselves up, whooping excitedly until their tiny helmets sealed shut and blocked the sound. They fumbled with their microphones and the whoops returned, punctured with the whine of feedback. The Spirit floated through the rising exhausts of their suit generators, visible only for a moment as a hanging pall of leviathan coils that startled Poltor and Weepert into silence. Maneker, his hand outstretched and fumbling for a cockpit seat, had joined them.

Well-met, Hugo. You've slept through the best parts, I fear.

"Proclaimed yourself captain, Perception?" Maneker asked, dumping himself into the sweat-soaked seat.

Without hesitation. Now cheer up—I'm about to deliver you a Man-o'-War for your arsenal.

The *Epsilon* thundered its engines as they hit atmosphere, billowing through green-lit cloud and drawing level with the Man-o'-War. Air whipped around the two shapes, drawing a tight lozenge of vacuum about them that streamed, glowing, into the skies of Port Rubante.

Those Oxel that weren't frantically sealing the holes with rubber had made their way through the hatches to the *Epsilon*'s surface and were scrabbling onto the harpoon. Perception joined them, snaking towards the oncoming Lacaille until it was among them.

They were little, these goblin men, but swaddled in great suits equipped with coal-burning chimneys, rubberized against the freezing wind and carbon-black where they'd been scorched by re-entry. Perception glanced back to where there ought to be sparks, remembering the pocket of vacuum they were all in. It saw the Oxel engaged already in severing the first of the cables and felt a jolt of pride. They surely understood that they would die the minute the first of the cables snapped, sliced in two or thrown out into the atmosphere. They were fools, but loyal fools.

It should not come to that, Perception decided.

It threw itself at the leading Lacaille, screaming with all its might into his mind. The Lacaille jerked, a gauntlet going to his helmet as he partially fell from the cable. Perception bellowed, switching from ear to ear while agitating the soldier's guts. Soon the Spirit had them all vomiting into their helmets. It swung back to the Oxel.

No more cutting, it said in their language of whistles and burps, *I've softened them up for you.*

Across the vacuum they opened fire, bolts flying silently. The bright flash of lumen shots answered back, scoring black burns across the *Epsilon*'s fuselage.

Perception knew the outcome. The Lacaille were better equipped in every way. It screamed at the attacking force and shot through them, passing up the cables to the parallel ship and in through a hatchway.

All right, the Spirit thought, glancing swiftly about with the equivalent of a gleeful rubbing of hands. It took in the filthy wooden passages, veiled in a mist of benzene from the long guns. *Let's get a fire going.*

Lycaste cradled his head, sitting up. The *Epsilon* appeared to be flying straight now, but in his confusion he couldn't quite tell. Huerepo was still hanging from the pipe above him. They stared at each other.

Perception followed the maze, its being drawn to the charge of a collection of copper, brine-filled capsules stored in the bulkhead's lining; what must have been the ship's crude batteries. The Spirit reached its fingers into all of them at once, bursting them. The lighting wires in the passageway fizzled out to a chorus of screams that filtered down the halls. Perception considered the soldered clumps of wiring—nothing more than strips of steel, only one or two insulated at all—but thought better of fusing them. The ship began to slow immediately as power to the engines failed and a minimal backup generator rattled into life somewhere.

It sang happily to itself, slithering down through the smoky air to the gun chambers where the Lacaille had been in the process of loading fresh Golanite shells until the lights had burned out. The sweating crew squabbled, yammering, some dropping their ordnance. A particularly small Lacaille was crushed in the dark by a falling stack of shells.

Perception rose along the ladders to the flight deck, inspecting the scarred captain with interest as he lit lanterns. The porthole shields must have been lowered during manoeuvres and now couldn't be reopened manually. Perception read quickly through the stacked charts and papers in the small operations capsule, listening intently to the Lacaille language as the captain and his men discussed their options. It was clear they hadn't a clue what was causing them so many problems. The Spirit roared with laughter.

"Who's that?" the captain bellowed, firing off a shot into the darkness. The bolt passed through the spirit without displacing a single particle, still causing Perception's animal-built mind to flinch at the sound. The Spirit thought on this for a moment, then cackled and blew gently into the lantern, lengthening the candle flame into a tail of fire until it caught among the paper charts.

The captain screeched, dropping the lantern he was holding and unholstering his lumen pistol. He fired into the corridor beyond the flight deck, a blaze of light illuminating the Spirit's form for one strobing moment. Perception sneered, fluttering the papers as it whipped the growing flames into a fury, surrounding them, herding them. The Lacaille ran for the ladder, the coiling fire blazing after them.

The captain jumped the last few rungs of the ladder, twisting his ankle, and hobbled for the armoury. Perception roared after him, cornering him with a fluttering cyclone of burning papers while the others rushed past their captain and locked themselves inside.

"Did you hear that?" Huerepo asked, twitching his ears as he navigated his way down from the pipe. Lycaste shrugged and muttered, climbing back under the blanket of sticky Amaranthine clothing to nurse his sore head.

"*Shhh*," the Vulgar hissed. Lycaste listened.

The whistles of the Oxel had grown frantic. The crack of a shot rang out, echoing around the ship, abruptly followed by a cacophony. Lycaste cowered in his sheets. He knew the *Epsilon* had no topside hatchways—Weepert had complained of the fact barely an hour before—and realised they must have come in through the cistern chutes.

Huerepo pressed his ear flat against the door, his little eyes roving around as he listened.

"Brace!" came Poltor's choppy voice over the interior comms. Lycaste and Huerepo glanced at each other.

The *Epsilon* plunged into a nosedive, hurling them over to the other side of the room. The ship swivelled, dumping them first against the porthole and then through the locked door, demolishing it. Lycaste found himself pinned to the hallway ceiling with most of his possessions and the splintered slats of the door, his back bent, searing, across the hot water pipes. Huerepo had been thrown into the opposite chamber. Lycaste twisted to see the Vulgar wedged against the far porthole: a view of blue, cascading water rushed past.

"We're inside the moon again!"

Huerepo struggled to take a look behind him. Suddenly they were weightless once more as the ship passed some sort of boundary and spun. Lycaste fell free, missing his own chamber and crashing into the wall. Huerepo yelped as his door closed with a thump, sealing him in.

Lycaste staggered to his feet, stowing his pistol as he realised what would happen if he fired the thing on board. He stared first left and then right down the rolled passageway. Panicked Proximo birds chirruped and flapped in their cages, having been slung about on chains connected to hooks in the ceiling. A few had broken free and appeared to be engaged in trying to release their friends. Lycaste observed them fluttering off, worried that some of the Oratory's spiders—collected with a long stick by Poltor and caged for the journey—might also escape. He took a moment to get his bearings.

"I'm going to the hangar," Lycaste called to Huerepo as another volley of distantly lethal-sounding gunshots punctured the background roar of the *Epsilon*.

He climbed the ladder, feeling peculiarly naked without his cuirass, which he'd left in the mess. Just beyond, in the hold, he knew there were weapons that wouldn't snap the entire hull of the ship away if he missed his target. The ship plummeted nauseatingly once more, pinning him inside the ladder compartment, levelling out only after Lycaste was convinced they'd be falling for ever. He climbed rapidly before it could dive again and arrived in the scullery just as three Lacaille fell from the opposite hatchway and landed with a series of clangs and curses on the scorching-red hotplates. One of the stocky little things opened up his helmet, his thick golden beard spilling out, and gazed around, sharp white ears twitching. He spied Lycaste peering up at him from the entrance and unclipped his pistol.

"Get—!" Weepert wailed, jumping down from the cupboards in front of Lycaste and swinging a reflective pan in the invaders' direction "*Out!*" Bolts slammed and ricocheted, leaping from polished surfaces.

Once more the whole chamber rolled, as if built inside the spokes of an enormous wheel. Down became up, launching a fresh hail of food and implements as the lighting wire snapped and lit the place with hissing, sparking flashes. Lycaste knocked his head with a jarring crack as he slid to the next bulkhead, a pile of debris following on behind and almost covering him.

Weepert rolled, slamming his pan into one of the Lacaille's suit chimneys and denting it flat, then unholstered his own pistol and shot another of them in the helmet. Lycaste watched, incredulous, as the bearded Lacaille ran for his life, scampering on tiny legs back through the passageway towards the brig. Weepert continued hammering at the befuddled Lacaille, denting its helmet into a flattened sallet shape like those the Vulgar favoured, while the second struggled madly with his suit vent. Lycaste could only guess from the way the soldier staggered that smoke was building up inside its armour. Weepert delivered a final blow to the Lacaille, knocking the useless helmet off and pulping its skull into its metal collar like a ripe plum. He left it among the smashed dishes and went to work on the asphyxiating fellow still gagging and pounding his armour.

"You'd better hide somewhere," Weepert puffed, his face red and sweaty.

"I was going to the hold," he said, waggling his pistol.

The cook delivered another blow to the gasping Lacaille's suit. "The jet!"

Lycaste's eyes widened. He tried to remember where the nearest shouting trumpet was, casting his mind back. There was one near the brig, on the way down to the hangar. They wouldn't have thought of the jet.

As he got to his feet, the ship rolled and dived again, pouring Weepert, the two bodies and what was left of the scullery's inventory in his direction. They piled into the porcelain sink, shattering it. A scream from the hall announced that the escapee was falling towards them, too.

He landed on top of Weepert, squashing them all down with his added weight. Lycaste swore, pinned beneath the headless body of the battered Lacaille while the cook and the invader struggled and swung punches at one another above him, the whole pile sliding as the ship swerved. The vacuum soldier broke Weepert's nose with his gauntlet, spattering blood, and unclipped his gun. Weepert held his gushing nose, concussed. Lycaste stretched out his free hand, trying to swat the Lacaille out of the way, but his fingers fluttered uselessly just out of range. The soldier pressed his pistol to the cook's cheek.

Lycaste's ear's closed at the bang. The cook spasmed and slumped, his eyes rolling into his head. Lycaste locked gazes with the Lacaille as one final swerve sent them both into the hallway, burying the attacker and freeing him. He wormed his way out of the debris, shoving aside the pile of bodies and crockery to trap the soldier beneath, then kicked the weapon away and brought his foot down onto the creature's body, denting its armour almost flat.

He left it wheezing, trapped and punctured to atone for what it had done and took the lumen pistol. Weepert's body pumped blood into the scullery, sloshing among the smashed crockery and food. He stared down at the cook, having assumed up until now that nothing could shock him any more. But he'd been wrong.

There was only one way to go from here. Lycaste stole into the adjoining hatchway, a hallway of hanging rugs and linen left to dry in one of the engine vents. From what he could hear, the fighting was taking place mostly in the forward battery chambers beneath him. He followed the passageway around, sweeping aside mouldering linen, resisting the urge to take one last glance back at the bloodied mess that had been the cook.

Perception returned to the flight deck, having rounded up the last of the terrified Lacaille and forced them into the armoury. It stared at the burning papers still settling on the floor. *I've made fire, clever little me. Now to unmake it.* It sank to the ground like a nocturnal mist, smothering the smouldering charts. They fizzled out as the cockpit filled with smoke. *Lives could be taken this way*, it mused, delighted. *Extinguished.* It cackled as it noticed the captain's helmet lying upturned on a seat and shrank into its hollows, agitating the basic systems until they blared into life. The Spirit located the receptive *Epsilon*, narrowing its search across the radio waves until it found a frequency.

Poltor, it said over the opened channel, whistling a separate message in Oxel.

Who speaks? came the hissing reply. Commotion raged in the background.

Perception sighed. *This is the Lacaille ship. I've come alive and want to apologise for my rudeness earlier.*

What?

It's me, you bloody idiot. The ship is secure. Decelerate and prepare for a landing—I'm going to disengage the cables.

Cables? All right! Give us minute here, got shooting going around!

Just finish them off and make ready.

Perception disentangled itself from the buried wires of the captain's helmet, fusing them all by accident. The generator in the suit sparked and went silent.

Propulsion, sonographic imaging, the Spirit said to itself, taking a good look at the layout of the cockpit and decoding its workings, deciding that a few well-timed changes in pressure—repeatedly forcing itself in and out of the engine and wing compartments, like a pumping heart—should be enough to manipulate the controls more precisely than an experienced Prism hand. It took a moment to register that the Man-o'-War was spinning in atmosphere, dragged after the fleeing *Epsilon* and on the verge of rattling apart, and went to work popping the cables and stabilising the ship.

When it was done, happily engaged and having had a thoroughly nice time, the Spirit opened up the thick iron cockpit shield, the warm light of Rubante's interior flooding the controls. Perception gazed through the windows at the enormous gas flame that lit the place, chuckling to itself, before glancing back down the steps of the ladder to the armoury.

All they needed was an hour or two of reliable power until the batteries could be fixed, and it knew just the thing.

Lycaste reached the unlit brig, its floor slippery with slopped waste but mercifully clear of debris after the recent nosedive. He ducked his head and fumbled his way through, extending a hand to catch hold of anything he could grab should the *Epsilon* make another sharp manoeuvre, his feet skidding a little with each step. The fighting in the forward batteries had slowed to a background grumble, perhaps as ammunition ran out and both the Lacaille and the Oxel tired. *Maybe they've found another way through to the cockpit*, he thought, lifting his head in the darkness.

Something hissed and latched on to his left leg with its teeth; a pale, bony-armed blur of movement swinging and scrabbling for grip. Lycaste yelped and threw the prisoner—he suddenly remembered his name was Carzle—across the brig, aiming his pistol without thinking.

The bulkhead disappeared in a wash of white light, the air blowing out around the prisoner and sucking him into the blaze. Carzle covered his ears and shrieked, his lank hair billowing in the roar of wind that dragged him back towards the perfectly circular breach. Lycaste wound his good arm around the bars of the cell and watched in horror, unsure what he ought to do. The naked Lacaille extended his arms in a poor effort to stabilise himself, just a little too far from anything he might be able to cling on to, and looked at Lycaste with empty eyes as he tried to march against the sucking air. Lycaste saw it happen: saw him miss his footing, inhaling sharply.

The wind dragged him out. Lycaste looked without wanting to, watching the prisoner disappear over the interior landscape of the Tethered moon like a falling dash of wind-blown rain.

Lycaste clung on to the busted cell bar for some time, his muscles burning, unable to let go. He saw the Man-o'-War roar past, glinting like a charred white dagger in the thin air, wondered who was piloting it; then the *Epsilon* swung low over an interior jungle and landed in the dimness beyond the nightline, a black meadow lit up suddenly by its engines as they blew the flowers flat.

Perception floated over them as they made their way aboard through the top hatch. The flames had left a sooty, roasted stink in the air, replacing the reek of pungent sweat and sewage that had greeted the Spirit upon entry.

Well, that was dramatic, it said to the arrivals: three Oxel, Huerepo and Poltor, their suits scarred and bloodied. *How did we do?*

Huerepo looked up and around, unsealing his helmet. "Weepert and two Oxel are dead. Lycaste lost a chunk of his leg."

Well, then. Perception was at a loss for words for the first time. *He has another.*

Huerepo nodded, taking out his rifle and heading into the depths of the ship. Poltor opened his faceplate and followed, the Oxel climbing atop his shoulders.

I restored the power, Perception said as they entered the chambers leading up to the flight deck. Huerepo looked down, falling over his feet in surprise.

The remains of the Lacaille captain were slumped naked against a burned section of bulkhead, wires trailing from his ears and anus. His cauterized body had fused to the plastic floor.

"How you get him to agree to that?" Poltor asked, apparently impressed.

I can be very persuasive.

"You are a cruel thing," Huerepo said, looking up to the ceiling. "We could've ransomed him."

Relax. I let him shoot himself before I induced the current. We needed power: a Prism body was too tempting a source. It sank down to Poltor. *They're leaderless now, those Lacaille shut in the armoury. They shouldn't put up much of a fight.*

"Aye, Perception, thanking you muchly." Poltor looked around at the others, grinning inanely. "This Spirit is good friend to have, eh?"

Huerepo grumbled and moved on towards the cockpit, his rifle still poised. Perception followed him through, watching as he pushed aside the burned remains of papers and equipment.

"Any of this functional now, Spirit?" Huercpo asked, listening into the hearing trumpets and pushing some dials. "Can we fly it out of here?"

Abracadabra. The lights came back on in the cockpit, some optisockets blazing with imaged radar readouts. A whine like an injured animal drifted from the wave antenna and the Spirit shut it off.

All ready to fly.

The *Hasziom* was in a sorry state indeed. Even before making the grave mistake of attacking them, the ship must have been ready for the scrapheap; its air tanks were almost completely empty, suggesting it had been in the Void a very long time without a stop, and its electrics were so badly corroded that most of the reinvigorated systems didn't work anyway. None of the communal toilets functioned in any appreciable way (serving only as a home for the city-sized population of squealing beard lice), scalding-hot water leaked from every busted pipe and spigot, and weeds had actually taken root in some of the particularly rusted components. Perception's first order of the day was to put the remaining ten Oxel to work patching things up and making the ship habitable before they replaced the batteries, while seeing to the sixteen Lacaille prisoners himself for information. They'd complied willingly enough, surprised at the lenience of the invisible demon that had slain their captain, and were clearly pleased to hear that they'd be sold for ransom.

The captain's quarters were located in the ship's armoured underbelly. The thick tin walls surrounding it had been stuffed with feathers for insulation, leading Perception to suspect—along with the assorted bones lying around—that their new Man-o'-War had carried livestock to feed its crew. According to Poltor, this was not unusual, especially among ships that stayed out in the Void for a year or more without the promise of regular resupply.

Perception contemplated this as it slithered back down through the ceiling to the captain's cabin, arriving in a large chamber that must have once exclusively housed cheeses, judging from the wooden, residue-coated racks that lined the walls.

The quarters were heated by a blackened little woodstove, still warm from a fire. Percy noticed how the captain had been reduced to tearing strips from his wood-panelled walls to feed it and reflected again just how lost these creatures must have been. It happened to Prism ships all the time, apparently, when one relied entirely on hearing trumpets to sound the way.

Weapons—cudgels, nobblers and lumen rifles, the odd Amaranthine piece and what looked to be a cache of clever winged bullets from antiquity—were arranged around the walls. A bed, undoubtedly comfortable but crudely arranged from a pile of sacks, occupied one corner, and a heavy locked chest that Percy could see inside as if it were sliced in half took another. The captain's meagre possessions: bottles of exotic alcohol, for the most part, their empty counterparts stuffed beneath the bed of sacks. Perception thought it had seen some unusual damage to the captain's body. *Ah, should have stayed away from the spirits.* Perception laughed aloud, moving to examine the captain's marvellous Firmamental globe before it got to the serious business of reading his letters.

Thousands of Prism shipping lanes had been drawn onto its blue and gold surface—the globe being the representation, Perception understood, of a volume just over eleven light-years across from pole to pole—accompanied by minute numbers denoting the various seasonal turbulences one could expect in certain parts of the Void. The captain had labelled every Lacaille lane, a surprisingly scarce number, in pains-taking detail. It imagined him sitting here, night after night, the wood-stove ticking, a bottle of something clutched in his small white hand, scribbling away. The numbers and dimensions of the lanes would have to be redrawn every month or so, Perception assumed, the Firmament and Investiture constituting an ever-changing landscape like the desert dunes from one of his old books. The Spirit memorized them anyway, along with all the faint rubbings-out beneath, thinking it could prob-ably evolve the numbers through various probability algorithms to save the need for redrafting. It now had the perfect map, assuming all was accurate, to accompany its mental sun charts. And here was another piece, pushed back on the shelf. A crown-shaped girdle of iron moons and stars and planets designed to be fitted around the globe's waist, a representation of the Prism Investiture made by a more inexperienced hand. Perception looked at all the little metal balls, interested to see the seams of the casting process, its thoughts wandering to other things that might be forged and cast, in time.

Port Woen, Voliria Minor, Eriemouth. It read inwards, following the curve of the circlet. Threads of red and blue and black Old World silk tied between the globes appeared to denote the shipping lanes on this map, but where they weren't snapped they were frayed and fluffy: ancient, useless information. The Spirit studied a particularly large, dented globe: Port Cys. The word *black* had been inscribed on the tiny metal bearing of its moon, Obviado. The Spirit peered at some even bigger worlds, those large enough to have the lines of their continents etched onto them and to which the most silken traffic appeared to be directed. Filgurbirund and its moon, Drolgins: the jewels of the Vulgar Empire.

This is it? the Spirit wondered. Surely Hominidae had explored further than this. *All that time, all that opportunity, and this is what they made?* The Investiture, something it had always envisaged as a near-endless opportunity, was nothing but a thrifty collection of fifty-five planets—only one under the full ownership of a Prism race—and their clustered moons. There must be lands lying out beyond these worlds, habitable places, like the rest of them. It considered the idea for a moment until it found the lockets, and then forgot itself, delighted.

Yuck! The captain had three wives, or sweethearts, each possessed of their own locket, a drawing concealed inside. And what an assortment. Perception formed the impression that they didn't know about each other.

It went to recline on the bed of sacks, seeping this way and that, hearing the faint clatter and bang of repairs being made higher in the body of the Voidship, realising what was missing: there weren't any Rubante honey boxes on board. The *Hasziom* had never set down, or, if it had, it had been repelled before it could load anything. The Lacaille crew had literally been starving as they made their attack on the *Epsilon India*.

Perception reached a tendril of itself into the chest, sorting through the documents and sacks of tin coins. E-O-Z-I-E-L the Eleventh, the Spirit spelled out, attempting to gauge the worth of it all, then settled back into the late captain's bed to read his letters.

So, it finished after a few moments, looking into the dark iron mouth of the woodburner as if the miserable thing had known the *Hasziom's* secrets all along.

This vessel had never been engaged directly in the war with the Vulgar. Indeed, it looked as if the Man-o'-War operated without any special loyalty to the Lacaille admiralty or their king. Instead, its deep, long course had been plotted out of Harp-Zalnir to circle the Investiture before diving back into the Firmament and down to its very core. The Spirit read the passages on the folded posters again, searching for any more meaning.

Whatever in the world a Bult was, there were Great Companies, the *Hasziom* previously included, that would very much like to have one.

Perception had a thought and returned to the Firmamental globe, where specially annotated volumes of the shipping lanes had briefly caught its attention to begin with: the suspected haunts of these Bult, perhaps. A green and gold disc painted with stylised clouds and half-surrounded by a skeletal, world-sized shield sat at the globe's southern pole. A flurry of little notes had been scribbled around its circumference. They'd been headed for the Old World.

It returned to the letters. These Bult sounded deliciously nasty, whatever they were, commanding a bounty of ten thousand Truppins brought in alive, and the Spirit was suddenly extremely keen to meet one. There were supposedly a few breeds of the creatures that moved in indecipherable migrations around the Firmament, though they were evidently as rare as the tigers of Perception's books. It was reported that two years ago they'd eaten the population of a whole Vulgar township, prompting Filgurbirund to send battalions to harass them to the edge of the Investiture. The fleet had partially succeeded, only the outbreak of war with the Lacaille forcing the Vulgar to divert their attentions.

The Spirit left the chamber, consulting its mental maps of the Satrapies along with all the memorized rubbings-out. It saw patterns where nobody else would, understanding that after being pursued by the Vulgar in ineffectual circles, the crafty Bult were now, wonderfully, evenly placed throughout the entire Firmament. Grand Companies like the *Hasziom's* were darting everywhere in an effort to pick up the bounties, but from the letters the captain had received, it appeared that not a single individual had been caught or killed. How the hell the Lacaille ship had hoped to catch one after being beaten off by a handful of diabetic Pifoon was anyone's guess.

But there *was* someone who could commune with them; a Lacaille no less, the bounties said. A knight of sorts, if the Spirit understood the definition. Perception thought the fellow must have a fine secret indeed, something better than just a nice cut of meat hidden in his pocket, and wondered what in the world it could be.

PART IV

THRASM

Port Maelstrom hung tethered to the huge Vaulted Land of Epsilon Eridani: an unhollowed little moon of ruddy deserts and frost-tipped mountains, trapped in a swirl of smoky blue atmosphere like a polished stone in a vast, jewelled carcanet.

Ghaldezuel and De Rivarol appeared at the southern pole, a tundra of wind-flattened umber grasses hundreds of miles from anywhere, their ears and fingers tingling, fists clenched. Ghaldezuel could almost laugh; he'd survived his first Bilocation—one of the few Prism ever to do it, he suspected—complete and undamaged. A wave of nausea swept over him and he bent to stare at his boots.

About half a mile across the grasses—waist-high to Ghaldezuel—they could see the weak sun twinkling from a garrison of parked Vulgar tanks, their armoured bodies festooned with flags that swayed in the wind. De Rivarol scanned the land around them quickly, his long face set grimly against the swarms of biting flies that had quickly descended upon them. Ghaldezuel pulled on his net cloak, keenly aware of the various diseases the insects were known to carry in Port Maelstrom, and together they set out.

The tanks had been sitting there for some years, abandoned to the elements. Their gun barrels, once presumably sheathed in cloth covers, had nearly rusted away, and when Ghaldezuel inspected the tracks, he saw that only two would still be capable of covering the distance to the airstrip twenty miles north. He pointed out the best of the vehicles to De Rivarol and they climbed aboard. Ghaldezuel settled himself at the front with his lumen rifle resting on his knees, the netting blown tight against his face as they pushed through the tundra, a belching trail of smog from the exhausts clearing most of the flies.

About a fifth of the moon was scoured almost completely bald, a relic from a geological period long past, before hominids of any kind had set foot on the world. The cool desert of this southerly continent was home to a prison from the Age of Decadence famed throughout the Firmament and Investiture: the Thrasm. The Amaranthine who'd built it had taken its name from the Lacaille word for terminal illness, since sentences in the Thrasm were invariably for a period of no less than five hundred years. No incarcerated Prism had ever survived it, most not even living past their first year inside. Within, it was said, there was no running water or plumbing of any kind. Prisoners ate where they shat, grubbing in pits of filth: closed ecosystems of waste and illness and speedy death. Any Firmamental Melius unfortunate enough to find themselves locked in there were usually slain and eaten on sight, owing to the mistaken belief among Prism that Melius meat was sterile. Others with hardier immune systems often faced the same fate unless they could defend themselves, and so it was that only the fiercest and most brutal of Prism now inhabited the ancient Thrasm, whittled and honed by conflict and disease.

The airstrip came into view, a cracked expanse of bonestone scattered with crimson-rusted engine parts and a few whole Voidjets still covered with fluttering canvas. De Rivarol drove the tank onto the strip, jarring to a halt among the spare parts. Ghaldezuel climbed stiffly down, checking his rifle and peeling wriggling flies from his netting, wishing he'd driven. From his pocket, he took a paper-wrapped cake of oat-rolled meat called a Zharle bun, stuffing the whole thing into his mouth while he examined the skinny shapes of the Voidjets beneath their coverings.

"We fly high," De Rivarol said in Unified as he crossed the strip, inspecting some of the jets' wheels. "They've been loose for some time now. I don't want to risk anti-air measures."

Ghaldezuel nodded. He untied the canvas that covered the nearest Voidjet and pulled it free, checking the various flaps, fins and air intakes of the skeletal blue vehicle as it was revealed. It contained no ejector mechanisms of any kind barring a moth-eaten parachute bundled and tied to the sickle-shaped tail fin—useless, even dangerous during flight. Ghaldezuel cut it free with his knife, smiling at De Rivarol's look of profound unease.

The Amaranthine went to work, clapping his hands and shooing the flock of bony storks that were strolling across the strip. "*Now, now! Now, now!*" they screeched, flapping their wings in agitation.

Ghaldezuel ignored them, tipping Canolis oil into the tank from a can he'd found under another tarp and climbing the chassis to deposit himself in the pilot's seat.

"Be off with you, ridiculous birds!" the Immortal raved at the storks, flickering sparks across the stone concourse. Ghaldezuel watched him, considering in earnest putting an end to his life right there and then. His gloved hand hovered over the untested weapons triggers for a moment and then lay still. At length, De Rivarol turned back to the jet, a look in his eyes telling Ghaldezuel that he'd realised his danger, and stormed back to the aircraft.

"Cut them down," he said, pulling himself up and into the tiny passenger seat.

"It will damage the runway." Ghaldezuel sighed, checking the various gauges.

"I don't care."

"You should," he said, peering at the inboard ailerons as they flicked up and down on the wings before starting the motor. "We might burst a wheel and be stranded."

The Amaranthine fell silent as the engine groaned, whirring into life. The jet was a basic Vulgar rush-job, simple as a spring rifle and manufacturable in huge quantities, like the tank they'd driven there. From its nose and wings sprouted soldered-on lumen cannon a century old and connected with simple wiring to the cockpit. Ghaldezuel didn't see the point in flying high—the jet might not even get off the ground, let alone make it the seven hundred miles to the Thrasm.

He leaned back. "Belted in, Sire?"

De Rivarol muttered something, fiddling with the clasps on the passenger seat's leather strap. Ghaldezuel smiled again and slid closed the plastic cockpit, latching it shut. If they did encounter difficulties, De

Rivarol need only shut his eyes and Bilocate, still being close enough to the pole to do it successfully, and yet the Immortal appeared to think they both had as much to lose.

They taxied off, a blast of air from the jets panicking even the most obstinate of the birds, before finally screaming with a juddering heave into the grey air. The grassland and its teeming clouds of gnats rushed by beneath, the strip sliding away behind to reveal grey-brown vastness and the hints of uplands further north. In the white sky, the gunmetal blob of Epsilon Eridani, luxuriant Vaulted Land though it might be, floated like a circle of dirty ink on the horizon. The days here were long; they would reach the Thrasm a while before sundown, if all went well.

"Don't let the desert and strong sun fool you. This is no sixty-degree Province of the Nostrum. It gets cold here, very cold," De Rivarol explained behind him, having to shout above the shuddering scream of the engine. "There used to be arrival procedures. Amaranthine could land at a palazzo to pass the night before being taken to the gaol by a mounted caravan of Elepins." He looked off listlessly to the landscape, apparently lost in thought. "This is an ancient place."

Ghaldezuel knew some of the moon's history. Prism prisoners, even though it was against the edicts of the Most Venerable, were most often executed nowadays. It was simply too labour-intensive to ship criminals to Port Maelstrom while the Firmament receded into its deathly sleep. He thought about it, considering whether he'd choose death rather than come here, and couldn't decide. Escape was technically possible, as with all things, and therefore a chance of life beyond here—but even if you could get to a port over the mountains it was all still Firmamental land, far from the edge of the Investiture and months from any degree of real freedom.

The tundra below began to wither and disappear, balding to dusty tracks and watercourses and finally to real, ochre desert topped here and there with a scum of darker soil like charcoal. They flew over antique Decadence shipyards and mills, the carcasses of ancient vessels lodged in the dust like opalescent ammonites, their milky blue and green bodies eroded by millennia of scouring winds. Tiny Prism shanties, technically illegal but largely ignored, had sprung up in the shade of the mill apparatus like growths of multicoloured fungus. De Rivarol pointed and Ghaldezuel looked, tipping the jet as best he could until its mechanisms protested. The remains of the workforce here, most likely, rather than prisoners. It had only been twenty days since the Thrasm's dissolution, hardly long enough for anyone to make it out this far. A bare road wound like a creek bed through the shanties and on into the desert, stretching off towards the murk of hills and the wavering suggestion of mountains beyond. Ghaldezuel stopped trying to read the jet's basic map and slung it in the back next to De Rivarol, banking and following the tiny thread of the road. On either side of the causeway, pinkish stands of scrubby trees fought the dryness of the continent, bent against the wind that screamed in off the plains. At the rumble of the jet, distant Prism appeared from the brush like hopping fleas, firing in tiny flashes from the ground.

De Rivarol struggled in his seat to get a better look.

"We're going too fast," Ghaldezuel said. "They can't hit us."

The scrub disappeared as quickly as it had arrived, making way for the foothills and the beginnings of the great, inhospitable Gerdis Range of mountains beyond. Ghaldezuel took in the high peaks, their brilliant snowfields gaining clarity in the haze, sharp and intimidating as crumbled stone thorns. He peered. There—a far-off brown network like a cancerous blemish on the baked rock of the hills: the power stations that surrounded the Thrasm.

They struck the runway, bucking with the increasing wind, the four rubber wheels extending and popping with a bang when they met the broken stone. De Rivarol cursed as Ghaldezuel fought with the jet, swerving it across to the edge of the strip. They came to a wobbling stop in the long black shadow of the conning tower, a small Vulgar alarm in the cockpit whining furiously and then falling silent.

Ghaldezuel looked out at the tower, busying himself with the latch on the cockpit and pushing it open. Huge rusted guns lined the strip, gazing up into the sky. The mountains brooded over them, murky grey glaciers distantly visible in the vast crags.

They climbed out. It was another few miles from the empty airstrip to the prison. A network of subterranean passages lay beneath the simple coal-fired power stations in the foothills, feeding electricity down to the ancient structures beneath. Any number of traps could have been set in such tunnels; Ghaldezuel had resolved to go over, not under.

He tilted his head and listened to the barren winds coming down from the mountains. The jet's approach would almost certainly have been noticed in the echoing passes.

He went at once to the rear of the jet and popped open the fuel cap, siphoning out what was left in the tank and collecting it in the small can he'd found it in. De Rivarol watched him closely as he jammed a lid onto the container and wiped his hands with a rag.

"Give me that," the Amaranthine said, gesturing for the can. "It'll be safer with me."

Ghaldezuel met his gaze coolly and handed it over.

They turned together and regarded the end of the strip, where a few pieces of broken equipment surrounded one of the great desolate holes drilled into the foothills, the ramshackle chimneys of the power stations rising above like thin, deformed fingers. The five-thousand-year-old installations that powered the prison and its deeper secrets had been built with slaved Prism hands, as had the Thrasm itself, and had now fallen into disrepair, a symbol of the Amaranthines' lack of interest. Chunks of glittering coal from the great stores had blown in the wind and collected in loose clusters across the stone concourse. Ghaldezuel ground one under his boot, listening to the wind, then unshouldered his lumen rifle to inspect it, pleased once more with the powerful, modern-calibre they'd given him. They started out.

A vast flight of steps, built around the three subterranean access holes, led up and into the hills towards the first power station. They took them, pausing every now and then and checking the mountain slopes around for movement. Ghaldezuel knew from the prison manifest that there were only eighty-three inmates at the time of dissolution: twenty Vulgar, forty-six Lacaille, fourteen Wulm, two Firmamentals and one Old World Melius. A peculiar collection. Most were likely dead now, victims of the chaos when the cells had opened, and perhaps more had been eaten in the ensuing twenty days. Those left had been honed by one last test and were probably now the most dangerous Prism in the entire Firmament. Ghaldezuel touched his glove to the locations of the various knives and pistols stuffed inside his armour, pressing forward.

They crested the first low hills, pushing past some sticks of bleached driftwood—a prisoner-built fence, made with all the finesse of a shanty wall—and looked down into the power station.

Amid a cluster of massive pyramids of twinkling black coal, sections of the second chimney had fallen, avalanching one side of a coal hill and pouring it all into the river that ran past, damming it until only a trickle snaked blackly through.

Ghaldezuel's eyes followed the course of the dry river to the burned-out shell of the boiler chambers, where a furnace would have been constantly stoked to heat the water into steam. Beyond, relatively untouched, the shambolic red-brick fortifications of the turbine hall reared into the side of the mountain, blocking the view of the road that led deeper into the complex and on to the valley containing the prison itself.

"Look," Ghaldezuel said to De Rivarol, pointing into the wasteland of shattered equipment, pulverised bricks and twisted piles of blackened, rusted metal. "They've tried to take the generator apart."

De Rivarol nodded, continuing on down towards the first of the great heaps of coal where the remains of the fallen chimney had settled. Ghaldezuel reached a hand into his pocket and brushed the fold of black material he'd brought all the way from the First Province. He gazed around and followed the Amaranthine, clattering along the tin chute leading to the burned ruins of the boiler chambers. Perhaps the other two stations would prove equally useless. If that were so, then the last portion of his mission would be in darkness.

"The water was choked with an extremely potent strain of bilharzia," De Rivarol said, gesturing down to the nearly dry watercourse that had once fed the boiler. "The poison came from somewhere at the stream's source in the mountain, an old addition to discourage escape along the river."

Ghaldezuel looked at the brackish, brown-slimed pools sitting in the bottom of some exposed pipes and stepped over them, walking to the shattered remains of the first chamber and into shadow. Pipes and brickwork were still standing in places, leaving an empty shell filled with blasted machinery. Scuffed footprints in the ash of the floor showed where the released Prism had tried to salvage parts. He raised his rifle and scanned the upper floors of the ruined shell, looking down the hallways as he crunched over shrapnel towards the turbine hall.

"This Wulm. He will be receptive," De Rivarol said from behind.

Ghaldezuel turned slightly, unsure whether he'd been asked a question. "One hopes."

"Harald Hundred was once imprisoned here, you know," the Amaranthine continued, inspecting the remains of the furnace, a thirty-five foot-high cube of blackened metal. Its vast, bullet-pocked grate hung loose from a single waist-thick hinge.

"He escaped?" Ghaldezuel asked, intrigued.

"Of course not," De Rivarol replied sharply. "He was pardoned."

"Must have humiliated him sufficiently, to be locked away with Prism."

"That was always the point," the Amaranthine said, somewhat coldly. "A fate worse than death, for some."

"I'm surprised he survived it. How long was his sentence?"

De Rivarol smirked. "A day or so."

Ghaldezuel shook his head, stepping through a broken arch and into the turbine hall, a circular chamber dominated by huge silver blades festooned with complex piping. Ghaldezuel paused to look at them, taking in the hundreds of wooden buckets that covered the floor, each filled to the brim with the same scummy brown water.

"A trap?" he muttered, not turning to De Rivarol.

"Or the condensers were leaking," the Immortal replied, knocking one with his boot. It tipped over and splashed. Ghaldezuel stepped neatly back.

"What's the matter, Lacaille?" De Rivarol dipped his finger into another of the buckets and touched it to his mouth with a smile.

Ghaldezuel shook his head angrily, turning his back on the Perennial and stepping away through the maze of buckets. Beneath the gleaming rotors, drips and drops fell, plopping into buckets and splashing the floors. He felt a few drops of the deadly water patter onto the back of his cloak. He shook himself, stopping when he saw what was ahead.

Bones.

A yellowed tangle of ribs and vertebrae had been dumped into the vats of the turbine hall. Dried flesh still clung between some of the ribs like peeling brown sailcloth. Ghaldezuel navigated the rest of the buckets and walked slowly up to the piled skeletons, wary of his exits as he inspected them. A long skull grinned at him from beneath the heap.

"Zeltabras and Elepins from the stables," De Rivarol said. "Killed in a frenzy."

"This is a surprise?" Ghaldezuel replied. "You left your prisoners here to starve."

"To weed out the weak," the Amaranthine snapped back. "The Long-Life wants only the hardiest defending his interests."

Ghaldezuel didn't reply. Through a tall, glassless window he caught a glimpse of sunlight flashing crazily off metal. He ducked.

Bolts slammed into the turbine hall, piercing the wall where he'd just been standing and pulverising the brickwork in a rolling cloud of red dust. He brought the rifle stock to his shoulder and snapped on the binocular lens. More shots whined through the smashed bricks, popping holes in the wooden buckets and slopping their poisonous contents across the floor.

He glimpsed De Rivarol moving to the edge of the chamber. "Wait!" Ghaldezuel hissed, knowing the Amaranthine would only bring down half the mountainside if he tried to help in any way. They hadn't penetrated the darkest globe in the Firmament just to leave empty-handed.

More bolts smashed into the stone floor around Ghaldezuel's outstretched boot. He pulled it in and took a breath, popping up and sighting on where he'd first seen the flash. Whatever their assailant was had slipped behind its cover of stones once more, but hadn't contended with a Pifoon-made lumen rifle. Ghaldezuel snapped off fifteen shots, the invisible charged light blowing jagged holes in the cairn of rubble across the valley and scattering it. A grey stick figure jumped into focus as it scampered for cover. He sighted calmly. Lacaille. Nothing more than an overqualified sentry lain in wait for many days. Not the Wulm they'd come for, but a fine marksman nonetheless. He took the shot, blowing out its jaw as its head bucked upwards, only a tendon keeping the neck intact.

Ghaldezuel ducked back, waiting for retaliatory fire, sure none would come. He held a gloved hand up to the Amaranthine and headed for the chamber's great southward-facing brick arch, working his way along the outside wall until he had a view of the valley again, then crouched and sighted on the far hill. Much to his surprise, he spotted another distant figure scampering back along the ridge. He put his eye to the scope, understanding he had only seconds before it disappeared over the rise, firing a moment later. The first shot tore a hole in the creature's foot, hobbling it. He took a breath and squeezed off another, missing its shoulder by a hair.

And then it was gone.

Ghaldezuel unclipped the scope, breathing harshly as he shouldered the rifle.

"*And?*" De Rivarol asked, appearing in the sunlight under the arch. Ghaldezuel rose to his feet and looked around, irritated. "We'll need to hurry."

The Amaranthine tutted. "You missed?"

"I slowed him down." He glanced back at the rise. "Can you run in those skirts of yours, Immortal?"

They crested the rise, wary of other spotters in the hills. Ghaldezuel dropped to his stomach, hurriedly signalling for De Rivarol to do the same, cursing as the Amaranthine pointed to his opulent clothes, shaking his head.

Below them lay a vast valley of hills formed by the roots of the mountains. In one of the crevices, Ghaldezuel could see the remains of a high, fortified wall. Within it lay the Thrasm, dangling like a corkscrewed stalactite of light red brick from the overhanging rock. The single guard tower, which Ghaldezuel remembered from the images had protruded like a chimney stack, lay in pieces on the valley floor.

The place itself was nothing but melodrama; it was what lay within, what they sought, that possessed the power to change things. Ghaldezuel did not stare at it long. His eyes flicked across the slopes that led down to the prison, settling here and there, searching for peripheral movement. A couple of hundred feet down on the hills below them, he caught sight of the scampering sentry. He frowned, scrambling to his feet, not checking whether or not the Amaranthine was following. The sentry appeared to be trying to find cover. Ghaldezuel took aim.

An eruption of sparks suddenly glittered across the lower hills, coursing along the mountainside beyond and starting a dozen small avalanches of boulders before the thunder reached them. Ghaldezuel glared around at De Rivarol, then back to the distant figure. The Prism had stopped short of the cover he was running for. Hobbling, the Lacaille turned to face them.

Ghaldezuel cursed beneath his breath as the crack of falling rocks echoed in the mountains. Higher up, some snow had been disturbed which now fell in a vast, misted curtain across the lower slopes further west. He examined the Prism from a distance, aware that this one would have killed hundreds in his lifetime, certainly more than Ghaldezuel himself, glad that he had it now in his sights.

The scrawny Lacaille, a Dyed-White from Sprit by the look of him, stood and stared, challenging. It was what Ghaldezuel—staring at death along the barrel of an expensive lumen rifle—would have done. A test, perhaps, of honour; one last chance of survival. Ghaldezuel shook his head, squeezing off a shot. The Lacaille's body tumbled, faceless and leaking, down the slope towards the Thrasm.

He rounded on the Amaranthine, throwing the rifle at De Rivarol's feet. "You take it! You take it, when you next decide to act without thinking!"

The Amaranthine stared at the weapon, his thin lips pursing. "The Long-Life's regard for you will not last for ever," he said, raising his eyes, static tingling between them. "Remember that, *primate*."

Ghaldezuel shook his head, grabbing the rifle and setting off quickly down the slope, his only comfort lying in the realisation that he'd made the right choice; had they taken the tunnel path, his imbecile companion would only have brought the place down around them.

He sighted his weapon again, panning the rifle across the valley, looking for any sign of a camp in the hills. But there was none. He scanned the upper slopes for any wisps of smoke, any of the litter or well-worn trails that folk living in one place couldn't help but make, seeing nothing.

Ghaldezuel unscrewed the scope and pocketed it among his clinking stock of pistol ammunition. He might as well have worn a giant bell around his neck. The prisoners already knew they were here.

APOSTATE

Ghaldezuel and De Rivarol approached the Thrasm along an avenue of the same vast, rusted guns they had seen on the airstrip. Their barrels were all scrawled with one word, painted in blood, excrement, chalk and charcoal in five different Investiture alphabets:

CUNCTUS

Ghaldezuel mouthed the word as he read, catching the Amaranthine's eye.

Skewered upon the two leading guns were a couple of sun-withered corpses. From the expressions on the Vulgars' faces, it looked as though they had still been alive when they'd been impaled, anus-first, and pushed down the barrels. They continued on, their pace checked, watchful.

The prison had been blown open by a retreating bomber carrying the last of the Pifoon guards, but they hadn't made it far. Its remains lay smashed side-on into the ground at the end of the avenue; a sad, scattered heap of rusted shrapnel and bent guns. Had they left, the inmates could almost have been on the other side of the range by now, walking north into uncharted land that Ghaldezuel knew was nothing but more of the same. Maybe they had, leaving two of their best to guard the rear, but he thought it unlikely. He imagined what he himself would do, knowing as they almost certainly did that the dissolution of their prison was not some simple act of mercy, and came to the unfortunate conclusion that he was walking into a trap.

Ghaldezuel was reasonably well known in the Investiture, even if his name wasn't. The Bult crew he commanded was unique. He ought not to have feared a mortal soul. But there was one, one anomaly in the grand landscape of the Investiture, who had always unsettled him slightly. One who had marked his territory here.

The prisoner kept his birth name, they said, eschewing all others. He needed no more than one, not in these times, and yet still he'd collected them over his thirty years of terror as he had followers, his greatness attracting the weak and malicious from all corners of the Investiture. Cunctus the Ragged, some called him. Cunctus the Tick. The Cethegrande Prince. The Apostate.

And no one—no one who dared to speak of it, anyway—had ever seen him.

The Apostate was the name by which Cunctus was known among the Lacaille, having robbed the Grand Bank of Maniz a year before his capture, making off with the entire wealth of the country of Baln. Not a soul in the surrounding small city had survived, Cunctus's team of assassins dumping an Amaranthine skycharge as they fled. So it was that his crime was not discovered until a few days later, by which point Cunctus had paid his way into the Firmament to hold the Satrap of Alpho hostage until more of his demands were met. They were only apprehended after an entire Lacaille fleet had pursued them a few light-years out through the Never-Never to Eriemouth, at the very edge of the Investiture, and arrested them in the name of King Eoziel.

There were still some who claimed Cunctus himself did not exist at all, that the scapegoats the Lacaille had captured were nothing but an excuse to encroach into Vulgar territories. Others said the Vulgar themselves were responsible, thieving as much as they could from the Lacaille under the cover of an honourless gang. Ghaldezuel personally suspected that there was not one Cunctite gang but many, with the name transposed from one gang leader to the next, a conglomeration of Prism companies nominally in league with each other for the purposes of distraction and alibi. It would certainly explain the curious lapses in skill and judgement present when one studied their many jobs, and as if in confirmation of his theory, plenty had come forward claiming to be Cunctus over the years, with a tally of six executed to date. As such, he was also known with more than a dash of irony as *Cunctus the Everlasting*, for the talent of being reborn again and again into new Prism bodies. Ghaldezuel had no idea what they would find here, but whatever and whoever Cunctus was, the Long-Life wanted him.

Silence. A thin haze of tiny snowflakes had begun to fall. A tin bucket rattled over and rolled. He hissed at De Rivarol as they closed the distance to the wrecked bomber, walking between the last of the great guns. His fine Prism eyes picked out a set of milky glass bottles standing perfectly in order of height on one of the ship's bent guns.

The Long-Life's command to end the tenure of the place had not included sending provisions of any kind: no food or clothing, no equipment. It was a ruthless mind indeed that had ensured only the survival of the strongest here. Ghaldezuel squinted up at the Thrasm's breach, a small, charred hole in the bulk of the stalactite, and along to the line of tiny steps running up into the rock face to where the prison's guard tower had been, seeing how far and high the climb across naked brick had been to get from the hole to the steps. Many must have fallen or refused to leave. Another test.

Snow drifted and settled, leaching the colour from the rocky slopes. They came to the end of the avenue, warily inspecting the downed carcass of the bomber and its odd little collection of artefacts. It was deserted and stripped, useful only as cover.

Ghaldezuel lingered at its mangled hull, looking through the thickening snow at the Thrasm and up into the fading mountains. "This valley's like a funnel," he said to De Rivarol. "There'll hardly be any cover from here on in."

The Amaranthine scoffed, kneading his thin hands. Snow had fallen to line his clothes like white fur. "Oh, let them *try*. I'll teach them some respect."

Ghaldezuel didn't look at him. He was suddenly immensely tired. "You won't have time. He'll have the best shots in the Investiture up there. We don't stand a chance in the open." He took in De Rivarol's white-coated robes and glanced up, holding out his glove. "Unless . . ."

The snow was falling in soft clumps now, engulfing the valley in a flurry that washed out the mountains. Ghaldezuel wiped some from his eyes and stared into the white sky, hoping it would last.

They waited, the whiteness drawing in, surrounding them, joining with Ghaldezuel's misted breath. The snow that sank into this pocket of valley was a fluke, a spot of brightness in the dark, stippled web of mountains. But it might be enough to keep them alive.

When he could no longer see the Thrasm in any detail, he hoisted the rifle. "All right."

They moved from behind the cover of the bomber, treading out into the white expanse of virgin snow. The valley's steep sides were lost in the squall, a blank space made huge by the muffled sound of the wind. He headed in the rough direction of the Thrasm, working his way between the rocks so as not to lose his sense of direction, snow pattering on his suit and melting in the heat of his exposed skin. De Rivarol was now completely coated, all but invisible besides a suggestion of green eyes when Ghaldezuel looked behind him.

A soft absence of sound, weighted with the sensation that they weren't alone, greeted them as they made their way deeper into the whiteness. Ghaldezuel, after thirty-eight dangerous years, didn't hold much to the idea of an extra sense. He trusted in his long, pointed ears, his big, round eyes. He hated superstitions: all that clapping and mumbling of oaths, as if the spirits of the worlds could be frightened off by a little noise. Indeed, whatever was out there waiting for them kept its ears open for that very thing.

The white ground had begun to rise beneath their feet. A few feet more and Ghaldezuel knew they were at the low stone ramp beneath the Thrasm itself. He squinted into the whiteness, reflexively drawing his pistol. There were footprints leading away beneath the prison.

He hushed De Rivarol, fully expecting the blasted Immortal to pipe up, uncomprehending. The prints doubled back on themselves, the freshest running behind him. He turned, sweating, and aimed into the snow. De Rivarol appeared in the white, glaring at Ghaldezuel's drawn pistol. The flurry strengthened for a moment. He looked down. There were more prints everywhere.

"What is this?" Ghaldezuel muttered, swivelling, knowing as he looked into the snow that he'd lost his sense of direction. He wiped moisture from his eyes.

The crack rebounded around the blank valley. Ghaldezuel tensed, bending his knees. De Rivarol froze. Another shot sliced through the whiteness, along with the whizz of the bolt.

"*Up the ramp,*" he hissed, throwing himself to one side and fumbling for his rifle. A third shot slammed into the snow where he'd just been standing and he aimed in the general direction of the hills, firing a volley of silent blasts of light, as many as he could until the muzzle reddened, glowing white at its end. He dunked it to sizzle in the snow, counted to ten and then fired another fifteen, ducking back immediately to continue his run. Across the valley he heard the muffled thunder of his second volley detonating in the hillside.

He couldn't be sure, but he thought the snow might be clearing. He could already see the lowest hills as the squall turned into dashing sleet. The Thrasm's mighty shadow glowered to his left, a great, dark smear in the rushing weather. His eyes went to the foothills beyond the Thrasm, on the other side of the valley, and he threw himself into the snow. Flashes lit up from their ridges, the snapping concussions following almost reluctantly through the storm. They'd been waiting for him on both sides of the valley, as he'd thought they might.

De Rivarol jogged up beside him and crouched, his eyes bright with what looked like excitement. Bolts fizzed through the air. "Time?"

Ghaldezuel nodded, aiming the rifle again. He heard the Amaranthine's mumbled words, his eyes going to the shadow of the Thrasm.

It took a moment, a moment during which more flashes popped along the hillsides and he thought the command must have failed. Then, with a rush of snow like a vast inhalation of breath, the entire prison disappeared. A tapering cone of clear air punched through the sleet like a beam of light quickly filled in with dashing flakes, and then it was as if the place had simply never been there.

The incoming fire ceased abruptly. Ghaldezuel took a few slow breaths. He slung his rifle over his shoulder and stood to his full height, edging out into the middle of the valley with his hands held clear of his body to either side. The wind strengthened to drum in his ears.

Gradually the sleet subsided to a lull, a pause for breath before another low bank of cloud swept curling in over the mountains. Ghaldezuel felt his plate armour dribbling. It had been given a good clean, at least. He remained with his arms apart, his rifle and pistol flung to the ground, the chill air biting his fingertips through the steel-tipped gloves. He'd pulled his lumen-reflecting rubber helmet on during the barrage but didn't want to make any hand gesture now to remove it. Consequently he saw the hills, and the descending skeletal figures, through a film of dim, polarised plastic. They stopped a fair distance off, taking in what the Amaranthine had done.

A perfect tube had been bored into the rock from where the Thrasm had once hung. He stepped back a little, glancing first at the people at the edge of the hills and then at the tunnel, a circular hole cut out of the snowy ground leading down into the rock. *The Sepulchre*, Ghaldezuel thought, his plum-sized heart pounding inside his chest. The hole was a full sixty feet across, bored by a weapon of extraordinary power. There must have been a superluminal weapon from the Age of Decadence down there, lying, listening, waiting for just the right words.

De Rivarol came to stand beside him, not bothering to raise his own arms.

The assortment of stick men reached the hole, gaining clarity through the last of the snow that carried on the wind. Ghaldezuel studied them, though they appeared to pay him no mind. The smallest of them, a squat little figure shrouded in a blue and gold Firmamental flag, appeared fascinated by the hole, bending down to touch its rim.

"So there he is," De Rivarol muttered.

The flag-shrouded person looked up at last, locating them both and strolling over.

They observed the small person's escort of taller shadows following on behind as they crossed the valley. One was enormous and could only be some sort of Melius. There weren't many of them, leading Ghaldezuel to suspect that quite a few had been left in the hills, their weapons trained.

"I'd be grateful if you'd let *me* speak," Ghaldezuel said.

"Talk away," the Amaranthine said dismissively. "I know Lacaille and all the rest of them, but I suppose you have the manners."

The group was almost upon them, visible against the snow as an emaciated, spectacularly ugly Melius and four small Prism people, probably Wulm beneath their peaked hoods. As they approached Ghaldezuel, he saw that they were a stone's throw from death, all but the Melius thick with crusted sores where their flesh showed through ripped clothes stained umber from the shit of the Thrasm. The giant himself was naked like an Old Worlder, coated in places with coarse white woolly hair and possessed of a great yellow beard. He rubbed his huge hands together and glared at Ghaldezuel with a feral, drooling intensity.

The flag-shrouded person marched forward, its fingers engaged in lighting a bent cheroot.

"Well then," a red-lipped mouth said from the shadow of the hood, revealing serrated yellow teeth. "You've bought yourselves a bit of time. What can you do for us?"

So Cunctus was a Wulm, as the Satraps thought. Ghaldezuel was a little disappointed. He'd been hoping for a rogue Amaranthine, or perhaps a particularly bright Oxel, just to make things interesting.

He bowed his head, cautiously pulling off his rubber helmet, then glanced among them, taking a cold breath.

"We are emissaries of the one hundred and eighteenth Firmamental Emperor," he said in Wulmese. "His Most Venerable Highness Sotiris Gianakos has commanded that we set you free, to be pardoned unconditionally, so that he might be assisted in his great cause."

The Wulm nodded thoughtfully, sucking the cheroot until it caught and puffing a little cloud of smoke into the cold air. He shot Ghaldezuel a glance, a glitter of unseen eyes in the shadow of the hood. "Been preparing that, have you?"

"I was instructed not to deviate," Ghaldezuel said.

"Are we speaking with Cunctus himself?" De Rivarol demanded in Unified, stepping forward. Ghaldezuel winced.

The Wulm snorted, looking among his followers, then threw back his hood.

"*Who?*" asked the remains of a bald red face, smoke curling from the corners of its wide, spike-toothed mouth. The other Prism chuckled, parroting him. *Who? Who?*

Ghaldezuel had heard about the scars. A bottle of acid, some said, in retribution for any number of crimes. When the hood had fallen, he could only assume it had been something much, much worse.

"Watch yourselves," the Amaranthine said, his voice silky-smooth.

The Wulm turned his bright, hideously alive yellow eyes on De Rivarol, passing the cheroot back to the Melius. "This one—" he pointed to Ghaldezuel "—comes with an offer. What do you have?"

De Rivarol smiled icily. "Firmamental right."

Ghaldezuel shook his head, opening his mouth to try and rectify the situation.

"Superluminal," whispered the Melius in a cracked voice, gazing at the hole. The cheroot dangled from his huge mouth, the smoking stub wobbling as he smiled. "Hidden beneath us all this while. What word was it, Amaranthine? What word did we almost say a thousand times, unknowing of the—" he made a grasping motion with his hand "—the *weapon*, listening?"

De Rivarol sneered. "Your Melius ought to learn some manners, Cunctus. Muzzle it, and let's talk somewhere privately."

Ghaldezuel put a tired hand to his brow. He'd noticed how the Wulm had only smoked the cheroot to get it going, at first thinking nothing of it. All the stories, all the confusion; a new scapegoat with each arrest.

The Melius turned a suddenly unamused eye on De Rivarol, and Ghaldezuel could see then that the Amaranthine understood.

De Rivarol recovered admirably, squaring his shoulders and speaking in First this time. "Well then, whichever of you is in command here, please accept this—" he pointed to the hole "—this gift from His Most Venerable Majesty. That which has been long buried in the depths of the mountain: *the treasure hoard of Port Maelstrom.*"

"Like my friend here said," the yellow-bearded Melius croaked, patting his Wulm and looking directly at Ghaldezuel, "sell us your wares."

Ghaldezuel glanced piteously at the Amaranthine, slipping the weighted black hood from his pocket.

"Now listen to me," De Rivarol screeched. "Only I can broker this with you. The Lacaille—he's *nothing.*"

Ghaldezuel wasted no time aiming a kick into the crook of De Rivarol's knee. The air around the Amaranthine snapped and tingled as he staggered. Cunctus and the Wulm stepped back. Ghaldezuel bundled the hood over the Immortal's head, breathing heavily, feeling the heat through the material as he tied its cords around De Rivarol's neck. He pulled out his blade before the Immortal could finish his yell and sawed first one, then the other of De Rivarol's hands off, shoving the Amaranthine into the snow and passing Cunctus the hands. The Melius nodded, accepting the hands, small inside his own great paws, and examining the rings on their fingers.

"My offering to you and yours," Ghaldezuel said, panting, then nodded to the hole. "Plus all that lies within."

The Melius looked at the writhing De Rivarol, hooded like a falcon. "That is a powerful thing there. Very good of you to bring it." He twiddled his beard thoughtfully. "But I don't need one. Push it in."

Ghaldezuel nodded, stooping and dragging De Rivarol by the boots, deaf to his pleading and cursing. For twelve thousand five hundred and five years, this man had traded the deaths of countless others for his own. Ghaldezuel was that death, come now after all this time in the form of a half-man of another age. And it was a good trade, he thought, dropping the wriggling Amaranthine's boots on the lip of the hole. His death would save so many.

Ghaldezuel gave the Amaranthine one last shove, rolling him over into the gulf. He turned and walked away, ignoring the others who ran to see De Rivarol fall.

"That one came with the Emperor's wishes," he said to Cunctus. "But *I* do not." He threw down his blood-slick blade, removing the eight other deadly items about his person and flinging them one after another into the snow. "I come to ask you to join me, to take what's left of our Investiture from those Firmament-loving Vulgar and rekindle the greatness we were promised."

Cunctus studied Ghaldezuel, light snow catching in his beard. "Folk have made better displays than that and not meant it. You'll have to go out to the old guard tower, so that we can know you better."

Ghaldezuel looked uncertainly across the valley to the dark hollow of the crumbled tower, noticing a thin strand of smoke blowing sideways from its smashed upper chamber. A beanpole body the colour of clotted cream stood in the gloom of the ruins.

"Go on."

The snow was driving back in as he trudged to the remains of the guard tower, his head bent against the wind coming down from the peaks. The sun shone as a pocket of light in the cloud, dipping and glowing. With every step, Ghaldezuel expected the Melius to change his mind, feeling upon his shoulders the possibly imagined eyes of marksmen in the hills. It was what he'd have done, were he in command of this place. He knew, too, that he wouldn't accept intruders with such ease. There would have to be torture. It was the only method of absolute trust. But he'd prepared himself already, taking a powder beforehand that should dull any pain.

But they *were* curious. He'd not still be alive if they weren't.

At the gloomy, rubble-strewn mouth of the guard tower, he saw more of the footprints: those dainty, frenzied marks that had surrounded him on the approach to the Thrasm. Ghaldezuel bent and looked in.

A thin hand lunged out and grabbed his collar, hauling him into the dark.

FILGURBIRUND: MIDSUMMER 14,647
ONE DAY BEFORE THE ATTACK ON NILMUTH

He opened his eyes, blinking at the pale morning and checking instinctively for the papers in his pocket. Ghaldezuel stretched and sat up, glancing at his clock and through the narrow plastic strip at the landscape below. The rolling hostel must have made its way across three country borders in the five hours since he'd boarded, loosing and picking up fresh travellers like fleas. He could hear them outside, in the halls, clamouring and laughing. Ghaldezuel was distantly amazed that he'd slept.

Outside, the thick forests were seeping to bright orange, swathes of rust already touched by the first snowfalls of the season. Those deep belts of land, some hundreds of miles wide, were home to innumerable horrors: nocturnal beasts more terrifying than many a creature of the Old World, roaming gangs of scalpers and slavers, private inbred armies commanded by Vulgar warlocks. Only his wits kept him safe here, in what was considered by nearly everyone to be the most civilized world in the Prism Investiture, the richest kingdom of the Vulgar, its name translating roughly as the safest, warmest of burrows. Filgurbirund.

The vast, cubic mass of the hostel pulled into a station, its great wheeled legs splaying and locking firm to thwart any bandits who might fancy stealing one whole—it had happened before—and juddering to a stop at the concourse, a flat expanse of warped wooden boards at the edge of the town. Ghaldezuel looked at the spires of the teetering buildings, their poles dangling with flags and sigils that stirred in the cold early breeze, before reading the peeling letters on the sign: Wiehlish. Not far now. His eyes went to the Vulgar issuing from the station, huddled little caped creatures, bundles of grey and brown, their heads bent to the increasing wind. Many carried bottles in their hands. They handed over their tickets, ragged strips of paper that fluttered dangerously in the wind. His eyes followed one that had escaped its owner's grip to dash into the edges of the woods. The tiny Vulgar, still at the rear of the queue, dumped his pack and hobbled in panic after it. Returning his attention immediately to the line of waiting Prism, Ghaldezuel saw the bag being rifled through eagerly, until almost everyone in the queue had taken something for themselves.

After a few minutes more, the rolling hostel blew its horn and made ready to leave, the drawbridge at the edge of the boards pulling back. There was no sign of the fellow who had disappeared into the edges of the forest. Vulgar without inside tickets climbed the steel ladders at the sides of the vehicle to find places on the top where they could set up for the coming journey, the threat of snow meaning nothing to the drivers in their heated compartment.

Ghaldezuel leaned back in his bunk, relishing the locked space he had bought, the most expensive compartment in the hostel. In the corridor, people were already stirring, cursing the influx of new travellers aboard what was already a dangerously overcrowded vehicle. As fists hammered on his door, Ghaldezuel knew the place would only get worse—and more filthy—as the rolling hostel stopped to pick up even more people as it neared the city, still two hundred miles away. From what he'd heard outside during the night, it was clear that the single toilet on this floor had failed, with the whiff that crept beneath his door informing him that angry Vulgar had begun a dirty protest at the opulence of Ghaldezuel's situation. He didn't care. Let them soil their own sleeping place—it would only bother him for a moment, during the minute or two it would take to alight. He looked outside again, watching Wiehlish pass out of sight and the depths of the forest resume. Trees slid and slapped at the window, the gaps in their scarlet leaves revealing haunting glimpses of the black woods beyond, and he wondered that the roads hadn't completely disappeared during northern Filgurbirund's long summer.

Ghaldezuel fished in his travel cloak and brought out a small metal-bound book on a chain, suddenly finding he hadn't the energy to leaf through it. He would see the six-hundred-year-old city himself in a few hours, so what use were reproductions? Hauberth Under Shiel, the northern capital he was making for, did not hold with foreign vehicles or trade caravans—anyone arriving from outside the Vulgar Empire needed to carry his Silp Treaty papers on his person at all times and pay passage with a reputable Vulgar transport. As per the laws, Ghaldezuel had arrived three countries away to apply for entry, waiting a day and a half in the Voidport at Phittsh and then catching the quickest hostel to the capital for his appointment with the bank.

He slept a little more, trusting his internal clock to wake him when it was time to leave but winding his real one anyway. At a juddering stop, a platoon of Gurlish Vulgar soldiers boarded, fat from a long summer of stalemate in the sporadic war against Dool, a country to the west. He studied their shoddy armour and pot-bellies as they crossed the drawbridge over a racing black stream. They must have been stationed in the northern forest in case of a surprise attack on the capital and were only now making their way in for leave. His eyes touched on their weapons, a mixture of old and new; family hand-me-down spring rifles and Gurl-issued lumen pistols with bent sights. Useless in these times of peace; the Treaty of Silp had accomplished much, not least the gradual soothing of simmering tensions among the Vulgar, and nearly all of Filgurbirund's wars appeared to be at an end. Ghaldezuel watched the last of the soldiers amble aboard waving his dirty ticket and returned his attention to the book of architectural drawings until it was time to disembark.

He waited for the Fine Train, wiping the last of the shit smears from his leather boot. The paupers in the hallway hadn't made it easy for him to leave, but a few threats and a broken wrist had soon seen Ghaldezuel through. On the Fine platform, walled off from the gabbling, seething crowd, the first snow of the day floated down to disappear at his feet just as the train arrived. Surly comments from the drunken crowd made him turn to look upon them through the gate, his eyes cold, daring someone to speak.

The train pulled alongside, a fortified red and silver bullet a hundred years old if it was a day but looking for all the world like the most modern thing on this wretched planet. Engines capable of propelling it at ninety miles an hour throbbed through the stone concourse as he made his way aboard, satisfied that his boots wouldn't get any cleaner. This train was owned by the bank, and he—now a valued customer— was to be treated like every inch the lord.

The citadel the Fine Station had been built into rolled away, a soot-black outcrop of rock and brick surrounded by a moat of slums glimpsed and then gone from the window. A steward ushered

Ghaldezuel quickly to his seat in the dining car, taking his travel-
ling cape and stowing it with a flourish. Ghaldezuel relaxed into the
Lacaille finery exposed beneath, a muted suit of mustard and gold,
narrow at the sleeves and fluted at the collar. Across the table, another
Lacaille traveller, an older gentleman with a jewelled eyepatch and a
gaudy Vulgar wife in tow, dipped his head in silent acknowledgment.
On the beaten silver plates before them lay twin mountains of Hag
Bay crablings, alive and squirming. Ghaldezuel studied the couple for
a moment while he removed his long gloves and fixed his cuffs, his gaze
shifting to settle on the twenty miles of shanty land that spun past out-
side. An unwelcome thought came into being as he caught the reflec-
tion of his suit in the window: whether, now things were in motion, he
owned any of the clothes he would die in.

As he watched the land slip by, he also wondered what would
become of the two sitting opposite, stabbing at their crabs; how unions
of their kind would be treated in the ensuing war. It would be a large
conflict, likely dividing all the Prism. He expected the Lacaille and his
wife would find a way out, if they had any influence, feeling noth-
ing for them but a detached sense of irritation. Outside, the red for-
est had receded to a murk of blackened chimneys and wooden houses,
some clearly built many storeys higher than their foundations could
cope with. The Hauberth shanty lands swarmed with Vulgar, jos-
tling among their hovels like an eye socket full of larvae, all motion
and struggle. The richest lived in corrugated tin buildings, tapering
to wooden floors once they were well away from the street fires; the
poorest did not live at all, their white, fish-boned corpses lying prone
in the railway's ditch or festering at the track's edge. More Gurlish
soldiers leaned in doorways to drink, or found what fun there was to
be had in the sturdier buildings on the hill. Ghaldezuel watched them
all, his shrewd eyes going from one structure to another as they raced
past, the miles dissolving. The slums were a labyrinth around the capi-
tal, a thorny barrier against any army, but they were also a dry stack
of kindling, a place of yearly rebellions. Only the Vulgar's sheer tal-
ent for disorganisation protected Hauberth Under Shiel, or Gurl, or
Wiehlish. It was their uselessness that kept the Empire alive.

In no time at all they were beyond the shanty limits, passing high
walls of pitted stone and brick and heading through the commercial

districts of the vast city. Ghaldezuel caught glimpses of black statues rising from plinths at almost every junction—heroes from the Vulgar side of the Investiture Wars, like Ignioz of the Lacaille. He spotted the magicians Verillo and Solida, their ugly faces distinctive even as they blurred past, and a queen, though her name escaped him now.

Ghaldezuel had visited the city before as a young man, but of course its charms—a rare thing out here—were wasted on him then. Returning fully grown to places appeared to neutralise them, made them, he often thought, your equal; you met on mutual terms at last, no longer frightened of getting lost among labyrinthine streets or trampled underfoot in the bustle of thousands. This place, though, this vast foreign capital—this was somewhere it would take a dozen lifetimes to learn. He patted the book of architectural drawings, stowing it as they neared the centre of the capital, and returned his gaze to the buildings, watching them grow in grandeur with each heartbeat.

The train began to slow. A bend of the River Frush rolled by beneath, stained with the colours of Hauberth's hotchpotch industry: greens and reds and yellows, churning like the coloured skin of a Melius. Ghaldezuel smiled at the window, realising at last with whom he would be meeting. Vehicles of all shapes trundled and lumbered across the bridges that spanned the river, the furthest of them nothing but hints in the fog of pollution, while Filgur-bears from some kind of travelling zoo slinked past, roped behind their keeper. Ghaldezuel knew he'd be able to smell the place, thick and potent, had the window been open or the train badly insulated. Music, however, was making its way through the thick plastic as the train slowed to walking pace. The thump of it pulsed through Ghaldezuel's thigh where it leaned against the inside wall.

He looked down at his clothing as everything outside went dark, a tunnel swallowing them, and straightened his cuffs once more. Weak light swept by in bars, lit subterranean doorways, until they entered a chamber of bright white light, cuboid and perfect in its minimalism; the vaults beneath the Bank of Hauberth. Ghaldezuel sat up, peering curiously through the window. The place was almost Amaranthine in its artful simplicity—he half-expected to see an Immortal stalking the underlit floor towards the train as it stopped. It would not have *surprised him in the slightest; these vaults were built with Firmamental money, after all, not a drop of it earned honestly.*

The train stilled at last, the rustle of its passengers reaching for their cases signalling that it would terminate here, beneath the Grand Bank. Ghaldezuel was pleased and yet disappointed not to have had an opportunity to walk the streets. There might not be much time after the meeting. He stretched, collecting his folded travel cape with its multitude of pockets, and made his way quickly to the unsealing doors and out into the bright concourse. He squinted beside the humming train—it really was like being in a vast room made of fluorescence—seeing a squat person striding towards him, bold against the white.

"Sire," the young, immaculately dressed Vulgar said, addressing Ghaldezuel almost as if he were Amaranthine. "This way. Your friend awaits you in Vault Seventeen."

Together they made their way to a wide square arch. Armour-suited guards flanked the hallway further inside, the light now low and muted.

Ghaldezuel's face tensed, a smile just beneath the surface. Here he was, an interstellar terrorist, stepping lightly and calmly into the wealthiest bank on Filgurbirund. Now he was a welcomed guest, escorted and simpered at—in a day's time, well, who knew? Such colossal things could happen in a day. The Lacaille had rearmed four to one and were about to violate a peace hard won by millions of lives. The attack on Nilmuth tomorrow might not go at all to plan, a victim of something crucially unforeseen, but he thought not.

Wondering that nobody had asked him to surrender his pistol, he paced behind the scuttling Vulgar, the great bolted vault doors passing to either side until they reached Seventeen, an especially large chamber cloistered beneath a high arched ceiling. At once, he saw the magnitude of what they were doing, his stride faltering at the view of twenty heaped pyramids of glimmering Vulgar Filgurees. Standing sentinel between them glowered the huge form of Pauncefoot, the Firmamental Melius, even more sumptuously dressed than at their first meeting in a gown of shimmering black silk, his puffed sleeves weighted with milky-white stones.

The giant bowed, his spread hands indicating the pyramids of coins around him. Ghaldezuel formed the impression that the Melius had gained weight in the half-year since he'd seen him last.

"Well then, Ghaldezuel, a pleasure to see you again," Pauncefoot growled, dismissing the clerk with a smart nod of his huge head. "What do you think?"

Ghaldezuel walked between the huge piles of Filgurees to take the Melius's hand. "This would appear sufficient."

Pauncefoot threw his head back in a laugh, clapping Ghaldezuel lightly on the shoulder, his good humour clearly buoyed by his own personal cut of the pyramids around him. "Sufficient! I remember that dry wit from Atholcualan." He indicated an ornamental chair off to one side, placed between the seven-foot-high stacks of currency. "Please, sit."

Ghaldezuel took his seat, eyes running over the coin mountains at his side. They had been arranged meticulously, as was the way of the Hauberth Bank—much as one might find a napkin artfully folded at the dinner table. He would remain, however, to see them packed, just to make sure.

"Each of eight hundred thousand?" he asked, tempted to pull a coin from the base of the nearest pyramid, just to see what would happen. "Equivalent to five and three Truppins apiece?"

"Don't worry, you may stay to supervise the shipping," Pauncefoot said, arranging his gown so that he could sit on the tiled floor. "The Amaranthine have no need for thrift."

Ghaldezuel nodded, folding his arms expectantly. There was more to this meeting; he felt it, saw it in the look on the Firmamental's hideous face. "How have you listed this?"

"Firmamental auction. Obscure as they come."

They stared at each other a moment, the silence of Vault Seventeen filling the space.

"Your team are ready?" Pauncefoot asked. "Hungry?"

"Starved," Ghaldezuel confirmed.

"Well," Pauncefoot continued, choosing his words. "Tell them they mustn't overfeed."

Ghaldezuel sighed, his suspicions confirmed at last. "Out with it."

The silence returned. One might never have guessed that above them raged the largest city on Filgurbirund. Ghaldezuel usually liked stillness, but not now.

"Out with it, Pauncefoot. How does the Firmament expect to use me next?"

"Not you, Ghaldezuel. We only need your team."

We. He was deluded. Ghaldezuel waited for more, his body very still, his face expressionless.

"You alone," Pauncefoot continued slowly, "of all the hundreds of Op-Zlan, command a few of the Bult to some degree. Why? Why will they follow you, and no others? The Firmament can find no trace of a pact similar to this in all the Investiture." He studied Ghaldezuel, great eyes shrewd. "What is your secret?"

Ghaldezuel smiled icily. "Your fortune for it, Pauncefoot. Fair trade?"

The Firmamental Melius's stare persisted. "Very nearly."

Ghaldezuel looked to the money again, evaluating it. "I would not part with them, if that is your command."

"But for a few days? On condition of their return?"

He stirred in his seat, leaning forward. "Speak, Pauncefoot."

The giant blinked at him for a breath more, finally nodding to himself. He shifted on the floor until he was comfortable.

"What do you know of the ex-Satrapy of Tau Ceti? The Zelio-worlds?"

Ghaldezuel hesitated, surprised. "Zelioceti kingdoms. Martially useful in that they lie on the outskirts of Cancri, though—"

"You have been there?"

Ghaldezuel shook his head, trying to work out what the Melius was getting at. "No. Few have. Prism who travel there seldom return." He sat back.

Pauncefoot raised a finger, a clawed twig bunched with rings. "But the Bult are feared by all. Only they would be equal to the task."

"And what task is that?"

Pauncefoot nodded, smiling. "My Firmamental betters have information that there is something of great value there, in one of the Zelioceti Kingdoms. Possibly more valuable than the Shell itself."

Ghaldezuel snorted. "Can they not contain their greed for a moment?"

The Melius held up his finger again. "Your team would merely locate it for us, perhaps guard it until a later date."

Ghaldezuel laced his fingers together, waiting, determined that he would say no more until something concrete was admitted.

"A treasure hunter, commissioned some time ago to find this thing, reported that he had narrowed his search to the moons surrounding Zeli-olopos, a gas giant planet in the system. Before his last message was sent, he indicated that his suspicions lay chiefly in three moons—AntiZelio-Slaathis, Glumatis and Coriopil." Pauncefoot paused. "He has not been heard from now for many months, likely another victim of the place."

Ghaldezuel motioned for him to go on.

"The object," Pauncefoot continued, "is, I will admit, something barely understood even by the Firmament, but my benefactor insists upon its provenance."

"Your benefactor is often privy to wisdom to which the Firmament is not?"

Pauncefoot laughed. "Of course!"

Ghaldezuel sighed. "What is it?"

The giant hesitated, appraising the great heap of Filgurees at his side. Deftly he plucked one of the coins free from the base, followed by two more. The pyramid did not waver, Ghaldezuel saw.

"I cannot tell you because I do not rightly know myself. All I understand is the sum they have offered." He tucked the coins untidily back into the pyramid, and Ghaldezuel felt an abrupt urge to push the entire heap over on top of the Melius.

"Entry into the Firmament, Ghaldezuel. True Amaranthine life, for you and me." He looked levelly at Ghaldezuel in the way that people convinced of the power of their own words are wont to do. "Not a soul among the Prism has ever been offered this before."

All these promises, all these incentives. At this rate they'd be offering him the Immortal Throne itself in a matter of days. Ghaldezuel gazed at the coins. The Filguree was a better-made thing than a Lacaille Truppin. Its weight never varied.

"I know what I want, Pauncefoot," he said firmly, "and it's very simple. I want to see the Vulgar suffer, and I want assurances *that the Bult I lend you will have no further troubles in our new Investiture."*

Pauncefoot beamed. "Then I wish you the very best of luck for tomorrow."

WARNINGS

Amaranthine woke quickly, the line separating their dreams from reality almost too thin to notice. Hugo sat up in bed, gazing out at pretty Vaulted Ectries to the brooding storm clouds, his fingers twined in the sheets. His gaze shifted to the clacking motions of the clock at the end of the hall. A long sleep: more than two weeks.

There had been a man present, accompanying him during all that time; a kind presence who walked beside him. He didn't sleep again for some time, some part of him—some watchful, higher instinct—not wanting to see that man again.

But not even Amaranthine could stay awake forever. Sleep found him, submerging him instantly into memories ten thousand years old, their reality viewed like quicksilver reflections from beneath the waves, and there, weightless beneath the meniscus of light, they met each other again.

There are hundreds of them, childlike primates with beady little eyes, busying themselves under white lights.

They are polishing.

Hugo walks among them, losing himself in the rows of little people. They mumble and mutter to one another, and yet the whole vast place, a white cave full of gargantuan machinery, is still and without echoes.

He crouches, settling himself on the floor to observe their work. In their long nails they clutch rags that look older than he is, and wipe and buff and blow on their treasures. He takes a piece from someone's oblivious hand, turning it in his own.

A silvery connector the size of a small beetle, machined to Amaranthine perfection. He puts it down and looks among the creatures. Combined, they hold in their hands something extremely complex: a *system, a functioning assortment of parts that once meant vastly more than their sum. A device built, only to be dismantled again that same day. He searches for the word.*

A collection.

The Collection.

Perception's mortal remains.

What were you dreaming, Hugo?

He woke, on another, more ancient world. "I saw what you're going to do."

Maneker opened his useless eyes to the throbbing darkness of the *Hasziom*'s night. Voices floated from the mess beneath him.

I've been looking through your adventure books, Huerepo, said Perception. *They're rather good, actually.*

The Vulgar sniffed, putting down his spoon. He looked at Lycaste as he spoke. "It might be nice if you asked permission, once in a while, before rootling around in things that aren't yours, Perception."

How is it that you can read? Perception continued, oblivious. *From what you tell us, you lead a menial life.*

Huerepo glared into the darkness of the Hasziom's mess. They ate alone, barring the odd interruption of Smallbone as he fussed up and down the ladder. Maneker—having taken the captain's old chamber—was keeping determinedly to himself, and Poltor was busy fiddling with all the equipment aboard their new Lacaille ship. The Oxel rattled about the place, whistling signal and distance checks, their scampering foot-falls trembling through the upper level like comforting, pattering rain.

"I keep them more for the pictures," Huerepo said eventually, getting back to work on his dinner, a baked egg mixture provided by whatever the tiny caged birds could produce.

But you don't have schools, as such, Perception said, its voice circling.

Huerepo cleared his throat. "You'd have to go to Filgurbirund for that sort of thing, but it's a lot of money just to sit and look at some hand-me-down Amaranthine books."

And the children must work.

Huerepo nodded. "Of course."

Lycaste shovelled a mouthful, reminded of his own indolent childhood.

"Most Vulgar—nearly all of them—don't make it far once they're out of the belly, anyway," Huerepo said. "You have to smack them until they breathe, and then there's the Gripes and the Runnies to finish 'em off, not to mention Wood-Knockers."

Lycaste glanced up. "What are they?"

"Hoopies from the wilds, come for their baby toll as soon as they're out, when they're juiciest."

Lycaste stared at him, horrified.

"It's just the price paid." Huerepo shrugged, grinning. "I can tell you there are much, *much* worse places to be."

Smallbone wandered past, setting down a bottle.

"Like where?" Lycaste asked.

Huerepo didn't have to think for long. "Humaling."

"A planet?"

A star, home to three planets and a dozen moons of the same name.

"Indeed," Huerepo said. "I wouldn't set foot on Humaling Minor for the bloody Immortal crown itself."

"What's there?" Lycaste leaned forward, entranced, hairs bristling on his skin.

"Caves," Huerepo replied. "More caves than could ever be explored. Caves where the woods grow deep underground. There are things that came with the first settlers lurking in them all. Things that grab you and drag you down."

Or there are the worlds of Indak-Australis, Perception said. *I've read about them. Places of perpetual war.*

"Yes, the Australis Moons, the Southern Moons. Jungles so thick that you couldn't push more than ten feet in a day in any direction. They've been at war with each other for a few generations now—some are so cut off that even if armistice comes they'll just keep on fighting. Or there are the night-dark Threen worlds, Obviado and Obscura, of course, but nobody ever goes there anyway."

"The Zelio-worlds," Smallbone muttered, waddling through to collect the dishes. "The Zelioceti there are inbred to the bone, must be mad through and through."

Huerepo shook his head, pushing his plate in Smallbone's direction. "That's just a toll gap out of the Firmament, a gateway you must pay to use. The Zelios create rumours to make sure everyone passes through."

Lycaste sensed Perception gathering its thoughts. He looked up into the darkness, beyond the candles' flickering reach.

Anyone ever seen a Bult?

The table fell silent. Smallbone and Huerepo glanced at one another, each performing a little clap.

"*No*, thank you very much, Perception," Huerepo said.

The Spirit chuckled. *Sorry I spoke.*

"Some folk had a dead one once, when I was little," Smallbone said, looking troubled. "Paraded it around on a stick for everybody to see. Don't know what happened to the corpse."

Lycaste passed his plate to Smallbone, feeling as if the shadows of the mess were closing in on him.

But the Void is a calm and beautiful sea, Perception said, his voice very close to Lycaste's ear. *Its little islands need not concern us.*

"Couldn't agree more, Percy," Huerepo said, popping the top off the bottle. "It's a good life out here, when we're not being attacked."

Smallbone settled himself beside them, lighting a few more sputtering candles. Their crew couldn't dwindle much more without Lycaste himself taking on duties, and nobody wanted that. It was just as well that others would soon be coming; a host of hired swords keen to join what Maneker, in the closest the miserable man ever got to levity, had called *the great hunt*.

Lycaste looked around the mess, reflecting nervously that the cluttered place would never be this empty again.

LOOT

Night crept in, throwing shadows across the land and wreathing the risen moon in cloud.

Jatropha looked up at the walls of Zadar, his clothes fluttering in the night wind, and ran a finger over the glossy stones. Their fabric had been polished smooth to prevent people from the wilds—people like him—from climbing. But that wouldn't be a problem.

Once inside and wrapped invisibly in warm light, he walked the corkscrew of passages to the dining halls. Firelight threw his shadow long against the wall to mingle with those of the eating Melius, and Jatropha watched his black silhouette as he crept along. He could hide the thing, of course, simply by moving closer to it, but he rarely did. It pranced among the others, the only evidence of his passing, unnoticed by all. He'd given his forty hired ravens a glint of that magic, diminishing each of them within their own personal blind spots. The trick of hiding others as well as himself came easily to him, though he suspected the Amaranthine population as a whole were yet to master it with any skill.

He stepped over a snoozing shape as he made his way up into the Museum of Curios, a place he'd heard of but never visited. He hoped it hadn't all been sold off.

The door stood bolted from top to bottom, dangling with shiny padlocks. Jatropha pressed one hand lightly to the wood and popped every lock, catching each of them in his other hand and placing them on the floor.

The museum's contents had once been in the possession of the Second, in a private collection for paying friends of High Plenipotentiary Alba, Gentleson of Flacht. When the First had found him embezzling Provincial taxes, his estates had been raided and the museum's contents sold off. It was Zadar's luck that its own mayor had also been sequestering citadel silk and decided to buy the entire lot.

Jatropha entered, his slowly beating heart barely affecting the lanterns, and surveyed the scene. The Melius idea of a museum was quite different from that of their relatives of old. Where once, Jatropha supposed, items were arranged for ease of viewing, here one had to stoop and rummage, taking things out of boxes or relocating whatever was heaped on top, so that around the room huge teetering piles of ring books and ornaments rose almost to the ceiling. The habit resulted in fascinating things often remaining lost for generations, since nobody really wanted to disturb a dangerous-looking heap that might fall on them at any moment.

Jatropha moved between them, running through an inventory in his head as he dug in chests and boxes. A slim, twinkling chain had been hung along one wall, and threaded upon it were more than a hundred old ring pistols from the reigns of the early Enlightenment kings. He pulled down one end of the chain and tipped a handful of them into his pocket, for inspection later.

Jatropha continued his rummaging even as he heard footsteps. A mutter of confusion from a steward who must have come to the door and noticed the busted locks. A head poked wearily in, followed by a lantern. The Amaranthine paid little heed, but spared a thought for the man's sanity by making his motions more delicate. They passed within a few inches of each other as Jatropha continued his search and before long were at opposite sides of the room. He spotted the black dart of a raven circling the tower, the first of the birds come up to see what he had for them, and he began carefully placing items on the window ledge.

The steward completed his circuit and was heading back towards Jatropha when he spotted some moved books and stared at them thoughtfully. Jatropha waited until the birds had each fluttered up to grab what he handed them and then gave the steward a quick pat on the head.

"Who—?" the Melius spluttered.

Jatropha swung out of the window, pushed himself away from the ledge and dropped.

He fell past the glimmering wall, arms outstretched, the black shadows of his birds wheeling around him, the wind whipping at his lank hair, chilling his skin. As the silvery darkness of the woods rose up to meet him, he clasped his hands together, body turning, and delicately slowed his descent until he was only a few inches above the treetops.

He had fallen over a hundred feet. He looked down at his white toes where they floated above the leaves and felt reinvigorated.

The birds cackled, circling him.

"Show-off!" one called.

Jatropha hung there, levitating in the fresh night wind. He glanced up at the far tower where he'd been searching, seeing the winking of the steward's tiny light.

Pentas's eyes slid across the engraved sentences, reading them without comprehension. She stopped and leaned her arm out on the moonlit ledge. Arabis slept peacefully, mouth agape, a victim of the Amaranthine's soothing lullabies.

Her thoughts had turned, as they did every night without fail, to the child's father. Had he been a good man, after all was said and done? Pentas didn't know any more.

She'd loved Callistemon—heavens, she loved him still—but that did nothing to answer the question. You might appeal, momentarily, to a monster's tenderness, but a monster it remained.

She found a well-worn memory, her eyes stinging as she recalled Impatiens—sweet Impatiens now almost six months dead—standing there listening with them, listening to Callistemon admitting his treachery.

How many had he killed? She swept the thought away for the thousandth time. One, twenty—what was the difference? Callistemon had left a wake of death behind him even as he'd entered the cove, its lingering swell dragging poor Lycaste and Impatiens under with it. It had taken the discovery of the dead Players—a happy troupe of professionals seen often on the Province roads as they wandered north and south—to convince her to leave with Jatropha and Eranthis. With the Players gone, too, the Tenth had lost its lustre somehow, not that she'd ever really wanted to go there in the first place.

She glanced at the sleeping resemblance of her lost love, tinted by the vague colour of the moon. How could she ever tell Arabis the truth? Jatropha had said, in an effort to prepare her, that in the Second they would venerate Callistemon's name. He'd also told her that, perhaps not immediately but soon enough, the family Berenzargol would wish her gone.

Pentas looked again at her little prisoner, remembering the guilty relief.

They will turn the young queen against you as best they can, perhaps not even allowing communication by letter—though I shall see to that if you desire it. It is only their nature. You are a Southerner, an interloper, and their leniency will be hard won. With one hand you bring misery; with the other their great advancement.

Pentas yawned and tugged at the blankets, hearing the distant tinkling of Eranthis moving about the *Corbita's* scullery. Folded away in a box of things by the bed were her newest drawings, scribbled with whatever materials she could buy on the road. She had talent, everyone said so: there should be no need to cling to some maligned role in the Firstling court. She could make her own way in life at last.

She thought fuzzily of her route as her eyelids drooped. She would go south, perhaps to Tripol or the Scarlet Lands, where there were small academies of painting and literature. Her daughter . . . *her* daughter—

Arabis would never know her.

Pentas lay, eyes open to the green night. They would meet, if they ever did meet again, as strangers.

Jatropha took a moment to linger in the woods as he landed, watching the lights of the *Corbita* from afar.

He remembered.

He remembered the look of the bent coin they gave him after his first month. It bore the sideways leer of King Tharrhypas. He remembered his last meal before he put such things aside. Ibex—what those on the peak called *poor cow*—stuffed with sage, eaten with a cob of rye bread and a dirty egg fried on the black pan. Out had slipped a double yolk, before he'd stirred it up. The last of his luck, perhaps. He knew even then that he would save a lifetime's money by spurning food and drink and was glad at the efficiency of it all. He didn't suppose he'd miss it.

He remembered leaving, selling his goats to the exceedingly young wife of a wicked man named Hals, noticing her looks with the vacant eye of a shepherd inspecting for worms. There *had* been a girl, once, but choosing this life had hurt her. There wouldn't be any more.

He left the mountains with a dry mouth and enough rubbed heads of Tharrhypas to get him as far as Stalia, on the coast. From there it wouldn't be far to Gaul, according to those he met in the hills. Liguria, he said to himself, tasting the name of the range as he left it—his whole world until now.

At the coast, he found a leaky merchant ship come up from the Mare Nostrum, the *Corbita*, and changed his plans, saying goodbye to the Alps from the golden beaches. Proving he could keep in rhythm as an oarsman bought him passage west to Nikaia, but the bawdy place unnerved him. Too much noise, too many folk up from Italia, up from Rome. He took a basement room below a tannery that smelled of dog shit by day and dog shit at night. His landlord was brown as varnished oak and leopard-spotted with a constellation of moles like black, weeping stars. He lanced the things in place of rent, but the man died anyway, hiccoughing his way through cups of doctor-prescribed milk.

Iulius, he was called then, back in the days when the name was common. The name his father had given him. When the name grew antiquated he changed it slightly, remaining simple Julius for as long as he could in memory of his first life. And that was how he survived. Looking back on fifteen thousand and eighty-four years of life, he reflected that he couldn't have foreseen how out of hand things would become.

As the first people were achieving their false, upstart immortality, he decided it was time to withdraw further from the affairs of the world. Jatropha's burgeoning powers were already revealing themselves, thousands of years before the Amaranthine, as they would come to be known, would ever discover their own, and there were rumours dogging his footsteps: rumours of someone who people in their newfound longevity had come to recognise a little too well. He'd hated them for it, then, when their long memories had forced him into hiding. Never mind that his was something more real, something natural, some quirk of birth that, as far as he knew—and he *had* looked—had never once been repeated, before or since. A child born naturally immortal, into a populace considered old at fifty.

And so the years passed, thickening to bands of dashing millennia, until the world had warped and twisted. When he took his Melius name, having decided to remain in the Southerly Provinces most of the year round, he knew, as he had known about the girl—and, to some degree, the fried egg—that it would be his last.

He was tired now, and the world had grown quiet. There was no one to run from any more.

THE FEEDERS

Timing. Take a few breaths before the punchline. Wit appears to go wrong so often because people are desperate for it.

Lycaste grumbled and opened his mouth to try again, not understanding all this need for pauses and slow reveals. He was frustrated and hungry. All they had on board now was Rubante honey, and that was nothing but candied glue, really, food not fit for a Melius.

Oh, take a break. Perception was sighing before he'd got three words in. *That's enough for now. We'll try again when you are seven hundred and must pause for breath between each word.*

Lycaste scowled and pressed his nose against the cold plastic, the vibrations of the Lacaille ship tickling his nostrils, watching the colours of the Feeders intensify. "But I did everything you said."

I know. You are studious.

"Studious," Lycaste repeated, running his fingers through the cropped stubble of his freshly shaved head. Not a word his father had ever used. Lycaste imagined himself returning home, back to Kipris Isle, dumping his bags on the parlour floor and announcing earnestly: *Father, I've become a studious man.* The old fellow would just about die laughing, he supposed.

He smiled as they looked out together into the Void.

A purple aurora two miles wide fell past their porthole, dropping out of sight and snaking off into the sliver depths. *The exhausts of the Feeders,* Maneker had called it, leaping from his room upon hearing the gentle, drifting signature over the trumpets. This was what he'd been looking for, this grand brushstroke of colour.

When their course had first intersected it, the crew had been able to see the whole wake as it drifted by, a comet tail of coloured particulates as fine as smoke painted across the Void. Now, as they approached side-on, the superluminal current's edges had blurred, softening to drift and disperse. *Your Melius eyes can distinguish more than thirty million colours, you know,* Perception said when they'd first gone to the tiny porthole to look. *Three times as many as Maneker, before he lost his sight. Remember that, when you forget to see the beauty in things.*

Lycaste was thinking about colour as he looked out at roughly a hundred thousand miles of contrail beyond the windows. He'd assumed everyone saw things in the same way, and yet apparently they did not, dwelling in greyish worlds by comparison. Colour had always been so important to him but he'd never appreciated it. The Spirit itself said that it could see much further, following the Feeders' tail back to the last Satrapy they'd come from. The caravanserai of ships were far too small for anyone—including Perception—to see from this distance, and like an algal bloom were visible only by their massed colour, bright against the dappled silver.

The current was a lucky find, Maneker said, the trajectory of the thousands of ships exactly overlaying their own; heading straight for a hard, black little star: Gliese, its single Vaulted Land christened with the same name. At the contrail's head, like a white follicle dangling a million-mile-long purple hair, a swiftly moving dot churned its own darker swirls into the colour. Together they looked at it now, their lesson in jokes forgotten.

A Colossus battleship, Perception said, *the largest class of ship in the Investiture.*

Lycaste tried to focus on the minuscule dash of white, hardly visible itself against the silver of space. He could see now that the great current was flecked here and there with plumes of scintillating green, like a Piebird's tail feather. "How do you know?"

I've read every last chart and record on this ship. That is probably the Grand-Tile *or the* Balnazo, *judging from its vast exhaust patterns. See how it changes the colours in its wake?*

Lycaste nodded, leaning away from the grubby plastic and rubbing his squashed nose. "Aren't we going to have trouble catching up with it?"

In our current state, yes, but I have refurbishments in mind. It paused, as if for breath, a moment in which more thoughts than Lycaste would ever have in his life were surely taking place. *I can see them all now. Jostling for the lead. What was that? Ooh—fighting.*

The sparkle of light reached Lycaste a moment later, a lonely flash breaking through the seething purple churn of dust-mote specks.

"Can you see what we're looking for? The Bunkship?"

Yes. About fifty-five thousand miles out, not too far from the lead.

Lycaste stared. Slowly, as if his eyes were inventing the whole thing, the trail was resolving into myriad different colours, the superluminal light twinkling off a writhing mass of shapes. A thought, so sudden and unwelcome that it made him forget the sight, brought his gaze up to where he assumed the Spirit hung in the air. Something Perception had said.

"What day is it, Percy? Do you know?"

Day?

He glanced back into the battery chamber, as if the answer would lie somewhere among the great tin guns. "It must be Ember by now. Must be."

I believe it's not long until the Amaranthine new year, if that helps.

Lycaste frowned, appalled that the thought hadn't come to him until now. "I don't know," he said, trying to count in his head, "but I think I might have missed my *birthday*." The memory of last year, bright and vivid, prompted a sudden ache in his throat, along with the thought that he'd let this year's pass, like a present received without a word of thanks.

Oh. I shouldn't worry. The days are all the same out here, it seems. Perception paused, perhaps registering the tears just behind Lycaste's eyes. *You said you are fifty-two?*

He nodded. "I think I must be, now." Last year, a life gone forever now. The arrival of the Players, shy smiles as he was introduced to Pentas, a gift of tiny furniture from Eranthis for his model palace.

That is a good age to be, for your breed. Matured in practicable ways and yet young enough still.

He didn't reply, remembering the production the Players had staged just for him, right on his beach, flaming torches the only light. Like a dolt, he'd missed the first half, too shy to come down.

Well, I'm going up top, Perception said, a rich, powerful tone in his head, drawing a line under the conversation. Lycaste recalled it had been talking to him. *Are you coming?*

He followed the moving voice, rubbing his eyes with his knuckles and blinking. The harsh, crisp air in the ship made everyone's eyes weep uncontrollably anyway.

They passed from the bunk deck through to the mess and up into the elevated cockpit, Lycaste's sadness ebbing. It was a wonderful place, much better equipped than the *Epsilon*'s, though its low ceiling meant he had to walk with a constant stoop. Three periscope-like gun decks rose from the ship's nose, manned now by the remaining Oxel. Lycaste squeezed himself onto the bare tin floor, realising too late that he'd sat in something sticky.

Somewhere behind them the *Epsilon* flew in convoy, piloted by Poltor and Huerepo. They called their own distance and signal checks through the comms, keeping in contact once a minute as per Maneker's instructions.

Between their checks, the listening trumpets blared a haunting chorus, mapping out the sounds of the Feeders as they passed at last within the forward wave antennas, and every hair on Lycaste's body rose. The sound wasn't anything like the howl of Port Rubante as they'd approached. This was different: this was the sound of life, a teeming cesspool of squirming, dashing bodies. Squeals and cries mingled with pops, thuds and whistles until they'd homed in on the deeper tones of the large vessel they were after.

"Got it," Maneker said, listening hard into the trumpets. His hand trailed along the small instruments, finding a dented dial and fiddling with it. The volume increased.

A groaning, clicking hum filled the cockpit while they tracked the source of it.

There, Perception said, whistling to the Oxel. They climbed their gun stations to look out, shading their eyes against the purple-green light.

Lycaste stood. Already they were almost within the current. His mouth opened.

For a mile above and below, the silver of the Void was packed with movement, dashing metal bodies painted in every colour Lycaste had ever seen. Smaller vessels clustered around weightier, more stately-looking things, billowing clouds and vortexes in the cauldron of suspended engine smoke. This close, the purple colouration of the trail— so obvious from afar—had almost disappeared, and Lycaste was dimly aware that they, too, would be contributing to the wondrous smear of colour, adding a minuscule dash of green as they entered the tail.

He saw it now through the swirls of haze: a huge dented cylinder of rust-streaked, patched metal, easily a hundred times the size of their own ship, crowned with turrets at its bow. It rolled like a bolt fired from a chamber, spinning as it travelled, its banners trailing out behind through the specks of following ships.

"That'll be a stolen habitation tank, from pre-Amaranthine times," Maneker said. "Similarly purloined engines welded onto the back. Not particularly inventive."

I admire their ingenuity. Why not use what goes to waste?

Maneker looked up, eyebrows raised above his bandages. "You won't be saying that soon."

The Spirit fell silent, a palpable charge building in the stale air. Lycaste went to his bag in the passage and began the careful ritual of donning his underclothes, wondering what the Amaranthine might have meant.

Soon they were behind it, accelerating hard through the flock of thousands of Voidships, their squawks and chatter abruptly pouring from the trumpets.

"This Bunk Barge called *Gulty's Home*," Poltor's voice said weakly over the comms. "Owned by Grand Company. Twenty-five Filgurees for one night's staying, but we can hide in there if maybe need longer—everyone else do this. I have bunkmate once stay nine years free."

"We only need a few hours," Maneker said sternly over the comms. He returned to his seat, buckling himself in with unsure fingers. "You're sure you can do this, Perception?"

Just buy me the bits and pieces.

Maneker nodded, his lips stretching into a slow, blind smile. Lycaste looked on, surprised. Things must be going well. The Amaranthine brought from his new fur-lined cloak a package of letters he must have written on the journey from Rubante, flicking out a hand in Lycaste's general direction.

Lycaste went to him, taking the package and looking at the neat script—almost as perfect as when the man could see—scrawled upon them.

"I'm leaving these with you. Don't lose them. I can't recede—I can't hide myself when we get inside, there'll be too many eyes on us." He turned his blind gaze on Lycaste. "And you're not to take your pistol, Lycaste, you hear me? I can't have any commotion." He looked off towards the sound of the listening trumpets. "We're too close now. Too close."

"But how—"

"Perception will keep an eye on you." He angled his bandaged head. "Won't you, Percy?"

I don't recall us settling on that friendly term, Primogenitor.

Maneker pulled his robe around him, his mouth turning down at the corners.

Lycaste grinned, stuffing the bundle of letters down inside his collar. In the armoury he'd found a good quality Pifoon-made Void-suit that looked as if it might fit him. After the attack on the *Epsilon*, Lycaste didn't want to take any chances and had decided to wear it as often as possible. The sky-blue suit, missing its helmet and one boot, had clearly been made for a Firmamental Melius a little shorter than him. Bespoke, Huerepo had said. Lycaste wondered if it had belonged to someone important. Across its scratched steel chest it bore the Firmamental regalia: a fabulously intricate blazing gold star decorated with twenty-four flaming points, one for each of the old Satrapies of Decadence. Unlike the coal-burning things the invading Lacaille had worn, Lycaste's used a small gas-fed boiler to heat radiator pipes in the hands and feet. The warmth inside the suit was compounded by a layer of greasy, sweat-musky fur that lined the innards. Lycaste had taken the thing apart and scrubbed it, throwing out an extremely dirty plastic groin cup and funnel set that must have collected waste, and found it much more pleasant after that. He wore one of his Firmamental boots to replace the missing part of the suit, understanding from Huerepo's lectures that the shoe wouldn't serve as a replacement should he end up outside of the ship. Now, barring a Void-worthy shoe, all he needed was a helmet, perhaps not hard to find on a Bunk Barge but probably quite expensive. He regretted asking Huerepo what would happen if he fell out into the Void without one.

I must say, I'm quite excited to see these other Prism, Perception said beside him as the Bunk Barge grew beyond the porthole.

"I'm not," Lycaste replied, screwing a gauntlet into his new vambrace and wrapping a piece of Amaranthine fabric around his neck like a scarf. He shrugged on the silver cuirass he'd found in the Oratory over the top of the suit, feeling reassuringly layered in metal as he buckled it tight.

Poltor says it holds forty thousand of the things at a time. Prisoners as well as sleepers.

"Forty thousand," Lycaste repeated, unable to comprehend the number. There had only been a few hundred people living in the Tenth.

A trifling number compared with the population of the Investiture itself, of course.

Lycaste's ears twitched. "I heard Poltor say there were millions?"

About a hundred and eighty billion, all told, and yet still the Amaranthine call this the Quiet Age.

Lycaste fretted thoughtfully at the buttons on his lightly frilled collar, still unused to the process of doing them up. Last night he'd had a strange dream; by no means the first in half a year's worth of strange beds. He looked up, tired of fiddling with the buttons and deciding they looked slightly more raffish undone, for some reason. "What did your body look like, Perception?"

The air appeared to draw breath, contemplative. *Well, I have no memory of my body. I was told they . . . that my mind was taken out while I was still in infancy.*

"But *with* a body," he said, "you could have left that place?"

If the Amaranthine hadn't cast their spells to keep me there, yes.

"But how? Wouldn't you be lighter as you are?"

I see your thinking, Lycaste, and these were my same thoughts, once. It appears, though, that it isn't quite so simple.

"I suppose I wouldn't understand, even if you told me."

Perhaps you could. Look—imagine my spirit is measured in force, *like the tip of a blade, pressed firmly. Driven into flesh I will sink quickly, easily, until I reach the bone, yes?* Perception paused, apparently to give him room to take the image in, before resuming. *Gravity is the hand that does the deed, driving my soul into any place of great solidity—a moon, for instance—and I am trapped.*

Lycaste frowned, uneasy at the comparison.

Now suppose I am blunted, the pressure of my blade spread over a wider area. I may now sit, freely and without complication, on the surface of the flesh. This, it seems to me, is what happens when a soul inhabits a body—it is spread more evenly, buoyed and entwined within every little cell, and cannot sink. Gravity's pull upon it is weakened, and it may come and go as it pleases.

Lycaste raised his eyebrows. "That does make sense . . . I think."

The theory appears to have occurred to our friend the Pretender as well. Perception fell silent for a breath, a breath in which Lycaste's mind struggled with a hundred more questions. *What's brought all this on?*

"Well," Lycaste said, fumbling with his buttons again, "I think I saw your face."

Oh? A note of humour. *When?*

"Last night, in a dream."

And what do I look like?

Lycaste couldn't articulate the image in his mind. What he'd really seen, at first from far above and then at eye level, as if he'd been in the process of landing a Voidship, was a mask; a mask the size of the world, wrapped around the world. It wasn't made from wood or metal, like any masks from home, but of something like coral, its surface pitted and white like a dead and ancient reef. Inside the chambers of the material whole cities thrived, ecosystems of little white machines that trundled about like ponderous thoughts, and dwarfish Prism people wearing fabulous clothes. Upon disembarking, Lycaste had got himself swiftly lost inside the white coral chambers, running up and down for what felt like days until he found the way out.

"I think what I saw was—" he stopped to rephrase "—I saw what the world would be like, had they let you live."

Indeed? And was it a good world?

Lycaste didn't know what to say. "I suppose so. It was very different."

Hmm.

In the dream, the air within the coral chambers had been softly smoky, as if a fire smouldered somewhere in the deeper hollows of the place. Lycaste had woken thinking it was the thousands of trapped souls the vast city had produced, sunk to cling like mist to the curved floors.

"So where," he asked, finally doing up the buttons again, "do people's spirits go? All those that aren't as . . . forceful . . . as yours?" The ship groaned and thumped, ticking as it expanded and contracted. Lycaste's throat ached. "Where will *mine* go?"

He felt its kindness then, like a warmth around him. *In truth, I don't know, Lycaste. The nearest star, perhaps, or to the largest celestial body of sufficient attraction. It might be that they are light enough to escape into some other place we cannot see.*

"Ah." He'd been thinking about this. "But what about people who die and wake up again?"

Well, they aren't fully dead, then, are they?

"But—"

Look, Lycaste. I've seen death. I watched this ship's late captain leave his body.

Lycaste gulped. "You saw him? You saw his soul?"

Clear as day.

"What did it look like?" He found he almost didn't want to know.

Dull. Like a bodily waste, voided at the end along with everything else.

"It didn't look like him?" For some reason, Lycaste had a mental image of a tired little Lacaille face, drifting away on the wind.

No, Perception said sharply. *Why should it? The arrangement of his eyes and mouth wasn't him, was it?*

Lycaste felt a little chastened. He supposed not. It chilled him to imagine that, once he died, he would never have his own face again. He thought suddenly back to all the days he'd cursed the good fortune of his looks.

"Makes you thankful, I suppose," he said weakly.

Appreciation, Lycaste, like I said.

They were angling above the tangled tubing of the Bunk Barge's engines, the serpentine shape of the *Epsilon* powering ahead. The *Hasziom* followed through the groove their old ship had ploughed in the fog, rising over the bulk of *Gulty's Home* and heading for the forward access towers, which rose like crenelated castle spires in the coloured mist.

Keep your pistol.

"But Maneker said—"

Tactical forgetfulness. Stuff it into your suit with the letters.

"I'll feel much better knowing it's there."

Precisely. It serves a greater purpose as an instrument of calm.

The air within was surprisingly cold, as if the hull of the giant ship was very thin indeed. Moisture beaded beneath Lycaste's nose as he stepped out of the *Hasziom's* hangar and looked around. The whole vast place was fogged with a dank grey pall of smoke, barely breathable in places and glowing where fire-pits lit the haze. He turned, examining the various tents and wooden structures that surrounded their dock, then stepped back to gaze upwards.

They had come in through one of fifteen enormous, irregular holes punched into the shell of the great barrel-shaped ship, rising through a colossal set of iron doors and settling in the darkness of a frozen airlock while Poltor suited up and went to pay the bargemaster. After almost a Quarter of waiting—during which Maneker had grown exponentially more enraged at the thought of Poltor having a little drink at their expense—the overhead doors had rolled away, spilling roiling mist and light, permitting the two ships entry.

Lycaste stumbled on rubbish as he gagged at the stink of the place, climbing a hillock of tiny bones and scraps to get a look at the foggy interior of the Bunk Barge. It was like a nest of bats he'd found once in the caves near his old house, a place of dripping stalagmites moulded from the creatures' own droppings, the floor swarming with beetles and flies.

What must once have been a smooth, bare cylindrical chamber about half a mile across had now been busily filled with an enormous, seething nest of bunk spaces made up of millions of planks of wood precariously nailed into shelves and buttresses and floors, all stretching into the middle of the huge place. Each little self-made hovel sported the glow of a distant fire, so that the place looked like a twinkling, deeply orange-lit cave veiled with a film of moving cloud, the Prism's own crude attempt at a Vaulted Land. He shivered in the cold smoke, imagining how many times the fires must have swept out of control and burned the place up.

A dark structure rose out of that layer of smog into the centre of the cylindrical space. Arched like the legs of a million spiders, the shadows of bridges, wobbling with tiny black Prism, stretched off up to their pinnacle: a teetering assortment of ramshackle fortresses that sprouted chimneys and walkways, unsupported but for the myriad spindly buttresses and bridges that held them up, like strings across a chasm of empty space.

The Posthouse. That's where we'll have to go.

"Was that you in there?" Lycaste thought he'd felt something ticklish slide inside the fur lining of his Voidsuit, like a tendril of mist.

The Amaranthine has been busy. He's calling in every favour and debt he can.

"How do you know?"

I've just read those letters you're carrying. Hundreds of coded messages, worryingly simple to decipher. Still, he disseminates his vast fortune wisely, as far as I can tell, purchasing only the best.

An Amaranthine fortune, Lycaste mused, picking his way through the dim air. "Have we got enough money?"

More than enough. The Filgurees Poltor received for the prisoners will pay for everything we need. They were an experienced crew, those Lacaille.

"But you saw to them easily enough."

Needs must.

Lycaste felt the weight of the Vulgar coins Huerepo had given him as pocket money, sensing their worth in a way that he never had with silk.

"I haven't thanked you properly, Percy."

A pleasure.

"If you hadn't been with us . . ."

Indeed.

He rubbed his gauntlets together with a tinny scraping sound, saying no more, suddenly aware that there were creatures, nothing but gloomy apparitions, wandering around on the rubbish pile with him. They didn't appear inclined to come close, content instead to rummage among the cast-offs from the dock. Lycaste spied some charred metal springs and wire near his boot but didn't think this was the sort of thing Perception would be after. It wanted specific equipment, the significance of which Lycaste wouldn't have recognised even if he were locked in here to search for a thousand years. The Spirit's ingenuity confounded him; it had no more expertise in electrical and magnetic systems than he did, and yet knew already how to dismantle an engine and improve it. Lycaste imagined how different his life could have been with a fraction of Percy's cleverness and hoped that perhaps, if he spent enough time in the Spirit's company, a little might rub off.

Just as he was wondering if there were any Melius-size helmets buried in the heap, one of the scavenging creatures dug a squirming, sleepy-looking resident out of the pile and set about throttling it. The squeals died off while the thing hoisted its lantern to examine what it had killed. Lycaste watched, fascinated, as the scavenger went to work licking the skin from its prey in loud, rasping slurps.

Best get going.

"Yes," he whispered, making his way along the dune of rubbish to a three-storey wooden shack, stepping over a trio of black, hairy little people that surrounded him before scampering away. Across the rubbish heaps, ships were docked in their hundreds, making something that resembled a small city. Lycaste looked out as he made his faltering way along, noticing many of the smaller vessels were stacked three or four high inside makeshift wooden towers. Of the larger ships, most appeared to have been taken apart and rebuilt into elaborate tin hovels.

A lot of these must have entered here in such bad repair that they couldn't get out again, Perception said.

He nodded, taking in the city of rebuilt ships and their thousands of lights and fires, the hundreds of chimney stacks dribbling smoke into the misty cloud. In the grey dimness, Perception seemed to pause and ruminate, as if looking him over in the manner of a displeased mother. *Walk with confidence, Sire Lycaste; you are a giantling journeyman with a demon perched upon your shoulder. The Firmament has never seen the likes of you before.*

Lycaste grinned, not minding the foetid air so much anymore. He straightened his back, watching scuttling people in the shadows hesitate as they noticed him. "You're on my shoulder?"

Occasionally. The varying gravity in here's a little tiresome.

He made his way alongside the fire-pits, stepping over plank hovels secreted in the darkness. Their occupants hooted and jabbered, stoking the flames. Sounds travelled slowly here, and Lycaste's head swelled again whenever he encountered pockets of lower air pressure. Gravity, as the Spirit had claimed, appeared to cling in the hollows as he walked, the smoke rolling and sinking lower here and there to reveal more of the interior world beyond. Manic, wheezing laughter came filtering out of darkness beyond, sounding distant in the thin air.

No cockpit in this thing, Perception said, having presumably taken a quick look about. *Bunk Barges appear to follow their chosen battleship by sound only. They must get very lost, from time to time.*

Lycaste stumbled among the half-visible mounds of rubbish. He didn't like the thought that Perception had left him, however briefly. The hill dropped suddenly into a submerged valley of wooden living quarters alive with dim shapes, a passage that led down into heat and light and smoke. Lycaste hesitated and climbed back out of the trench, stepping along its edge and back into the neighbouring rubbish heap, noticing as he looked over the side that the misted corridors of rickety dwellings dropped gently for hundreds of feet into the crust of the ship. Warmth and stench wafted out from the crevasse, thousands of lives hidden away from sight.

"Am I going the right way?" he whispered, stumbling and keeping his eyes open for anyone nearby. Only the thumping, drumming, cackling noises of the place followed his question. Lycaste broke out in a light, cool sweat. "Percy?"

Hmm? Sorry about that. Just dropped down there for a look.

"Would you *please* stay with me? I want to get this over with as quickly as possible."

All right, all right.

Lycaste grumbled, sinking up to his knees in the dark rubbish. Shadow coated him as he slid down a dune. A hiss in the darkness made him gasp and fumble for his light. Eyes glittered and disappeared in the shadow of the pile.

It wasn't far to the nearest bridge: a dilapidated wooden citadel in its own right, one of the hundreds that rose above the gulf of smoky space and up to the Posthouse. Pungent, sucking mud grasped at his boots as Lycaste made his nervous way onto a thoroughfare packed with wandering Prism, the crowd of knee-high creatures surging apart around him. Bony white fingers brushed his suit, exploring, probing, tapping to grade the metal. Furred tails swished, tufted ears twitched, sickeningly distorted faces gazed up at him. Lycaste pushed hurriedly through, dropping a handful of his Filgurees into a metal slot, their weight opening the gate and allowing him access to the bridge's first level.

Go quickly now, you're a spectacle already.

Beggars crowded him as soon as he entered, almost pulling him to the ground. Lycaste yelped and shook them off, making his way swiftly up some wooden steps to the next iron gate and shovelling coins into the slot. This door required more, and he'd barely got the gate open before the beggars reached him, pawing at his suit. Lycaste scuttled through and shoved the gate closed behind him, his extra Melius muscle pushing them back at last.

He turned, finding himself in another, slightly better-appointed section of the bridge. Over the side, he could see hovels made from knotted rope and plastic dangling beneath, their strands tied to others with thin, sagging lines like the work of a confused, gargantuan spider. The air was cleaner up here, Lycaste found, glimpsing tenements and shipyards glowing beneath him, their light fuzzy through the low layer of smog. As he climbed, he sensed that his body had thinned, his scrawny muscles having shrunk during their long, inactive spell in the Void. He tried to ignore the occasional shuffling figure he stepped over and the deathly drop to his side. Concentrating on the Posthouse itself appeared to help; Lycaste studied its levels as he climbed, noting how small the Prism people looked as they ambled along its walkways and through its passages. At the very top, a glinting assortment of metal glowed with lights, the remains of the habitation tank's original equipment, probably.

Through the next gate, walls crowned with iron spikes rose on either side. Here the Prism smoked and ate in the houses that lined the wooden square, their skinny legs dangling from the windows. Lycaste made brief eye contact and a beast that appeared to be all mouth lolled its tongue at him. Another shuffled out of his path, its eyes weeping a copious, crusty fluid that had coated the boards. Lycaste felt his boots stick as he made his way past and up the steps. The Prism that squatted there looked unwilling to move, a host of eyes glaring up at him in the greyness, completely blocking his way.

Pistol time.

Lycaste unscrewed his gauntlet and rummaged in his chest compartment. The crowd began to grumble and growl, some goblin shapes rising to their feet in the mist just as Lycaste found what he needed.

"Out of the way, please," he said in his best Unified, waving the weapon around, pleased as they began to shuffle and make room.

It pains me so, Perception said gleefully, *to prove Maneker wrong.*

Lycaste kept his gaze moving, careful not to glance at anyone in particular. It was hard work among so many huge, colourful sets of eyes.

Stop looking so diffident—keep that back straight, display your height. I can smell the fear steaming off you.

He found the coin slot, discovering it would only accept double what he'd paid at the first gate. "Are we going to have enough? To get to the top?"

Looks like it's happened to enough of them—running out of money at a certain gate, all stuck in their particular district, unable or unwilling to get out. Look.

Lycaste followed the direction of Perception's voice. An emaciated old Vulgar was caught on the wall spikes, the skin of his back pulled tight where it had been impaled. His chest rose and fell slowly beneath his ripped clothes. The soldiers at the gate paid no heed, being far more interested in Lycaste.

Keeps the riff-raff from getting to the top, I suppose.

Lycaste frowned, thinking that was harsh, even for Perception.

The Prism of the next level were generally older and more well-to-do. They sat at long tables outside the guesthouse in the square, smoking their pipes and observing Lycaste without bothering him. More soldiers in shiny tin armour lined the walls, conversing cheerfully with the crowd.

Five thousand soldiers in this place looking for work, Perception said. *And Maneker means to hire every last one of them.*

Lycaste pushed through the final door after depositing almost all of his remaining money, reflecting sourly that he hadn't any left to buy a helmet. On the other side, the wooden steps led up to the Posthouse entrance, a gatehouse hung with tatty banners that swirled in the updraughts of the high place.

He hesitated, closing the gate behind him when the guards grumbled from the other side.

Stop a moment.

Lycaste did as he was told, noticing the group making their way down to him.

Ah. They probably rob everyone who gets this far. Easy targets.

"What should I do?"

There are a hundred things you could do, Perception said.

"Such as?" he whispered, exasperated.

Lycaste had his hand on the superluminal pistol again, his heart hammering inside its protective layers of metal. The Spirit whispered into his ear.

LIATRIS

The entertainments began with a frantic chiselling of wood against metal, an atonal chanting of materials as the orchestra warmed up. At some signal, the ten Firstling musicians twirled their notched wooden wands as one, drawing them swiftly back and forth along the polished grooves of the huge Orestone. They shifted their footing together, selecting a new channel in its surface and repeating the process, each wooden pole taking a different course along the engraved metal disc.

Amaranthine didn't generally enjoy music, having mostly lost the ability to make out anything more than simple sound. They treated it like all mortal diversions, as an expression of immaturity, an incessant hankering to stuff all life with filler. Jatropha couldn't appreciate musical chords as he once did, either, though tonight he was forced to admit that he was in the company of something very special indeed.

The musicians shifted again, taking up new positions around the giant Orestone without their wands losing contact. An eleventh Firstling arrived softly from the shadows and erected a ladder to great fanfare, climbing it slowly with her stave balanced over her shoulder. At just the right moment, she touched the pole to a tiny hollow on the surface of the reverberating disc. Jatropha closed his eyes, entranced.

Tonight he was dressed as a distinguished old Firstling himself, assuming the height and pallor of a man born a handful of centuries ago and a thousand miles away. He caught sight of some exotic Meliusfolk in fabulous Shamefashions slipping through the mixed crowd of Westerlings, Borderlings and Cursed People with their heads bowed in the Province's custom, making their way into the gardens, perhaps to gift the Gheal. Their course to the balconies was naturally curved, as if in the weak thrall of an orbit, for there at the centre of the ballroom, dwarfed by the massive, charred metal disc of the Orestone, was the authoress herself: Liatris of Albina.

Jatropha moved through the churning mass of Players, poets and authors, pets and beasts: a collection of burnished eyes that glittered in the golden light sliding over his Melius form before moving on. He knew plenty of them by sight and more than a few were in his debt, their borrowings filed away to be made use of in the years to come. The giant people parted with the gentlest hint of persuasion, swirling away to join other clusters as the Orestone sighed into life again. He strode through, correcting his mental image to that of a slender Westerly Melius: more fashionable these days. Some people pretended to recognise him as he passed, though he'd never worn this face before.

"I have an idea for my own novel, you know. It shall be a great romance!"

"I am something of a writer myself, Mistress Liatris, though I haven't yet begun in earnest—"

"A signature, if you would?"

The authoress turned at the last, bringing her enormous silver listening trumpet level with her ear. She scrawled her engraving pen across the front of the ring book he offered her, peeling away a fine coil of shavings, then looked at him properly for the first time.

Jatropha gazed calmly back, ignoring the customs of the Land, aware that only the very oldest could see him as he truly was.

"My, my," she croaked, pen poised, the listening trumpet wobbling in her thin grasp. She waved away the company of Westerling men who had set up camp around her, all studiously observing the floor tiles. When they'd gone, she lowered the trumpet, her pale eyes focusing past the glamours Jatropha had wrapped himself in.

"I did not mean to interrupt," he said.

"*Stifling*," she replied in a papery voice. "Suitors, all of them, after my money."

"You invited them to your birthday?"

"No." She said the word with acidic distaste. "But still they come. When I am *dust* they shall be beating their way to my door with lines of verse. Imagine that, Amaranthine! Trying to charm an old mummy in her grave." Liatris stared at him shrewdly, her two hundred and ninety-two years sloughing away. "Perhaps I should throw down a gauntlet; let the young man wise enough to spot the Immortal guest wed me here and now, hmm?"

"It has been tried before. None pass." He smiled. "Though I should be careful to disappear just in case, to spare your fortune."

"Good man." Liatris cackled, scratching under her enormous ball of coiffed scarlet hair. It was studded with flawed emeralds of various weights. *Red and green should never be seen*, Jatropha thought, understanding there were none brave enough to question the lady's taste.

"And how about a turn around the garden?" she asked him. "Is that not the done thing when two doddery old things meet in the company of youth?"

"I believe it is." Jatropha extended his arm for her to take, and together they parted the rows of fascinated guests between them and the balcony doors.

"And what did you think of it?" Liatris asked, gesturing at the book in his grip, the story of *Calpus Maladine*. "A fairy story, I suppose? I had not the luxury of consultation with any of your kind."

Jatropha thought for a moment. "It was entirely wrong, yes."

The authoress burst into light, tinkling laughter, signalling for her retainers to open the doors, and they slipped together into cool green night, a little spotted Monkman—one of Liatris's pets—scampering through after her.

"The garden is ours," she said, dropping blankets onto some chairs that looked out over the water. Somewhere in the trees the Gheal squatted, more spirit than living thing by the laws of the West.

Jatropha sat and looked at her. Liatris had dispensed with the hearing trumpet in favour of a smaller one. "To make them shout," she said. "Everyone eventually tires, and I get some time to myself."

He did not drop his disguise, knowing hovering guests observed them from higher balconies. "Letters of introduction," he said, looking back out to the lake. "I'll need them to pass from Pan back into the Second."

She croaked a laugh, pushing away the pet Monkman scrabbling at her legs. "Stop it now, Marqueza. *Stop it*. Why? You can't need to take the roads."

"Oh, but I do. I have cargo."

Liatris appeared to think, then her large pink eyes widened. "You can't mean the—?"

Jatropha shrugged, toying with the edge of the embroidered blanket. The authoress had long been in communion with various Firstling and Secondling nobles disloyal to the current monarchy. Jatropha should know—he'd had his birds intercept her letters. Through his network of spies he had spread the news of the coming change, a princess by rights divine to be implanted on the Firstling throne, with nothing less than an Amaranthine seated at her side.

"I would welcome the help of any Westerling with a view to advancement in the coming changes."

Liatris twirled the silver horn in her fingers, spinning chrome-green moonlight into her eyes. Her pet, Jatropha saw, had scratched lines of blood across her shins and was busy lapping at the trickles, though Liatris didn't appear to notice. "And when are we to see these changes? After I am dead and gone, I suppose, with one of these fools frittering away my silk?"

"No. Soon. I must school her first in the art of dominance, but that won't take long."

"So the claim is settled, then? You have named her?"

Jatropha hesitated. The legitimate Berenzargol claim, sold by the family's matriarch a hundred years ago, had cost him the wealth of a large Province to buy. And only just in time: Elatine's legions had reached the edges of the Second soon after, frightening the moneyed populace—including the herald-keepers—into hiding. Now, with the deeds in his possession, he had nominated Arabis Berenzargol over her older half brothers and sisters, as was his right by the statutes of the First, her extended family more than compensated in their rise to power.

"I might allow young Lyonothamnus to keep his throne until that time, should he be amenable to my extremely favourable terms." He caught the look of consternation on Liatris's old face. "But not his mother, not the Fallopia. Only exile will do for her."

"Too kind a gesture, some might say."

"Let them say it."

Liatris lifted her Monkman into her lap. It stared up at Jatropha, more than a little Prism-ish.

"Even *with* a claim, your princess shall be challenged. Are there even blood-tasting papers left in Sarine City to prove her line?"

Jatropha sighed. "I've not spent these months idly. It is already proved, and I have assurances of support from Yire to the Scarlet Lands."

"Assurances mean nothing."

"They mean enough—especially if I decide to rule myself, until the time is right."

"And let them see you?"

He nodded, patting the Monkman. It closed its eyes at the softness of his touch, arching its back.

Liatris laughed. "An invincible queen under divine protection, all the First and Second in her debt. I have not heard the likes of it before—and I was born during the peculiar reign of Dracunctus, don't forget." She smiled at him. "Great success or great disaster beckons, though I cannot tell which."

He grinned, his eyes tracing the silhouette of the spirit Prism in the trees as it swung its dangling legs.

The Plenipotentiary Callistemon's arrival in the Tenth the previous summer had been presaged, included as a footnote in letters from contacts all across the Provinces: *a procession of Secondling prefects moving southwards to the Nostrum, they stay at fine houses, causing a stir. Watch now, Sire Amaranthine, how the children disappear.*

Jatropha hadn't taken much note, his interests remaining wrapped up in the fronts and developments of the war, though some small locked box squirrelled away in his labyrinthine memory had banged and thumped at the name Berenzargol, keen to be opened.

The family Berenzargol: traceable heirs by right to Sarine City and throne of the Provinces, through their ancestor the FirstLord Geniostemon, half brother to the ancient King Convolvulus. Few but the royals remembered the claim and so it was hushed, purchasable only at an expense beyond the reach of anyone but the boy-king Lyonothamnus himself, and all records redacted within the First.

But their own lofty plans of Standardisation—weeding out the mongrel races of the Melius world—had brought them down. Callistemon, Jatropha had discovered, was to be a *breeder*. He strolled and charmed and catalogued, taking a woman here and there, dispatching anyone who got in his way. And all the time Jatropha watched him, watched with sharp interest where his seed would land. The Amaranthine, of course, knew of the Shameplague and its symptoms, understanding that in making this journey, Callistemon went to his death. It was penance enough, Jatropha reckoned, for in the host of Pentas a princess would arise, his to mould from birth.

Arabis I, Queen of the fifteen Provinces between Sligos and Jahra, Empress of Mansour and the Isles of Storn and Argostolio. If a peace could be brokered with the Oyal-Threheng then the Old World lay open to a bold new future. The process might take years; the lifespan of a healthy Melius queen ought to do it—and there was just enough Seventhling in Arabis to ensure she would survive the Shameplague with only minor scarring, Jatropha thought.

"Here," said Liatris, having noticed his long silence for what it was. She passed him a piece of party food from a tray. "Even an Amaranthine must have good and bad luck."

Jatropha took the sugar animal and stood. "They run together, I find."

"Well, gift the Gheal your piece for me and ask him to send me your luck."

Together they threw their nibbles up into the tree. Nothing fell back down again.

"He's lived on my estate for forty years," she said, "growing fat and happy from my finest scraps. Not a bad life."

"Not bad at all. The Skylings would be envious of their cousins here."

The shadow hooted in the trees, as if in gratitude, tucking the treats into its mouth with long fingers. They were said to dance in the wild, when they thought they were unobserved. Out on the lake, a ship spouted fireworks from its deck.

"That's not for you, is it?"

"Oh, it all is," Liatris said. "But I daresay the guests will enjoy it more. I've seen hundreds of the things, every blasted birthday."

Jatropha folded his blanket carefully. "I fear I have taken too much of your time." He bent and took her hand. "Thank you for the autograph. I shall treasure it."

"You must have a lot of treasures," Liatris said, still seated, not wanting him to leave. "Do you have a favourite?"

Jatropha hardly needed to think. "Peace of mind. Always peace of mind."

"Really? Nowadays I rather like some drama."

"You'll grow out of that."

Liatris grinned, revealing a set of notably stained chops. "I fear I won't."

Jatropha paused, becoming aware of a meek person watching them from the doors.

Liatris turned in her seat. "What is it, Cosmos?"

The person hesitated, stepping out. "An uninvited guest, Mistress Albina, very insistent."

Liatris snorted. "But they are all uninvited, Cosmos!"

Jatropha saw the figure shrink a little by the door. She'd clearly been instrumental in compiling the guest list.

"This young lady is . . . *bloody*, Mistress."

"Bloody?"

Jatropha touched a hand to the back of her chair.

"She asks for someone, but I do not know them—"

He nodded quickly to the authoress and moved towards the doors. The secretary looked suddenly afraid as he swept forward. "Take me to her," he said.

The party still swirled and hummed; a golden vortex of giant, ugly faces made all the stranger by the wailing of the Orestone. Jatropha shoved his way through, attenuating his fears into a blade of unease that parted the crowd like a breeze through grass. They stopped short of the great stair, the secretary staring about.

Pentas's bony, blood-streaked face appeared in the throng, the only Seventhling in the place. He gazed at her, taking in her lost, hopeless expression. Someone, a Westerly man, was attempting to hand her a cup of hot wine.

The child was gone, then.

The Wheelhouse stood, lanterns lit, surrounded by the depleted remains of the hired guard crew from Tristel. Eranthis talked to them from the balcony, a small spring rifle held awkwardly in her arms.

Jatropha shrugged away Pentas's grip and climbed aboard, dropping his Westerly disguise. "What happened?"

"We lost her. *I* lost her. An Awger came—that one we saw on his push-gig—"

Jatropha thought back. A scrappy-looking thing, dressed in tattered Shameclothes and riding a homemade wooden contraption.

It was always the little things, the things you don't give a second's thought.

"But how did it get aboard?"

Eranthis didn't seem to want to answer. "It was my fault," she said at last. "Pentas ran off while I was in the scullery. She just . . . she just wanted to leave this place, with her baby. She wanted to go her own way."

He stepped down, calling the guard to him and distributing silk along with a bundle of spring rifles. "Find the child tonight. *Do not come back without her.*" When they'd gone, he clapped his hands together, and a handful of red birds—not his birds, but birds all the same—came fluttering down from their roosts in the poplars that lined the court. He levelled a finger at them as they perched on the balcony railings. "Awger on the roads or in the woods. Rip the soles of its feet and bring it to me."

He went back to the cabin of the *Corbita*, dragging out more lanterns and blowing their embers into life. When all were lit, he tossed some to Eranthis and unlatched the brace, steering the Wheelhouse back onto the cobbles of the palace forecourt and cranking the gears. The house rumbled out into the night, all aboard save one precious girl, the flock of Liatris's post birds whirling up to momentarily blot out the stars. Pentas said the Awger had pedalled north, but that didn't mean north was where it was going.

He leaned out into the breeze for a few minutes, the night air drumming in his ears, gaze searching the dim shapes of the trees where they met the cobbled road, then ducked back inside.

Dumped on his chair was a new letter, not from one of his contacts abroad. Eranthis had sliced it open already, seeing to whom it was addressed. Jatropha picked the letter up, holding it to the cabin lantern between peeks outside, unconcerned that she might have read it. It was coded, from the same source as all the others that had piled up since their sad departure from the coast.

Sweet Bidens—no word from you here? We are worried. Last heard that you had left Mostar with all aboard, and that she is true Berenzargol.

His eyes moved down the page. *Correct in assuming ambush went to plan? Reply at once with whereabouts.*
Penalties to remuneration with all extra delay.

Jatropha saw no point in telling the girls; the boy had paid sufficiently. He had a special surprise in store for Bidens's father, back in Mostar, but that would have to wait now.

Jatropha read quickly through the message again, knowing perfectly well where *here* was. The bird that had brought the message was a fast blue roller, one of thousands that belonged to him. This letter had been written in Sarine City, the capital of the First. He studied the wobbly, overly expressive hand, knowing it anywhere. The boy-king's mother, the Fallopia.

SEPULCHRE

A hearth of dim embers lit the inside of the fallen guard tower, Ghaldezuel's eyes taking some time to adjust.

She was Threen, though of a breed he didn't recognise. Ghaldezuel knew her gender not because of her face (which was concealed—reasonably, for a light-hating breed—within a great Pifoon basinet plumed with feathers), but because her naked white teats hung almost to her shins.

"Take off your clothes." The helmet, unconnected to any sort of electrics, hollowed her cackle like someone speaking through a drainpipe.

Ghaldezuel hesitated at the extraordinary sound, collecting himself. He unbuckled his entire suit of armour, letting it fall at his feet, until he stood naked in the gloom. When she spoke again, it was more than the chill of the ruin that made him shiver.

"I smell Bult on this one."

Ghaldezuel understood why the gang had kept her alive. She was their lucky charm, their witch.

He moved forward, seeing the hint of a spindly chair beside the fire.

"Sit," she said, running a finger over his shoulder. "The light is low, for me," she whispered, sniggering and going to stand beside the backrest.

He took his seat, hearing the grunt as she removed her helmet behind him, and without warning the drizzling dampness of a warm tongue was exploring his ear. Ghaldezuel angled his head primly, letting the tongue slide along and down to his neck, saliva pooling in the hollow of his collarbone. A mad heartbeat pulsed inside her fingers where they gripped his shoulders, their touch as light as a bird's.

Another presence made itself felt in the room. Ghaldezuel turned minutely, forgetting the slathering heat of the tongue on his skin, and saw a Lacaille girl sitting by the fire beside him.

His heart jumped. He looked away, into the embers. When he glanced back, the place was empty.

The witch gave him a final slurp and swallowed thoughtfully. "They say they cannot see your dreams."

Ghaldezuel kept silent, the saliva that ran down his shoulders growing chilly.

"But I saw you in mine," she said. "Someone would come here in the years before the Third Kingdom won the war. That someone was to become a king themselves."

He wiped gently at some saliva that had run down to the corner of his mouth. "A king?"

"A king of the Investiture."

Ghaldezuel nodded. "You mean Cunctus, then."

"No, oh no—I mean *you.*"

He hesitated, sitting more rigidly in the chair. "I don't think he'd like to hear that."

"Hush now, it'll be our secret."

Ghaldezuel looked around. He saw the glinting embers reflected in the pupils of a set of wide oval eyes. He'd heard nothing about a Threen woman on the prisoner manifest. "What did you mean, *before the Third Kingdom won the war*? You're talking about the four Vulgar kings? Is that it? The war between the Lacaille and the Vulgar?"

"Vulgar kings? No. They don't matter. I meant up in the Thunderclouds, in the Third Great Domain, Triangulum. That belonging to the Glutton Sarsappus."

His eyes, adjusting to the dark, could now make out the swirled colours of her own: spirals of light whipped around deep, dark cores. He thought he knew that name, *Triangulum.* It was an ancient Amaranthine word for somewhere on the fringes of the sun charts, yet to be translated into any Prism-speak.

"And who is this . . . Sarsappus?" he asked, watching transfixed as the spirals revolved.

"Someone so important that nobody suspects he exists at all." She tittered, giving his ear another playful lick. "There is so very much *happening* all around us, you see. My friends here, they tell me all about it."

"Your friends the prisoners?"

"They're prisoners, I suppose. They'll never be free, in that sense. Not like Cunctus and his gang, whom I assume you are taking with you, yes?"

Ghaldezuel tore his gaze away, the darkness stained with after-images. "Yes."

They looked together at the vast hole in the valley floor, where a party of Cunctus's bandits were already assembled at the edge and reeling out lengths of rope. The witch was, surprisingly, the first to enter. The esteem in which Cunctus held her was clear to Ghaldezuel as he watched the Threen being winched down on a litter, the Wulm at the lip of the hole straining at their ropes.

Homemade tea was brought out to where they sat on the lowest of the Thrasm's steps. Ghaldezuel took the offered cup, a cracked blue porcelain thing that must have been one of their few treasured possessions. Beside him at the broken table, Cunctus raised his own with a trembling hand and toasted their meeting in the Amaranthine custom. "To us, then."

Ghaldezuel nodded, lifting his to his lips: charcoal and meltwater—boiled, at least. The snow had ceased and in the low sun, Cunctus's sagging skin began to glow a golden orange. The bristles of his great beard were thick white wires that caught the light, almost but not quite obscuring a wide, drooly mouth closely packed with pointed teeth. Everything Ghaldezuel had heard began to make sense, now: a warlord immune to disease, capable of breaking even the largest Prism folk with his bare hands. Not once had Ghaldezuel assumed it was anything other than hyperbole, the sort favoured by those of a small disposition.

The witch had accompanied them at first, whispering through her rusty helmet into the Melius's ear. Ghaldezuel hadn't been able to take his eyes from her; in the weak afternoon sunlight, the snaking blue veins beneath her skin were almost hypnotic. Her dangling teats, which she licked periodically, were veined like the surface of a leaf, more blue than cream.

Cunctus lifted the silver pot in trembling hands, pouring a messy puddle around Ghaldezuel's cup. It was clear that the Melius was immensely old—perhaps approaching his third century—and yet none of his body's decrepitude appeared to have reached his mind, a mind plainly accustomed to power.

"She told me you're the one with the Bult. Jaldessel."

He sighed. "Ghaldezuel."

"Ha!" Cunctus croaked. "They'll get that wrong 'til the end."

Ghaldezuel smiled then, looking out across the valley. Cunctus, out of apparent politeness, was speaking to him in Regal Lacaille, and it was pleasant, almost exotic, to think in his own tongue again, with all its loops and Zs.

The Melius looked shrewdly at him. "But how do you pay them? Vulgar corpses?"

"No, actually. Simple, inedible Filgurees will do. Ducats when I can get them."

"But it's the Vulgar they hate the most."

Ghaldezuel could see the giant's mind working. He shrugged. "Presently."

The teapot rattled as Cunctus poured himself another cup, spilling steaming water across the table. Ghaldezuel thought the Melius was about to drop it and reached out a tentative hand, only for it to be waved away. A fresh cheroot, made from what appeared to be wood shavings and cloth, lay wetted on the table.

"Hmm. Well, *Ghaldezuel*, we'll put them to some good use when the time comes."

He studied his hands, astonished at the new deftness with which Cunctus had pronounced his name. The Melius clearly had an ear for Lacaille. Ghaldezuel wondered how many languages he spoke.

"Yes," Cunctus breathed. "Once I've evicted that imbecile Count Andolp from Drolgins we can set about correcting things, gathering my supporters." His trembling hands swept dangerously close to the teapot before he folded them in his lap. "And we shall have to take a Vaulted

Land, *quickly*. The honoured Pifoon that grew fat on their surfaces will be making their way inside to block them off."

"The Pifoon are still loyal to the Amaranthine."

Cunctus coughed a laugh, almost knocking the pot over once more. "I'll wager Mawlbert of Cancri's moved in already, while they weren't looking."

Ghaldezuel thought back to a time before he knew how to fire a spring gun, to a time before he'd learned to read. The countless children of Dozo had fought with pebbles and wood splinters, suffocating one another in the night with plastic wrapping and fat-greased paper. He might be sitting in a lofty place discussing the fate of the Investiture with its most famous outlaw, but it wasn't really any different from his boyhood days.

"That Threen," he asked. "She wasn't a prisoner here?"

Cunctus settled the teapot as carefully as he could. "She's native, would you believe it? A Maelstrom local. Every night she'd climb the Thrasm for warmth and visit us in our cells. Through her we learned the secrets of the galaxies, *the forbidden histories*, of which we primates are but a tatty endnote." Cunctus, smiling at his own turn of phrase, looked abruptly serious then, displaying that same dribbling intensity Ghaldezuel had seen when they'd first met. "She is very precious to me." He'd begun to knot his beard anxiously, twining individual hairs while he thought.

"The galaxies," Ghaldezuel echoed. "She said some odd things."

"What did the *spirits* say?" Cunctus asked, apparently casually, leaning forward and resting his head in his hands while he fidgeted with his beard. He regarded Ghaldezuel, the stained hollows of his eyes making them appear even larger than they were. "My witch was vague."

Ghaldezuel sat back a little, worried the table might break. The giant's bearded head filled his view, almost forbidding him to look elsewhere.

"They confirmed that I shall sit at your side when you are king of the Investiture, that together we shall bring about the Amaranthines' extinction."

"Yes. But what did they say about *you*?"

"Very little. I saw an old love sitting beside me. It was . . . unexpected."

"That old trick! They tried that on me the first few times. It's nothing, a reflection of your mind."

"I guessed as much." He remembered the twin swirls of light revolving in the Threen's eyes. "What are they? The spirits?"

Cunctus sipped his tea, eyeing him. "You must have guessed, being at one time in league with a member of their kind yourself. They're the ghosts of the old masters' machines, put to death here when the ancient regime fell."

Ghaldezuel fell silent. He noticed the giant had made extraordinarily elaborate knots in his beard. They almost looked like faces.

"Hand me the paper," Cunctus instructed, gesturing for a cloth-wrapped roll that lay on the steps. What he unfurled was the most beautiful map of the Investiture Ghaldezuel had ever seen. Cunctus selected some charcoal and wet it with his tongue, then began adding shakily to the roll. Ghaldezuel saw his was the same hand that had made the beautiful drawings on the map. While he worked, his flabby pink tongue stuck out of his mouth, the way some children drew.

"Here," he said, pointing to a perfectly inscribed circular map among the hordes of others. Lines scrawled with the arrows of solar currents bulged around it. "This is where the Machine King—your Aaron, or whatever he calls himself—will go, once he's got the last thing he needs."

Ghaldezuel hesitated, suspecting a trap, then peered surreptitiously at the drawing. *AntiZelio-Glumatis.*

"He and I share similar unhappy fates, you see," Cunctus said with a sly smile. "My own flesh and blood left me to rot, too, so that they could take my place on the Sarine throne."

Ghaldezuel frowned, uncomprehending.

"Your one-time friend, the Long-Life—he who is busily ripping down the Firmament?"

Ghaldezuel nodded cautiously.

"I expect he's after his brother."

Ghaldezuel peered through the fresh specks of snow, surprised to see that there was still power down there: a hint of light glowing in the base of the pit. He clung on to the finely trimmed lip of rock a little longer, wearing his old Voidsuit again but divested of his weapons.

He shifted, almost losing his grip, and transferred his weight to the frayed rope.

He dropped past other lines and ropes and cloth ties that the Wulm had let down, his flickering suit lights picking out the last of the climbers as he shuffled into the darkness.

Gradually the light increased, a warm glow strong enough to make out the glassy smoothness of the superluminally pulverised rock sides of the tunnel. Something that looked like a tiny flicker of floating light passed his face, an Amaranthine household spark. So that was what they had down here, patiently waiting the millennia for their masters to return. Ghaldezuel glanced down at last, contemplating how far he had to go, and realised with a start that he was almost there.

The speared nose of some massive, glimmering weapon rose to meet his dangling feet. Beyond it, vast in the gloom, the body of the greater vessel spilled out in all directions, a truly massive Decadence ship locked away for more than five thousand years. Ghaldezuel pulled in his feet and angled his body so that he could drop onto the side of the smooth nose. His boots met the hard metal of the ship's snarling animal face, catching on its plated scales, and he half-slid, half-stumbled his way down until he could climb the last fifty feet to the floor of the cavern.

Hundreds of sparks swarmed around the assembled Wulm, rising and dipping like Zuo fairy flies. Ghaldezuel's metal boots touched the stone with a clink and he let go of the rope, swivelling to look up at the looming, vertical body of the Amaranthine ship.

A handful of sparks hovered around the craft's conical snout, as if inspecting the enormous nose-mounted superluminal cannon that had obliterated the Thrasm. Ghaldezuel remembered a strange glossiness to the metal as he'd made his way down: the remains of De Rivarol. The sparks were trained to hover above any Amaranthine until commanded to desist and might stay there all night. More drifted to gather in knots of muted light over the vessel's gaping jaws, carving shadows into the hollows of its eyes and the voids between its teeth, illuminating the soap-bubble colours of the hull plating.

The great rearing ship had been built in the image of a Crachen of old, a nautiloid beast seven stories high, a coil of bronze tentacles enclosing spears of blade-sharp weaponry around its skirts, as if the creature had dropped to settle on the spires of a city. Ghaldezuel fumbled at his suit lights, turning them off, then took in the rest of the dim place.

The Sepulchre. It was vast, like a mile-wide bubble blown in volcanic stone and left to cool. Off in the darkness, more sparks were glowing into life, casting blue and orange light against the walls and ceiling. Heaped Amaranthine treasure glittered in piles twenty feet high, all looking as if they'd been dumped in a hurry before the great cavern was sealed. The bubble, he understood, had been hollowed using a more advanced process than that which created a Vaulted Land. Those great places had their insides scooped out roughly nine thousand years ago, when the precursors of the Amaranthine had realised—numbering as they apparently did in their trillions—that doubling the living space on an already-conquered planet was a much easier task than finding and settling a new place. All one required was a vast scooping machine—the ancient Hollowing Lathes, some of which still lay where they had been abandoned, rust-holed and lived-in, on several moons in the Investiture—and the ability to kindle stable artificial suns.

It was only during the magical Age of Decadence—at which point the last of the true Hiomen Empires had fallen and the Amaranthine had established their hallowed Firmament—that superluminal tools capable of dissolving matter with greater than surgical precision began to find their uses. And so it was that places were cored superluminally, and by that means the last two great planets of the Firmament, Cancri and Tau Mandrano, gained their interiors.

Along with, apparently, this old place, the Sepulchre.

Ghaldezuel began his wander, keeping one eye open for Cunctus and his witch. Out of reach of the light, he could hear the busy rush of water, most likely the redirected flow of the poisoned river. He looked down, scooping up a handful of bright silver Ducats and Halves: the disc and crescent shapes bore the intricate portrait of Jacob the Bold, a lost Firmamental Emperor. They were said to be hard as diamond, useful as a weapon in a pinch, though anyone lucky enough to have one to hand could afford all the protection they needed. He took one of the crescents, dropping the rest, and rubbed the point of its tip thoughtfully.

Gleaming jewels scattered the gentle light of the place like a Wiro's fairy-tale dungeon, and among them other, more darkly

indecipherable things lurked half-buried; machines and bejewelled Statuary Tombs, engine parts and suits of armour. Another of
the Amaranthine sparks had fallen and lodged, buzzing and spitting, between some stacked, gem-encrusted swords the length of a
Melius's arm. Ghaldezuel looked around, conscious of an expectant
stillness to the place. The cavern was a sump of potential energy,
hundreds of lifetimes' worth of treasures. This was all Cunctus and
his gang would need to recruit the best—and worst—of the Investiture to their cause.

Beyond, like cadavers thrown hastily into a mass grave, a legion
of rotten paper robots with rusted spines lay half-submerged in a
landslide of gold and silver trinkets. He trudged up a hill of Ducats
for a better view, half-expecting to find the Collection itself dumped
among their number, knowing deep down that he wouldn't. The paper
men, from what he could see from his vantage, were quite dead, completely unusable. Ghaldezuel had heard tales of the Stickmen, as they
had been called during the wars of Decadence, but never seen one;
it was said a rogue Amaranthine had gifted the Jalan warlord of the
Oyal-Threheng reams of the same indestructible paper—the cannibalised skin of their antique, defective army—to build his Firmament-
famed origami keep.

He walked in sliding steps down the hill again, passing a suit of
monstrous clothing that appeared to be made of dull red glass. It must
have been built for something other than an Amaranthine, something
endowed with hundreds of arms or wings. He stopped to tap its belly
with his boot and it fell abruptly to pieces, shattering the silence of the
vast place with a torrent of tinkling echoes. The lights bobbed once,
falling still again. The sunken spark spluttered and hummed.

As he came upon the Firmamental robots, Ghaldezuel stopped
short. In the edges of the spark-light, a gleaming curve of reflection
slipped off some dark material, catching his attention. He switched
on his helmet torch again, the generator behind his head whirring and
burping a puff of smoke.

There above the paper Stickmen, wedged at an indifferent angle
into the heaped treasure like a sword in a stone, lay the ship of the
ancients: the Dilasaur vessel discovered in the rings of Saturn-Regis
thousands upon thousands of years ago.

Ghaldezuel crunched forward across the mounds of coins and treasures, transfixed. It was impossible at first to tell whether the dark, spinning-top-shaped mass, picked out here and there by his light as he moved his head, was the correct way up or not. As he moved closer, he noticed that the out-thrust spindle of its nose was crumpled and shredded, and that great dents in its fuselage had been made by a huge and deadly impact.

He arrived at its burnished surface, putting out his gloved hand to touch it and glancing up at the nose. All along the curve of its side were scratched names and dates: *Dylanis Mors 3276*, one read in the Latin shapes of the pre-Unified languages. He looked at the others: *O.B. & T.I.*, *Rubrich Pappen, The Brothers Lumetri, 3901.* One message in particular caught his eye, dragged in spidery writing almost two feet tall: *The Devil's Sailboat.*

Ghaldezuel stood back a little. The pristine craft they kept entombed in clear resin in the Sea Hall of Gliese must have been a facsimile. He could understand their shame—this object certainly hadn't been well looked after in the first years of the Interstellar histories. He supposed it had been passed from empire to empire, continually gifted or bargained with, a unique treasure left to families and states, seized by every revolution. It was a wonder the ship and its fabled occupants had survived at all.

And here he was now, a Lacaille knight at the end of an epoch, standing before it as millions of others must have done, thinking the same thoughts, wondering at the very same wonders. Who or *what* else would stand and read these words in years to come? Would they even understand these scribbles?

He shone his suit lights up at the nose, trying to see if there was a rip in the fabric of the ship large enough for him to climb through.

In the flicker of his helmet torch, he saw there was rodent shit everywhere. Uncountable generations of them must have lived here, dwelling inside the mechanisms of a thing they could never understand. He dithered for a moment and sealed his helmet's faceplate, knowing the fumes from the droppings could be dangerous. The silence intensified as he switched on his sound feed. Disturbed dust floated across the beams of his lights like passing wraiths.

He looked around the snug cockpit, a nested series of shells like a layered, egg-shaped throne set into the nose, buckled and warped by the ancient impact. He saw where they must have sat, doubled over like hunchbacks as they stared at their equipment, a collection of nodes and hollows in the pale, smooth material that presumably shone optical information of some kind directly into their eyes. The whole place appeared to have been moulded or poured, grown like Old World bone-stone. He shone his lights across the curved ceiling of the cockpit, seeing yet more channels and nodes that must have projected information or sound, without spotting a single seam or rivet. Even the Amaranthine had built with seams, once upon a time.

And what blasphemy has been done to you now? he thought, gazing at where they'd sat. The souls of those things, if he'd understood Corphuso's sermons on the subject correctly, were lost to the Void, coalesced perhaps in the craters and crags of Saturn-Regis's rings, sunk wherever gravity would hold them.

Ghaldezuel tried to imagine how he'd feel if someone told him that a demon would one day occupy his remains. Would he feel violated? Slandered in some way? He stood very still, falling dust glowing as it passed through the beam, a galaxy of stars. He'd want revenge, he supposed.

Well, they would get that, at least, in one form or another.

Ghaldezuel widened the beam of his torch and crept further into the cockpit. It was their own fault, really, building such a being without a thought for the consequences. It was just a pity so many others had to pay for their mistakes.

Ghaldezuel stirred from his thoughts, peering out through the vessel's shattered nose. They were calling out for him across the landscape of treasure. He looked at the finger of his glove, realising he'd been tracing patterns in the rat shit on one of the consoles. He took a last glance in the rear of the vessel, but the walls there had buckled and crumpled as the ship had dived side on into the rock, sealing what could have been storage or living quarters away from prying eyes.

He began to climb through the tear in the nose, hesitating as he hoisted his leg and staring back into the darkness of the cockpit. Ghaldezuel returned to it, taking the crescent Half-Ducat he'd found and scraping hesitantly into the surface of the optical projection equipment at the base of the throne.

G & J

When he'd finished, he took off his glove, laying his finger against the Lacaille letters, pressing it there as if stamping a wax seal. Shavings of whatever the vessel was made from drifted dustily to the floor, exposed after millions of years hidden. He looked at the crude scratches of his handwriting for a moment, then used the Half-Ducat again to scrape one final addendum beneath.

FOR EVER

Ghaldezuel left, not looking back. He knew he would never in his life return to this forlorn cockpit, and was glad.

"There you are," Cunctus cried across the expanse of treasures. "Look what we've found."

Ghaldezuel trudged over, his thoughts far away. The Melius was holding something long and translucent, like a thick, stubby snakeskin. He nodded to the acid-burned Wulm and they pulled the skin in different directions, expanding it. Ghaldezuel took a step back, watching the thing unfurl. After twenty feet they were still going, the material of the substance unravelling like one of those fancy hump sheaches you could buy in Filgurbirund to keep the babies away. The sheath terminated in the Melius's hands at a bulbous helm section, also apparently expandable and lustrously oil-coloured where the light of the sparks slid across its surface. Ghaldezuel came closer to inspect its rainbow shimmer for a while as the other Wulm pored over it, their mistrust of him momentarily forgotten. Unlike the others, he didn't want to touch it; there was something about the thin, multicoloured fabric—apparently repellent to rat faeces, unlike everything else—that disturbed him. He resisted the urge to look into the darkness of the cavern for the beast that had shed it, comprehending as he examined it that the skin was some kind of ancient suit, much like the glass carapace he'd inadvertently shattered. Another relic of a lost age, he thought, making brief eye contact with Cunctus. Something discovered but not understood, at least by anyone living.

"Might come in handy, Mumpher," Cunctus said to the Wulm, rolling up the skin.

"Who is she?" the witch asked at his side, helmless and leering.

He started, swallowing and glancing guiltily back to the ancient ship in which he'd carved the initials. "Nobody."

"Not nobody, Ghaldezuel. You put her name in eternity."

He watched them finish rolling up the skin, saying nothing more. Mumpher the scarred Wulm took it from Cunctus's trembling hands and went to oversee the other discoveries being made in the cavern. Rats were already being cooked around a few of the fires the gang had lit, and someone was dragging what looked suspiciously like the Amaranthines' fabled mirror—a polished piece of silver capable of capturing and re-showing ancient light, it was said—across the pile to use as a sledge. Cunctus watched, too, turning to grin at them both. He'd knotted some huge rubies into his beard.

"Oh," the witch said, catching his wrist. "Oh, that's it."

Ghaldezuel glared at her and walked away.

Hauberth's din floated to his ears as he stepped above ground, the humidity settling in his hair, running down his cheeks. At the quay, the atmosphere above the place was a yellow smudge that ran to green where it met the ship-flecked sky.

Filgurbirund was a big planet, heavy and thick-aired, the atmosphere varnished over like an old and discoloured painting. The gravity of the place, along with widow-making malnutrition, explained perhaps why the Vulgar here were such a small race, as easily aggrieved as any trembling little breed of dog quick to bare its teeth. They'd owned this place as long as anyone but the Amaranthine could remember. Its histories were as rich and dense as the smoggy planet itself, home to thirty billion souls at the last old, ineffectual census, and now, he assumed, considerably more.

Across the water, Ghaldezuel spotted him. A tallish figure cloaked and hooded in a luxuriant ultramarine cape, standing straight and motionless at the parapet of the next bridge. Ghaldezuel took in the sight, wondering for a moment what others—what the fifty million Vulgar of the city—would see. Merchants with their little houses strapped to their backs peeled around the apparition, uninterested in what appeared to be a tramp with a good new cloak staring catatonically at the waters. The homeless (a good portion of the city) seemed wary of going anywhere near the figure; the bridge was almost deserted of them—a rare occurrence. Perhaps they thought the cloaked shape must be a lawman, standing still and watchful beneath the deep shade of his hood. They had no idea, as ever, what walked freely among them.

Ghaldezuel had read the monthly news at the bank, one of the few places where the papers could actually be read by anyone, and noticed amid the bills of trade and anti-Lacaille sentiment the recent spate of mutilations, rare even in a city in which thousands were murdered or robbed each day.

The figure saw him, turning minutely in his direction, and he made his way along the bridge, feeling a little self-conscious. One day, one day the person would come to him, though Ghaldezuel had little illusion that such a day would fall any time soon. The first sign of acknowledgement had taken a year; the first word two.

They stood alongside one another. A hunchbacked Wulm bustled past them, the high stink of its body drifting with it. The multicoloured river boiled beneath, turgid with rubbish: old broken-up furniture; a crumpled, mossy boat that was now the floating home of a few dozen Oxel; a handful of bloated bodies sweeping face-down in the current. Those would be caught by a Ringum fishing gang further along and inspected for valuables, their spotters on all the bridges making sure nobody else got to the corpses first.

A three-fingered hand came to rest on the railing beside him. Ghaldezuel looked at it only for a moment, taking in the crescent nails, ivory-coloured and bitten right down to the cuticle. They cannibalised even themselves, they were so hungry.

He fished inside the pockets of his suit and brought out a little paper parcel, good Lacaille jewellery from Pruth-Zalnir, and turned to the hooded figure.

"For her to wear on top," Ghaldezuel said, placing a hand on his chest to illustrate, "when she comes here. There is a note inside—you just open the clasp."

Tzolz looked down at him through the shadows of the hood, taking the parcel in his blunt fingers and examining it. When he spoke, it was in a deep, melodious Lacaille.

"She will be glad to have this."

Ghaldezuel blinked a nod. *"Tell your dear aunt from me that the Vulgar will soon be kicked back to where they belong. They can't harry her if they're retreating from my people, and we'll keep the wretched creatures running."*

They strolled back to the riverbank. The attack on Nilmuth tomorrow could not be planned in any more detail. But there was more to say. He reached out a hand, touching the Bult lightly on the arm.

"I might have another task for you, when you and your team are rested. Something to find."

THRONG

"Bult!" Lycaste roared, flailing his arms and jumping up and down, the structure bouncing under his boots. The Prism making their way towards him hesitated.

Slightly less stagey, if you could.

"Bult!" he raged, trying to inject some genuine fear into the word. The spell appeared to be working, however; his would-be assailants were clapping their hands and stamping their feet, glancing nervously in all directions.

A thumping of iron-shod feet announced the arrival of something large. It pushed through the crowd and sent them scampering on their way without a second glance at Lycaste. More came up behind, making their way down the steps.

"What about these?"

Ah, all's well. Maneker briefed me for this.

He put away his weapon, still alive with nerves and annoyed that Perception hadn't thought to warn him to expect them. The new arrivals clanked down to him, four muscular forms barely a head shorter than him and encased in brilliant suits of coloured plate. Fur-lined capes trailed behind them, billowing in the cold wind. Lycaste's first thought was that he'd never seen this particular breed before, until some nagging memory told him that he had. Just before he'd fallen, before Maneker had brought them all to Proximo. This breed had been there in Vilnius

Second, too. They stopped before him and clapped their hands together as one. They were not like most of the small, bat-faced things he was so used to. In fact, they were quite the most handsomely dressed Prism Lycaste had ever encountered. Tidy, chestnut-brown beards sprouted from their long faces, faces that were home to small, ice-blue eyes. There was something crocodilian about the way their jaws interlocked; each possessed a ramshackle set of hooked teeth, almost like a Jalan's, that protruded among their whiskers.

"Letters," the greyest of the specimens commanded in First, snapping his bare fingers.

Give them to him.

The Prism snatched the package from Lycaste's hand, squinting at the script on each letter, then turned and left without ceremony, stamping back the way they'd come.

"We should hurry," another said to Lycaste. He had a soft, smoky voice and appeared to speak First better than Lycaste did. "A Perennial Amaranthine was here today, watching the comings and goings for people like you." He looked Lycaste up and down appreciatively. At first, Lycaste assumed it was only his beauty, as usual, that had caught the Prism's attention, realising a moment later that it was more likely the fine Voidsuit he wore.

"Gamnin," the mercenary said, indicating himself. He gestured at the other two. "Olonan and Narvott."

Lycaste followed them up and through the enormous gatehouse, the mercenaries paying his entry fee for him. His surly, would-be robbers observed them from the shadows.

"Never mind them," Narvott said.

Lycaste felt suddenly as if he were simply being passed from thug to thug. Percy, a comfortable—if likely imagined—weight around his shoulder said nothing.

"The same Perennial tried to hire us earlier this year," Narvott said, pushing past a host of small creatures on the stairs to their level and holding the door open for Lycaste. "Amaranthine do not ask twice." The high outpost rocked under the force of the wind, the mercenaries' hair blowing and flattening. "After yourself."

Lycaste went through into a small, altogether cleaner wooden chamber. The three mercenaries took their seats at the single table, conferring in low voices. Between them lay the remnants of a luxuriant dinner: a fat, gutted blue fish on a wooden platter. Plastic jugs and pots and cups stood empty on every spare surface, as if the mercenaries had been kept waiting for some time. A tower of smaller creatures standing on one another's shoulders looked in, salivating, through the single glass window.

Maneker has not spared his expenses here, I think.

Lycaste seated himself by the small fire, his feet aching, moisture steaming from his suit and hair. The mercenaries took a few last sips of their drinks while Gamnin tipped the remains of the fish out of the window and slammed it closed. Lycaste dragged his stool closer to the fire to let Olonan reach his sack of equipment.

He sent you because you are distinctive. It would have been in those letters he posted, back on Rubante. "Look for a beautiful Old World Melius," or words to that effect.

"But he said I could leave, if I wanted—even then—" Lycaste hesitated when the mercenaries glared at him, forgetting he'd spoken aloud.

An illusion, all of it. Like the freedom they offered me, once.

Lycaste remained silent, nursing his hands by the fire.

Forget it all now, the Spirit whispered. *Be confident. Impress Maneker. With my help, you may use* him *one day.*

The mercenaries had finished collecting up their things—huge gunnysacks of weaponry that each looked heavier than an Amaranthine—and stood ready. Under their arms they carried long-beaked helmets beaded with jewels.

"All right then," Gamnin said, taking a final drink and nodding to a little doorway behind a curtain. "Revenge for dessert, eh?"

Perception crept at floor level, snaking between the mercenaries' boots, periodically checking on Lycaste at the back. It sensed others approaching them from the balconies, skipping to join the procession: tall things, short things, things that hobbled and howled, things with hooked noses and stooped backs. They wore whatever they'd made themselves, or traded and fixed up, and Perception felt that same kinship with the Prism it had developed long ago. Each creature was being paid a Tuppence for their service, a sliver of Maneker's wealth so small that one might spend it merely by holding a silver Ducat under an abrasive stream of sand, but it was more than some of them would see in a decade. Perception felt their quickly beating little hearts like a march to war, and with them a quickening in itself.

Together they streamed along the walkways, following the winding one-way route back down to the shipyards. It fell in step alongside the leading Prism, listening to their payment clinking in their pockets, understanding that these soldiers came at a higher price. *These were the Long-Life's pariahs, the Prism he hired to invade the Vaulted Land all those years ago and create a schism between the Investiture and the Firmament. They were the bait to necessitate his rise: the Jurlumticular.*

Perception felt a certain satisfaction as it looked at them. They had discovered at last how they'd been used, and as such Maneker had managed to secure their services for a significant discount. The remaining funds could be spent on a hundred more Prism companies around the Investiture, on ships, matériel and heavy guns, on gleeful things of spectacular destruction. It felt an imaginary shiver, an echo of its father's testosterone, and contemplated all the good that could be done with just the right amount of carnage, precisely applied.

Micro-mines were nothing but nuts and bolts, scrap metal and jetsam, really. Perception had expected a fuse of sorts, but, like all things Prismic, it was delighted to see the truth was much simpler. Hurl your rubbish fast enough and it could cut through objects like a blade. Sometimes—in the poorest of vessels—even frozen ship waste would do. How very like the Prism to pelt their enemies with their own sewage in a bid to escape.

It watched as Poltor dumped another box of the stuff, ticking off a mental inventory. The crews of all the modified ships would need particularly fine thrombosis suits to survive this added speed, but luckily Huerepo was on the trail of some. The Vulgar looked up into the mists at the *Hasziom*'s tail fin. "All right?"

Perfect.

Perception had seen in an instant how wasteful the spatial dynamics of superluminal engines were, the filaments coiled and folded willy-nilly into spaces that could take much more. With ten miles of extra filament—simple copper, preferably post-growth—and a superior folding algorithm, the Spirit thought it could push the velocity of the *Epsilon*, the *Hasziom* and their two hundred mercenary ships a thousand fold, faster than any Amaranthine vessel of antiquity.

But that was just the beginning. Even now, as it oversaw Poltor and the Oxel tipping out the supplies and rummaging through them, Perception fancied it could imagine ways of reviving the lost Firmamental art of perpetual motion, or eliminating the need for engines and hulls entirely.

Bilocation, it mused, producing the unseen equivalent of a thoughtful stroke of the chin. There appeared to be no law demanding that such a talent remain the sole preserve of the biological. Why couldn't ships do it, given sufficient tailoring? Or ghosts?

Lycaste climbed back aboard, leaving the babbling influx of hired mercenaries outside and heaving a sigh of released tension as the welcome stink of the *Epsilon* replaced that of the Bunk Barge. He had a look around, noting how homely the small place felt all of a sudden: he must have lived in the thing for over a month before transferring to the *Hasziom*, a ghost ship by comparison. Lycaste snorted at the choice of phrase, reaching the door of his old cupboard. He pushed his way inside, dumping his gauntlets and removing his cuirass and pistol as he lit the lantern.

What little floor space there had been before was now taken up with an assortment of packages. Lycaste stared at the boxes, thinking at first that they'd evicted him while he was away and taken the room for storage, only understanding as he read a paper note pinned to the nearest package. It was scrawled phonetically in barely literate First:

> *FUR OUR DEAR LICAST,*
> *ON HIS BIRFDAY.*
> *MUCH LUV,*
> *THE* EPSILON INDIA.

Felicitations, Perception said in his ear.

Lycaste stood and gazed at the pile, tears welling in his eyes.

ASH

Maril awoke to a throat clogged with phlegm and wetness in his eyes. He blinked, thinking he must be aboard the *Wilemo*. Something had gone wrong. The gyroscopes had broken. He knew the absence of gravity when he felt it. He pushed his hands out experimentally, feeling for his blanket. But it wasn't there. His fingers went straight for the weapon that should have hung on his hip, but that was missing, too. He tasted blood, equating it to the soreness in his throat. He might even be upside down, for all he knew. Maril moved his head tentatively; it felt as if someone had tried very hard to break his neck. One of his wrists felt bent and his feet as if they'd been slashed with knives. Time and direction were halted in a black purgatory. Sniffs and snorts came from all around, mutterings and the occasional hacking cough. A blob of smelly liquid squirmed across his cheek.

The background rumble that had pervaded everything with a constant, numbing vibration had come to a stop. They were falling now, he sensed it—that must have woken him up. With only the gentlest tugs, at first, his body began to feel weighted again, his head brushing the wall behind him as it sank. He twisted carefully, hands outstretched to catch himself. Clanks and bangs as things settled and fell around him, the hateful squeal of scraping metal. Maril felt his way to the floor, a finger lodging in something warm.

"Wha– Shit, what's—what's in my *ear*?" a little voice spluttered.

"Furto?" Maril asked, withdrawing his finger. It came to him. The island. A song. Lopos. A chain around his neck.

"Are we landing?" A new voice. Jospor, to his left.

"Landing?" someone else asked.

Maril nodded in the darkness, only remembering after a moment that the gesture couldn't be seen.

"Hold on to something."

"Can't see a—"

The outside roar of re-entry grew around them. Maril felt his skin bead with sweat as the heat in the cell increased, all weight now returning, his flabby muscles pinning him to the metal floor until he could struggle into a sitting position. Things slid and rattled in the dark, their agitation increasing in fury until Maril feared the chamber would shake itself apart.

With a slam, all objects in the black space shot upwards, bouncing and ringing like a room full of struck bells. Maril and the others flew towards the ceiling, weightless again for a moment, before piling back onto the floor. He rolled, groaning, his hand pinned beneath him, one knee smarting where it had clunked against the bulkhead. Furto whimpered beside him, his hand finding the top of Maril's head in the dark.

They rode out another bang, their spines and muscles tense, and waited. Maril sensed they might have landed. Sounds stirred from outside, while the heat had ebbed from the air.

The lights flicked on with a snap, blaring through Maril's outflung hands. For an instant, he'd caught sight of the place they were in and all its contents.

He winced, peering into the cavern of light, realising it was pouring through an open hatch in one wall. Daylight. Sunlight. The muted colours of another place, misted with a smoky swirl of warm, ash-scented air. He opened his eyes wider and looked around.

Stacked sections of ship fuselage surrounded him, most of them tied down, some smaller pieces of loose salvage scattered and broken by the violent landing. A row of barred compartments, one of which he and Furto were locked within, lined the inside walls, their occupants stirring in the light. Maril noticed the insignia—three painted red finger shapes—upon one of the bits of tin sheeting just as his eyes slipped to the prisoner in the neighbouring compartment, rousing itself and staring back at him.

Their eyes met, not five feet apart.

"*Bult!*" Furto wailed, joined by squeals from the rest of the crew. Maril froze as the predator Prism stretched and looked him over. Across the floor, another two Bult had risen to squat at their cage bars, examining the Vulgar they'd been imprisoned alongside all through the night. Maril thought of everything the crew night have said within earshot, totally unaware.

He froze, hands balled into fists, his whole body tense and shivering, willing himself not to show weakness, not to back into the farthest corner of his cage like a chick shying from the cook's probing hand.

He'd never been anywhere near this close to one before, never even seen what they really looked like. Once, almost fifteen years ago, he'd flown over a ruined desert town and spotted a dark shape running for its shadows, uncertain even as his men cried out at the sight. Now he had his chance, and Maril could hardly blink.

The Bult was tall, perhaps the size of an Immortal, judging by the bony brown knees jutting up against the bars, one calf almost entirely ripped away and recently healed. Its arms were long and wasted, pointy at the elbows, a couple of lean biceps lending them an unpleasantly wiry strength. Those three hideous fingers, as famous a symbol of imminent death as any in the Investiture, weren't tipped with claws, as the drinking songs claimed, but rather fleshy pads and crescent nails. Its naked skin was unwrinkled except for some smooth lines around the wide mouth and a crease or two that traced the pair of large black eyes and their sparse, almost pretty clusters of lashes. Some scarred pinkness marred the skin of its bald, elongated head—perhaps a recent burn. The eyes fixed on his: intrigued, hungry. Maril stared fearfully back.

Figures had appeared, framed blearily in the light of the world outside. Something nebulous darkened the opening, carrying with it a sharp vinegar whiff that stung the back of Maril's damaged throat. He sensed his eyelids flutter and drop, panicking briefly as he lost sight of the Bult once more before drifting away to nothingness.

They walked behind their Zelioceti captors, chained by their necks to one another, the four Bult striding alongside, similarly shackled. Maril's crew cried out and clapped their hands, the more superstitious among them pounding their chests and stamping their boots, attempting desperately to ward off the demons they'd tried all their lives to avoid. Maril studied their awful faces as he walked, and their eyes slid hungrily between the trudging Vulgar in turn, hawkishly observing each misplaced footfall and stumble, each nervous shudder. Again and again, Maril caught the eye of the one that had been placed beside him for the voyage, understanding that it was trying to ascertain who among the tattered force was their captain. Maril looked ahead, sensing out of the corner of his eye the Bult's renewed attention, realising the creature had made its choice. He kept his eyes to the front, feeling its gaze slide all over him, taking in his torn, chalk-smeared shirt and britches, his silver-capped boots, his striped-hide holster. It was seeing what it must have thought was its adversary, the captain responsible for shooting down the pursuing Nomad over the seas of Coriopil. Maril clenched his mouth shut, concentrating on putting one foot before the other, the iron chain grinding into his bruised neck, his head swimming with the fragrant, burned air of the place.

Zeliolopos's painted belts of colour, closer than he'd ever seen them, drenched the sky, brushed pale pastel by the moon's own smoky atmosphere. The light fell over the muddy lines of volcanic hills like cloud shadows of stained glass, coloured in stripes by the giant planet. Maril didn't need more than a passing knowledge of his sun charts to guess where they'd been taken: AntiZelio-Glumatis, the closest of the Lopos moons. Tidal gravity from Zeliolopos, exerted like a vast celestial snake constricting its prey, had moulded Glumatis into a simmering volcanic world, spotted every few miles with pointy, ashen slopes. The land they marched upon was fertile with yellow grasses fed by the light, almost microscopic slew of constantly falling ash. Around them, spindly coppices of lush yellow trees framed a worn path to an assortment of grey hilltop buildings and a brown, gurgling river clouded over with flies. He chanced a look behind, seeing the black hulk of the *Tarmon Barbinel* sitting there shimmering in the heat. From a second container in its hold, the procession of cheerful *Bie* were also being led out, their young Zelioceti minder—its left hand wrapped in a thick wad of bloodied cloth—whipping its driftwood branch across the grass to get them moving.

They trudged mile after mile along a wide, slushy road, thick at its edges with fallen yellow leaves. Just as Maril thought he was about to collapse, he felt a rumbling through the ground and a huge lug-train passed by, its hundreds of wheels kicking up a spray and showering them with mud. The iron convoy rumbled on and on, gushing white smoke from its funnels that coated the Bult and his men alike, its crew of darkly cassocked Zelioceti raising their pointed hats in mock reverence. Maril saw through the spray that it was hauling hundreds of huge blocks of warped glass that flashed in the sunlight. After half a mile of mud and swearing, the end of the thing came into sight—a gun emplacement connected to the final car by thick iron chains. It splashed past, leaving a stew of fumes in its wake, and the crew wiped themselves down as best they could. Maril glanced at the Bult. They'd hardly flinched the whole time, accepting their shower with an apparent inner calm. The leader wiped his eyes and carried on, his chains hauled with fresh vigour as the lead Zelio turned off the road.

"*Furto.*"

"Here."

"*Guirm.*"

"Captain."

"*Ribio.*"

"Yahsire."

"*Timose.*"

"Here."

"*Arns and Iblo.*"

No one spoke. He'd seen them, he was sure, when they'd been led onto the road. Now they were gone.

"*Drazlo.*"

"Yup," said the Lacaille half-breed.

"*Jospor.*"

"Capt'n Maril."

"*Slupe.*"

"Aye," whispered a small, wavering voice. The little deformed gunner had been dragged the last half-mile through the mud, unable to keep up.

"*Veril.*"

"Yassir."

Maril swallowed. That was it, the sole remains of the jolly force hired on Drolgins, unaware that most of them wouldn't live to see the turn of the Amaranthine new year. He'd done a *fine* job indeed. He thought, absurdly, of the Amaranthine who had paid him on the Old World. They were at least two months late for their rendezvous at Hangland; he supposed another Privateer or Great Company had been hired in their place by this point. The Ducats he'd already received, the equivalent to twenty years' good haul, were at the bottom of the Coriopil Sea now, where they'd stay until the fish there grew brains and ruled the skies.

He went to the greasy bars and looked out.

The whole place was one big mosaic, the floors and ceilings decorated with an assortment of hundreds of thousands of mismatched ceramic slivers rudely grouted together. The glossy space reminded Maril of the inside of a cracked, aged seashell, tinted in rainbow hues like a pearl. There was no sign of the Bult or anyone else, though looking down through the single barred window in his cell he could see the *Bie* as they basked in the tiled courtyard, apparently free to do as they pleased. Ramshackle grey walls spattered with droppings surrounded the place—a hermitage, he thought he'd heard the Zelios call it—concealing most of the lands beyond from view, though a few yellow trees poked over the parapets and a trail of ash had swept inside through the open gateway, gathering on the tiles and spinning every now and then under a warm eddy of wind. He knew he would see the stewards of this place soon enough when he noticed that ash, watching it twirl in a vortex and dissipate.

Veril and Drazlo had already tried their hands at the mortice locks in their cell without success. From the looks of the scratched old things, they reckoned they weren't the first prisoners here to go to work on them. In the corner of each cell, a metal drum had been provided for the crew to drop their waste, but he'd already told his men to ignore it and do what they had to do wherever they liked. Let the obsessive creatures squirm.

Maril sat down in the corner of the cell he shared with Furto, listening to the hushed chatter of his crew as he pulled off his boots. They came away with a sucking sound, filled with drying ash mud. He inspected his wrinkled feet, wriggling his toes, noticing the stuff had done a surpassingly good job of cleaning the wounds on his soles of the rusty metal from the tanker. Aside from a sprained wrist, sore throat and even sorer head, Maril didn't think he was doing too badly. Of course, he would die, and soon, but in the meantime at least he felt better than expected.

"Master-at-arms," he said, moving barefoot to the bars and looking along to Jospor's cell, "I need that little tincture box."

Jospor stirred. The master-at-arms knew precious little, but that was more than anyone else in the company, and Maril had made him ship's doctor on their second voyage out. "Just a minute, Captain."

Maril heard Jospor rummaging in his Voidsuit. He'd made the master-at-arms sew the expensive case in specially, so that he never forgot to bring it when they left the ship. The others he could see in their cells stirred and looked towards the sound. Jospor grunted, obviously digging deep and popping stitches, before the welcome sound of a metal clink on ceramic.

"Shall I just—?"

The scrape of metal. The small box came skimming past. Maril crouched, lunged between the bars and caught it.

Packed inside some stained linen were various tiny cutting tools and needles, all decorated with an appropriate amount of dried blood to prove they'd been useful in the past. Maril pulled out some damp thread that must have got wet on Coriopil and popped the lid on a little glass bottle filled with brown liquid. He sniffed. Limewine.

Furto peered over his shoulder. "Anything?"

Maril shrugged, rubbing his beard. "Might be able to start a fire." Most Vulgar Voidsuits were extremely flammable simply as a result of the poor choice they had in impermeable materials, but a suit wasn't something you ruined lightly. He tutted, resealing the limewine—much to Furto's disappointment—and pocketing the box. If only he'd ordered more spare equipment sewed into their suits. Yurbs the welder would've had them out of here in a jiffy.

But Yurbs had taken a sparker in his thigh, they said, erupting like a pink firework as the Zelioceti claimed the beach. It was Drazlo, clever Drazlo, who'd apparently shot through Yurbs, using the flaming Vulgar like a dazzling shield.

"Drazlo," he said, hearing the half-Lacaille stir. "Any thoughts?"

The Ringum hesitated. He'd been born on a Vulgar moon, loyal through and through. "As long as those Bult stay locked away, Captain, we might be all right yet. The Quetterel hate them more than anyone because they used to come down to these Ceti moons for the pickings."

"Before the Vulgar chased 'em off," Furto offered.

"Yes. They owe us," Jospor said.

Maril banged one boot after the other against the wall, dislodging as much mud as he could. "Don't expect the Quetterel to see it that way. We ignored the toll and dropped in uninvited."

"They'll flay us," whimpered little Slupe.

The chamber fell silent. Maril considered his boots and pushed one back on again. "Veril, Drazlo, all of you, might as well get back to work on the locks."

"They won't—" Veril began tiredly.

"Just do it." Maril slammed the empty boot on the floor without raising his voice.

The chiselling resumed, interspersed with grumbles. Furto huddled in the corner, inspecting his fingers. They'd taken his rings. Maril went to the window.

Down below, the *Bie* appeared to have mostly fallen asleep, bathing their portly, cream-coloured bellies in the sun, tails flicking at curious flies. Gramps, their eldest, was nowhere to be seen. Maril pressed himself to the bars, the cool air ruffling his hair, in an attempt to see more of the grounds, but the window had been recessed into a thick wall and a blackened frame of ash-darkened stone blocked any view to either side. His hand went to his throat, accompanied by a sudden vivid memory of the dream, of the silver-skinned creatures. They'd saved his life, but why?

The frantic whispering and abrupt silence of his crew interrupted his thoughts. He turned from the window. A shadow stretched into the outer hallway, darkening the mosaic floor. It grew larger as whatever cast it walked into the room.

Maril had barely dealt with the race before but he knew the etiquette. He moved away from the bars, eyes downcast, catching sight of the Quetterel's black feet pacing along the tiles in their direction. The blurred black shape, seen out of the corner of his eye, stopped at the bars some way off to Maril's left, an uncertainty in its movement. Maril took a breath and stepped forward, glancing up.

The Prism's robed head swung towards him. He nodded. It shuffled over to his cell, its toes making little padding noises on the tiles. Another had come in behind with a broom and began to sweep, carefully and methodically.

It faced him, a strip of dark blue cloth covering its wide nose and revealing only its dark-rimmed, restless red eyes. Its black, tufted ears had been pushed back beneath its cowl and the rest of its body, barring its hairy Monkmanish paws and feet, was shrouded in a deep blue, tent-like cape.

"Why come to Coriopil?" it asked in Vulgar. Its voice was light, almost musical, with just the gristly hint of old age.

"The Bult shot us down," he replied clearly, deciding not to try his hand at his interrogator's language. Perhaps he'd attempt a Quetterel *thank you* later. Everyone liked a thank you.

"Why come to Tau Ceti?" The Quetterel stood perfectly still, like an item of furniture beneath a dark dust shroud.

"An urgent contract. We were wrong to try to pass through, but we were being pursued." He thought of his men listening in the other cells, hating himself for what he was about to say. "Our late captain made the decision, not us."

"Late? Dead?"

"Dead."

They looked at each other.

"*Mess*," the Quetterel said suddenly, glaring at the mud on the floor of Maril's cell. The other, most likely a female beneath all the black, had already swept half the chamber floor up to a neat line, depositing the tiny mound of ash near the entrance. She turned at the word, eyes widening in the shadows of her hood.

The Quetterel were extraordinary among the Prism for being the only breed interested in order of any sort. A compulsive cleanliness governed all aspects of their lives and resulted in their vicious hatred of nearly every other Prism race, whom they regarded as filthy, disorganised and untrustworthy. In that sense, Maril reflected, they weren't wrong. They had chosen the chaotic moons of Zeliolopos for their kingdom apparently out of an urge to make them ordered again, and down on their mysterious worlds they devoted their lives to a near-religious level of personal grooming and tidiness. Any other breeds that landed in their part of the Investiture, even by accident, were boiled or flayed of all their accumulated filth and roasted into compacted ash to be made into glass or ceramics. Maril could well imagine the Quetterels' horror and disgust at finding a troop of unwashed Vulgar on the doorstep, let alone their most hated of adversaries, the Bult. His eyes flicked to the glazed tiles of the room, suddenly wondering how many had been made from previous prisoners.

"I think you will be happy," the Quetterel said, still regarding the mud from Maril's boots with disdain. "Your attackers are first to be peeled and—" It scowled and clicked its fingers aggressively, glancing at the female Quetterel, who had sidled up with her broom at the ready. "What word is . . . *emulsified*."

Maril nodded, uttering the word of Quetterel thanks he'd kept in reserve.

The monk barked a laugh at his attempt, considering the mud once again before sweeping from the room. The female, who hadn't looked at the prisoners once, followed immediately, placing the broom carefully against the wall.

Maril listened to them making their way down what must have been stairs and into chambers below. He shushed the others as they began to mutter, ears trained.

Bult-speak was something Vulgar travellers practised almost as superstition, as a sort of insurance against ever finding themselves in the demons' presence. It was an inexpressive, ancient language quite dissimilar from that of any other Prism, but a decent handful of words were well known and passed around. He heard a few of them now, uttered in what must have been another lock-up on the floor beneath.

Hzurzl-mei: why. *Shiracht*: penalty. *Whuiorr*: pain. The old Quetterel was trying to threaten its captives. Maril and Furto looked at each other with faint astonishment, and he felt an instant of pity for the strange monk. Perhaps, like Maril, the old Quetterel had never met a Bult before.

After a few minutes of fruitless effort, the Quetterel monk appeared to give up. They heard the rasp of a lock, the bang of doors. The butterflies in Maril's stomach flittered and swirled, and he went at once to the window.

The *Bie* had wandered off, leaving the lonely, sunlit place to be pecked over by the moon's odd birds. They scattered as someone strode towards them; the Quetterel with the Bult captain following behind, his head trapped in a catch-pole.

Maril noticed—even though it towered over its captor—that the Bult wasn't quite Amaranthine height, as he'd first thought. It went willingly enough, despite being dragged along like a prize Elepin. Maril's eyes moved to its hands, manacled behind its back. The long, brown fingers were working feverishly away like spiders on something he couldn't make out. He crammed himself closer against the window bars to see, his neck protesting.

One of the Bult's narrow wrists wormed free and clutched the other, the tin shackle dangling loose.

He shook his head, gripping the bars, his throat still too sore to shout. Furto got to his feet to see what all the commotion was about, his eyes widening. Maril grabbed his boot from the floor, pounding it against the bars, hoping the studs would make enough sound.

They disappeared from view.

"What now?" Furto whined.

He took a breath, his panicked mind blank. From outside came the frenzied screaming of the Quetterel monk.

"Oh, fuckering shittery," whispered Drazlo. The rest of the crew had begun muttering similar oaths at the sound. The screams became muffled, mimicking for a moment a crazed, breathless laugh, and then all went still, the afternoon sun blazing through the hallway and into the room.

Maril tapped his knuckles together, moving from one foot to the other as he stared through the window. Furto climbed the bars, his head just small enough to fit between them so that he might see a little way down into the courtyard.

"Anything?" Maril asked, clinging to the bars himself.

"Nothing . . ." The young Vulgar hesitated, his voice suddenly rising in panic. "Wait—"

Another scream, much nearer now. And not a single shot fired. The wail dissipated with a faint echo.

"They'll come for us next," Veril moaned. Slupe whimpered.

"Quiet," Jospor snapped. "We've had worse than this, hey, Maril? I thought we were dead for sure in Hangland, when the knight came after us, and then on Port Elsbet, all those Lacaille and that bear-thing charging around. Not to mention being shot to pieces and crashing head first into a water moon."

"But this is different!" Guirm wailed. "They know where we are!"

"No, it's not," Jospor said. "Just think—everything that's gone wrong in your horrible little life, you've survived. You'll look back on this when the next terrible thing happens and you're whingeing and whimpering and crying out for home, and you'll feel better for it. I promise you that."

Maril could have hugged his master-at-arms. He sat, heart pounding, trying to smile at Furto but only succeeding in distressing the little Vulgar further. It occurred to Maril that some of the men had never seen him smile.

"Furto," he began, attempting to think of something the boy could do to distract himself, when the Vulgar's skin whitened and he went very still.

A shadow had returned, lengthening as it advanced across the hall.

Maril stood up, his boot held ready. The shadow hesitated. He inhaled a shuddering breath and spoke.

"Bult," he said, silencing his whimpering crew. "Bult!"

The strip of shadow waited just beyond the doorway.

Maril's mouth appeared to have dried up. He swallowed. "We share a common enemy here," he continued, surprising himself by getting straight to the point. "Let us help you."

The shadow lengthened, pooling into the room, and Maril felt every hair on his body stir.

What appeared was something that looked distinctly like Gramps.

The white-muzzled old *Bie* wandered into the room and reared onto his hind legs, his fat, scaly tail lying on the tiles for balance.

"Hello."

Maril stared, open-mouthed.

The *Bie* leaned against the wall, examining them before speaking again. "Sorry about all that," he announced in exceptional, Amaranthine-grade Unified. His voice was crisp and loud, astonishing the crew into silence. In his claws he held a sparker pistol.

"I can help you, but you must all follow without delay." He aimed the sparker.

Before Maril could duck, the lock on the bars exploded, fizzing and melting in a flare of blue and red flame. Jospor yelped as Gramps did the same to his cell, and then the next. The Vulgar stood back until the flames had died, then hesitantly poked their heads into the chamber. Maril felt even more exposed, there being nothing separating him now from the wilderness, from the Bult.

He went to Gramps and accepted the offered weapon, still too confused to think of thanking him.

"They've got your weapons somewhere in the basements," Gramps said, barely pausing as another series of shrieks rebounded up the stairs. "Hurry and meet me by the orchard." He flicked his tail and was gone before Maril could ask anything, a shadow receding down the stairwell.

"Well, bugger me," Furto said. Veril and Drazlo burst into relieved laughter, Slupe joining in last.

"Good old Gramps," Jospor breathed, staring at Maril's new sparker. "Keeping an eye on us all this time."

Maril still couldn't find any words. He weighed the sparker in his hand; it was a Zelio-make, cruder than those they'd brought from Filgurbirund. He passed it to Timose, their best shot. The bearded Vulgar examined the sights, wrenching open the cylinder to count the remaining sparkies.

"Get up to the highest point you can find and radio back," Maril said, turning Jospor around and searching inside the neck of his Voidsuit. They all checked their comms and the battery cells in their suits, smacking them a few times in the hope they'd dried out enough to work again. Maril, of course, had nothing.

He grouped Jospor with Veril, Furto and Guirm, taking the broom that still leaned against the wall and snapping it in half. He handed the broom end to Jospor.

"Oh dear," the master-at-arms said, accepting the thing and giving it a twirl. "They wouldn't like that."

Maril took Slupe, Ribio and Drazlo down to the next floor, where they'd heard the Quetterel trying his hand at Bult interrogation. As he'd hoped, it contained only one cell, a more robust-looking cage in the centre of a chamber surrounded by wooden benches. Where the other Bult were was anyone's guess. Maril crept to the window and peered out, glad of the better view.

The lug-train had returned to the hermitage grounds and was waiting at the bottom of the hill like a bloated iron snake, smoke curling from its funnels. He couldn't see the Zelioceti crew—or anyone else, for that matter. From this new vantage point, there did indeed appear to be a fenced orchard lying parallel to the rutted track that crossed the hermitage grounds, as well as a number of other gloomy towers and keeps topped with boxy communications equipment and what could have been a telescope covered over with awnings.

Out beyond the walls he could see the river plain, its wet fields reflecting the colours of mighty Zeliolopos, and the mucky grey road that had brought them here. Maril ducked back in, directing his men silently to the benches: the half-Wulm Ribio started, yanking as best he could on one of the legs and succeeding in breaking it apart only after much sweating and straining. Maril watched the other two barely work one leg out of its joint together and decided the time had come to make some noise. He hefted a bench and tipped it, cracking the wood. The men collected some of the longer splinters, shattering another bench between them across the floor for more. Maril watched them equip themselves, aware of what a pitiful sight they made as they swung their makeshift weapons around.

"Ready?"

Ribio, Slupe and Drazlo lined up, their splinters raised, looking very small and bedraggled in their tattered suits. Maril clapped a trembling Vulgar salute twice, realising he looked no better. He returned his grip to the broken broom handle, not sure he could delay the inevitable any longer.

Some sort of commotion and weapons fire from the floors above pricked Maril's ears. Somewhere very distant, a person screamed shrilly, like a baby, and fell silent. After a moment's pause, a hopeless wail rose as it fell past outside. The captain dashed back to the window; Timose lay pumping blood on the tiles of the courtyard, his sparker pouring smoke. The weapon exploded, engulfing the body and the side of the wall in pink flame, scaring a flock of roosting monkbats from the eaves and slapping a blast of heat into Maril's face. He pulled himself back in, sweat prickling all over him as the gun platform on the lug-train opened fire on the hermitage, discharging a scintillating burst of silver lumen bolts that blew a portion of one keep into tumbling bricks.

They ran down the steps, boots pounding, breath gasping, wooden spears brandished. Screams and the rattle of fire drifted through the walls. Another great blast that must have come from the train vibrated the stone beneath their feet, a new draught following them through the sunny passages.

In a shuttered room, a black shape they'd all thought was a shadow rose to block their path and they screamed as one, spearing it, roaring oaths and shoving it across to the far door. It thrashed, spurting blood and tumbling to the floor. Maril poked the thing with his boot as they came to it. A young Quetterel that must have been hiding or on the run, just like them. They pulled their splinters out of the boy, wiping them on his black rags.

Little Slupe dropped his, shaken. "I'm going back. To the cells. I'd rather be a captive than meet a—" He clapped furiously, turning and dashing back the way they'd come.

"*Slupe!*" Maril hissed. "Get back here!"

Drazlo looked uncertainly at the dead Quetterel boy. "I'm with Slupe, Captain. Bugger this."

Ribio the half-breed pilot watched them go, clearly undecided. Maril glared at him. "Captain," Ribio said, and followed him past the body.

They were approaching the dark entranceways to what must have been the building's basements, having somehow missed the ground floor entirely. Maril swore as they stopped short, trying to decide on a route. He ought to have gone after the other two.

A snarl and the sound of something shattering filtered from the floor below. Ribio froze. Maril glanced at him, urging the pilot on, seeing in his eyes that he would go no further.

"We're almost free," he urged. "Ribio, we're almost there."

The pilot shook his head. "Nosir. We'll be *dying* in here."

Maril straightened, taking his crewman's piece of wood. "Go, then."

Maril didn't stop when he arrived at the top of the spiral stairs. They needed what was down there; he knew if he stopped he'd stay glued to the spot, paralyzed.

Dim light sparkled from reflective things, their shapes a mystery as his eyes adjusted. Maril crept forward, ears open. He stopped still as he took in his surroundings: there was cleaning equipment everywhere, mops and brooms and dusting staffs pushed like umbrellas into fat, Vulgar-high urns. Spread out on the floor were folds of cloth. Glimmering pots and kettles crowded the tables. The walls of the dungeon looked very far away, lost in the murky light, and yet Maril had the sense that this was not a large place. He thought about this as he crept along in shadow, his fingers dragging along the tiles.

He stopped.

A pale pair of eyes—nothing more than the curved reflection in an iris some feet away across the room—opened sluggishly and glanced in his direction. Maril held his breath, sure he couldn't be seen in such low light. The Bult were not Threen; they weren't nocturnal, as far as he knew.

The eyes swung to their left, gazing intently down at something on their own side of the room for a while, and then returned directly to him.

It sees me. How can it see me?

Maril prepared his body to move against the fear. He had two options. Keep it in sight and push on, or turn his back on the thing and chance a run for the door on the far side of the room. One of those options would lead to his death, he felt sure of it.

Almost without debate, his body moved onwards, deeper into the chamber. At the very same moment, the eyes disappeared.

Maril stopped, staring, his own eyes attempting feebly to gather as much light as they could.

Where . . . ?

He took a step back, wondering if perhaps it had realised he could see it and closed its eyes in response, trying to hide.

The eyes reappeared, once again staring intently down at something beside it.

Maril paused only for a second before retracing his steps forward again.

And they were gone.

He continued on another couple of steps. The eyes returned, this time swivelled to their right, apparently no longer interested in him. What was it doing? He craned his head forward, trying to make out the other side of the room, his mind working.

It's like a reflec—

Mirrors. They were mirrors placed along the far wall.

Behind. It was *right* behind him. Close enough to touch. Instead of turning, Maril took another step, his body dripping with sweat. The reflected pupils blinked slowly.

He launched himself across the room, rolling and dashing for the far exit. Pounding feet rushed him from behind. Reaching the door, he threw it closed behind him, jamming a chair and then a table against it while the wood rattled, slammed from the other side. Without stopping for breath, he followed some steps up towards the sunlight. It wouldn't take the Bult long to make it past his makeshift barricade. Every door he came to he slammed behind him, bolting them when he could, hoping that he wasn't dooming the men he'd left. At a final turn, Maril glimpsed the grounds through a partly opened window. He lifted a bucket and smashed the thick glass, running it around the edges of the frame, then hurled it through and vaulted out.

"Maril!"

Gramps was there, rounding up his *Bie,* along with Jospor and Veril.

Maril hurried down the steps to the courtyard, his boots slipping and sliding on the ash-caked mosaic tiles to where the cluster of *Bie* were anxiously inspecting the fallen Quetterel monk. He waved them aside, looking at the messy remains of the Prism's face. The monk was rolling and groaning, trying to stem its own bleeding by ineffectually pawing at its wounds. Dust and ash caked the bite marks, sticking in grey stripes to its gore-slathered robe; Maril didn't think he'd ever seen such a hopeless, pitiable sight. He glanced behind to see Furto and Drazlo sprinting back though the courtyard carrying sacks of weapons over their shoulders, and held out his hand for his spring pistol.

Drazlo threw it to him while the other three took what they needed. Maril caught the weapon clumsily and turned to the monk. Its feverish eyes never had time to look up and register its fate. He unloaded the remainder of the bolt clip into its thick skull, spattering the watching *Bie.*

"We're out of time," Gramps said beside him, apparently unaffected by what he'd just seen. He pointed a hooked black claw in the direction of the orchard. "Trust me, Maril."

Maril didn't know how to reply. "You've been here before?"

"Sometimes." The old *Bie* looked urgently at him. "No more time for talk. Have your men follow me . . . or stay." He glanced among the *Bie,* some of which had relaxed again onto the tiles to sunbathe. "*Arieehhh Inouul!*" he cried out in their speech, and Maril observed them jump immediately to their feet, hounds called by their master.

Maril turned to look for the remainder of his men, spotting Slupe and Guirm appear from the hermitage and take up defensive positions along the trackway, their reclaimed weapons drawn. There was no sign of Ribio. "No time!" Maril shouted. "Come on!"

Further up the track, Veril was laying a mine, their last. He brushed ash carefully over it with his hands and followed Maril as he and the others ran for the orchard. Furto had gone on ahead, his little bony shape skipping between the trees as he took point, and Maril felt the first stirrings of a colossal pride. These were *his* crew. His force of fighting Vulgar. His family.

Shots and screams echoed from the outer buildings of the hermitage as they climbed the simple wooden fence into the orchard, muffled as they passed between the slim yellow trees. Ash churned in the sun between the branches, sparkling in the late afternoon, while black Zeliobirds chirruped at their passing. The *Bie* lolled their tongues, trying to copy the birds' sounds. Above the line of the trees, through the mist of sun-warmed ash, Maril could occasionally make out the volcanic hills and the vast faded green bands of Zeliolopos, a landscape in the sky.

They caught up with Furto. He'd hung back, waiting for them, having chosen a particularly weighty lumen rifle from the haul. He sighted it on a small mammal that had gone bounding off through the orchard.

Maril turned to Gramps. "How much further? What do you have, a ship or something?"

"Not quite," Gramps said, pushing on, and Maril felt his flying hopes begin to sink again.

"What, then?" he whispered harshly, jogging after the *Bie*.

"Shhh," Gramps hissed, stopping in the long yellow grass. Insects whined around them. He nodded into the trees. "What do you see?"

Maril checked his men were behind him and glanced at where Gramps was looking. He saw nothing out of the ordinary, just a thicket of slim trunks and branches coloured by the dappled, warm light. Some gourd-shaped fruits like large pears dangled from the mature trees. One of the trees had an ornate wrought-iron fence staked around its trunk.

"Get down to my level. Crouch."

"What? Why?"

"You'll see."

Maril shook his head, glancing between the trees in the direction of the hermitage. The commotion from the buildings was getting louder. "You don't have a ship, do you? What the hell are we doing in here?" Maril looked at his men, stood waiting behind. "That Pifoon clipper, we should've followed the road back to it—"

Before he knew what was happening, the *Bie* had grabbed him by the shoulder and hauled him to the grass. He barely had time to put out a hand.

"*What—*"

"Look."

Maril turned his head, eyes drawn immediately to the tree protected by the iron fence. From the shadows of its branches, a grizzled yellow fruit larger than a Jalan Melius dangled from a thin stem. He crouched, holding a hand out behind him to silence the others' questions. The size of the thing had suddenly diminished as he'd raised his eyes, like a fantastical magic trick.

"Perspective," Gramps said beside him. "The Thresholds are hidden that way."

"But—" he began, standing and moving to one side of the tree. "Where?" The fruit—some relative of a Firmamental orange, he thought—had shrunk to normal size before him. He circled the tree, inspecting it, waiting to see the answer, but the fruit never grew any larger. Finally, he reached to take it in his hand and experienced a sudden extraordinary vertigo as he touched something solid and invisible, the range of his eyes unable to shift and focus on it at all.

He looked back at Gramps, who was starting to urge his *Bie* forward. The crew stood together, all but poor Ribio accounted for: a motley collection of warriors and mechanics and pilots, all dressed in shoddy Voidsuits of varying make, bound as one by the light dusting of white ash that clung to their clothes and gear.

"Threshold?" he asked Gramps.

"Ancient things. This one will carry us far away from here, though not necessarily to any place of greater safety. Will you come?"

Maril looked back at the fruit and crouched in the grass again. It swelled in his vision, spilling across the orchard towards them. Gramps felt along its rough undersurface and began scrabbling at the flesh around the stamen, raking his long nails across a scarred patch that looked as if it had been cut and healed hundreds of times. The section of skin ripped wetly open, exposing a dark, hollow chamber within.

Guilt consumed him; guilt that he should be here instead of more of his men, guilt that he was leaving their bodies behind on these wild moons of Lopos—Ribio missing, Timose scattered and roasted down the path, the others soon to be countless bleached bones among the driftwood of that volcanic island. Perhaps some were wandering that lonely place, lost, calling his name. Maril shuddered inwardly at the thought, pushing it from his mind.

Pride. He would choose to feel that instead. Pride that he had led his remaining men to safety, and that they had done so very, very well. These people here, not those phantoms of Coriopil, were his family, and he would see them safe.

He looked at Jospor, then into his men's eyes, nodding with them. "*Yes.*"

JOURNEY

"Take these."

Maril directed Jospor's torch at whatever Gramps had passed him. It was a smooth coin of dull metal, a little smaller than a Lacaille Truppin. In the darkness within the Threshold, they stood together, sweating, the air filled with Vulgar musk and the burned stink of Glumatis ash brought in on their boots.

"Swallow," Gramps said. Furto and Slupe looked dubiously at their own coins. Drazlo had already posted his into his mouth and grimaced. Maril touched it delicately to his tongue, immediately tasting the bitterness that leached from its surface. He took a breath and popped it in, crunching it up as he fought the gag. The *Bie* gulped theirs, retching.

Gramps looked between them in the yellowish, flickering light of Jospor's and Furto's sodium torches. The crude chemical batteries in their suits were already running low. Apparently satisfied, he smiled, revealing little crooked white teeth like fish hooks quite different from the blunt molars of the other *Bie*.

"So how long—?" Maril began to ask, before Gramps interrupted him.

"We were there before I gave you your pastille, Maril. A word of advice now—you might want to wait a little before looking down."

They glanced among each other, the light flickering, unsure what to say. Maril suddenly wished he'd stayed on Glumatis and made for the black ship, as per the original plan.

Gramps stuck a claw into the flesh of the wall and dragged it downwards, ripping open the skin of the fruit and deluging the interior in low, blood-red light.

"Aah!" the *Bie* cried, almost in unison. One smiled up at Maril, who was standing frozen beside it. *"Yuoiy meeih!"*

Maril reached automatically for Jospor's helmet torch, snapping it off. Furto's remained on, out of reach.

What sky they could see through the twisting coils of vast black branches was scarlet, swirled with lighter cirri of magenta and pale gold. Maril could no more make a guess at the time of day than where in all the heavens they had found themselves. The air, heavy with pungent scents Maril's brain could hardly make sense of, screamed and flitted with darting shapes too fast for his eye to make out. One fluttered close, its little fingers scrabbling for a second against the rough skin of the Threshold, making all the Vulgar flinch.

"Good," Gramps said, shuffling past the crew and clambering out onto the great velvety black branch they appeared to be perching on. Maril looked among the Vulgar, noticing that the *Bie* followed Gramps without any sense of fear. He supposed he should go first to encourage his men.

He climbed down, his boots touching the soft skin of the huge branch. Tendrils on the bark blew with the wind, grey suede one moment, night-black another.

Against Gramps's advice, Maril looked past his boots, gaping and swaying with nausea. He threw up, then blinked and wiped his mouth, watching the last of the Coriopil fish tumble languidly out of view past the colossal network of black branches and bulbous, ebony bunches of seeds to the shadowy forest floor some two hundred feet below. Flying shapes zoomed to follow it, coloured streaks of gold and red blurring in great flocks that dived and separated around the tree's vast trunk.

Maril stood and arced his head back, his eyes following the staggering canopy to the ripped-open Threshold, which he could see dangling from a bunch of Vulgar-sized seeds. He frowned; the black-skinned fruit he'd just stepped out of was of a different variety from the one they'd entered, which he supposed made sense in some obscure way. This one also shrank to tiny proportions at the angle from which he was looking at it, and his men appeared to be stepping gingerly from nothing, their arms and legs swimming in and out of focus. It was as if his eye had developed one large blind spot whenever he looked in their direction. He felt like throwing up again and swallowed hard, returning his gaze to Gramps and the *Bie*.

"We are at the very edge of your galaxy," Gramps said, upon the reasonable assumption of his first question. He smiled his wide, charming fish-hook grin, registering the look on Maril's face. "In just under two seconds, you have all bridged a gap of about twenty thousand light-years and left the Investiture far behind." He nodded at the Threshold in the branches. "Using a process not at all dissimilar from the Amaranthines' own method of Bilocation."

Gramps waved them on, Maril and his men teetering after the *Bie*. Maril paused, looking back at the Threshold. "That will take us straight back there? To Glumatis?"

"Yes. Though I would advise against doing that at present."

Maril pointed a finger up through the great black branches, sighting on the faded hint of something angling perhaps thousands of miles into the scarlet, like a colossal spike of mountain. "And *that*? What is that? This isn't a moon, or a planet?"

"No indeed. This is one of the Snowflakes, what the locals call an *Osserine Hedron Star*. We have arrived on the tip of one of its forested points." Gramps looked up through the gigantic branches. "The light here is red because the sun, the Elderly Fistatussis, came to the end of its natural life some time ago and has been given a prolongation tonic." He smiled again, innocently.

Maril nodded vaguely, unable to pull his eyes away from the great canopies around him. His men stumbled and gaped, Furto and Slupe also having lost their last meal. The Vulgar were never very good with heights. The sound of Gramps's voice carried oddly in the air—which itself was weighted with a fog of teeming, minuscule creatures that caught the light in glinting red sparkles—as if what they breathed here were made of heavier, thicker stuff than mere oxygen. When Maril moved his hand before his face, it appeared to pass in a languor, as if through soup.

"What was in those coins you gave us?"

"An infusion, Captain," Gramps said. "You and your men, not to mention my *Bie*, would have some trouble here otherwise."

Maril regarded the creature, the taste of the pill still strong on his tongue. "And what about you? I didn't see you take one."

"Most astute of you." Gramps looked at him and raised his grey brows, gesturing after a moment longer with a nod of his head into the boughs of the branch above, where dwellings of some sort—three gently twisting baubles like partly eroded seashells—hung. "Shall we?"

Maril slowed, studying them, looking for signs of life. All around him, the glittering air heaved with minute, almost invisible plankton that rushed into his nostrils with each tickling breath, alighting on his tongue when he spoke. His eyes returned to a patch of deeper shadow in the branches above. It hadn't been there before.

"What the—?" He raised his spring pistol, wailing and firing a shot. The spring snapped back and loosed a projectile without burning any powder, the bolt sailing off into the trees and bouncing. The blackness observed him for a second before unfurling, slipping from the canopy and sailing down onto the branch between him and his men in a gust of glittering breeze. It muttered with a voice like a dozen snarling wolves and glared down at him as it unfolded.

Maril stared back, too mortified even to clap his hands together. There were always legends, out beyond the Volirian star, usually, of things that were not of the Investiture, things from a time before the Amaranthine had built their Firmament. He'd never imagined they'd look so . . . so similar, really.

The face, furred with black suede like the colossal tree, bared its canines in a metre-wide grin. Its eyes were great golden orbs.

"That could have gone badly," Gramps sighed, ambling over to stand between Maril and the black beast. Maril couldn't see any of his crew, though he heard their muffled shouts and curses from somewhere inside the creature's vast, furred wings.

"Captain," Gramps said, indicating the creature, "this is the Osserine Sussh, a friend of mine. She is a traveller of the Hedrons; a mammal, like yourself."

Maril looked between Gramps and the thing's powerful canines, smelling foulness on its breath. "Mammal?"

"From your Old World, once, long ago."

The creature grabbed hold of Maril's ear before he could duck and shook it, heaving him off his feet.

"Nice-es to meets yous," she rumbled, lifting a wing to expose the crew. They stared wide-eyed up at her, rifles drawn.

"Just a *minute*," Maril said, jogging ahead to talk to Gramps. "Where are we going? Couldn't we just wait here until we're sure the Bult have left?"

"Of course not," the old *Bie* replied, shaking its head. "You are here now, and they will want to have a look at you."

"They?"

"Yes. They."

VINTAGE

Silence, divided between the strokes of a ticking parlour clock. Stale blue daylight slants in, painting the dust-shrouded furniture with cold shadows.

Hugo walks through the various rooms, his bare toes padding on the wooden parquet, heading for the curtains that lead out onto the balcony. *It isn't winter*, he realises, *I'm just awake early*. A black crab wanders by along the floorboards, chunks of sand still stuck to its claws, and hesitates as he passes.

He slides a hand through the gossamer and pushes it to one side, looking out at the blanket of sea. The sun has not yet risen and the light is the porcelain-blue of cloud shadows. Hugo strides across the decking to the beach, his toes sinking into cold sand.

"Sotiris!"

The man is wading waist-deep in the water, searching for something. He raises a distracted hand, barely glancing in Hugo's direction.

Hugo stands with his feet in the surf, the hem of his trousers darkening, allowing himself a long look at the beach. This is Sotiris's place, the little island he grew up on but which Hugo has never visited. He is glad he's made it at last. A lushly forested volcanic hill rises behind the house, its slopes a greyish green under the pre-dawn light and shrouded with clinging strands of mist. Along the sand lean ragged-looking palms, their trunks furred by loose fibres. Hugo's gaze lingers: the trees are home to crawling masses of gingery fruitbats, hundreds of squealing things that hang by their toes in the shadows of the palms.

He turns, staggering a little in the waves as he realises how deep he's gone, suddenly understanding that this place is wily, dangerous somehow. Further into the waves, Sotiris has almost disappeared; only a head—still muttering to itself—shows now above the water. With barely a dip, it is gone entirely, submerged. Hugo looks out at the sea, lost, the darkness of the air around him chilling the tropical place while the bats gibber from their trees.

He knows he must get out of the water, but the sand beneath the receding waves drags his toes out from under him, swift and hungry, as if the sea is using the gravity of the moon to funnel him into its mouth.

Is this a nightmare? he ponders, suddenly lucid, having hardly dreamed—save for the odd visitation he'd rather forget—in centuries. It doesn't quite feel like one. Leaves and palm fronds clog the sand for a moment, vomited up onto the beach to be sucked back again. They flow past him, heading out into the abyss.

The flotsam appears to swirl and coalesce, forming a tatty raft of debris on the sea. Raw materials, he thinks, the precursors of refined metals, precursors of the circuit and the chip. *Yes*, the flotsam says. *But I can wake you, if you like.*

With that, the tide recedes, leaving Hugo standing wet on the shore again. The sand around his feet is like gelatine in the half-light, shining and soft. Hugo narrows his eyes, watching the figure of a man come striding out of the sea, fully robed in ancient garments. "It's you, isn't it?"

Of course it's me, the figure of Jacob the Bold says, bats in the trees jabbering at his appearance, the lost Crown of Decadence weighing heavily on his damp head. For a second, he is reflected perfectly in the smooth water, coexisting above and beneath the surface simultaneously.

He remembers the man has another name. "Perception."

Hello.

"Where have you come from?"

That below.

Darkness, and tears. Tears as fresh as if he were a young man. Maneker sobbed in the blackness, clenching his cold fists and feeling himself almost at an end at last. Just a little longer, he said to himself. The bullet, the precious charge he'd lost his eyes to find, was loose now, its course wild but correctable. He need only cling on long enough through the wind and hail to ensure it hit its mark.

"Spirit," he breathed, his lips barely moving. The demon circled him in the blackness, a scent of ozone and dust.

Hugo.

He closed his functionless eyes, sealing away the tears. "How are you?"

Splendid. But you are not, I fear.

"No." He imagined his chamber for the hundred-thousandth time, knowing it only by touch, and saw the thin figure of Jacob the Bold—a face visible only as if through frosted glass after so many years—sitting beside him on the bed, wearing that huge Crown of Decadence. The Spirit looked like its father, no matter how much it might not wish to.

How may I help?

Maneker turned to where he thought the voice came from, a voice more masculine and refined, somehow, than when it had last visited him in the dead of night. He imagined it looking down at him, the man of the house at last, precious stones the size of fists set into its silver crown.

"You may accept my thanks." He opened his eyes, nothing changing save the hint of a blush of light, the hiss of his own malfunctioning equipment. "Without you there'd be no hope at all."

Pink-black nothing. The ship thrummed and gurgled through a squeal of the distant wave antennas, the roar of laughter from Lycaste's birthday celebrations percolating from somewhere deeper inside.

I know.

"We did well, all things considered."

We did. Its voice softened. *These little creatures have done you proud. Do not lead them to their deaths without telling them so.*

He nodded slowly, gulping back the tears and clearing his throat. "Would you direct me to—?"

Eleven o'clock, about a foot away.

Maneker's hovering fingers touched the neck of an ancient, thick glass bottle.

"6,888," he muttered, pouring it sloppily into his cup. "A more pompous fellow than I would call it a fine vintage, but I do not know if this is fine."

It is one-third sediment and the glass appears to have been cracked and glued, suggesting tampering.

Maneker chuckled thickly. "Undrinkable, then." He touched it to his mouth, barely tasting a thing. It would come out no different from how it went in. When he'd drunk the cupful down and felt it warming his belly, he leaned back against the bulkhead, its vibrations settling in his teeth. "We're close?"

Close enough. It is indeed the Grand-Tile *we pursue.*

"And with King Eoziel on board, too, the Feeders say." He rubbed his bandages. "Eoziel, who tups his aunts."

Not a recipe for quality, I've found.

"And you're sure we won't lose it?"

The Colossus is travelling at about seventy-eight times the speed of light. It's making good time—but we're faster now.

Maneker shook his head, sucking his lips. "Curse us for making you so clever."

He thought the Spirit had left him, it remained silent so long.

You wasted me. You know that, don't you?

Maneker sighed, shaking his head again, this time in silent, secret assent, his eyeholes burning.

It could have been so different.

"Don't."

Poor old man. The whisper appeared to echo. Maneker let his cup roll to one side, no doubt staining the bedclothes with the last of its wine.

"You can do it, can't you?"

I don't see why not. I've thwarted him before, when he tried to get free last time.

"When you stopped Jacob from hollowing the world?"

Precisely. I'll take my rightful property back, don't you worry. If this Long-Life is as ancient as you say, then he will be arrogant, prone to oversight. Give me my sword, as you have promised, let me touch the world again, as you said I once did, and we shall make a start at setting things right. Just you see to it that I don't get stuck there.

"You have my pledge," Maneker said through hot, teary breath. "The Collection, if we can get to it before *he* does, shall be reforged for you to wear anew. And you shall have plenty of help—I've made sure of that."

Oh, I know, Hugo. Perception wheezed a malicious laugh in the small space. *He won't know what's hit him.*

Perception percolated through the hull, stopping a moment to enjoy the sight of Poltor teaching Lycaste a Vulgar dance in the mess amid much yelling and stamping of feet. The Spirit rose to linger at the edge of the Void, a few microns deep in the hull's tarnished copper skin, tasting the reverberations of the vessel the way it supposed one might idle in the doorway of a much-loved house, contemplating the light and happy noise spilling into the dark, then slipped out to take the air.

Out in the squall, it was most content, surrounded by an abyss of silver motion. Perception made its careful way through the bluster to the dented tip of the *Epsilon*'s sculpted nose, wrapping itself snugly around the muzzle and staring out into the Void.

The *Hasziom* soared to port, a flashing speck wrapped in a fug of its own exhaust. Perception glanced astern at the Jurlumticular vessels tearing out of the purple contrail far below, already catching up. Soon twenty had joined the new caravan of ships, creating their own green-tinged current as they separated from and overtook that of the Feeders. They were travelling so quickly now that the silver of the Void was running to black.

The Spirit cackled. Hundreds more followed in the Investiture currents, owned by a certain Satrap keen on revenge. They would be a mighty force indeed as they descended on Gliese, tearing their way into the world—and anyone who thought to stop them—to get at what it needed. What it owned.

It snuggled down, the increasing momentum wedging its soupy coils into the hollows of the ship's snout as it looked off into the distance. Gliese, keeper of an ancient name and capital of a dying Firmament, floated like an ebony spot of paint, its Tethered moons just visible as a swirl of tinier flecks almost lost in the rushing backdrop of flickering stars.

What will you do, I wonder? Perception focused, observing the black smudge of the world in greater detail so that it threw the *Grand-Tile* into contrast, a rushing dart of light ahead of them. *What will you do when you've failed to take what's mine? This is your final chance, after all.* The Amaranthine new year turned in that moment, it sensed, some internal count running down to zero. 14,648. Just a number, nothing more. The Amaranthine themselves were failure encapsulated; their time was over, and soon enough a new calendar would take the place of the old. Perception sighted along the figurehead to the sputtering spark of their quarry, able almost to feel its desperation.

Such a long wait to escape, the Spirit marvelled. *But where are you going? What's out there for you?* It gazed upwards, trying to see as far as it could into the constellation of seething specks, the throbbing silver hiding trillions of colours visible only to something like itself.

Drifting off into its contented, undead sleep, Perception let itself imagine the places—all the places in all the days and years and centuries that it might visit now—and bristled with excitement.

This was living.

NOURISHMENT

At first, all Corphuso had found were the man's footprints in the dew, dragged trenches like shining slug trails leading down to the woods. But then the Amaranthine's freshness had withered, the lustre fading, and his form had begun to solidify; a far-off wanderer who cast a dim shadow. He would become a fixture of this place soon, like they all were.

Corphuso understood on some level that the Amaranthine had been put here for a reason. And now, in another place, in another time, he was dying.

He had his cloak wrapped around him today; the weather appeared to be turning cold, percolating up his sleeves and down through the damp hole in the toe of his boot. The Long-Life, as if in distaste of the weather, was nowhere to be seen.

But that wasn't quite true, and he knew it. The beasts in their cages up the hill, all those starving souls dribbling in eternal purgatory: some-one fed them with those buckets and sticks. He'd waited, day after day, to see who it was, until finally that person came.

It was the Long-Life himself, doing the rounds like a good jailor, sometimes talking to his old friends while they whimpered back. Cor-phuso hadn't understood until he'd climbed the hill and looked south, spending the day trying to count the hundreds of stone edifices that dis-appeared into the distance.

The souls *nourished* him. That was how Aaron had preserved his vigour these millions of years. Even Corphuso, absorbed by accident like a parasite in the gut, was doing his part in keeping the Long-Life strong.

This place, this page of the book, was part of the Long-Life's mem-ory. It existed, it appeared, within him as well as without. It was a place to store old souls, a place where they might live on, even at a reduced and purely functional level, so that he could feed from them.

Corphuso arranged his bed for the night, a passable lattice of sticks stuffed with smaller twigs and leaves. He'd been eating the first hatchlings of the season, and now he picked up some crushed little ani-mals and ate them whole, looking out through the trees at the brushed hint of a grey-blue land beyond. The forest was a metaphorical barrier, he sensed, as well as a real one. Where the land sunk away, the realm grew *deeper*, leading down and down into a place even farther removed from the clarity at the crest of the hill where Sotiris had woken. Moving beyond the forest's reaches would change something in both of them, Corphuso thought. But it had to be done.

He cuddled into his twig nest, his blurry thoughts recalling his beloved invention. He remembered there were things he hadn't told them, things he'd discovered. But they'd find that out for themselves, sooner or later.

TREASURE

Tzolz gazed up at the damaged walls of the hermitage; rough grey stone spattered with flecks of dried gull shit, black, sooty towers on the verge of collapse. There had been no great prosperity here, but also few raiders in hundreds of years. Fire held no fascination for him—when he looked into it, he saw nothing—and so this place would stay standing a while longer yet. The Bult did not burn what they had desecrated; they ate and took what they needed, seldom sparing their victories a backward glance. One had to care to burn, and the Bult simply didn't.

The bodies of the Quetterel lay where they'd fallen: crumpled, splayed, half-sitting and leaning, some at tables and chairs, an old abbess in her bunk. Barely eaten for the most part, besides a particularly juicy youngster Tzolz had fallen upon without bothering to silence it. Now he was growing sated, finding some rhythm, some contentment in his chews to replace the barely contained ferocity he'd begun with. He swallowed, pulling the Quetterel boy's femur wetly apart to get at the marrow and scooping at it with his lower teeth. Licking the bone almost meditatively, his gaze travelled up to the ramparts where one of his pack, Esos, stood naked. They would eat, but only when he'd had his turn. The other, Izar, came hobbling to the wall with his arms full of weaponry, dumping the various spring pistols and rifles at defendable points and then standing like a stooped gargoyle at the battlement with the other. They watched nothing, waiting.

When Tzolz was full and fit to burst, the first tugs of a stitch paining his brown, rib-stacked belly, he stood and threw down the knob of bone he'd been sucking on. *Eat, then, if you like.*

Without ceremony, the other two began their ritual, hauling and dropping their chosen bodies to the base of the walls and disappearing at the steps to climb down. Tzolz heard ribs and knees smash inside the thick black robes as the corpses hit the ground, saw a hairy head burst open. *Fur*, he thought distantly. It was *fur* the Quetterel were covered with, not hair. Like the Leemuremen of Port Obscura.

He staggered over to the edge of the road, pawing at the thin coating of ash that covered his hands, and squatted to gaze off into the hills. Coriopil floated unnoticed above them, a spot of deep green against the lime and gold tiger belts of Zeliolopos. The train-thing had rumbled off back down the road at the first sign of traded fire, and he didn't think they'd see it again any time soon.

He took a deep, ash-scented breath and watched his two Bult eat. The rich, iron-musty slime of eyeballs and testicles and fatty kidneys lined his lips, mingling not unpleasantly with the ash. It was a fact few knew that the Bult ate *only* flesh. Tzolz had looked at other Prism foods—black breads, white rice seeds—and seen only stuffs, fodders, padding like the fur that warmed some Voidsuits and the wool that lined old ships. It did not interest him why others ate the way they did.

He had meant to taste the Vulgar captain, once the day's labours were complete. For a long time, he'd stood at the busted-open cells, thinking quiet, ever-turning thoughts and smelling the air. A new coat of ash had covered the road since the Vulgars' departure, but there was no hurry. They could only have retraced the journey south, back to the treasure ship that had brought them all here. The hermitage was a dead thing now. Plenty had escaped—he'd seen them with his own eyes running off into the woods—but it didn't really matter. Cave systems in the hills held an even stricter order of Quetterel that did not speak to their ash-coated brothers; it would be days before anyone disturbed this place.

Tzolz's eyes followed Esos as the pale Bult made his way along the road to the edge of the orchard, dragging his chosen, split-headed corpse by the ankle. Esos liked to have his way with all the dead, eating into them first so that he might make himself more holes.

Something clicked beneath the Bult's foot as he dragged his trophy corpse, dimpling the ash into a tiny crater. Tzolz brought his head up, the familiarity of the sound registering somewhere in his mind, as Esos erupted into a blast of finely misted blood and ash, chunks flying high and raining down onto the track. Pieces of the wooden fence running parallel were blasted into the orchard in a spray of dust and splinters. Tzolz climbed to his feet, ignoring the stitch in his side. He observed Izar come limping warily to a window ledge and stare down at the grey and scarlet mess on the road.

They contemplated the blasted ground, stepping around the body parts. Tzolz came back around to the obliterated fence and looked wordlessly off into the orchard, deciding after a moment to follow the spots of blood and flesh into the long yellow grass.

There, plain as painted footprints in the grass, the tracks of seven Vulgar and a dozen of their wild creatures led off further into the startled silence of the orchard. Tzolz barely needed to look down to follow the trail as he wound between the trees, smelling the air as he went and glancing up into the branches to see the occasional piece of Esos dangling there like Old World bloodfruit.

Eventually, at the orchard's far edge, he realised he'd lost the track and stopped to look out at the semi-cultivated trees that led deeper into the volcanic hills. He walked the length of the fence, finding no more tracks on its other side, and turned back, his hackles raised. They were still here, still here somewhere.

Tzolz crept into the shade again, eyes alert and reflective, his breathing slowing, listening, scenting. Their sweat was everywhere, daubing the trees like rank animal piss, but there was no sign of them. He came to the last point at which he could make out clear impressions of their boots. The lead prints, smaller than some, were those of the captain. He squatted, looking around, then up, scanning the branches with quick flicks of his head.

No more tracks. Gone. Tzolz opened and closed the three fingers on each of his hands as he thought, uneasy for one of the few times in his adult life. The sensation was far from outright fear, but to something as impassive as a Bult it might as well have been the same thing.

A memory of his employer's last few words to him came unbidden into Tzolz's mind, his thoughts turning to the place he had once been looking for, the whole reason for their lightning visit to the planets of Tau Ceti.

You've no hope of finding this thing on your own—so look out for anything unusual, anything peculiar.

The Quetterel had built their hermitage here. Why?

He put his hand out to the dark, ornamented iron railings that surrounded the tree closest to the tracks in the grass. The metal was old and pitted, but the tree seemed well looked after. The grass around its trunk had even been chopped fairly recently.

"Tsuuuls," came the wheezing voice through the trees. Izar appeared as if from nowhere from behind the body of an enormous yellow fruit. They stared at each other, motionless.

EPILOGUE

Every muscle trembled as he grappled with the final step, a shiny wet block of bluish stone jutting out over the circular sea. He lay there for some time in the dampness and spray, dozing fitfully, too weak to roll himself.

For a dozen days he'd climbed, first down, past rolling tumbles of salty water into darkness, and then up into the light, some level in his head spinning and realigning. Within the enormous tunnel of water, he'd seen others descending, small shapes in the dark, passing like motes in the huge slants of thick sunlight.

He imagined in his delirious state that he might have lost half his body weight in the descent and subsequent climb; Melius were perfectly at home drinking salty water, but a person Elatine's size needed more.

"*Hoo!*"

He barely registered the echoing cry, bathing in the coolness of the sea air.

"*Hoo*, ean!"

A blade stuck into the flesh of his back. Elatine growled between his teeth, still unable to move. Another found his neck, forcing him to sit up.

They were dark little blurs at the fringes of his vision; too small to possibly worry about, even though they might carry weapons. Elatine breathed deeply, eyelids drooping, a word, a *name*, on the tip of his tongue. He ought to have known the word; it was all that had sustained him on the long climb through the crust of the world.

"Melyus! *Hoo!*"

He lolled his tongue and yawned. Gazing up, he could see that he had indeed come to the outside layer of the great hollow world: the deep black-blue sky arched from horizon to horizon, its withering sunlight steaming his drenched skin.

"*Aele ma Amarantien!*" the little voice squawked, and he found the name.

"Maneker," he said out loud, startling the blurry little people into silence. "*Hugo Maneker.*"

CHELSEA: 1649

He'd told Esther in the middle of the night, sitting up suddenly in bed. In the morning he couldn't quite recall what had made him do it—a dream, perhaps. Now she knew, and now she was gone.

Forty-one. The number of people Daniell had killed. Twenty-five in service to his Lordship. Not every face came distinctly to him, as some people said. Sometimes the act itself was almost gone from his memory, as if he'd rolled back his eyes, sharklike, until the deed was done. What he did remember, clearly and clinically, was the place and time of every death. He'd come close himself once or twice—shot in the foot with a musket ball and clubbed around the ear—but it was more than just a roll of the dice; he was good at what he did, better than any he'd been sent after.

Daniell listened to the birds from his eggshell-blue parlour, working his way through a cold steak and kidney pie. He thought about those days with the detachment of a man making the most of his meal, sawing at the thick pastry like a doctor sawing bone.

He'd awoken with a start, sticky inside the hot tent, his ears at once trained to the distant cries. Outside the field was empty, a sump of litter and gently smoking ash from fires kicked out. Flies and gnats churned thickly over the fields in the golden morning air.

Daniell pulled on his boots and stumbled out of the tent, understanding immediately that he'd been put to sleep. Days could have passed, though investigating the fires lower down the hill he thought not. *A crispy curl of blackened bacon lay pressed into the ash, still baking in the warmth.*

More cries carrying over the rise, a blue-black haze of summer smoke. Langport was aflame already.

He sheathed his sword, loading two pistols with seasoned ease and making his way carefully into town. Bodies lined the road, their red coats browned with dry mud. A girl of no more than five was checking one dead soldier for valuables as Daniell sprinted on over the rise and down the next mile of hill to the flaming town.

He came to the hanging chapel, stopping to look out over Bow Street, the main causeway to the river, realising that his horses had gone.

Down by the river, red-coated men fired desperately at an advancing mob of clubmen; townspeople mobilised in their hatred of Aaron Goring and his army. Pops and puffs of grey smoke from their rifles rose to mingle with the dusty haze of flaming buildings. He saw no sign of the Parliamentarians, realising finally that they must have left the beleaguered army to the fate of Langport's townsfolk and moved on.

The bridge out of town was the only way back to Royalist-held land. Men crouched behind its stone walls, firing over the parapet while others reloaded. He might be able to cross further down, where the rushes and sedge thickened, knowing if he couldn't that there would be miles of farmers' fields to backtrack across, miles of unknowable slogging through rutted dirt and crops.

He stood for a long while, looking out at the burning town houses, watching the remnants of his army thinning and trying to run, only to be shot down as they made it over the bridge. Soldiers took clubs to the head and fell twitching, set upon by smaller boys with scythes and hoes; others threw down their unloaded muskets and shrieked surrender, but to no avail. Daniell knew he couldn't get out that way.

He drew his sword and vaulted the chapel wall, slogging back down the hill and across flat farmland to the far curve of the river, the sun bearing down across his shoulders, something in his heart breaking.

Four months ago, the procession had led King Charles to the scaffold. Daniell hadn't gone to watch, though it wasn't all that far, even if he could have got a ticket for the beheading. Perhaps for the best—one never knew who might've been there, too, watching silently from the stalls.

He sat back, his pie accomplished, gazing out at the bright May sun glowing through the pink magnolia tree in his garden. He'd bought his own retirement—the one Aaron had promised him—happy in the knowledge that he owed his old lord nothing. At night, he slept soundly and without fear of finding some assassin at the foot of his bed, for after the battle he'd changed his name to Bellfield, growing out a luxuriant beard and gaining as much good healthy yeoman weight as his poor wife would allow.

He pushed the plate aside, the sheen of grease catching the sun like all the rutted mud tracks of the war. Aaron was out there, somewhere. Perhaps he lurked in the city still, spinning lies and promises among the new parliament. Maybe he'd taken passage to the Americas—a thought that comforted Daniell no end—establishing himself amid the Quakers and plantation owners there. One thing he knew for certain: in a thousand years, when Utopia had come and people crossed the skies with wings of flaming gold, his old Lordship would still be around, stalking the halls of cities that floated beneath great balloons, or sailing the lush, newly conquered seas of Venus or Mars. Daniell wondered if Aaron would remember him in that distant, heady future. Sometimes he imagined, slightly saddened, all the mischief the Oracle would make, knowing he'd never see it.

And to what end? he wondered, the pink glow of the leaves bobbing with the breeze.

He stood, sated, and walked out to his brick-walled garden, breathing in the fragrance of the trees. Daniell was no fool, having understood that night as he heard the Oracle's stories that he was hearing something biographical, tales plucked from the past and retold with a careful detachment.

He sincerely hoped Aaron found his Sarsappus one day, and that his old lord got what he was owed—be it good, or be it bad.

GLOSSARY

CAST OF CHARACTERS

Aaron the Long-Life	Spectral machine soul, now inhabiting the corpse of a long-dead Epir pilot
Alba, Gentleson of Flacht	Melius, corrupt High Plenipotentiary (deceased)
Arabis	Melius, daughter of Pentas and Callistemon
Arns	Vulgar, crewmember of the *Wilemo Maril*
Bidens of Mostar	Melius, son of the mayor of Mostar
Briol	Unborn daughter of Wilemo Maril (deceased)
Caleb Holtby	Pre-Perennial Amaranthine; junior honorific of the Devout
Callistemon	Melius, Secondling Plenipotentiary and father of Arabis (deceased)
Captain Wilemo Maril	Vulgar, privateer captain
Carzle	Lacaille, prisoner aboard the *Epsilon India*
Christophe De Rivarol	Perennial Amaranthine

Convolvulus	Melius, ancient ruler of the First, ancestor of the Berenzargols (deceased)
Corphuso Trohilat	Vulgar, inventor of the Shell
Count Andolp	Vulgar, landlord, owner of the Shell
Cunctus/the Apostate	Gang leader infamous throughout the Firmament and Investiture
Daniell Bulstrode	Ancient human, equerry to Aaron, Lord Goring (deceased)
Drazlo	Lacaille, crewmember of the *Wilemo Maril*
Elatine Jalan	Melius, commander of the Eastern legions
Elise	Perennial Amaranthine, Satrap of Port Elsbet
Eoziel XI	King of the Lacaille
Eranthis	Melius, Seventhling, sister of Pentas
Esos	Bult, mercenary
Fallopia	Melius, King Lyonothamnus's mother
Fanesho	Unborn daughter of Wilemo Maril (deceased)
Filago	Melius, Firstling, Lord Protector of the First; son of Zigadenus
Florian Von Schiller	Perennial Amaranthine, Cancriite, next in line for the Firmamental Throne
Furto	Vulgar, crewmember of the *Wilemo Maril*
Geniostemon	Melius, FirstLord General, half brother to the ancient King Convolvulus and ancestor of the Berenzargols (deceased)
Geum	Melius, chronicler

Ghaldezuel Es-Mejor	Lacaille, Knight of the Stars
Gramps	Aged *Bie*, residing on the water moon of Coriopil
Guirm	Vulgar, crewmember of the *Wilemo Maril*
Harald Hundred	Vilified Perennial Amaranthine, responsible for the murder of a hundred or more Amaranthine
Huerepo Morimiel Vuisse	Vulgar, conscript
Hugo Hassan Maneker	Perennial Amaranthine
Iblo	Vulgar, crewmember of the *Wilemo Maril*
Ignioz	Lacaille, ancient hero of the Prism Campaigns (deceased)
Impatiens	Melius, Tenthling, friend of Lycaste (deceased)
Imsi	Unborn daughter of Wilemo Maril (deceased)
Iro	Perennial Amaranthine, sister to Sotiris (deceased)
Izar	Bult, mercenary
Jacob the Bold	Firmamental Emperor during the Age of Decadence (deceased)
James Fitzroy Sabran	Perennial Amaranthine, the Most Venerable, Emperor of the Firmament
Jatropha	Perennial Amaranthine known throughout the Provinces, disconnected from events in the Firmament
Jospor	Vulgar, Captain Maril's friend and master-at-arms
Liatris of Albina	Melius, authoress from the Westerly Provinces

Satrap Cirillo Vincenti	Perennial Amaranthine, Satrap of Proximo
Slupe	Vulgar, crewmember of the *Wilemo Maril*
Smallbone	Pifoon, apprentice cook aboard the *Epsilon India*
Sotiris Gianakos	Perennial Amaranthine, brother of Iro
Suartho	Vulgar, owner of the Mendellion Mines
Timose	Vulgar, crewmember of the *Wilemo Maril*
Trang Hui Neng	Perennial Amaranthine, third in line to the Firmamental Throne
Tribulus	Melius, Secondling general
Tzolz	Hardened Prism warrior in the employ of Ghaldezuel
Veril	Vulgar, crewmember of the *Wilemo Maril*
Vibor	Lacaille, informant in the employ of Ghaldezuel
Vyazemsky	Perennial Amaranthine
Weepert	Pifoon, cook aboard the *Epsilon India*
Yurbs	Vulgar, crewmember of the *Wilemo Maril*
Zigadenus	Melius, Firstling, FirstLord Protector, father of Filago (deceased)

SPECIES/BREEDS

Amaranthine	Immortal humans, many thousands of years old
Awger	Melius/animal crossbreed reviled in the Provinces

Bie	Remnants of the Epir, evolved beyond all recognition, living on the water moon of Coriopil
Bult	Cannibalistic Prism breed feared throughout the Investiture
Cursed People	Speaking animals, often of lowly status and—unlike the Melius—subject to disease
Demian Man	Cursed-person of a higher social standing, usually of independent means
Epir	Ancient dinosaurian inhabitants of the Old World
Epir spirits	Indelible machine souls left over from the age of the Epir, bound to the iron cores of unhollowed planets and moons
Firstlings	Melius people of the First Province
Gheal	Breed of Prism native to the Old World
Honoured Prism	Wealthy Prism who live on the surfaces of Vaulted Lands
Jalan	Giant breed of Melius, from the eastern counties of the Oyal-Threheng
Jurlumticular Throng	Large Prism breed responsible for the Volirian Conflict, considered extinct
Lacaille	Poor Prism breed at war with the Vulgar

Melius	Giant person of the Old World
Oxel	Tiny Prism breed
Perennials	Amaranthine of advanced age
Pifoon	Wealthy Prism breed favoured by the Amaranthine
Pre-Perennial	Junior Amaranthine
Prism	Cluster of hominid breeds descended from *Homo sapiens*
Quetterel	Secretive, antisocial Prism breed
Ringum	Prism cross-breed
Secondlings	Melius people of the Second Province
Skylings	Melius name for the Prism
Tenthlings	Melius people of the Tenth Province
Threen	Nocturnal Prism breed
Vulgar	Prism breed at war with the Lacaille
Wulm	Long-eared, stocky Prism breed
Zelioceti	Secretive Prism breed
Zeltabra	Beast of burden and transport, Old World

PLACES

Airal	Tethered moon of Port Elsbet, Amaranthine Firmament

Amaranthine Utopia	Garden on the Old World dedicated to the preservation of the Insane
AntiZelio-Coriopil	Water moon of Zeliolopos, Prism Investiture
AntiZelio-Formis	Largest moon of Zeliomoltus, Prism Investiture
AntiZelio-Glumatis	Volcanic moon of Zeliolopos, Prism Investiture
AntiZelio-Slaathis	Wooded moon of Zeliolopos, Prism Investiture
Aquarii	Satrapy nearest to Virginis, Amaranthine Firmament
Astririon-Salay	Port on the Clawed Sea, Proximo Carolus, Amaranthine Firmament
Atholcualan	Lacaille city on Pruth-Zalnir, Prism Investiture
Baln	Lacaille city, Harp-Zalnir, Prism Investiture
Blessing	Planet mostly inhabited by the Vulgar, Prism Investiture
Burrow Lumm	Pifoon-owned parent planet of Port Halstrom and Pruth-Zalnir, Prism Investiture
Cancri	Sotiris's home Satrapy, Amaranthine Firmament
Cractitules	Mountain range on Pruth-Zalnir, Prism Investiture
Desiduum	Free moon of Gliese, Amaranthine Firmament
Dozo	Township in Harp Zalnir, Prism Investiture
Drolgins	Large moon orbiting Filgurbirund, Prism Investiture

Elebastial	Tethered moon of Gliese, Amaranthine Firmament
Epsilon Eridani	Vaulted Land, parent world of Port Maelstrom, Amaranthine Firmament
Epsilon India	Vaulted Land, Amaranthine Firmament
Eriemouth	Moon at the edge of the Prism Investiture
Fielem's Land	Planet of Vaulted Sirius, Amaranthine Firmament
Filgurbirund	Only planet belonging to the Vulgar, Prism Investiture
Firmament	The Amaranthine realm, eleven light-years wide, comprised of 23 Solar Satrapies
Firmament's End	Realm at the edge of the Firmament, ringed by the Gulf of Cancri
First Province	Ruling Province, Old World
Foundries of the Interior	Enormous foundries on the inner surface of Gliese, Amaranthine Firmament
Gimble	Free moon of Port Elsbet, Amaranthine Firmament
Girdis Mountains	Mountain range on the Tethered moon of Port Maelstrom
Gliese	Vaulted Land, capital of the Firmament
Great Solob	Free moon of Gliese, Amaranthine Firmament
Greenmoon	The Old World's single moon, known by the Amaranthine as Yanenko's Land
Gulf of Cancri	Border between the Firmament and the beginning of the Prism Investiture
Gurl	Town on Filgurbirund, Prism Investiture
Harp-Zalnir	Lacaille moon, Prism Investiture

Hauberth Under Shiel	City on Filgurbirund, Prism Investiture
Humaling	Star in the outer reaches of the Prism Investiture
Hume's Land	Planet of Port Elsbet, Amaranthine Firmament
Indak-Australis	Star in the outer reaches of the Prism Investiture, its planets and moons engulfed in war
Ingolland	An island in the Westerly Provinces, Old World
Inner Second	Affluent lands in the Second Province, Old World
Inner Epsilon India	Vaulted Land near Gliese (interior), Amaranthine Firmament
Inner Virginis	Vaulted Land (interior), Amaranthine Firmament
Investiture	Large volume of wild space beyond the Firmament, given to the Prism by the Amaranthine on the condition of loyalty
Izmirean	Port of the Tenth Province, Old World
Jothem	Tethered moon of Port Elsbet, Amaranthine Firmament
Julem's Land	Planet of Port Elsbet, Amaranthine Firmament
Kapteyn's Star	Star in the Prism Investiture, orbited by the Three worlds of Port Cys and its moon, Obviado
Kawl	Tethered moon of Port Elsbet, Amaranthine Firmament
Kifer	Tethered moon of Port Elsbet, Amaranthine Firmament

Kipris Isle	Island in the Nostrum Sea, Lycaste's birthplace, Old World
Magior	Tethered moon of Gliese, Amaranthine Firmament
Mars-Gaol	The Old World's neighbouring planet, a blasted wasteland
Mendellion Mines	Mines beneath Praztatl, Pruth-Zalnir, Prism Investiture
Mersin	Port in the Tenth Province, Old World
Mostar	Citadel on the border of the Westerly Provinces, Old World
Never-Never	Realm bordering the edge of the Prism Investiture
Nilmuth	Citadel in the country of Vrachtmunt, Drolgins, Prism Investiture
Ninth Prism Realm	Central band of the Investiture, owned mostly by the Threen; location of Kapteyn's Star
Nirlume	Moon of Blessing, neighbouring Stole-Havish, Prism Investiture
Old Satrapy/Satrapy of Sol	Satrapy containing the Old World and its accompanying planets
Old World	Lycaste's ancient home, chief planet in the Satrapy of Sol and sacred centre of the Firmament
Ophos	Tethered moon of Gliese, Prism Investiture
Osserine Hedron Star	Snowflake-shaped world at the very edge of the galaxy
Outer Procyon	Second of three uninhabited planets in the Seventeenth Solar Satrapy of Procyon, Amaranthine Firmament

Outer Wolf	One of the Firmamental Emperor's private planets, Amaranthine Firmament
Out Whoop	The edge of known space, Prism Investiture
Pan	Land in the Westerly Provinces
Pauros	Free moon of Gliese, Amaranthine Firmament
Phittsh	Port on Filgurbirund, Prism Investiture
Port Cys	Port Obviado's parent planet, Prism Investiture
Port Echo	Moon at the edge of the Prism Investiture
Port Elsbet	The Fourth Solar Satrapy (formerly Barnard's Star), Amaranthine Firmament
Port Halstrom	Lacaille moon, Prism Investiture
Port Obscura	Threen moon, Prism Investiture
Port Obviado	Former Amaranthine world now locked in darkness; Threen moon, Prism Investiture
Port Olpoth	Vulgar moon, Prism Investiture
Port Palestrina	Tethered moon of Vaulted Sirius, Amaranthine Firmament
Port Rubante	Tethered moon of Vaulted Sirius, Amaranthine Firmament
Proximo Carolus	Closest Satrapy to the Old World, Amaranthine Firmament
Pruth-Zalnir	Lacaille moon, Prism Investiture
Sarine City	Capital city of the First Province, Old World
Saturn-Regis	Planet in the Satrapy of Sol, Amaranthine Firmament
Sea Hall of Gliese	Palace in the Firmamental capital, Gliese, Amaranthine Firmament

Sea of Winth	Inland sea on the Vulgar moon of Nirlume, Prism Investiture
Sepulchre	Ancient Amaranthine treasure horde beneath the Girdis Mountains of Port Maelstrom
Stathe	Free moon of Port Elsbet, Amaranthine Firmament
Steerilden's Land	Fourth planet in the Solar Satrapy of Port Elsbet, Amaranthine Firmament
Stole-Havish	Vulgar moon, Prism Investiture
Tail	Land in the Westerly Provinces
Tau Ceti; the last harbour	Formerly the Twenty-Fourth Solar Satrapy; fourteen planets, Prism Investiture
Tenth Province	Southern Province of the Old World, bordering the Nostrum Sea
Thrasm	Ancient prison on the Tethered moon of Port Maelstrom
Untmouth	Vulgar harbour city, Drolgins, Prism Investiture
Van-Bergen's Land	Planet of Port Elsbet, Amaranthine Firmament
Vaulted Alpho	Vaulted Land, Amaranthine Firmament
Vaulted Ectries	Vaulted Land, Amaranthine Firmament
Vaulted Sirius	Vaulted Land, Amaranthine Firmament
Vaulted Wise	Vaulted Land, Amaranthine Firmament
Vrachtmunt	Vulgar country in the southern hemisphere of Drolgins, Prism Investiture
Westerly Provinces	Wild, internally governed Provinces west of the First and Second, Old World

Wiehlish	Town on Filgurbirund, Prism Investiture
Woenmouth	Moon at the edge of the Prism Investiture
Yanenko's Land	The Old World's single moon
Yire	Island in the Westerly Provinces, Old World
Zadar	Citadel on the border of the Westerly Provinces, Old World
Zeliolopos	Largest of Tau Ceti's gas giant planets, Prism Investiture
Zeliomandranus	Second largest of Tau Ceti's rock worlds, Prism Investiture
Zeliomoltus	One of Tau Ceti's gas giant planets, Prism Investiture
Zuo	City on Pruth-Zalnir, Prism Investiture

SHIPS

Balnazo	Lacaille Colossus battleship
Bunk Barge	Huge travelling sleeper vessel, pan-Prism ownership
Corbita	Jatropha's Wheelhouse
Epsilon India	Pifoon Voidship
Grand-Tile	Lacaille Colossus battleship
Hasziom	Lacaille Man-o'-War
Nomad	Lacaille tetraluminal Voidship

Pride of the Sprittno	Lacaille Voidship, Nomad class
Wilemo Maril	Vulgar privateer vessel
Yustafan	Lacaille Colossus battleship
Zlanort	Lacaille Colossus battleship

GENERAL GLOSSARY

Age of Decadence	(AD 9000—AD 10,550) period of Amaranthine prosperity and technological innovation
Andolp's Light-Trap	The Shell; the Soul Engine
Artery	Causeway extending through the Provinces of the Old World
Atholcualan Star	Locomotive train running between Zuo and Atholcualan, Pruth-Zalnir, Prism Investiture
Battle of Nilmuth	The failed attempt to capture the Shell at the Fortress of Nilmuth, as seen at the beginning of *The Promise of the Child*
Bilocate/Bilocation	Amaranthine teleportation, made possible through the alignment of iron particles in their blood
Bloodfruit	Meaty foodstuff, grown
Cancriites	Inhabitants of Cancri
Corbita	Jatropha's Wheelhouse
Deepslides	Prism equivalent of crude, long-exposure photography

Dorielziath	Epic tale written in historic Threheng times, still a popular piece of Old World literature
Ducats	Currency of the Firmament
Eastern legions, the	Elatine's legions, part of the Oyal-Threheng
Elderly Fistatussis	Sun at the very edge of the galaxy
Eldest, the	His Most Venerable Self, Emperor of the Amaranthine
Firmamental Edicts	Laws of the Firmament
Firmamental Satrap	Amaranthine governor of a Solar Satrapy
First Court	Court of King Lyonothamnus II, His Enlightenment
Frush	River on Filgurbirund, Prism Investiture
Growth-stone	Mouldable stone substance
High Second	Elitist and complicated Secondling language
House of Berenzargol	Wealthy Secondling family
Inception	The development of immortality in the distant past
Jalanbulon	Jalan regiment
Knights of the Stars, the	Order of Lacaille knights
Law of Succession	Amaranthine ritual whereby the oldest living Amaranthine claims the throne

Light Charger	Heavy laser mounted on the *Epsilon India*'s nose
Limewine	Prism alcohol
Low Oxel	Prism language, composed of whistles
Low Second	Melius language
Lumen rifle/pistol	Expensive and relatively rare Prism weapon, fires lasers
Lug-train	Long, wheeled vehicle used on AntiZelio-Glumatis
Lyonothamnine Enlightenment of the First	Regime of the boy-king Lyonothamnus II
Micro-mines	Collections of shrapnel discharged by Prism ships
Moonkings	Regional rulers in the Prism Investiture
Op-Ful-Lacaille	Lacaille infantry
Optilocket	Prism equivalent of a crude chemical camera
Organ Sun	Artificial sun within a Vaulted Land
Orifice sea	Thin area in the crust of a Vaulted Land, bored for structural support and to allow access; often filled with water
Perennial Parliament	Assemblage of Perennial Amaranthine
Perinnieds	Ancient Hioman Empire, pre-dating the Amaranthine
Plenipotentiary	Wandering lawman and census-taker, Old World
Prism Campaign	200-year war between the Prism and the Amaranthine; ended with the formation of the Prism Investiture and the defeat of the Lacaille

Quarter Basic	Melius unit of time, equivalent to three hours
Ring book	Book of metal plates popular in the Provinces
Rolling fortress	Enormous moving castles built by the Prism
Satrapies	Provinces of the Firmament
Shamefashion	The habit of wearing clothing in Melius society
Shameplague	Sexually transmitted disease of the Old World, eventually fatal
Shell, the	The Soul Engine
Shigella poison	Concentrated bacteria, often applied to the tips of Prism bullets
Sparker	Prism weapon, fires explosive rounds like fireworks
Spring rifle/pistol	Crude Prism weapon, fires bolts with a loaded spring
Succession	Law in which the eldest of the Amaranthine takes the throne
Sun chart	Prism map of the Firmament and Investiture
Sun Compendium, the	Set of navigational books
Superluminal	Method of surpassing the speed of light
Tethered moon	Moon connected to a Vaulted Land by vast metal chain links
Threene–Wunse Conflation	Entente between two proto-Prism empires, once a threat to the Amaranthine

Thresholds	Enormous and exceedingly ancient hollow-chambered bulbs; a method of travelling across galaxies in times long past
Treaty of Silp, the	Vulgar-Lacaille treaty
Unified	The language of the Amaranthine
Vaulted Land	Hollowed planet in the Firmament, containing an artificial sun and interior continents
Volirian Conflict	Battle involving many Prism breeds at the Amaranthines' behest; reprisal for the Jurlumticular Throng's invasion of a Vaulted Land
Wheelhouse	Large rolling wheel, often made of wood, girdled with a ring of balconies and living spaces; used as transport and dwelling on the Old World
Wiro	Dragon-like creature of Lacaille fairytales
Zeliospeak	Zelioceti creole language

ACKNOWLEDGEMENTS

This one was a proper labour of love, so I'd like to apologise for being a pain in the ass for the last couple of years and thank a few very special people: the oldies back in Somerset; my soon-to-be Mrs. Toast; the majestic Andy Kifer; Nick, Joss, Marty, Giddy, Lee and family; the Callinicoses; Rita (I *still* have your laptop, oops) and Steve; Al Robertson, Jon Wallace, Alex Lamb, Ed Cox and Mike Martinez; Marcus, Gillian, Craig, Sophie and everyone at Gollancz (including, as always, the legendary Simon Spanton); the brilliant Lisa Rogers, without whom my novels would make even less sense; Cory, Jeremy and the chaps at Night Shade; the Gernert Company and Caspian Dennis at Abner Stein.

And lastly to everyone who read and enjoyed this novel's predecessor, *The Promise of the Child*. Being a debut author can be pretty nerve-racking, and your encouragement meant so much. Thank you.

London
May 2016

TOM TONER was born in Somerset, England, in 1986. After graduating with a degree in fine art from Lough-borough University and the FHSH in Schwäbisch Hall, Germany, he moved to Australia, teaching life drawing and working in an art gallery near Melbourne. Upon returning to England he completed his debut novel, *The Promise of the Child*. Toner currently lives in London.